Chapter the Last

Originally published as *Det Siste Kapitel*
Copyright © 1923 by Gyldendal Nordisk Vorlag, Oslo
Translation copyright © 1929 by Alfred A, Knopf, Inc.

Front cover: *Sanatorium* (detail) by Edvard Munch
Source: Munch Museum, Oslo, Norway

Back cover photo: Knut Hamsun, 1925
Source: National Library of Norway

ISBN 979-8-218-54825-4

This edition published in 2025 by
Tough Poets Press
Arlington, Massachusetts 02476
U.S.A.

www.toughpoets.com

Knut Hamsun
§
Chapter the Last

(Det Siste Kapitel)

Translated from the Norwegian
by Arthur G. Chater

Tough Poets Press
Arlington, Massachusetts

I

Truly we are vagabonds in the earth. We wander by roads and trackless wastes, at times we crawl, at times we walk upright and trample one another down. As with Daniel: he trampled others and was himself trampled.

It is no trouble now to go up to Torahus, where he lived; but one year it was a dangerous business; you had to take a gun and keep your eyes open. It lasted only a few days, but he was king of the mountain that time and he shot folks; it's a long while ago, it was when we were all younger.

Originally Torahus was a sæter* belonging to his father's farm; it was badly run and was finally given up; it had now been deserted a good while. His father mismanaged everything he had, including the main farm, including himself. It is so easily said, but there was a reason for it; his sorrows began when he lost his wife, and his sorrows increased for a score of years; then his riotous life came to an end and the farm was sold up. Daniel managed to save the sæter and one or two beasts, moved up there, and made it his home; it suited him well, he was healthy and strong and something over twenty. An old maidservant from the farm went with him out of devotion.

It is so quickly told, but it was a long and painful process to leave the village in the sight of all and move up to the sæter, and Daniel had a tough job before him at the new place. He set to work like a man, digging ditches, breaking new ground, clearing forest, turning the stream into a new bed; he took an enormous quantity of

---

*A mountainside summer farm.

stones out of his land. Nobody had believed Daniel was such a plodder; he had never worked too hard on the farm, probably because he saw it was hopeless. When he got a place of his own to look after he showed himself in quite a new light; he became a worker, he was his own day-labourer, so to speak, and earned his wage, whatever may have been his private reason for it, but no doubt he had one.

A couple of years went by, Daniel was frugal and trustworthy, dull and uninteresting perhaps in his garb, as in his speech, but staunch to his purpose. Wars, epidemics, and earthquakes in the world at large did not concern him, he read nothing and never dusted a stone before sitting on it.

After a couple of years the place had grown, Torahus was a farm on a small scale—Torahus: the Home of Thunder. He knew no discontent, he had a life after his own heart. Here was solitude without emptiness; the view was magnificent, of mountains miles away, with a wealth of forest between. His work took up his time; when he was thirsty he went to the stream with his tin pail, emptied it, and carried it back full. Here was silence, with a background of eternal sound; here were fine stars, not the golden trash that you saw through the mist down at his father's farm, no, but twinkling lights, they were so pretty; there is something luscious about stars; they are like little girls. He did not feel poor and forlorn, as he really was; why, all the stones he had cleared looked just like a crowd of people around him, he was personally related to every stone, they were acquaintances every one, he had conquered them and got them out of the ground.

He used to go out again after supper and stroll about, looking at the forest that grew so nicely and the bogs that lay there and would have to be drained; could he have afforded it he would have had a horse; ah, but that would come in time; as it was, one day went by after another and the place was good.

When the old maid had had time to go to bed in her little closet

CHAPTER THE LAST

and the two beasts in the byre, he went in again. The hut received him as it received anyone else, but it was his own hut and no other man's; it sheltered him with the impartiality of a cave, but at the same time it was his hiding-place, because it was so small and close. The walls were of logs, the roof was low; he came from outside, where he was getting cold; the fire was burning on the hearth; he gave a little shiver of comfort, and he could do that because there was nobody to see him. Outside was solitude. A stream murmured a few paces from the houses. He went to bed in peace.

A couple of years went by, but of course this hard-and-fast round could not be kept up.

In the third year he began to go down to the village more, to his acquaintances, and to little parties, to church, to auctions, and then there was his girl too. He was still a young lad, too full of fire to take life at an unbroken walking pace; he ran to his girl. The distance was no short one, but it wasn't impossible either; even as children they had found the way to each other, she from her home, he from his; the forest was full of little brooks which they jumped over, here and there were patches of green, hazel-bushes with nuts, squirrels, ant-hills, and sweet-smelling hedges. He went by the same path now that he was grown up, and he was happy here and sang in his quiet joy at the familiar rocks and knolls and brakes; they made him light-headed, so that he would leap into the air and behave as if he had only a few more steps to go instead of three or four miles. Sometimes he met her before he got there, and both were bashful at having gone out to meet each other and invented explanations which resolved themselves into nothing. This was more especially in the time that followed their school-days and confirmation; later on there was more seriousness and less play in them; his father's farm was doing badly and she on her side may have thought it a little precarious to see too much of his company. Not that they had ever been sweethearts, any more than they were now, but they still had kindly looks for each other.

One day two strangers called at Torahus. They had gone up the mountain to shoot. One of them said he was a lawyer, the other a doctor. They chatted with Daniel and watched him at his work.

Why, he had quite a little farm here, they said to him.

Daniel gave a little laugh at this; it was not much of a farm yet, only feed for a couple of cows.

But if he went on as he had begun, it might feed a couple more?

Oh ay, Daniel didn't think that altogether impossible.

They were asked in and given milk; they drank and got their breath and drank again. The old maidservant got a whole two-crown piece. Free-handed folks, lots of money, Daniel felt quite at home with them. He joined them and carried their game-bags down to the village.

On the way, there was more talk of Torahus and they asked him if there was enough timber on the place.

What, for fuel? Many times more than enough!

How much of the mountain did he own?

Daniel pointed: a good four miles on this side and as far as the next sæter, the other Torahus, on that.

As they parted down in the village, the gentlemen asked: "Will you sell your place?"

Daniel repeated: Sell it? The gentlemen must be joking, they were free-and-easy folk, liked to be pleasant—

"It isn't altogether a joke on our part," said the one who was a doctor.

"Sell it?" said Daniel. "Oh no, I'll have to keep it."

They went their ways and Daniel went home again. He had got a whole five crowns for his trouble from the one who was a lawyer.

No indeed, he couldn't sell Torahus; wasn't it his own tiny farm? He had no other. But he was pleased that Torahus was the kind of place that other people would like to own. He busied himself with the houses and put them in order, made new drinking-troughs in the stream, built long stone fences; no one could say he had not been industrious. And when he went down into the village he could ask anybody to come up and see him on the mountain, they needn't be afraid. But it takes a village an immense time to change an old, rooted idea for a new one. Daniel was the only child of an old farm and he had come down to a sæter. That was his fate, he couldn't get away from it.

The girl's name was Helena. She was no beauty, far from it; she was one of those with a pimply face and bloodless complexion. But, apart from that, she was very well shaped and she listened so nicely when he talked to her. There is a difference between listening with attention and listening with toleration. She was a little slow, rather sluggish of nature, and seemed to think over what he said; that was how she made so good an impression on him. And she was nice enough and to spare. He would like to have her, he said.

She thought it over.

For now he had a place of his own and it was not a bad one. Besides, he could build on to it in time, another room.

"Won't you soon come down from the sæter again?" she asked.

"How do you mean?"

"And live here in the village?"

"No. I've got what I've got. Isn't it good enough for you?"

"Oh yes," she said thoughtfully.

They had several talks of this kind, and nothing was settled, At last he got so much out of her that she dared say she might take him; but she rubbed her eyes when he wasn't looking, to have some tears to show.

He did not take this as a refusal; there was no idea of giving up and expiring on her grave or anything of that sort; on the contrary, he thought he had gained his point.

Some weeks later he was down at the store and met Helena there.

He walked home with her, and as they went he asked her when she was coming up to see him, by which he meant when they were to be married.

She didn't know. It depended.

Ah. Well, but if she didn't think him any uglier and more dangerous than lots of others, she might as well take him right away and have it settled.

At this she laughed and only made a jest of his being ugly and dangerous. She didn't go into the question of time, she avoided that; no doubt this was her form for letting him down easily. She did not say it in so many words, but he surely ought to have understood that she was not going to leave a farm for a sæter. Why was he so persistent? Her whole attitude of late as good as told him that if it was all the same to him she would rather have no more to do with him. Couldn't he ever understand that?

Good. But this time again she listened with a certain fondness to what he said, and when they parted he thought there was a little twinkle in her eyes. Or perhaps not exactly a twinkle, but she dropped her eyes slowly, as though a little sad at parting with him.

Good again—Daniel walked home contented and without any special reason began to hum to himself.

A couple of weeks later, when spring was already come, with goslings in the sedges, Daniel heard a remarkable piece of news:

"Well, so she stuck to the Sheriff's officer."

"Who?"

"Who? Don't you know? Helena."

Daniel couldn't understand it, didn't believe it. Helena?

"Their banns were asked last Sunday."

"Helena? Last Sunday, do you mean it?"

"He's applying for a post and he'll be made Sheriff. So Helena will be a fine lady, I can tell you!"

"I had a kind of idea I'd hear some news today," Daniel forced himself to answer. "The thrushes shouted at me so as I came along!" And then he laughed with white lips.

He went home to Torahus with the purchases for his housekeeper and came straight down to the village again. He was not long on the way. Now, what was it that brought him back to the village? He didn't know himself, he simply walked, ran, stood still a moment, and ran on again. There was an absent-minded air about him. "Have you forgotten something?" they asked him when he appeared again. "Yes," he replied. He met a young neighbour who asked him to come along. There was a back room at the store, where they could go and be supplied with drinks. This was a good friend of his, Helmer was his name, a neighbour from childhood, the same age as himself, a young lad. They sat there awhile, others joined them and made a little party, talking of their affairs and concerns; how one of them was going to change his place next hiring day, and another wanted to send a carcass of veal to his brother who lived in Christiania. Just so, affairs and concerns of life in a small way.

They all kept a quiet eye on Daniel; they knew what had befallen him, it was common knowledge that he was to have had Helena and now he had lost her. There was no help for a thing like that, life wasn't all it might be. They avoided mentioning her name; instead of that they showed their sympathy for Daniel by drinking his health again and again and talking about his sæter, about Torahus, which he had made into quite a little farm. He was the boy!

Daniel himself said nothing and let them treat him like a sick man. This kindness on the part of his acquaintances was very agreeable; maybe he was a little inclined to show off and seem more staggered than he was; the long walk up the mountain and back had worked off some of his excitement, and now the good drinks had begun to take effect and set him free.

At last he could contain himself no longer, and asked: "Were any of you at church last Sunday?"

Yes, several of them. What made him ask?

Nothing.

"There were three christenings and one funeral."

"Ay, and the banns were asked for the Sheriff's officer," one of them said at last.

Another tried to pass it off; he turned to Daniel and remarked: "I hear you've already got feed for two cows at Torahus. Are you going to get a horse?"

Long silence. They were beginning to chat of other things, when Daniel said: "Am I going to get a horse? What do I want with it? What do I want with the whole of Torahus now?"

He was sitting among neighbours and companions of his own age; perhaps he ought not to carry it too far with his airs; these young lads were ordinary peasants, they wished him well, but they wouldn't see that a disappointment in love might deprive a sæter, a mountain farm, of its value. They would soon be getting bored with his melancholy mood, and in order to assert himself Daniel had to use a little bluster: that he didn't give a damn for it all, but he wasn't to be trifled with, certain people had better beware!

"Yes," said the boys carelessly; "good luck!" they said, and took no more notice of it.

One after another went out, as things were getting dull, and the man who wanted to send the carcass of veal by train had to get the store-keeper to help him with this difficult business. Daniel and Helmer were left alone smoking.

"Helmer, I'm going to set fire to a house," said Daniel and smoked calmly on.

The other opened his mouth. "H—no!" he said at last, with a smile and a shake of the head.

"I'm going to," said Daniel. "She shall feel what it's like to have a good fire of dry sticks under her."

"Oh no, that's all nonsense."

Daniel merely nodded.

His friend thought of an objection: "It's too far away from the Sheriff's."

"How do you mean?"

"You have to report yourself to the Sheriff one hour after you've done it."

"What's that for?" asked Daniel, interested.

"Because if you don't you'll be hunted down and caught and condemned to death."

"I'll chance that!"

"Oh no, it's dangerous to do a thing like that so far away from the Sheriff's!" Helmer concluded. And to put more stiffening into the other he added: "And besides, do you think she's worth all that? Come on, let's go!"

They walked together till their roads parted and then said goodbye.

"I say, Helmer," Daniel called out; "I'm going to do it!"

"Nonsense!" called Helmer in reply.

Then they parted, one to go home and the other to set fire to a house.

He arrived at the place at nine in the evening and sat down in a corner of the field to wait till it grew dark. It was the usual early spring weather, cool towards evening, but the drinks had warmed Daniel internally so that he did not feel cold. Smoke was still rising from the chimney of the house before him, but there was no sign of life about the farm, everybody had gone to bed. The sight of that house, of a certain bedroom window, his memories, the after-effects of his drinking, began to soften Daniel's heart; he wept and wagged his head in self-surrender. At last he fell asleep.

He woke up shivering, mistook the faint light, and thought it was the dawn. "It's too late to do anything!" he thought, and began to walk homewards. He had gone a good way when he suddenly stopped: why, this wasn't morning at all; on the contrary, it was about midnight, just the right time! Had it been the dawn, the birds would be singing already. What a fool he had been! But as for going all that way back—he couldn't do it, he was slack and down in the mouth. It would have to wait till another time.

Nothing came of the arson; no, no, nothing came of it but empty talk and bombast. But Daniel gained a notoriety by his talk; it leaked out that he had uttered these threats, and the villagers shuddered; to think that Daniel should come to this, a lad from a big farm!

They looked rather askance at him now when he came down to the village, Daniel could see very well that he had lost the goodwill of his acquaintances. To be sure, his neighbour Helmer was still the same and did his best to counteract the gossip, but we know that a village takes a long time to change its point of view and would rather believe the worst.

So Daniel again stayed mostly at home at his Torahus and put it in order and did a man's work. It was springtime now, and, as he was single-handed, he had enough to keep him busy. And who would have believed it? Daniel got over his disappointed love pretty quickly, it cost him neither sleep nor appetite. Not that it hadn't been bitter enough at first, but it was a thing by itself; he pulled himself together, pinched his arm, and felt that he was the man he was. Pluck it, smell it, and throw it away, that was what she called love! And then her lying way of letting it drag on for years with hums and ha's, and often with kissing and patting, and never meaning it to be for life! But that was all one. He had planned an addition to the sæter hut, and, by God, it should be built, nothing should stop it. Hadn't he all the timber ready, one log here and another there in Torahus Forest? He had felled these trees in the evenings, now one, now another, when he was taking his walks after finishing his work, mountain fir, solid wood that sang under the ax, imperishable timber. Oh yes, the addition was coming. Perhaps it was no immortal deed, it was an ambition turned upside-down; no one would think he had use for a big house now that Helena had broken with him—quite correct, by all means, but oh yes, there was going to be a house.

A powerful young lad couldn't be satisfied with leading a blindman's life when he could see, could he? Was he perhaps to go rotten here on the mountain, without aim or purpose? He had seen this house in his mind's eye for years; it was not to take anyone's breath away with useless ornamental flourishes, but it would be just as big as was wanted, one floor, three windows looking towards the village.

In the autumn the two sportsmen came again, the lawyer and the doctor. For the look of the thing they carried guns and gamebags but they had no dog with them and had shot nothing.

They asked Daniel if he would sell his sæter, his farm.

"Oh no," he replied with a smile.

"Not this year either?"

"No."

But he could say how much he wanted, he could name a price.

No.

That's that, they said. There you have the peasant, obstinate as ever, they must have thought. Then they began to dangle before him the possibility that they might of course buy the companion sæter, the other Torahus.

Daniel had no objection.

There was just as much land with it, only it lay rather high up, on level ground and not on the hill-side, that was the only disadvantage about it.

"Wouldn't that be just as good?" asked Daniel.

No, not for the use the gentlemen had for it.

Silence.

But, they said, the mountain was the same as here, it was Torahus Fell all the way, wood enough for firing, water, a fine view twelve hundred feet up.

Ay, said Daniel.

Silence.

So there was no business to be done with him?

Oh no. It would have to stay as it was.

A few days later a rumour came up from the village that it was quite correct, the neighbouring sæter had been sold, the two gentlemen had spoken the truth. They were going to establish a sanatorium up there, an institution for invalids and sick people; they were not speculators, they were benefactors and philanthropists with great plans in their heads. And one day, a couple of weeks later, when Daniel was clearing stones from an outlying meadow, he heard a sound of axes from the direction of the other sæter, followed the sound, and came upon four men working on a road up the mountain. They were village folks, Daniel knew them and fell to talking with them.

Yes, it was quite correct, what he had heard; there were great doings now on Torahus Fell, bless his soul! They pointed over their shoulders; over there they had started digging cellars and laying the foundations of an immense castle.

Daniel blurted out that the gentlemen had been to him first, but he wouldn't sell.

Then he was a silly fool, the men told him; the gentlemen had paid a big lump of money for this sæter and still the grazing rights over the whole mountain were not interfered with.

How much had the gentlemen given?

The men named a by no means fabulous sum.

Well, he might be glad of it too, the man who got it; and it was his old neighbour the farmer, Helmer's father. Good luck to him!

Daniel walked homewards considering the matter deeply. Big changes surely, but what of it? He who had not bowed to Helena's wishes, should he have sold and given up Torahus, his little farm, and returned to the village homeless? Was Torahus no longer good enough for him? He would show them! He had his own plans.

As the carpenters from the village had promised him time after time to come and build his house and never came, Daniel got two men from the next village. He had himself squared and dressed the logs in advance; the two carpenters worked with a will and put up the new building in a couple of weeks; there was another sitting-room and another bedroom, as nice as could be and all he wanted, so white and proper. The men were to make the two doors and three windows at home and bring them by sledge on the winter roads. All went according to his wishes. Oh, there was sense and meaning in everything, all went well, next summer the heifer would calve, then he would have three cows. A horse? Why yes, when he had four cows he would begin to think about a horse; till then he was a good enough horse himself.

A couple of outlying meadows gave him a lot of work, but rich promise; they were bogs, fearfully waterlogged, but grand soil; they wanted elaborate drainage. Daniel stuck to it.

II

Load after load went up the mountain all the winter, convoys of loads for the building of the sanatorium, all the horses in the village were employed; in fact, many men bought horses simply on account of this job and sold them again when the winter was over and there was no more carrying to be done.

Some folks shook their heads at these tremendous preparations, but they were folks who had no idea of anything. How should they know what it took to build a castle! What about the timber, the planks, the cement, the nails, what about all the pumps, all the paint, all the roof-tiles? There were two hundred windows in the main building alone, and there were five more buildings, great and small; how many loads did that mean of nothing but window glass? On top of all that there were some fifty stoves, how many loads did that make? And as for movables, there were all kinds of furniture, carpets, lamps, bed-clothes, wall-papers, table-cloths, glass and china, a thousand things, many thousand things. Finally came the food-stuffs, they made a caravan by themselves, in cases and barrels, in live animals, a whole farm-yard of cattle and sheep and poultry. Now there was nothing more to come but the guests, the patients, and after the opening ceremony they came too.

But what had it not cost to get it all finished, the castle with everything in it, all the other houses, the annexes, as they were called, and the roads and terraces round about! It took one's breath away to think of so much expenditure. But nobody seemed to give much thought to this, the undertaking was so soundly established, one thousand shares of two hundred crowns, capital fully subscribed, general meeting, statutes, and all. Nothing was lacking to its perfection, and when all the staff was assembled the guests began to arrive, all the wheels started and went round quicker and quicker, oh, so prodigiously quick that they flashed with it, they were like staring eyes, the wheels, so quickly did they go. On Sundays folks came up from the village and looked about them and stood stock-still in their bewilderment, they couldn't take it in, their standards failed them. Never before had they seen such fearsome dragons on the roof of any human habitation, never before had they seen so many pillars in one place, and the pillars carried one balcony after another, right up to the attic. And up above the roof of the attic a little flagstaff pointed to the sky with its shining ball of lustre. When all was said and done, the spectacle was just barely imaginable to the peasants; these verandas and balconies standing on pillars, on pins, reminded them of a game you play with matches, they were outside the laws of gravity and showed no disposition, no character. Oh, those peasants! They lay on their stomachs and squinted up at the castle and thought it was just imagination, all that they saw; it couldn't be possible that these houses should be left in this state. Was it right for houses to grow up out of the ground like this and be finished and then look as if nothing had happened? Why, they stood there threatening to go for you! The cow-house had a big dome on its roof, but no church bell in it; the barn, in old Norse style, had a tower, but no dinner-bell. Perhaps these bells had been thought of and were to come later? Oh, but nothing was to come later, nothing at all; the cost of building had already been greatly exceeded, it was said, but this again didn't seem to matter, Torahus Sanatorium was equal to a few supplementary estimates, no doubt.

But as the villagers lay there on their stomachs and squinted up they got a sort of impression that the people strolling about the paths and courtyards were also only imaginary people. Good Lord, many of them were shadows, hardly any were well, there were men with blue noses though it was not cold, and, to make up for that, there were one or two children with bare knees though it was chilly. What was the meaning of it all? There were ladies who shrieked hysterically if they got an ant on the sleeve of their dress.

Oh, but the people were real enough, there was nothing wrong about that. They walked about, they talked, they had clothes on, some of them coughed so that you could hear them a long way off. Some were as thin as ghosts and were not to take any exercise, but sit still in the sun; others struggled with a kind of machine fixed to a rock, a "try your strength" machine, to get their fat down. There was something amiss with them all, but God had distributed the ailments among them; the worst were the neurotic ones, they had every disease between heaven and earth at the same time and had to be spoken to like children. There was Fru Ruben for instance, she was so broad that she could scarcely get through the door of her room, but she never took it ill if anyone ignored her size or even went so far as to deny that she was particularly fat—no, that only made her smile sweetly; but if the doctor doubted her sleeplessness, if he joked about her nerves, she was furious and glared at him fiercely. One day the doctor said in passing: "It's extraordinary what a recovery you've made here, Fru Ruben; there's nothing the matter with you now!" Fru Ruben made no reply, but spat after the doctor and went her way.

For that matter, there were others who spat after him, who despised that man, whatever may have been their reason. He was a busybody. There was practically nothing for which he would not give you a bottle of medicine, though he must have known it was no good; probably he did it to be obliging, he was so over-anxious to meet his patients' wishes. As it was this man who, together with Lawyer Robertsen, had conjured up the whole of Torahus Sanatorium, one would have expected him to behave with dignity and authority; but no, he shouted "Good-morning!" a long way off and bared his head with such an exaggerated air that he seemed to sweep the ground with the flourish of his feathered hat. And you needn't think there was any chaff about it; no, it was all friendliness, familiarity. Many people turned away to avoid this officious politeness, but it was no use, the doctor shouted at their backs. He was also very fond of showing his wit, he made delicate and proper jokes and it sounded so hopeless; ah, he was just a good-natured peasant lad who had passed his doctor's examinations. But there was no doubt he meant it all for the best, he showed that in his solicitude for his patients. Who could have been so kind a friend to all the world as he? Very often he overdid it and belittled himself to serve others, nay, in the interests of others he was even capable of obliterating the importance of his position as doctor and saying, for instance, that with your culture and intelligence, Herr Bertelsen, you can cure that trouble of yours with massage more readily than I can with my medicine. Could a doctor say a thing like that without losing by it? The consequence was that Herr Bertelsen, who believed in physic, ceased to believe in his physician. Doctor Oyen's fault was that he talked too much, he did not preserve a mysterious silence; one ought to be able to regard a doctor with superstition, he ought to give you the idea that he knows a good deal more than his A B C; but what idea did Doctor Oyen give?

One day a gentleman and a lady came running home from the forest, and the gentleman was Herr Bertelsen, the lady Fröken Ellingsen, a tall, good-looking lady who was only a little overworked at her telegraph transmitter. This couple came running in to look for the doctor. It can't be denied that Herr Bertelsen grumbled a little: when for once the doctor's wanted he's not to be found! It looked as though Herr Bertelsen was in a hurry, he held his handkerchief to his cheek, moaned feebly, and showed signs of terror. "He's got an ant-bite!" somebody said jeeringly. When at last Herr Bertelsen found the doctor, it was not a case of an ant-bite, but a hat-pin that had run into his cheek, Fröken Ellingsen's hat-pin! It looked dangerous, fatal, his cheek swollen to double its size, the lady in despair: "Oh, it's septic," she wailed.

"Let me see," said the doctor. "A hat-pin, you say? Pooh, then it's nothing!"

"Oh yes, I'm sure it's septic," the lady insisted.

Now instead of putting on the mysterious air of a medical man and running to his dispensary for acids and brushes and cottonwool, the doctor laughed at the whole thing and said to his patient: "You go down to the stream, Herr Bertelsen, and pour a little cold water on your cheek. But, after all, you can save yourself the trouble; the swelling will go down of its own accord in twenty-four hours."

That was really taking it pretty lightly. Herr Bertelsen was disappointed and didn't care to have shown terror for nothing; he asked: "Then is it entirely out of the question that there can be poison in it? When it swelled up like that? I think the point of the pin—?"

"Absolutely out of the question!" And now the jocular imp got hold of Doctor Oyen again; he couldn't help showing off and said: "I cannot believe there is anything poisonous about you, Fröken Ellingsen, you don't look like it!"

If he had stopped there and not gone on, perhaps he might not have lost by it; but he rode his witticism to death, he turned the hatpin into a Cupid's dart, shot by Fröken Ellingsen; it became more and more impossible to listen to him, and Herr Bertelsen turned to his companion and said: "All the same, I'll go and put some boracic on it."

"No, there's no need for that," said the doctor. He explained just what had happened: no doubt it was blood that had caused the cheek to swell, but that blood was only under the skin. If he opened the wound again just a little, it would let the blood out and the swelling would be gone, but when the wound closed again, the blood would

CHAPTER THE LAST

collect as before. "Leave the cheek alone," he said, "then the blood will go back to its proper place."

Jaw, jaw. No doubt perfectly correct jaw, but jaw.

"Shall we go?" Herr Bertelsen asked his companion.

And now the doctor impaired his authority still further by calling after the couple: "You can quite well use boracic if you like, quite well. A boracic compress will be a good thing."

"Did you ever hear the like!" said Herr Bertelsen to his companion with a snort.

Herr Bertelsen was dissatisfied with himself and with the whole business. He had heard quite well what the mockers said about an ant-bite, but the mockers had only said that out of envy, because he was the rich young man from the timber firm of Bertelsen & Son, the first gentleman of the sanatorium, its very lion, to whose share the best-looking lady fell as a matter of course. The mockers were unable to change the situation, he could not be shaken. And over and above, it happened to be his firm that had supplied the timber for the sanatorium buildings and on that account had had to take a good many of the shares. So how could young Herr Bertelsen be shaken? It was actually by his favour that the mockers were allowed to be here, a nod from him—and the whole crowd would have to clear out. He did not give this nod, he was a superior person.

Herr Bertelsen's relation to the sanatorium was no secret, he himself had made no secret of it, and in a place where there was nothing to do but gossip about one's neighbours, it soon became public property. Now, one would have thought that the envious mockers might be grateful for his correct and tolerant treatment of them, but no. Look here, they said ill-naturedly, what was this Bertelsen doing so close to Fröken Ellingsen's hat-pin? What the deuce did he want there? A hand, why yes, you could imagine that, maybe her hat caught in the branch of a tree; but his cheek, breathing in her face? Damn it, what a disgusting fellow! And it was no use his putting on side with a broad turn-up to his trousers and white spats and having the best room in the sanatorium; all that was only because his father was a big timber merchant—while he himself was nothing but a tailor's dummy in the business.

"Ah, but he's been made a partner," said a peacemaker.

"What of it?" asked the others, glancing at him furiously.

"I only mentioned it. So he's part-owner of the business."

"Well, what of it?" they asked again. "When his old father dies he'll be the owner of *all* his planks!" They didn't see what this had to do with the question.

But the one who thus broke with the band of mockers may have done so intentionally, with ideas of his own, God knows. He was a young man who played the piano, Eyde, with the Christian name of Selmer, Selmer Eyde to wit, quite a nice boy, but delicate and of a blue complexion, rather weak-looking. When he sat at the piano and you only saw his thin back he made a morbid impression. But he was all fire and flame at the piano and he was indispensable to the patients when they gathered in the drawing-room in the evening to listen to music. Fru Ruben asked for Tchaikovsky and got it, Fröken d'Espard asked for Sibelius and got it. He was at everybody's service, and in return the sanatorium took him at half price.

This Fröken d'Espard had lately arrived and was taking a holiday; she was not a patient, but was a lively and frolicsome lady with dimples in her cheeks and brown eyes. What was she doing here? The story was that her family had seen better days, but had now fallen from consideration. This was true, as likely as not. Probably one fine day an immigrant had arrived in this country, where it is more distinguished to be foreign than native, and it only took the name on his visiting-card to get him on here. Of this mystical Monsieur d'Espard it was known that he had scraped along with one thing and another, chiefly by giving French lessons, and thus gained the entry into good houses, made a name for himself, earned money, and inspired everyone with respect by the mere fact of being a foreigner. Then he got engaged, and all might have gone well, he might even have been married, but against this his wife at home raised a protest, and after that he had to disappear.

That was the founder of the family.

But his Norwegian fiancée, she was left with her shame and her growing disability; she was about to become a mother.

The child was d'Espard number two, a girl; she acquired the inestimable name and nothing else from her brilliant father, only the name. Her mother was forced to go three steps down in order to get married at all; oh, but little Julie d'Espard, she has her name which raises her two steps up. She sits in an office in Christiania because her name is d'Espard and she has been about and learnt French. She knows nothing to speak of, she talks the colourless Norwegian of the middle class, she can't sing more than anyone else, has never learnt to keep house, can't do a day's work or make her own blouses, but she can click at a typewriter and she has learnt French.

Poor Julie d'Espard!

But she is so pretty and brown-eyed and lively! Perhaps too she makes a point of being a little livelier than she is; how else is she to show what race she belongs to? She is of French extraction, and not merely French, but southern French, and be it as it may with her irregular origin, she is at any rate a love-child. Happy Julie d'Espard! And, strangely as things turn out, from the day she arrived at the sanatorium she became somebody; Fröken Ellingsen was no longer the only pearl of womanhood at Torahus.

Fröken d'Espard could do things which nobody else did, she could quite well express an opinion about the salad at dinner, saying it was not as it was in France, oh, very different indeed! When the ladies sat and listened to music, they left the choice of pieces to the pianist and were indulgent with Fru Ruben when she asked for Tchaikovsky, because she was rich and suffered with her nerves. But

Fröken d'Espard would ask for Sibelius, though she was poor and had nothing the matter with her. A deuce of a girl, but what did she know about Sibelius? "Don't you think we ought to ask Herr Selmer Eyde to play what he likes?" asked an indignant old maid. "Yes, certainly," said others. And then they started cackling about this in half-whispers. But of course they all understood why Fröken d'Espard had asked for Sibelius: it was because she was sitting on the sofa with a Finn, her attendant squire, an aristocrat with an ancient name, Fleming; it was to him she wished to show an attention.

A deuce of a girl, that d'Espard! When the music was over, it was bedtime for all reasonable people, but Fröken d'Espard went out. Nor was she content to go out by herself, but dragged the Finn Fleming along with her, though he was forbidden to stay in the cold night air on account of his chest. They went to look at the weather forecast, which was hung in a case with a glass door; as far as they could see in the dim light it was a triangle: dry weather.

"Ah, but it's cold," said Herr Fleming, turning up the collar of his coat.

The young lady remarked that they would just have to walk a little faster. She herself wore so ridiculously little, and nothing round her throat.

But Herr Fleming asked if there wasn't a notice in the hall requesting patients to be in bed by ten o'clock?

Of course there was. There were notices about everything under the sun.

Herr Fleming laughed at that and said she was walking him to death. He had difficulty in getting his breath, put his hand to his chest, and coughed slightly.

They sat down to rest.

That was another of the things he was forbidden, he explained.

That too?

Yes. Walking fast so as to make him cough and sitting down to rest were both forbidden.

"Everything is forbidden," she said, as though to herself. Then she explained that the notice in the hall was only intended for the old people who couldn't sleep. It didn't refer to them, the young people.

She got up and they walked on. They went towards Torahus Sæter and looked at Daniel's little farm and its houses. It was all so still, not a dog, not a sign of smoke from the chimney, the people must be asleep, the cattle in the byre must be asleep.

To think that there were other people living up here! the lady remarked thoughtfully.

Yes. And who could tell if they were not actually living happily up here? mused Herr Fleming.

The lady walked on in the twilight to have a closer view: no paint on the log walls, no curtains in the windows, every house roofed with turf. Why didn't they hang white curtains in the new cottage even? Then it would look still neater with its three windows. People of that class had no idea of comfort.

"I dare say they make themselves comfortable in their own way," thought Herr Fleming. "And God knows if it isn't the very best way—the comfort of few needs."

They discussed this further on the way home; Herr Fleming spoke gently and calmly, disillusioned as invalids are in the first stages; later on they get over this and make a fight of it, unwilling to die, but in the first stages they are disheartened and crushed by their fate. The lady tried to cheer him up by getting him to talk of his home, the great estate in Finland, a property with a castle built of stone, and leagues of fields and forests. They came back about midnight, it had been a long walk and Herr Fleming was coughing a little. The place was shut up, but Herr Fleming tapped gently on the glass with his diamond ring, and the door was opened.

All might have been well, they need not have disturbed the bad sleepers, but Fröken d'Espard wanted a book she had left in the drawing-room or somewhere and she began to roam through one creaking door after another, found one of her books, but it was not the one she wanted, searched on and found another, but that wasn't it either, so she had to go back again and be content with the first book.

Oh, those books of Fröken d'Espard's, they were always left where she had been sitting, French books all of them, novels, yellow covers and cheap paper. All this literary mediocrity was the most important part of the lady's baggage, it was the books that made it heavy, made her driver strain himself lifting her trunk. Every book was inscribed with the lady's name, Julie d'Espard, so that there might be no mistake about who it was that knew French at the sanatorium. They asked her sarcastically if she read several books at once, as there were so many of them trailing about.—No, she didn't do that. And she said in her Norwegian: "But I thought that if there was anybody who would like to borrow a French book they're welcome."—"As far as I'm concerned I haven't even time to read a twentieth part of our own books," was the reply.—"Oh, our own!" said Fröken d'Espard.

It was stupid of them, but several people took offence at the young lady, she was so foreign and superior, she set herself above her surroundings. Old maids out of country parsonages thought it was sufficient to believe in God and go about decently dressed, but no. They did not tear round at night, opening and shutting doors, but Fröken d'Espard did. In the morning they complained to the manager, the manager had a talk with the matron, the matron went to the doctor. Well, the doctor thought it over and agreed that the nuisance must be abated. With the old ladies he took it in his usual light and playful manner and praised them for being so much better since they came to Torahus; with Fröken d'Espard he held up a warning finger and made her laugh. Oh, he got nothing out of her, she had a way with men. So he went to Herr Fleming,—a man with a weak chest ought to be in bed at night.

"You ought to go out in the day-time instead," said the doctor to Herr Fleming.

"Yes."

"In the day-time when the sun shines."

"Oh yes, but what is the use of it all? Why should I make such a fuss?" asked Herr Fleming, pale with morning chills and dejection. "Look at my nails, how blue they are!"

"Your nails? Pooh! You ought to go trout-fishing in the lakes up above."

"You can't go trout-fishing when the sun shines."

"Oh yes, with a fly. There are several people who fish with a fly, Daniel of the sæter is one. We'll find some good spots. I'll go with you."

"Look here, doctor, I noticed my chest again last night: the left side has fallen in."

"Ha ha," laughed the doctor. "No man has both sides of his chest alike, no man, I tell you. No, don't worry about that. You have no hæmorrhage?"

"Fallen in a great deal," repeated Herr Fleming. "I have night sweats too."

"But no hæmorrhage?"

"But I cough. I coughed last night when I was out."

"Just so!" cried the doctor. "Is it Fröken d'Espard who leads you astray like this?"

"No, no, it's my own doing, I enjoy her society."

"Very well, enjoy it in the day-time as much as you like."

"Since you mention Fröken d'Espard," said Herr Fleming, "I am grateful to her for keeping me company. She's so cheerful and full of life, I depend on her. We talk about lots of things, I tell her about my home."

"Now, look here," said the doctor to cut him short; "you are to go to bed at ten o'clock and get well again."

Herr Fleming repeated with a doubting smile: "Well again?"

"Well again," said the doctor with a decisive nod. "Now I'll give you a cough mixture."

A hope was kindled in Herr Fleming's eyes, his lips quivered as he asked: "You don't believe I shall recover, do you?"

The doctor stared at him: "Not recover? Are you crazy?"

"It would be too splendid—too splendid—"

"There, now come along and get your cough mixture."

As they went along, Herr Fleming began to incline to the doctor's opinion, possibly he would recover. "No, I really haven't any more hæmorrhage," he said; "you're right there. What on earth can have done that? A month ago I had a hæmorrhage, not much by the way, a few mouthfuls, but we have some quarts of blood in us, so what is a mouthful? And since I came here I have had no hæmorrhage. Do you think it's stopped?"

The doctor halted Herr Fleming, made him stand straight up and look him in the eyes. Probably it was a doctor's trick or he wanted to produce an impression. Suddenly he broke into a merry laugh and said: "You with your powerful build, a giant, with inherited stamina! I don't know anyone better endowed by Nature. We have just to plaster over the tip of that left lung, then you'll be as well as ever."

Herr Fleming smiled with surprise and gratitude. "Thanks, thanks," he said.

"But no wandering about at night in the raw air, remember that!"

Then they went to get the cough mixture.

Yes, it was true enough, Herr Fleming was well endowed by Nature, but Nature seemed to have gone back on her word, to have withdrawn her promises; it was pitiful to see a young man so changed. The doctor's consolation was very acceptable, he wanted it badly, and all that day he was in a brighter frame of mind. It would be a joke if he cheated Fate, a grand joke, really! He sat down to write a cheery letter home: A remarkable place, this Torahus in Norway; sick people got well here, one after the other. But, then, they had a doctor here who knew his business; such cough mixtures he made up, such an air of knowledge and security there was about him! he wrote.

In the evening, when Herr Fleming went to bed, it seemed very plain to him that his chest had fallen in still more; what could be the reason of that? It couldn't be that his chest was in a serious state after all? He examined himself in the glass, measured himself closely with the eye, pressed in the right side to make it equal to the left, but still the left was lower. Only a little, nothing to speak of, a sagging from the tip of the lung downward, but enough to reawaken Herr Fleming's suspicions. He lay down, but for a long time was unable to sleep for thinking; he had the odd idea that Fröken d'Espard would have cured him if she had been a doctor, he ought to have married her, then she would have cured him right enough! His thoughts led him on, growing more and more ardent; as usual after he had gone to bed, they became fiercely lascivious, intolerable; he writhed for hours before falling asleep. When he awoke during the night, he was bathed in perspiration.

Morning came. Was he one of those creatures who cannot open their eyes without laughing and singing? No, no, what should have made him do that? He took his place at the breakfast-table without cheerfulness and without the slightest appetite. He looked at Fröken d'Espard's plate; she had not breakfasted yet. What did he want with her? Nothing; she listened to him and did not give him the go-by, did not leave him to his own devices, she was pretty and sound, a tempting fruit. By the time she came in he was already tired of her and greeted her grudgingly.

"Slept well?" she asked.
He only shook his head.
"We'll go out for a bit," she said.

III

Torahus Sanatorium went its way. Perhaps not the way it should have gone in every respect, with band playing and flags flying and a good dividend, but that was not to be expected at the start, that would come later. The management had the best intentions of serving a good cause, the doctor was a worthy soul, concerned for everyone's welfare, the matron was a lady with experience of nursing-homes and sick-beds, the manager an old sailor, a first-rate fellow who would take a hand at cards or even drink a glass with those patients who required to be cheered up.

Then there was Lawyer Robertsen, who together with the doctor was responsible for the whole thing; he came constantly up to Torahus and inspected the establishment and went through the books, for it was he who was chief director. A clever fellow, a man of ability; he greeted the staff as equals, though of course he was the master; he did not push his way among the guests, but stepped aside and held the door open for the ladies.

And now he arrived at the sanatorium in swell company, an English Cabinet Minister's wife and her Norwegian maid. Lawyer Robertsen bowed deeply, arranged about rooms, gave orders to the staff, and did all he could for the Minister's lady. She on her side accepted all his attentions as a matter of course and thanked him accordingly. She was a lady getting on in years, divorced from her husband, but with reserves still in hand, powder on her cheeks, a tight-laced corset, and a smile. The lawyer was proud of this guest and instructed the matron to look after her, she could just ask the Norwegian maid, her interpreter, whether she wanted anything.

Not that there was anything the matter with the lady, she was just a fashionable person who had taken a fancy to visit the Norwegian mountains and could well afford it, to judge by her baggage and her jewellery. Be this as it may, Lawyer Robertsen did not forget to speak to the doctor about her, saying he had better pay her a visit, she was a magnet that would attract many guests to the sanatorium; in fact, the lawyer went so far as to enjoin the manager take off his hat and stand bareheaded as the Minister's lady got into her carriage. And Manager Svendsen, the rogue, he had been a sailor and could speak "Mylady's" language: "Very well!" he said.

That ended Lawyer Robertsen's business of this time.

Then came Selmer Eyde, the pianist, and asked to have a word with him before he left. Oh, the lawyer knew very well what Herr Eyde wanted, but all the same he replied: "At your service, Herr Eyde!"

They went into the private office and the pianist stated his business: it was the old song that what he was doing here led to nothing, he must go abroad, it was the only thing, but days and weeks went by and he was no nearer getting to Paris. Couldn't Herr Robertsen hit upon some scheme for him this time?

"To Paris—yes. I say now, as I said before, that I respect you for it. Hasn't anybody come yet that you can apply to? But they'll come in the course of the summer, you may be sure there'll be people with money at a big place like this!"

"I had thought of Herr Bertelsen," said the pianist.

"Have you spoken to him?"

"No. It only occurred to me one day."

"Yes. I dare say. Wait now till the autumn, there'll be some solution, I know."

And although the lawyer looked as if he knew a lot more than he would say, Herr Eyde exclaimed impatiently: "No, it's months to the autumn, I must get away now, time flies."

"Now? No, you mustn't do that. Do you know who's just arrived? An English Minister's lady. There, that's a public to play for! She's quite likely to take an interest in you."

"But the English don't care about music," said Herr Eyde superciliously.

"Don't they? Anyhow, it would look odd if you went away just as she came. Perhaps she would actually ask for music and then you'd be gone."

"I expect there are plenty of ladies here who can strum."

"Yes, but she will certainly want good music, let me tell you; I understood as much from her. Look here," said the lawyer suddenly; "we'll call it a bargain that you stay here till the autumn, then there'll be somebody at the sanatorium who'll find your expenses."

"Who?" asked the pianist, waking up at once.

The lawyer answered: "I ought not to tell you, really. But go and speak to Herr Bertelsen. You know who Herr Bertelsen is, firm of Bertelsen & Son, a very rich man and a connoisseur. Give him my compliments and say you've spoken to me."

How did it come about that Lawyer Robertsen negotiated with this piano-player as if he had been the most indispensable of chambermaids? The young man must naturally have got the impression that he was something out of the common, he must be unique, like nobody else on earth. He was aggressive, his tone was strangely familiar, as though he had been promised something several times over and had never got it. And the lawyer put up with it. If there was anything behind this, it was not explained, as the lawyer went away at once.

There can't have been anything behind it, except that Lawyer Robertsen liked to talk and smooth things over and didn't want to quarrel with anyone, not even with the sanatorium's musician. He had got hold of this pert little fellow and didn't want the trouble of replacing him. The lawyer was a born host, liberal and obliging to his fellow-creatures.

When he had already taken his seat in the carriole, he was called in again and had to settle one or two things more: there was a question of the visitors' mail, they must have a regular postman with gold lace on his cap; and there was the skittle alley, which was already warped from the damp ground and had to be put right. There had been complaints about it.

But after that the lawyer left.

There were at present only twelve or fourteen visitors at Torahus, so that they had no use for the big dining-room with long tables for eighty persons. That would come later. Meals were still served in the ladies' drawing-room, which, however, the ladies never frequented, preferring the gentlemen's smoking-room. There they liked to sit and drink their coffee and glance at a paper and give little coughs because of the smoke. Mylady, as they called her, on the other hand, kept her distance, and, as she took her meals at utterly different times, the others saw little of her. She had dinner at eight in the evening and drank tea at all hours of the day; her diet consisted mainly of ham and eggs and toast.

So these twelve or fourteen people were boxed up together, conversing no more than was necessary and telling each other about their ailments. Oh, it was not for nothing they had tried mountain air, they were forced to, they had tried other things first. One had a ruined digestion and took pills and salts at every meal, another was rheumatic, a third had sores on his face, a fourth spat blood. If they went out of doors they wrapped themselves up in different ways, some took care of their chest, others of their back, others again of their feet; some wore black flaps over their ears, others blue or smoked spectacles. They all protected themselves, none of them wanted to die.

Ah, but there was one who wanted to die. He had to be watched, he had shown a tendency to suicide. A prompt and ready-witted fellow at times, at other times a prey to musings and taciturnity; the doctor had to speak seriously to him now and again. Properly speaking, no doubt, he ought to have been in a more suitable institution, but he had money and could pay his way. For that matter, the doctor did not believe he would lay violent hands on himself.

There was nothing pretty about this man, he was so unfinished, powerful enough about the shoulders, but with skinny calves; he looked as if he had been begotten by a pupil, a prentice hand, and bred from a servant-girl. He had come into his money. The patients called him simply the Suicide.

When the doctor spoke to him he was never at a loss for an answer. At first the doctor thought he could take him as he took all the rest, in a light and playful vein, but he soon had to give that up.

"It'll be all right," said the Suicide with a nod.

"What will?" asked the doctor.

"Only something I was thinking of. I'll find the way all right, if not today, some other day."

"Do you mean suicide?"

"Of course. That's what we were talking about, isn't it? I'll find a way, you'll see."

The doctor smiled and asked him: "You mean you can accustom yourself to the idea?"

The Suicide gave him to understand in a hurt tone that this was something the doctor knew nothing about. "I am seeking a valid form for it," he said; "I don't simply go and take my life without more ado."

"You're right there!"

The Suicide looked at him furiously: "Be quiet, Doctor! You come here with your petticoat ideas and talk about hidden things. It's nothing to put a noose round your neck; but has it ever occurred to you that a suicide may bring disgrace upon murder?"

At this staggering question Doctor Oyen was silent.

"You see, you don't understand that that thought may hold one back. Because there's nothing in hanging, it's a thing anyone can do for himself. You could do it."

"No, thanks."

"You could manage the movements anyhow. You don't even have to take aim."

"But now look here," said the doctor, trying to speak weightily; "couldn't you drop all this rubbish, Herr Magnus? There is more in this trifling business of death than you seem to think. We doctors have seen enough of it."

The Suicide retorted instantly: "You doctors haven't seen a scrap of what I mean."

"Well, but do you know just what it means to die?"

"No," replied the Suicide, "not from personal experience."

And with that he waved the doctor away.

Left to himself, he seemed tickled at the answers he had given. Or indeed his gassing about suicide's being a disgrace to murder may have been only bluff, an excuse for not hanging himself. Altogether the Suicide's talk did not always sound as sincere as it might be, there was too much smartness about it. But at the same time he had a harassed look, his young face was wasted with brooding and suffering.

The patients had nothing to do, they were reduced to wandering about the neighbourhood, reading notices and finger-posts, to joining one another in a whisky and soda, or hanging about one of the long verandas in the sunshine and brooding over their troubles. They were always hunting for sympathy and as a rule it was not long before the right people came across each other and were like old acquaintances. "Ow!" one of them would say; "I wish to God I could get rid of this rheumatism!" "Yes, it's not pleasant," another would answer; "rheumatism's one of the worst plagues there are." That was a help, it gave relief; then it would be the other's turn to get *his* bit of sympathy.

There were not many peculiarities about them. Patients are always alike. Perhaps the Suicide was the queerest. Another curious figure, by the way, was the man with sores on his face. His sores had lately begun to break out, they were hard lumps on the skin, which burst and formed running sores. When these sores were healed in one place, they broke out in another; at last they had attacked his eyes, his sight even; his whole system seemed to be infected with a poison. The man was of about the same age as the Suicide, young both of them, under thirty, and these two kept together.

The man with the sores was no fool either, he was capable of making fun of the other visitors and of himself and his sores. He was the son of an auctioneer, he said, and was not exactly rolling in money, but he could pay for his board, no trouble about that, and pretty often he had a letter from his father with an extra ten-crown note in it; this was for cards. So he went about among the rest, fighting for his life with mountain air and medical attention, inelegant enough in a brown jacket and a sports shirt which was held together over the chest with a brown shoe-lace, tags and all. His name was Anton Moss. He accused the Suicide of drinking too much, though that poor fellow never drank, but only took a whisky and soda now and then.

"How can you expect to get rid of your fixed idea if you drink?" said Moss.

The Suicide was easily riled; he replied hotly that in the first place he had no fixed idea, in the second place he didn't want to lose it, and in the third place he didn't drink. "You can just mind your filthy scabs and hold your tongue!" he said.

"My eruption is only on the skin, but you're sick inside."

"There's nothing the matter with me."

"No? Then what are you here for?"

"Be quiet!"

"There must be something wrong with your head, your brain."

"Aren't you ashamed of yourself?" cried the Suicide. "It's your own head there's something wrong with. Go and look in the glass!"

Moss was subdued at once, he dropped his swollen face and was silent for a moment. A moment—then he was the same again. "I have practically only one sore that won't heal, and it's this one!" he said, holding out a finger with a rag on it.

The Suicide looked at the finger in disgust and took a pull at his glass.

"I keep this, you may say, as my pet sore, for special occasions."

"Ha ha," laughed the Suicide.

"I should miss it if I hadn't this lifelong bandage on my finger. Shall I take it off and show you?"

The Suicide scowled askance at the terrible rag and hurriedly took another drink.

Moss went on: "You will remark that this is not an ordinary rag, it was given me by my mother. With a total disregard of expense, it is a silk one, originally red silk. Now it's a little faded; well, it can't be helped, I'm fading, you're fading. Though as far as you're concerned, you're looking fine today; you must have slept splendidly?"

This little appreciation seemed to have a good effect, the Suicide nodded; yes, he had slept splendidly. They began to talk sensibly about these everlasting sores; what kind of devilment could it be? It looked horrid. And now his ears were bleeding.

Here Moss nodded assent, his ears were bleeding. He must have torn off the scabs in the night, he thought.

Hadn't he any ointment?

Yes, Moss had been given an ointment. But this happened to be a case where Doctor Oyen chose to employ the expectant method, as they call it, he would wait and see. Oh, yes, Moss was given an ointment; vaseline, if the truth were told.

That was extraordinary!

Yes. But it just showed how harmless the whole thing was. He was supposed to have got it originally from sneezing against the wind.

"Ha ha," laughed the Suicide. "Will you have a whisky and soda?"

"Yes, thanks."

Thus these two squabbled time after time and made friends again. They were never enemies in earnest and they could not be away from each other for long at a time. Some days Anton Moss came down in the morning with his face in an awful state from tearing at it in the night; but he held his head just as high as usual, and on meeting the Suicide he would say: "Well, so you didn't do it last night either?"

"Be quiet!"

"No, it's not so easy to hang yourself. In the first place you have to find a stout nail."

They went out into the veranda. There were some people out there already, among them the lady who was always wringing something between her hands. She wrung her handkerchief and her gloves, everything she took up she twisted into a rope. It was nervousness with method in it. Perhaps she never considered how ridiculous and futile her efforts were, but she was certainly industrious, as though the work had to be got through. If she hadn't anything else she twisted her fingers till they cracked.

Anton Moss said to the Suicide: "Go and tell that lady to stop."

"I? No."

"It will give her relief for a while. I'm sorry for her."

"Go yourself!" said the Suicide.

Fru Ruben came out into the veranda, chose the broadest basket-chair, and sat down in it, made it her home. In Algiers she would have been reckoned the belle of the place, she had lovely, dark eyes and was so inhumanly fat. Her bulging brown fingers, with their diamond rings, seemed to have no bones in them.

"Are you going for a walk?" she asked the lady who was wringing her gloves.

"Yes, if I have someone to go with. Will you come, Fru Ruben?"

"Unfortunately I can walk so little."

"But you've got much thinner, Fru Ruben."

"Do you think so? Well, I think myself I have reduced, but yesterday when I weighed myself I was just the same. But it may be that I had thicker clothes on, thicker boots. Then you really think I'm getting thinner?"

"Absolutely. Anyone can see it. I think you ought to come for a walk, Fru Ruben."

"Don't be absurd! A healthy young woman like you dragging me about! Herr Svendsen, come here!" she called.

The manager came up, took off his hat, and asked: "Were you able to sleep last night, Fru Ruben?"

"No," replied the lady. "No more than any other night."

"Not any better?"

"Better? How could it be better? And I must tell you that I'm quite unfit to bear any shocks and alarms at night. I can't bear it."

"No—"

"No. But last night again the servant-girls made a terrible rumpus in the attic over my head. Like a lot of savages, I thought."

"No, but, Fru—"

"What, do you say no? Do you mean to deny it? But you must know that that noise in the attic is liable to kill me at any moment. Yes. And last night again I hadn't a wink of sleep because of that noise in the attic."

Now the fact was no servant-girls had been sleeping in the attic Fru Ruben spoke about, it was perfectly empty; but the manager had learnt wisdom from experience, and as soon as he could get a word in he just told her right out that the servants had now been moved.

CHAPTER THE LAST

"Have they been moved?" asked the lady.

"Moved yesterday; they sleep in the annex now, in that building over there."

"Well, what then?"

The manager said no more.

But now Fröken d'Espard had come up, that scandalous and graceless person who only found grace in the eyes of men; yes, she had come up and stood listening to the conversation. "How is it—how is it—?" she said in a flurry.

Fru Ruben looked her up and down: "What do you mean?"

"All I mean is—Herr Svendsen can't have understood you. You were kept awake last night when the servants were moved yesterday—?"

Fru Ruben thought it over. "Well, then, it was the night before last," she said. But all the same she was beaten. Another woman might have had recourse to tears; that was not Fru Ruben's way, but she turned crimson in the face. And at this juncture the lady who wrung her gloves got up and gave her cover: "Excuse me," she said; "there's a little nail sticking up in that chair you're in, it tore my blouse the other day. There it is!"

"Thank you," said Fru Ruben. But now she had recovered herself and called to the manager as he was going away: "Then you've really moved the maids?"

"They've been moved," he replied.

"It was none too soon!"

So each had something to attend to, something to take care of, fixed ideas, imaginary evils, and real ailments. Alas, all the ailments were real enough, all brought suffering, and all were alike incurable. It was pitiful to see this assemblage of ill health in all its variations.

The lady sat down again and made a rope of her gloves. Anton Moss seemed sorry for her and said: "She stopped for a moment while she was talking to Fru Ruben, now she's started again. No, I can't go and speak to her, I haven't the looks. But you could do it."

"It doesn't matter," replied the Suicide curtly. Now he was brooding and brooding again, one of his gloomy fits had come over him, it was ridiculous to bestir oneself about anything, futile, to do anything with one's hands, to get up, to talk. "Be quiet!" he said to Moss.

Moss said: "Look at that man coming out!"

The Suicide did not look up.

It was Herr Fleming, the consumptive Finn, who stepped out into the veranda, well dressed, hollow-chested, bowing to Fröken d'Espard and the others. He had scarcely had a good night, the marks under his eyes were very dark, but he bore it decorously, with a smile, was polite to the pianist and offered him a cigarette from an expensive case.

Now Fröken d'Espard came up and gave him her hand; Herr Fleming took it, without interrupting his conversation. "Good-morning," she greeted him. "Good-morning," he replied.

Herr Fleming was consumptive and easily irritated; he now knew Fröken d'Espard too well to stand much on ceremony with her, he took it for granted that she would make allowances for him, had in fact asked her to do so. Oh, he didn't want to lose her, she was very far from being unnecessary to him, she was the only one he cared about; but she did not keep out of his way, Fröken d'Espard, he never had to go and look for her, no, and the consequence was that now and then—as after a sleepless night—she had a taste of his bad humour. Not that he wouldn't have let her feel his displeasure even if she had not been visible on the veranda when he came out. Whatever she did was wrong, for he was consumptive and irritable. An excellent person, this Fröken d'Espard, who could stand him in all humours.

They went down the steps together and left the sanatorium.

Where were they going? To Daniel's again, where they went

CHAPTER THE LAST

almost every day? What did they want there?

It was Herr Fleming's idea, he liked going to Daniel and his sæter, it was so simple and easily grasped, you had to duck your head going through the door, and then you found a bed, a table, a couple of chairs, and a fireplace for cooking, Stone Age fashion. Wouldn't the lady and gentleman rather go into the new parlour? No, thanks, the consumptive gentleman preferred this old sæter hut. Here he sat on the wooden stool and had milk in a bowl, or curds and cream in a wooden dish; it tasted of childhood and primitiveness; it was even to the taste of the lady who came from town and wrote on a typewriter and knew French. They talked together, Daniel and his housekeeper on one side and the two from the sanatorium on the other; simple talk, a blissful ignorance of life's riddles, they had not many ideas to exchange, it was a relief to sit here and chat about things that didn't matter. What a difference from last night, when there was no sleep to be had for cogitation: Where is the road ahead? Nowhere. But, then, where is the road back? Nowhere.

He paid, paid well for the milk, and asked to be supplied regularly with curds and cream. Yes, he was more than welcome! He charmed the people of the house with nice behaviour and silver coins. Might he come back every day? Yes, at his service! "Don't let me keep you from your work," he then said; "let me stay in here a little while. I should like to sit here at the table and think something out and perhaps write home. Fröken d'Espard, you can explain!"

He was left alone, and as though he had already thought it out he began to undress, shedding tears of sentimentality and abandonment as he did so; he was ill and short of sleep. Was it himself standing here? Then a true instinct must have led him away from human beings and great buildings, back to the cave and the shelter.

At that he smiled, smiled through his tears; O God, how weak and pulled down he was! But there was healing in the very air of this hut, perhaps bacteria of a beneficent kind dwelt in these old walls;

God knows, a soporific, a yeast fungus, red corpuscles, health and life.

It did not trouble him that the window of the hut was uncurtained, he lay down in his blue silk underclothes and pulled the skin rug over him.

And then, to be sure, Fröken d'Espard explains to the people what sort of a man he is: a great Count who lives in a castle, he knows French, nay, he knows Russian, it's only his nerves that are a little out of order, they'll be all right again after a while. "Do you see that ring on his finger? Oh, if you had that ring, Daniel, you wouldn't have to do another stroke of work all your life!" "What should I do then?" asks Daniel, bewildered. No, he can't understand that.

The young lady strolls out with Daniel into the fields and watches him building his stone fences. You see, he explains, the fences are never high enough and never strong enough, they're an everlasting worry; the goats clamber up them, the cows jump over them, and the sheep rub against them! He gives this information in a jocular and slightly superior tone; he wants to show that he too knows something, not such fine things as she, no, no, but what he has to know he knows down to the ground. He lets it be seen that there isn't a man down in the village who can teach him anything about the running of this sæter. He is glad to talk about his place, about Torahus Sæter, Mountain, and Forest; as he says, it's all his, all round here. "What, all this?" she asks, deeply impressed, echoing him. "My goodness!" she says. This encourages him to go on. The lonely lad doesn't often get a chance of letting his tongue wag up here on his mountain and is not going to let it slip, he answers all her friendly questions very readily.

It amuses the lady to listen to him, he has such an odd way of talking. Besides, he's a plucky fellow, he laughs at a sore hand of his. She sees nothing comic in a sore hand, and that makes him laugh all the more. As she seems to be interested in such trumpery things, he tells her how his hand got caught between two stones in the fence and crushed till it was all blue and bleeding. It might have been much worse, only he saved it with his other hand and his knee. Oh, a thing like that would often happen in outdoor work.

He ought not to have bragged, Daniel, and perhaps he was not bragging either, but was only grateful to have a listener. And no doubt he would have been mistaken if he had thought she listened to him for his own sake; of course it was in order that the patient in the hut might be left in peace. She had gone past the window once or twice without seeing him, and when at last she looked more closely she discovered that he was in bed and asleep. She returned to Daniel and went on chatting with him. Daniel was in a shirt, a pair of trousers, with worn-out leather braces over his shoulders, and wooden shoes without stockings, that was all he had on. He was a dogged worker, a stone was a stone and he didn't give in if it was a little too heavy. Presently one of his braces burst. That wasn't anything either, he just unbuttoned it and made shift with the one he had left. Fröken d'Espard looked on and admired his resourcefulness. What if a lad like that were well washed! His mouth was too broad, but he had good teeth, his hair was thick and greasy, unclean. God knows, perhaps he'd look like a monkey in evening dress.

The housekeeper came up with every sign of bewilderment. "He's lying in your bed!" she said.

Daniel looked up.

"Taken his clothes off and gone to bed!" said the old servant.

Fröken d'Espard also showed surprise: "Oh, then he must have been very tired!"

Daniel began to laugh, but his housekeeper murmured: "No sheets and nothing!"

"That doesn't matter;" said Fröken d'Espard; "just let him alone, he must have been dead tired."

The housekeeper left them.

"Ah, but he might have gone to bed in the new cottage and had sheets," Daniel persisted. "For I have sheets in the house," he added. He was not flabbergasted or fretting over what had happened, but he let her understand that he had more than one sheet. Oh, Daniel was not poor, he was contented. He knew what there used to be at his father's ruined farm and he knew what he had himself, and that was quite good enough for him. Down in the valley there were bigger farms, oh, quite big farms, but they had mortgages on them; Daniel's sæter, mountain, and forest were free of debt! He chatted away frankly and confidently as he went on with his work, and the young lady kept him going with her questions.

Now, hadn't he a girl down in the village?

Ha ha. Oh well, that might be!

Why yes, he must have had some idea with the new cottage? This question inspired him with respect for the lady's intelligence and he thought he might just as well tell her the whole story. Oh no, he hadn't any girl really, but it leaked out of him that he had had an idea with the new cottage, for he once had a girl, Helena, a farmer's daughter, but nothing came of it. That was all one! Daniel was red in the face, he was working desperately hard, of course he was angry. But even at that moment he could not refrain from making some parade of his rival; it was the Sheriff's officer, he would be Sheriff himself and make a lady of Helena. So she was one of the better sort. And but for that, why, he—Daniel—would never have cared about her.

No, of course not.

"He takes his fate like a man," thought Fröken d'Espard, and when she praised him for this he took his fate still more like a man and was lofty about it: Ah yes, Helena would soon be a Sheriff's wife, while he—Daniel— struggled on here at Torahus the same as yesterday and the same as every other day. What else? Was he to make a fool of himself grieving about a girl? Never! There was a lad down in the village, he was thrown over and he couldn't put up with it, he got thinner and thinner and after a few years he was a corpse. There was a way to go on! He might have been alive yet.

"Did he die?"

"Right off. One day he was finished!" And Daniel grew wise and overweening, he spoke in proverbs: "Oh no, it doesn't do to be too grand to stick it out with life!"

Fröken d'Espard liked this and perhaps took it for his own original view of life. That it can't have been, but it was just as good, for all that. She had never talked to the people down in the village and did not know that many such wise sayings were current among them.

Then Daniel reciprocated by asking if the Count in there was her sweetheart, and the lady did not go so far as to deny it. But no, he wasn't her sweetheart exactly, they had only met at the sanatorium and had kept together from the first. They had so much in common.

"Then something will come of it one day; you'll see!" said Daniel with a nod of encouragement,

And Fröken d'Espard answered: "What may come of it one day I don't know, but nothing has come of it yet. And what should come of it anyhow? No, it won't come to anything."

But now Daniel had already yawned several times and that was a sign that he was hungry, then he looked up at the sun and hinted that it was feeding time. As they walked back to the houses, Daniel asked what it was like at the sanatorium; very grand, wasn't it?

"Oh yes. So so. Not like it is abroad, of course, but still—"

"There's an English Princess come there, I hear?"

Fröken d'Espard could have no objection to living under the same roof as a princess and answered: "So they say."

"Well, to think that they should make a castle and a royal palace out of the old sæter over there!" said Daniel, shaking his head. And once more he began to set forth how it was he who had received the first offer, that it was his sæter they wanted in the first place. He did not seem to regret having held out and refused to sell, but people might as well know that it was the real Torahus Sæter, Mountain, and Forest that was first chosen for the sanatorium. Naturally, for this was the spot. Over there at the other sæter they had nothing but rocks and north wind.

The housekeeper met them with the intelligence that Daniel would have to have his dinner in the new parlour; there was cold porridge, cold milk, cold potatoes, pickled herring, she had been able to cook nothing, the stranger was still asleep in the hut where the fireplace was.

"Is he still asleep?"

"Asleep? He hasn't even turned over!"

Daniel laughed good-naturedly and went in to his cold dinner. And verily Fröken d'Espard was a wonderful woman; she waited patiently through the whole dinner hour, and when it was over she went out again into the fields with Daniel. Who but a loving woman could sustain such an ordeal? When at last Herr Fleming came out, late in the afternoon, the first thing that encountered him was her happy face. He smilingly shook his head as though apologizing for his conduct, nay, as though he had no words to excuse it.

"Have you slept well?" she asked.

"Yes," he replied. Then he thanked Daniel for his lodging and gave him a bank-note; oh, he was full of praises, he had not had a better sleep since he was a child. "Can you understand it, Fröken d'Espard? And will you let me come again, Daniel? No, no sheets, nothing elaborate, just as it was today. Thanks."

On the way home he was still talking about the sleep he had had. And fancy, he was hungry! He had not had an appetite for his meals for ever so long, now he could eat dry bread. That was the result of sleep. How many hours had he slept, anyhow? And without perspiring, almost without getting moist.

Fröken d'Espard could not help seeing the streaks of moisture that had run down from his temples, but were now dried up; she said hum and ha to all his high spirits and only forced the pace so that he might not take cold.

"Oh, I shall get better, you'll see; I feel it, I'm stronger already. Yes, that's right, let's hurry on, you're hungry, we're both hungry."

They were too late for dinner at the sanatorium, but Fröken d'Espard was quite equal to getting a meal served at odd times and she lent a hand by carrying it in from the kitchen. So they ate their dinner and drank wine with it; there was joy in the heart of the consumptive man, he thawed, colour came into his cheeks, and life into his eyes.

The day wore on. There was still joy in Herr Fleming's heart and later in the afternoon the couple took another glass or two of good wine. In the evening he seemed to have no idea of separating, though the lady showed every sign of tiredness; no, he himself was fresh after his good sleep, the night would be long, what should they do about it? They discussed this for a while; the very act of undressing, of unlacing his boots, appeared to him insurmountable. This made her laugh. They sat so long in the smoking-room that the last of the visitors left them and went to bed; then at last they too got up and ascended the stairs; Fröken d'Espard could scarcely keep her eyes open.

Then he took her hand and she said good-night, good-night!

No, that wasn't it. He wanted her to come on with him, to his own room, into it.

She wouldn't.

But he would find the night so long, so disconsolate, a desert of wakefulness. Look here, he had had some wine sent to his room, they could go on drinking wine.

Thanks, but not now. No, thanks.

Then might he come along to her room? They could sit there. Otherwise it would be such a long night.

"No, good-night," she said, and "You'll sleep all right," she said. "But all the same I might come along and take your boots off for you."

"Ah, thank you so much! You're so kind!"

On entering his room they both whispered cautiously, but she would not let him lock the door.

"It's only in case the maids might think fit to look in," he explained.

"Yes, but I'm going directly. Now sit down!"

She untied his shoe-laces and paused for a moment in surprise—which perhaps was what he had intended: this fine gentleman wore silk socks; as far as she could tell, very expensive silk socks. To cover her confusion she remarked carelessly: "Your socks are too thin for the mountains."

"Do you think so?"

"Yes. You want woollen ones here. There, now you can do the rest yourself!"

She got up, went to the door, and disappeared.

IV

When Lawyer Robertsen visited the sanatorium he had many things to see to, a word of encouragement here, of advice there, he had occasion for patience and goodwill, he was such a good-natured man that he very seldom used his authority.

The first one he asked after was Mylady, and, thank you, she was quite well. She was stylish and exclusive; read magazines, took her bath, went for little strolls with her interpreter, the Norwegian maid, got up at noon, and had dinner by herself at eight in the evening. She seemed quite comfortable. Oh, Mylady must have had something on her mind like the rest of them; she was not ill, but her Norwegian maid could bear witness that she sometimes shed tears and was sad at heart. So there must have been something amiss with Mylady too.

"She's running up a big bill," said the matron.

"Is she? That's grand!" replied Lawyer Robertsen. "The bigger, the better!" said he.

That was a matter he could dispose of on the spot. Other matters might be more complicated. The doctor spoke to him about the Suicide. That devil of a Suicide had his obstinate fits: why should he get out of bed anymore, why should he put his clothes on, why eat, talk, use his legs? Sooner or later he'd be dead! At other times he was in excellent humour, like anyone else, and would even join in a game of skittles. He was a man of regular habits and paid his bill promptly.

"Well, I don't see what more we can do for him," said the lawyer.

The doctor replied that no, they couldn't do any more. On the other hand there was the fact that occasionally he made foolish threats and wanted to put an end to himself. One could never tell.

"Whether he puts an end to himself here or somewhere else is all the same, as far as that goes. That's my opinion. But he might do harm to the sanatorium."

"Precisely!" replied the doctor. "If he carries out his threat he'll make a disturbance among the visitors, and the whole place will lose in reputation."

"Do you believe he'll hang himself?"

"Perhaps not that he'll hang himself exactly, that may be doubtful. But there are other possibilities, you know. His own idea is that he has got to discover some extraordinary and subtle way of killing himself."

"How do you mean?"

"Oh, it's all nonsense. He has a notion that suicide is inferior to murder, so the problem is to exalt the manner of his death."

"Is that what he says?"

"Something of that sort. Exalt it so as to bring it up to the level of murder."

Both doctor and lawyer laughed, the laugh of natural and sensible men. "Well," said the lawyer, "shan't we pay respect to murder, shan't we *exalt* ourselves to murder? Priceless!"

They agreed to keep this quaint character a while longer at the sanatorium and see how things went.

Then there was his good friend Anton Moss, the one with the eruption. It was not altogether comfortable to have him about the place, his face was no ornament to the veranda or the dining-room, but he did no harm either, and the other visitors did not seem inclined to leave the place on his account. Manager Svendsen thought a great deal of him, he would help with the book-keeping in the evening and was afterwards ready to take a hand at cards if any of the visitors asked him.

One after another the sanatorium patients were passed in review and discussed, and the lawyer came back to Mylady, the English Minister's wife: there was still nothing the matter with her, was there?

Oh well, the doctor had given her arsenic pills to brace her up and powders to make her sleep. She was not quite sound in her mind. The doctor had had several audiences of her and had received certain impressions of her condition: one time she had been provoked because the sanatorium postman had stood before her with his cap on, another time she had been annoyed at some washing which was hung out to dry and was visible from her windows. Well, neither of these trifles was particularly striking and both were put right. In the ordinary way Mylady was easily managed, she kept to herself, came and went with her maid, and interfered with nobody. When Doctor Oyen found it difficult to talk to her direct, the interpreter stepped in and it went quite well, that Norwegian maid was as sharp as a razor at translating his answers. Though indeed Mylady did most of the talking; thus she said there were some things, like these sheets and underclothes on a line, that were liable to turn her hair grey. On a later occasion she explained why she lay in bed till noon: it was because the morning light shouted at her, she said, howled at her, she said. Oh, it was terrible! "Imagine, Doctor, the morning after a ball: the evening has been lovely, the night soft and soothing, rocking one to sleep—and then to wake up in the morning to daylight!"—As concerned her general state of health, she realized herself that it was declining, she was overstrained, but she had no idea that she was near her death; she smiled and said: "It wouldn't be like me to die!"

"Has she asked for music?" asked the lawyer.

"On the contrary, she has asked to be spared it. Not that she would prevent the other visitors' having music; but when the pianist, Selmer Eyde, sent to ask if she would like any particular kind of music, some of Sullivan's for instance, the titled Englishman's, she replied that she didn't want any music at all. As far as I can see, Selmer Eyde has nothing more to do here," concluded the doctor. In fact, the same Eyde was going about in a very discontented frame of mind, in spite of his being boarded at half rates.

"In my opinion," said the lawyer, "Eyde is very useful here. It's one more advantage over the other sanatoriums that we have a permanent musician to play to the guests. Don't you think the same?"

"Oh yes," replied the doctor, falling in with his views. That was what he was for.

Lawyer Robertsen stretched his legs and said: "I have already boomed our permanent musician. It'll be in the papers one of these days."

The doctor smiled, shook his head, and signified his admiration. And the lawyer swelled with importance: "We'll make a good place and a fashionable place of Torahus, it's interesting to work at. Don't you think it's a satisfaction to see one's labours crowned with success? I attend to the practical side, you to the scientific. We'll make it go!"

"Certainly we will!"

"To jump from one thing to another—I can't find Mylady in the *Almanach de Gotha.**"

"No, no. But what of it?" the doctor innocently asked.

"No, you're right, what does it matter? Nothing at all!" The lawyer then propounded his views on this question: she was at any rate a Minister's wife—Princess he had called her in one of his notices. They must make the most of Mylady's stay at Torahus, she must positively be made to pay. Princess So-and-so and suite. The newspapers

---

*A directory of Europe's royalty and higher nobility, also including the major governmental, military and diplomatic corps.

were very obliging. If only it were possible to do something more for her, something extra. Couldn't they get up a rustic wedding for her, with master of the revels and village fiddler and national costumes?

The doctor doubted whether that would attract Mylady. She took no notice of the people of this country, the Norwegians.

Did she never speak to anybody?

Yes, to Fru Ruben. To Fru Ruben, curiously enough. She had even visited Fru Ruben in her room.

"Well," said Lawyer Robertsen, "that's not so strange; she goes where both her language and herself will be understood. Fru Ruben is cosmopolitan."

"But so are some of the others. Why doesn't she talk to Herr Fleming, for instance?"

"God knows. By the way, we've forgotten Herr Fleming. Is he getting better?"

"He's not really better," replied the doctor. "He picks up and slips back again, there's no lasting improvement. It wouldn't do for such a prominent patient to go and get worse here, to find the air too keen, to die perhaps."

Should he be advised to try a change? But on what grounds? That the locality did not suit him? No health resort in the world would turn away a valued guest on that ground. Wasn't Herr Fleming likely to recover?

The doctor explained that Herr Fleming had improved during the last few days, his spirits had risen, he reported that he was sleeping better. A queer fellow this Fleming, too; he went every day to the neighbouring sæter and drank sour milk. And no doubt he slept there some days. In short, the last few days had done him good. The matron hinted that he had even been larking with the maids; well, well, it was only with Fröken d'Espard.

"Oh, the devil," said the lawyer; "then he's going to recover!"

They agreed to keep him at the sanatorium as long as possible. Afterwards the lawyer found time for a personal chat with him and was very favourably impressed with the state of his mind; Herr Fleming was thus able to joke about having become a regular subscriber for curds and cream at the neighbouring sæter. It did him good, he said, helped him to recover. The only thing he missed at Daniel's was a young and pretty housekeeper.

All playfulness and good spirits.

And after that the lawyer was so cheered that he even arranged that matter of Selmer Eyde, the pianist. It came easily to him, he simply acted in his most natural manner.

It began by Bertelsen's coming up, pale with annoyance or fury or whatever it was, and exclaiming rudely, without answering the lawyer's greeting: "I'll be much obliged if you won't saddle me with any more petitioners."

The two gentlemen were good friends in Christiania and the lawyer therefore thought himself entitled to hit back. He asked: "Haven't you had your morning beer?"

"What's that got to do with you?" replied Bertelsen. "But you shove a starving piano-thumper on to me to try to get me to pay his expenses abroad."

"Oh, Eyde!" said the lawyer. "I couldn't make out what you were driving at. Has he been to see you?"

"Yes. And you sent him, he said. But I simply won't have you sending me people like that, so now you know!"

The lawyer admitted the justice of this: "No, I can quite understand that. This young man is rather apt to push himself forward, he's an artist and excitable, can't wait a moment. I did not send him to you, of course; it was he himself who mentioned your name."

"The fellow comes straight to me and asks what about that travelling scholarship and when can he have it."

"Ha ha ha," laughed the lawyer; "he's mad about that. All the same, I can't help respecting his enthusiasm and his wanting to get abroad. And I'm sure you respect him for it too."

"Yes, but he's not going abroad at my expense, I'll see him damned first!" squealed the exasperated Bertelsen. "I think you're crazy, both of you. He said he came from you."

At this moment the lawyer sighted Fröken Ellingsen in the offing and behind her Fröken d'Espard and Herr Fleming. Here was his escape; he said: "Of course he didn't come from me. But when the man himself mentioned you, said he thought of going to you, I probably said something like this—'Yes, do! At any rate it won't be the first time Herr Bertelsen has had an application of this kind.' Something of that sort I must have said."

Bertelsen was slightly mollified and said: "But it's a rotten trick to make a dead set at me like that."

"Good-morning, Fröken Ellingsen!" said the lawyer. "We were just talking of Herr Eyde."

Bertelsen turned round and faced her, but gave no greeting. A moment later they were joined by Fröken d'Espard and Herr Fleming; there were now five of them to discuss the musician. The lawyer warmly pleaded his cause, whatever may have been his reason; he praised the young man's enthusiasm once more and respected it. "What do you think, Fröken Ellingsen?"

"It isn't his enthusiasm I'm complaining about," interrupted Bertelsen. "It's his behaviour. What have I to do with his travelling scholarship?"

"Well, well, don't make yourself out any worse than you are," said the lawyer, slyly. "You know very well it's not the first time someone's been after you. And as far as I know, it wouldn't be the first time you'd assisted talent. I ask your pardon for disclosing this characteristic of yours to the company."

Bertelsen was now much mollified, that devil of a lawyer had twirled him round and made him into something more than an ordinary timber merchant. He stole a glance at the others and then dropped his eyes.

"He plays splendidly!" said Fröken d'Espard, speaking of Selmer Eyde. She knew least about it and therefore talked the most. "Doesn't he?" she asked, turning to Fröken Ellingsen.

"Yes."

"Well, what's the question?"

The lawyer replied: "It's a question of going abroad, Fröken, of studying in Paris."

"It's a question of a pretty considerable sum," said Bertelsen.

Then all at once Herr Fleming asked: "How big a sum?"

Everyone was silent for a moment, whereupon the lawyer reckoned up in a low voice: a year's keep, journey there and back, tuition fees, sundries—

But now Bertelsen scented danger, as though Herr Fleming might step in and take the wind out of his sails; he quickly intervened with firm decision: "Good, I'll give him the travelling scholarship!"

They all looked at him. A flush spread over Bertelsen's face, and the lawyer came to his aid, murmuring: "I knew it, oh, I knew it!"

"But on condition that he goes straight away," said Bertelsen. "That he gets out of here straight away."

"I'm sure he'll be more than glad," replied the lawyer. "But why?"

"Why? I don't want to have this fellow running after me here. No. I won't have him asking me day after day when he can have this travelling scholarship. It's just as if I couldn't pay it. He can have the money at once, I'll write a cheque."

"That's grand, that's extremely generous! I take the liberty of thanking you on his behalf."

"Well, we won't talk about that," concluded Bertelsen. "Just let me know how much he's to have for a year's stay in Paris."

They looked one at another, and all were silent again, Fröken d'Espard, who had been in France, looked as if she wanted to say something, but the lawyer proposed that they should all go indoors and discuss the question.

They did so and went to Bertelsen's room, which was the best and most expensive in the place, a little salon with an alcove. There were paintings in gold frames on the walls and curtains to the alcove, a gilt bronze lamp with pendants over the table, heavy curtains which shut out most of the light, a carpet on the floor, an ottoman, plush chairs.

"Come in, ladies and gentlemen, and sit down!"

Bertelsen, occupier of the swellest room in the sanatorium, ordered cakes and wine and was generous towards the musician, wanting to give him a decent allowance.

"I knew it, I recognize your way!" said the lawyer, the sly dog.

When all was arranged and the cheque made out, the party did not break up, it was as though these five people had met for the first time. Naturally their talk was of the other patients and visitors and it was not all innocent trifles that they had to say of them. Bertelsen was very free-spoken in his utterances both about Mylady and about Fru Ruben; these two ladies offended his eyes, one by her grand ways, the other by her bulk. "Good God!" he said, "it ought not to be allowed! The rest of us have our rights as human beings, and what's the use of all those grand airs and all that fat?" Fröken d'Espard seemed to be the only one who saw the logic of this; she laughed and exclaimed: "It's true, it's true!" Altogether Bertelsen and Fröken d'Espard found they had more and more tastes and sympathies in common, they were of one mind about the theatre, about languages, about good manners.

More wine and cakes were brought in, this casual festivity evidently suited Bertelsen's humour; and though both the lawyer and Herr Fleming looked at the clock, they were asked to sit still, on the ground that Bertelsen liked to have their company.

"We're very comfortable here," Fröken d'Espard chimed in, agreeing with him once more.

Poor Fröken Ellingsen was rather left out in the cold in the midst of all this agreement; God knows, perhaps something had come between her and Bertelsen today, otherwise he could hardly have neglected her thus. It was noticeable that he avoided listening to her words, talked them down and reduced them to nothing, he didn't even take the trouble to contradict her, evidently thinking it not worth while. Not that Fröken Ellingsen lost anything by it; Herr Fleming took up the conversation with her and carried it on smoothly and naturally, he knew what he was talking about. Oh, but Fröken Ellingsen was uneasy and far from being herself; Fröken d'Espard changed over to French and started parleyvooing with the timber merchant, and then who could tell what she was saying? It was beyond Fröken Ellingsen.

"What are they saying over there?" she asked with a smile of indifference. "What secrets are they talking?"

Herr Fleming smiled back with the same indifference and replied: "They're only practising."

But the devil was in it, something seemed to have come between Herr Fleming and *his* lady, it must have been an unlucky day for devoted couples, pique and resentment were in the air. Herr Fleming knew how to keep his countenance, but he could not entirely conceal the fact that Fröken d'Espard's behaviour interested him. Poor little Fröken d'Espard! Oh, a creature of temperament, a girl with sex appeal! She could lean against the one she was talking to, so as to make him feel her body, she was quite capable of taking up Bertelsen's hat, which was hanging on the back of a chair, gazing at it musingly, and then replacing it; the effect was that of something done to Bertelsen, a tenderness shown to Bertelsen. That was her winning way.

"I can read a little French," said Fröken Ellingsen, not to be quite out of it. "But unfortunately I can't speak it."

"Of course you know French," said the lawyer. "Otherwise you wouldn't be in the Telegraphs?"

Just then Bertelsen and Fröken d'Espard had a private laugh to themselves, and Fröken Ellingsen had a sort of shock. She asked them straight out what they were laughing at so that she might join in, but received no answer. Then Fröken Ellingsen turned in desperation to Herr Fleming and hinted that she was beginning to miss her work at the transmitter. He mustn't think it was uninteresting, no, no, she preferred it to this loafing existence, the telegraph was life in extract, she was forced every day to be a party to her fellow-creatures' weal and woe; oh, the telegraph was an inexhaustible well of secrets.

"I hope you don't know too many bad things about me, Fröken," said Herr Fleming in jest. But at the same time a little colour came into his withered face.

"I hope the same as regards myself," joked Lawyer Robertsen.

She passed it off: No, nothing bad about either of the gentlemen! But they might be sure she knew a lot of things. State secrets? Of course not; but they might be serious things all the same, mightn't they? There had been times when a shiver ran through her, sitting there as an intermediary, as a humble instrument, between one of our Ministers and the Department of Foreign Affairs.

Both gentlemen were listening.

But, Fröken Ellingsen went on, perhaps the most interesting of all were the telegrams to and from the police in different countries, the tracking of murderers, forgers, swindlers, gangs of thieves. There were fashionable ladies involved, noblemen, French politicians, banks, poison, politics—

The gentlemen were now listening in astonishment. This Fröken Ellingsen, who up to now had simply shown herself tall and good-looking at the sanatorium, hardly speaking, hardly ever asserting herself, now suddenly appeared with a radiance about her, a nimbus, she had the gift of acting, knew how to use her hands discreetly and to drop her eyes as though she produced her words from the depths. "Yes," she said, "life goes its way and God no doubt goes with it. Some men make a long journey with a railway ticket, others a yet longer one with a revolver bullet!" She related love tragedies, reconstructed whole dramas in which the telegraph had played the part of intermediary and accessory. There was the story, for instance, of the two foreigners and the shooting-cart:

"Well, two foreigners arrived in Norway, a gentleman and his valet. They proposed to shoot here, they had brought their own shooting-cart and intended to travel about by themselves in our valleys and forests. A few days later the telegraph gave the alarm: 'Keep an eye on the gentleman and his valet!' They were now in one or other of the dales. Foreigners imagine that our dales are made to hide in, that our whole country is out of the world, our dales undiscoverable. Good. But the gentleman, the valet, and the cart were in Hallingdal. A week or so later another gentleman arrived from abroad, an emissary dispatched after the two. He received the following order by telegraph from his country: 'Let gentleman and valet escape, but arrest shooting-cart.' Our police went with him, they found the persons, but the shooting-cart was gone. The emissary then telegraphed home: 'Shooting-cart vanished, alleged stolen by Hungarians, gipsies.' Then came a hunt for the gipsies, they were found on the way to Valdres, and there was the cart. Yes, it was the shooting-cart all right, but the gipsies asserted that they had bought it of the gentleman and his valet. The emissary then buys back the cart and reports home that the cart has been taken to an out-of-the-way spot and opened, taken to pieces—but it was empty. The cart had been emptied before the gipsies got it! It appeared from the report that the contents of the cart were not gold and precious stones or anything of that sort, but papers, nothing but papers—imagine, little black words on white, but more precious than any valuables, immensely important, fraught with destiny, life and death. And now the papers had vanished!"

Here Fröken Ellingsen broke off and asked: "Do you care to hear any more?"

What did she mean? Naturally they wanted to hear more, they were just coming to the exciting part.

"Oh well, but there isn't much more," she said. "The emissary and the police had to go back to Hallingdal, they searched fields and forests, in vain; finally they had to apply to the gentleman and his valet to tell them the hiding-place. Then they bought back the papers."

Her listeners felt rather sold: "Oh, so they bought back the papers?"

"Yes."

A curious change had come over the lady; she had lost the thread as it were, there was nothing more in her. How had that come about?

Then Herr Fleming had the charity to ask: "But why didn't they arrest the gentleman and his valet at once?"

"Don't know," replied the lady hesitatingly. "Perhaps they were nearly related to the victims of the robbery."

Silence.

"But the valet?" asked Herr Fleming.

Fröken Ellingsen seemed to have collapsed, but pulled herself together for a final effort and replied: "The valet—well, you see, it was a lady."

That made it a little better and the gentlemen exclaimed involuntarily: Ah! But a moment later they were puzzled again and asked questions: But the whole thing—what was the idea of it? A shooting-cart? And why didn't they arrest the conspirators?

Fröken Ellingsen didn't know, she said, didn't know at all. She seemed at her wit's end. All at once she hit upon a fresh idea and said mysteriously: "Why didn't they arrest them? It might be that their Government wished to give them a chance of shooting themselves with their own guns."

Ah. Yes, that might be. And the gentlemen accepted that. There sat Fröken Ellingsen, they felt sorry for her, they did not want to worry her. To let her down they began talking of something else. The lawyer returned to the topic of Mylady and asked Herr Fleming whether he, as a nobleman, had a copy of the *Almanach de Gotha*.

Herr Fleming seemed slightly embarrassed at the question and asked in return: "What? Why?"

"It was the *Almanach de Gotha*. If you have a copy I would ask you to look if Mylady's in it, if you don't mind. I can't find her."

Herr Fleming gave a laugh of relief and replied: "I don't even know if I'm in it myself. You can be a prince or a princess and not be put in. No, I haven't a copy."

But Fröken Ellingsen was still sitting there like nothing at all and Herr Fleming then told her about the bull belonging to the sæter, Daniel's bull. Had she come across it in her walks?

No.

That was a good thing, he was dangerous, not very safe anyway, best to give him a wide berth! Yes, Daniel had got this bull, a whacking brute with great horns, a smooth brown coat, and a monstrous ugly look. Daniel himself said he had turned bad-tempered and was not to be trifled with.

No, thank God, the lady hadn't come across him. Ugh—it made her shudder!

"If the animal is a danger to visitors at the sanatorium, Daniel ought to get rid of it," said the lawyer.

"He wants to keep the bull till the autumn and then sell it for slaughtering," Herr Fleming informed him.

"I'll send our porter over and buy it at once," the lawyer decided. "Our visitors must not go in fear of the beast. There's no sense in that."

It can't be denied that Lawyer Robertsen now felt something of a Mæcenas in his turn, a benefactor to a whole sanatorium, and when Fröken Ellingsen thanked him in a few words, he probably thought that one appreciation was worth another. He therefore said to the lady: "What you were telling us—that remarkable affair of the shooting-cart—it's strange you haven't written about it."

"I? No."

"You ought to write it. There was tension and life in it. Don't you think so?" he asked Herr Fleming.

Herr Fleming nodded assent.

The lady recovered herself; it seemed her story had not missed fire altogether and now she recovered herself. No, no, she couldn't write, she smilingly acknowledged that; but she could sit at a telegraph instrument and listen. That was all she was good for. And afterwards when she was by herself she thought over what she had heard. It was not without importance to her, it provided food for the mind.

Just so, then she did write it down?

Well, she couldn't altogether deny it. Of course she had tried, and in fact she had a good deal of manuscript put away, she might as well admit that. But how did the gentlemen know?

It was not very difficult to guess. Such lofty flights of narrative.

Fröken Ellingsen was now feeling pretty happy over this appreciation, this acuteness of perception, and for a time she forgot the parleyvooing couple, in fact she even got them to listen to her after a while. She ejaculated with unexpected conviction and as though the matter was of some importance: "No, what interests one in the Telegraphs is not the cheap little crimes, how one man swindles another over a consignment of timber; that's only rascality and smartness. But one day your instrument ticks out something different: out of the way there, England calling, the Duchess of Somewhere has disappeared, she's run away or been carried off..."

Another long story. It only came to an end when the lady again broke down and could go no further.

They had all been listening, Bertelsen and Fröken d'Espard stopped parleyvooing and listened. Once, at the beginning of the story, Bertelsen, the timber merchant, interrupted, declaring that rascality and swindling over a consignment of timber was out of the question. And Fröken Ellingsen agreed and excused herself; it was only what came into her head, she might have mentioned another trade, horse-dealing.

Later in the story Bertelsen asked: "But haven't you taken an oath?"

"An oath? Yes."

"An oath of secrecy?"

The question put her out a little; she floundered: What? Oh yes, she had signed a declaration. Not for anything in the world would she violate her oath. Had she done so?

"No," replied Herr Fleming.

"But, all the same," Bertelsen went on, still persecuting her, "I can't make it all out. Was the Duchess here, in this country?"

"Here?"

"I seem to have read something like it in a detective story. Is that the way you remember things?"

Here Fröken Ellingsen protested hotly, as a dark flush spread over her face: Certainly not, she had read very few detective stories in the course of her life. But the fact was they belonged to the age, they invaded everyday life, the telegraph was full of them. And as concerned her oath, she had mentioned neither names nor places, the Duchess might be anywhere you pleased. They must have noticed that she broke off suddenly and would tell no more? She had done so purposely, when she could go no further on account of her oath.

Bertelsen was pitiless. "Strange!" he said; "in the shooting-cart story you mentioned place-names offhand: Christiania, Hallingdal—"

This was too much for Fröken Ellingsen and she burst into tears. She did not get up and go, she simply collapsed in her chair under Bertelsen's words, like something speechless and submissive. She was shaken with hysterical sobs.

"Good God!" cried Bertelsen, dashing to her side; "what's the matter, what is there to cry about? I didn't mean—but of course it was stupid of me. Damn! What do I know about your oath and all the rest of it? But you must know that, not I. I wish you would stop worrying about it, I do sincerely. There, it's all right now, isn't it?"

"It's nothing!" she sobbed. "No, sit down, do you hear? It's nothing! You're not to console me, you were partly right, mainly right, perhaps altogether from your point of view. It was only that I felt faint. Don't let me disturb you, it'll be over in a moment. I felt a little faint, the room was going round—"

The gentlemen then managed among them to give Fröken Ellingsen time to come round. The lawyer expressed his admiration for Herr Fleming's appearance, his healthy appearance; how he had recovered, how he was putting on flesh! And Herr Fleming replied that, thank God, yes, he would soon lack nothing, except a sweetheart, he-he.

Fröken d'Espard had witnessed the unfortunate scene with Fröken Ellingsen at a distance, with an expression half of surprise, half of scorn; now she got up and went over to the distressed lady, spoke to her in whispers, and stroked her hair. The gentlemen tasted their wine and tried to restore an air of cheerfulness by talking more loudly than was necessary. And in this they were successful, by degrees the ladies joined in, the festive spirit was restored, more food and drinks were brought in. Yes, all was well again, there was no longer any misunderstanding between Bertelsen and his lady, he moved his chair close to hers and entertained her. He got on his feet and made a speech in praise of the place, of Torahus Sanatorium, and Lawyer Robertsen returned thanks as host. Herr Fleming grew more and more lively, he leaned back in his chair, pulled his waistcoat down over his shrunken stomach, and smacked himself on the chest. Look here what he could do; he couldn't have done that a few weeks ago, this was the home of health! He asked the company to join him in a cheerful telegram to his mother.

His home and his mother were always in his thoughts, a strong emotion appeared in his face, an enthusiasm; no one had any idea what a good mother he had, they just ought to know what she was like! He sat down to write the telegram with a heaving chest and they all signed their names to it. Thanks! he said; they would be witnesses that his mother need have no anxiety about him!

He even ventured to talk to Fröken Ellingsen again as though nothing untoward had befallen her; indeed he went straight to the Duchess of Somewhere and complimented the lady on her story. He did it very nicely, without any exaggeration.

"Oh, I know a lot more," she replied; "I could tell you what happened to her in the end if I dared. But I am bound to secrecy. Didn't you notice how I had to break off?"

"Yes. And I admire the self-denial which made you interrupt a good story."

There was a rumbling of wheels in the courtyard below and Bertelsen said in chaff: "Now you'll have to go down and do the honours, Robertsen!" But as no new arrivals were expected, the lawyer simply laughed and kept his seat. "You needn't joke about it," he said; "I've put in the papers that we have a count and a Princess here, that'll fetch them!"

Then it was that something happened: the Count made a nodding movement of the head as though he had got something in his throat, he pulled out his handkerchief and held it to his mouth, looked at it, and seemed to disbelieve what he saw; he rose and went to the window and looked at it again.

"What is it?" asked Fröken d'Espard anxiously.

Herr Fleming made no reply.

"What is it?" she repeated, jumping up.

Herr Fleming wiped his mouth and put away his handkerchief. "It's nothing!" he replied, and resumed his seat.

But they all saw that it was something, it could not be hidden. Herr Fleming raised his glass and emptied it; he had turned grey in the face.

"You have a little streak there," said Fröken d'Espard, pointing.

"Where?"

"There, at the corner of your mouth. If you'll give me your handkerchief—"

"Thanks, I can do it!" He got up and went to the glass to wipe his mouth. Fröken d'Espard followed him with her eyes, and the others became more observant.

He carried it off well, his words and gestures showed no hurry, but his face was relaxed and lifeless. The rest of the party showed no sign that they suspected the worst, but Fröken d'Espard stared at the sick man with terrified eyes and went so far as to lay her hand on his in tender distraction. Their eyes met. "Thanks!" he whispered. If there had been any tangle in their relations earlier in the day, it was now straightened out.

"I'll run for the doctor," she said.

"The doctor," he repeated, trying to show surprise. "Not at all, it's nothing. But since you say so, perhaps a little ice—"

"Are you unwell?" asked the lawyer. "The doctor shall come instantly!" He rose and rang the bell and gave the maid orders to find the doctor.

While they were waiting everyone tried to be calm and hopeful, and Herr Fleming refused to leave the company and go to bed: why should he be the first to break up? Once again he had use for his handkerchief and went to the glass to wipe himself; he did it in the same quiet and natural manner as before, making no disturbance; but the gaiety had left Bertelsen's room, the festivity was at an end.

Manager Svendsen knocked and announced that the Consul was downstairs, if the lawyer would like to speak to him.

"Who?"

"The Consul, Ruben, you know—Fru Ruben's husband, he's come."

The lawyer knew nothing about Consul Ruben's coming, but he got up at once and asked the others to excuse him. He turned to Bertelsen and repeated his prophecy: "You needn't joke about being short of visitors here; now we're getting the consuls!"

As the manager was going out Herr Fleming called him back. Oh, Herr Fleming looked grey as Death itself, but he was still alive, he still thought and felt. He could blink his eyes, breathe with his mouth, use his brain. He could open and close his hands at will, he was not dead. Now he handed the manager the telegram for his mother in Finland and enjoined him to send it to the station that same day, immediately.

That telegram was perhaps not altogether truthful anymore, Herr Fleming could no longer boast of his recovered health with a clear conscience. And yet—he sent this telegram to his mother. And it was actually his conscience that seemed to encourage him to send it.

V

Now several things occurred. People flocked to the place; and then Death began to play havoc, striking promiscuously and arbitrarily.

Herr Fleming lay in bed—at first with ice in his mouth and on his chest on account of his hæmorrhages, but when these ceased he was well enough to sit up in bed and pass the time by playing patience. Fröken d'Espard had been over to Daniel with a message from Herr Fleming that he had caught cold and could not come for his curds and cream for the present, but as soon as he was better he would resume his visits.

It was on this occasion that Fröken d'Espard was exposed to the bull; it came bellowing after her, and the lady arrived at the sanatorium very short of breath.

Yes, the bull was still out in the field; the sanatorium had offered to buy it at once, but Daniel would not hear of selling it before the autumn, when it was well fattened with summer grass and worth more. So one day went by after another and nothing was settled. And now Lawyer Robertsen had gone back to his office in Christiania. Nor did it excite any particular attention when Fröken d'Espard was pursued by the bull; the lady was not so generally popular that anyone took her part; on the contrary, the other ladies thought Fröken d'Espard might just as well have kept away from the field where the bull was; what did she want there?

More visitors kept coming. Consul Ruben had arrived, a couple of others came the same day, and finally at the end of the week a party of half a dozen people came down from the Dovre Fell and put up at Torahus. Lawyer Robertsen seemed to be turning out a true prophet: his paragraphs about the permanent pianist and the aristocratic visitors, a Princess and a Count, were drawing people to the place. "Where's the Count?" asked the ladies. And "Where's the Princess?" asked both ladies and gentlemen. The mountain sanatorium was becoming fashionable, a great place; the castle threatened to be full, and what then?

It became apparent that more rooms would have to be furnished by the autumn in order that the sanatorium might be fully prepared for next spring. For the present there were rooms enough, but they were not all ready, they wanted furniture and fittings, some of them wanted stoves. There was no immediate hurry; some visitors could not spare the time, others the money, for a long stay at Torahus, they left after a few days or a week and made room for fresh arrivals. The beds changed hands while they were still warm.

Consul Ruben had come to visit his wife; he was one of those who were pressed for time and could not stay long. The very first evening, as he sat in his wife's room, he showed signs of impatience and asked for the lady—"Well, where's the lady?" he said.

Fru Ruben, immensely stout and short of breath, got up and went to the door. Oh, she was so heavy she waddled in her gait like a wader; even going downstairs she puffed as much as going up. She opened the door, peeped into the passage, and closed the door again. All was safe.

"The walls are so thin here," she warned him; "don't speak too loud! The lady? She is no ordinary lady, she'll come when she chooses or not at all, we can't send for her."

The Consul was not pleased with this fussiness or with the whole business: "Why have you had this extra bed put here? Couldn't I have a room to myself?"

His wife evasively: "It was the maids. I didn't know—perhaps the house is full—"

"Rubbish. There's no room to breathe in this rabbit-hutch. What does the lady want, I ask you?"

"What does she want?" Fru Ruben entered into an explanation of the lady's position: she found herself in a great dilemma, she could not sleep at night, she was all adrift, unhappy woman, divorced from her husband, without a home or anywhere to go—

"That's bad!" said the Consul.

The lady had been in here several times, had knocked at the door, smiled, and apologized, otherwise she never spoke to anyone. The first time the lady came, Fru Ruben had been so surprised that she forgot to get up and curtsy.

"Where does she come from?" asked the Consul.

From England. Didn't he know that? She was a Lady, her husband was a Lord, a Minister, he was in the Government.

"Oh," said the Consul, "then she's the one I read about!" But the Consul attached no importance to it and showed little interest.

His wife tried to stir him up, going straight to the point: "What does she want? She is in a fix, she wants money."

"We all want that," replied the Consul.

"She is much to be pitied, she's absolutely on the rocks, can't get help anywhere."

The Consul leaned forward and fixed his eyes on his wife's hand: "A new ring—let me look!"

Oh, Fru Ruben had just stroked her hair and put it straight with that hand, her husband could not fail to notice the fine gem. "Isn't it lovely?" she said. "I didn't want to take it, God knows I didn't, but she pressed it on me. Have you ever seen such transparency?"

The Consul merely nodded, saying: "Ah, then she's got some more rings to sell?"

Fru Ruben was hurt: "You can't mean that! Of course she doesn't want to sell rings, she doesn't propose anything of that sort. She applies to you as Consul, a different thing altogether. As she neither can nor will go to her own Consul, she comes to you. No, she can't go to her own Consul, he would simply side with her husband and the Ministry, that's a matter of course."

"But she must have some connexions. Has the husband washed his hands of her entirely?"

"I don't know whether that's the right way to put it; she spoke quite nicely about him."

"Ah yes, the usual thing!"

"How do you mean?"

"Why, they always speak nicely after the divorce—when they begin to regret it all."

Again Fru Ruben was hurt. It was still no ordinary person they were talking about, but a Lady; the Consul was a little too ready to assume that all women were like the typist girls in his office. No, she had nothing but nice things to say of her husband, Fru Ruben continued; in a way he had done his part, even now he was not exactly opposed to her, but he maintained an attitude of stiffness and never replied to her letters. What a way to behave! And as for connexions, there seemed no doubt that she had forfeited the sympathy of her husband's family, and she herself had no relations who were in a position to help her.

"Then she was quite beneath him?"

Fru Ruben took up her defence: "How can you speak of 'beneath' in England, where everybody can marry whom he pleases? The King can marry any commoner if he likes, so I suppose a Lord may be allowed to marry an actress?"

"So that was what she was?"

"Something of the sort, it seems. A dancer, perhaps."

"Better and better! And so—I am to intervene as Consul? Of course I can't, it's out of the question, not in my power. You must be a pair of fools if you think I can."

Fru Ruben set herself to appeal to her husband's vanity. He must see that when a Lady applied to him, she distinguished him above all others, it could mean nothing else. She made almost a confidant of him, asked him a friendly question or two, put herself on an equality with him for the time being. As the soul of Consul Ruben was not affected by this distinction, his wife had to try another way. "So you see she must have money," she repeated calmly, ignoring her husband's objections. "And money she will get, there is no doubt of that. She has what is worth a very big sum."

"How big a sum?"

"It depends on what you reckon an English Minister is worth. It may be a question of success or ruin, life or death."

"That's a whole heap. What kind of property has she got?"

"Papers. Letters."

If the lady had expected great results from this piece of information she was disappointed; so far from flaring up, the Consul only yawned. But she was not to be beaten. Strangely enough, she seemed to have made up her mind to stand by this foreign lady and she was going to see it through. What was the reason of this constancy? This person, Fru Ruben, suffered from chronic nervousness, she was destroyed with fat, her bulk imposed on her inactivity, not as an indulgence, but as a terrible burden; all this was true. But it appeared that Fru Ruben was capable of kindness and helpfulness to others. What had she to do with this English lady? Racial sympathy? Perhaps. But in that case didn't her husband, the Lord, belong to the selfsame race? And she was working dead against him!

The Consul said: "I can't take action here simply because you've been given a ring."

"No," said his wife, yawning in her turn. The ring was a trifle, it had pleased her the first day and no longer. But could she without discourtesy have declined it in stronger terms than she had done? And was it the custom to be in earnest about refusing the gifts of persons of rank? Fru Ruben had rings already, far too many, they were a nuisance and in the way. Like himself she had had to shift them all to her little fingers.

Yes, by degrees, as all her other fingers became thumbs.

His wife bent her head and replied: "When I was eighteen—"

"Oh yes, I know all about it," interrupted the Consul. "But you're not eighteen, you're double! In more than one sense double, many times over."

"When I was eighteen," his wife continued, not to be beaten, "I had fingers as thin as your typists'!" For the second time she mentioned the typists, not merely in passing, but definitely, like something significant. And for the second time the Consul heard her with indifference and shrugged his shoulders.

"These papers," he said, "private letters—I am a Consul, these letters mean scandal, blackmail—no, I won't touch them!"

His wife insisted that the scandal would be less if a great Consul made a discreet use of the papers than if the Lady acted for herself and indubitably brought about her husband's fall.

And—whether it was the effect of the flattery or of the good sense in the lady's last argument—the Consul asked, in order to have done with it: "Where are the papers?"

He examined them till far on in the night. Now and then in the course of his reading he shook his head, kicked out his legs in excitement, waved his hand, raised his eyebrows; he was getting some entertainment. Yes, this full-blooded, bull-necked man found here as much as he could ask in the way of impure thought and candid expression. Why so little delicacy, why so much direct coarseness in these letters? A miry mess it was for the Consul to plunge into; this retired dancer must have had quite exceptional experience to tolerate such licentiousness from her husband without holding her nose. There were letters from India and other parts of the world, politics, Egyptian orgies, personal conflicts with the Government, private trading in doubtful commodities, purchase of a title, Army contracts—all lumped together, and all with a shocking bad smell.

Fru Ruben observed her husband in silence. The letters grew shorter and shorter, it seemed as though the writer no longer had full confidence in his wife or had found another confidant; the last letters contained allusions to the Lady's relapse into her dancing life, to a visit to Scotland with the manager of an obscure place of amusement. The Lady seemed to have denied this, but the next letter from her husband upheld the accusation and ended in a breach. The last two letters were finally decisive. Finished!

Fru Ruben guessed that the Consul's interest was cooling down as he approached the end. This was no longer to his taste, but seemingly it was very much to hers. The worthy Lord had made his start with the help of his wife's, the dancer's, money; it was she who had put him on his feet with the little fortune she had accumulated by her dancing, by her legs; he had then turned it into brains and action and it had carried them both to the top of the tree. But now what was the use of it all?

Fru Ruben was immersed in her own reflections and recollections. Was she in a similar situation to the Lady, discarded, superannuated by her husband? What else? It was too unreasonable that she should espouse a stranger's fortunes so warmly from purely altruistic motives, even if it were a question of racial kinship. The Consul evidently had no misgivings; had he looked up he must have suspected the growing excitement of his wife's eyes; she sat watching him from the side, with a soft and stealthy look in her almond eyes, a sign of activity within her bloated head.

"Phew!" puffed the Consul, "that's a messy business! How old is she?"

"Yes, it's a messy business," replied his wife.

"I can't have anything to do with it."

His wife said nothing.

"How old is she?"

"Oh yes, you could do something if you liked."

The Consul with sudden heat: "How old is she? I ask. There's the deuce and all of a mystery about it."

His wife with a wry smile: "How old is she? I haven't asked her. Nor do I know whether she's good-looking, according to your taste. I suppose that's all the same, that's not what interests you."

The Consul, with great irritation: "No, that doesn't interest me. Neither the lady nor her scandals interest me. Look here, it was a most extraordinary idea of yours to make them put an extra bed into this garret. It's a good thing it's only for one night. I don't understand what you wanted to drag me up into the mountains for, anyway."

Yes, there was no doubt his wife was following a definite plan and working on her own account, otherwise she would not have spoken as she did. Oh, she seemed bent on carrying her point; in spite of all her hopelessness her attitude was firm, come what might!

"Did I upset your plans?" she asked. "You didn't upset mine by coming here."

"Can't you reflect for a moment? Have you a business here, mails, an office, a big staff?"

"No, I have nothing, only myself, never anything but myself!" And she continued querulously: "I came here on a Thursday and wrote at once, and then one Thursday went by after another and I heard nothing from you. I wrote and wrote again. No. Then it was that I telegraphed."

"You don't seem to understand," he replied, "that I hadn't time. Just now I have a great deal to do, my people are having holidays in turn, their work has to be done, I myself have to find time to eat, I want a little sleep too."

Silence.

"But you don't understand that," he repeated, beginning to undress.

"If you say so, it must be right," she replied.

"It is right. And now it's late, let's go to bed. No, I won't be mixed up with that affair of the dancer. You see that, don't you?"

Silence. At last his wife said: "She must have a reply from her husband; nothing is settled at present, she is too heavy now to take up dancing again. She is waiting for an answer about a little poultry farm; why doesn't he answer? Her husband's a mighty man now, he simply says nothing; her own lawyer is getting slack and seems to have gone over to the other side. So where is she to turn?"

"It just struck me," said the Consul, "—are those letters the originals?"

"Yes, I suppose so. Why not? What makes you ask? You don't suspect the letters, do you?"

"No. Now you go to bed too."

His wife sat still for a good while, then she went over to her bed and busied herself there another good while; meantime the Consul lay puffing and blowing and turning about.

"Aren't you ever going to bed tonight?" he asked.

No answer.

Perhaps it then dawned on him that he had been unfriendly. "If you would go to bed and put the lamp out we could get some rest," he said.

"Yes, you shall have some rest!" she replied, with unexpected incisiveness.

Now a scene was enacted: the Consul must have been alarmed, he guessed there was something wrong, his wife's tone struck him as strange, he flung himself on his back and for the first time looked her full in the face. What the devil was she up to? She had been standing by her bed, now she suddenly came towards him with a hurried step, perhaps she was so intent on saying something furious that she forgot she had a pillow in her hands. What was he to think?—a big pillow in her hands! Her face showed distorted in the lamplight, with a squint of hysteria, of insanity, of course she must be quite beside herself, as she couldn't even get out a word. Then the Consul rose up in bed with a start, perhaps not so much in order to have a better view as actually to defend himself; but at the same instant a queer change came over him, his features collapsed, his hands were paralysed, he sank back heavy and lifeless, knocking the back of his head against the rail of the bedstead. And there he lay.

Another state of things altogether, with a crash! His wife checked herself and stood still; it took her time to gather her wits, she did not look round for a chair to sink into, but maintained her aggressive attitude, as though she would say: "There, you see!" She had not accomplished anything wrong, what had happened was just as it should be and was based on justice. She must have seen already that there was no longer any sense in her words, but she actually said to her husband: "There, that's enough!" As he did not move and showed no sign of life she simply went on as she had begun; blood was issuing from one of his ears, perhaps from the other too, which she could not see; then she thought of the doctor and looked about the room to see if it was tidy for him to see. "Answer me, do you hear?" she said aloud to her husband. She saw that his head lay awkwardly, against the end of the bed, with his chin thrust into his chest, but she did not straighten it; on the other hand, she carried her pillow back to its place, hid the Lady's letters, which were lying on the table, and waddled out of the door to find the doctor.

The first death at Torahus Sanatorium.

Extraordinary chance: a man arrives with a little hand-bag, night things, and tooth-brush, he has come to see his wife, who is staying at the sanatorium, he is in the place a few hours and is then struck down by death!

No wonder if perhaps his wife found the fortuity somewhat far-fetched, a mere fluke, almost a fabrication. Her husband might indeed have maintained that he had good reason for dying: he had been worried till late at night with an English scandal and was thus in a fit state to misunderstand his wife's coming at him with that pillow in her hands, he might have thought it looked dangerous, he imagined something about smothering, the hysterical look in her eyes got the better of his sound judgment—oh, the husband might have established his claim that he was not killed by a foolish figment of the brain.

On the other hand, the wife might argue that that was not the intention, a fatality was out of all proportion. When she reflected upon herself with that innocent pillow in her hands, she could not be solemn about it, the whole thing was comic, she couldn't help laughing, ha ha. And in the same way one was bound to see a comic touch in her husband's being in such a hurry to get home, ho ho, the very next day, the very next morning, and then dying instead. Yes, life was not without its comic side, nor death either.

Of course Doctor Oyen and the rest of the sanatorium people tried to hush up this preposterous fatality, but failed entirely; the news passed from room to room and even reached Herr Fleming on his sick-bed. How could that have come about? Fröken d'Espard sat with him several hours daily and kept watch; he must have heard it through the wall from the next room, where a lady paced up and down wringing her handkerchief, her gloves, her fingers, and talking to herself aloud in a voice of despair.

Herr Fleming said to Fröken d'Espard: "I can tell you a piece of news: a visitor died here a couple of nights ago." He announced it quietly and calmly, as a matter of no importance at all.

Fröken d'Espard rose abruptly, took off her hat, and hung it up. Turning her face away, she replied: "Oh, a visitor? Did he die? But perhaps it was a lady?"

"A lady? No, wasn't it a stranger, a Consul from Christiania? I don't know. Haven't you heard? It was the man who arrived while we were in Herr Bertelsen's room a few days ago."

"No, I hadn't heard."

"Oh. Well, now sit down, Fröken, I intend to be invincible today!"

And they sat down to their customary game of bezique. For a table they had a sheet of cardboard, laid across Herr Fleming's bed.

He was all there, counted the points accurately and marked them on his scorer, nothing suggested absence of mind, no, for Herr Fleming was so enormously better the last two days, almost well again, and had plucked up courage—a death in the place was no concern of his.

Was Fröken d'Espard disappointed that he took the Consul's death so calmly? Was she afraid he had not noticed her solicitude and delicacy as she hung up her hat and turned her face away? Oh, the wiles of human nature! She said in a tone of inquiry: "There seems to have been a great commotion in the sanatorium the last day or two?"

Herr Fleming murmured indifferently: "No doubt it's on account of this death."

"No doubt. And since you mention it—I seem to have heard something about it. Anyhow," she broke off, "it doesn't matter! Did you sleep well last night?"

"Yes, thanks, I sleep well every night now."

Silence.

"Well, perhaps he was a Consul," remarked the lady. "But he died of a stroke, not of an illness."

"It comes to the same thing. Let me see—four knaves!"

"Fancy, he came one day and died the same night! I wouldn't have mentioned it, but as you had heard it already—"

"Heard what? Oh, yes. I didn't know the man, did you?"

"No. Well, of course I know who he was, a big man in Christiania, huge business, I know some of the ladies in his office. Yes, it was a terrible thing to happen!"

"Are you really going to play that ace?" asked Herr Fleming.

"No, I'm sorry! So Consul Ruben was Fru Ruben's husband—you know, that fat person who's been staying here. Now she has left with the body."

"I see."

"And Mylady went with her, Mylady and her maid. So now there'll be no more of the everlasting teas and lunches here. And now we can play the piano again—"

And, to be sure, they played the piano and they hummed on the stairs and tried to laugh unconcernedly at the dinner-table, but it did not quite come off; even a week after the ladies and the coffin had been driven away the visitors continued to talk of the great calamity. It was a bomb bursting in the midst of a troop of weaklings. "The first death!" said the Suicide with a nod, just as if he had several more up his sleeve. This dismal person was hardly the one to raise the spirits of the health resort.

None of the visitors went into mourning exactly over the departure of the three women, but all the same it thinned their numbers, they left three empty rooms. What then? It was all perfectly correct, they paid their bills and left, none of them did a bolt, they were not that kind of people. Even Mylady settled her bill and tipped profusely, a regular ransom in fact. You see, Consul Ruben had provided himself with a gorgeously fat pocket-book before he left home; it was found in the inside pocket of his waistcoat, on the left side, where it had lain in his lifetime encompassing his heart. And now this pocket-book came in very handy when the ladies settled their accounts, Fru Ruben paid for the whole party. It's an ill wind that blows nobody good.

And after a week or so a fresh party of visitors arrived, they filled the empty rooms, they overflowed the sanatorium and created a housing famine, so serious that the doctor, the matron, and the manager had to put their heads together to find a way out of the difficulty.

The manager was sent to make a round of the place. He went to Room No. 7 and the lady was at home. What he came to say was, would she be so kind as to move for a few days and take another room?

What?

Another room. It had no stove, but otherwise it was just as bright and pleasant as this one. They would put in a camp-bed for her. Might he be allowed to show her the new room?

The lady began to twist her fingers and asked why she was to move.

Well, the sanatorium was overcrowded this afternoon, they were short of rooms, didn't know how they would manage.

The lady seized her gloves from the table and twisted them now. Her face grew rather long and blue and she looked at the manager in a bewildered way.

They wouldn't have asked her, he said, it had never occurred to them. Only just as the house was filled up, another little party arrived, among them a clergyman and his two sons; they felt the cold and asked for a room with a stove.

Well, said the lady, very well, she said, wagging her head. She was not unaccommodating, she gave in. It would never do for anybody to be cold.

No, would it! the manager agreed. And she had only to go where there was a fire and stay there, in the drawing-room, for instance. At any rate the change of room would only be for a short time, the manager promised, thanking the lady cordially. Whereupon he showed her the new room.

Encouraged by his success, the manager went on and found the Suicide. He was sitting in the big veranda, chatting with Moss, the spotty-faced man. The manager had played cards with these two cronies and could approach them in a free-and-easy fashion;

he was the bearer of mournful tidings, he said facetiously. But on remarking that the Suicide was by no means in the right humour he changed his tone and asked if the gentlemen had any objection to doing him and the place a great favour?

Both men looked up.

Would they consider changing their rooms for a short time?

How? Why?

On being given the explanation the Suicide refused point-blank to oblige him, couldn't think of such a thing—he had never heard such a bare-faced proposal! Moss asked for further information, and this time the manager trotted out three ladies, three school-teachers; they had arrived that afternoon when the house was full and what was to be done with them? Imagine three nice young ladies, they had come over the fells, were battered by the wind and starving, they begged and implored to be given a couple of rooms with stoves.

"Then did you intend to put me into a room without a stove?" asked the Suicide with pale lips.

Only for a short time, perhaps only a matter of days, somebody would be sure to leave soon; there was a clergyman and his two sons among the new arrivals, perhaps they would leave in a week's time.

The Suicide was furious; was that a way to treat people, and was it a robbers' nest he had come to? He had never heard such unbridled impudence! Oh, that Suicide! He proved himself a young man who was glad enough to be alive. "No, don't cock your nose so high, Herr Svendsen!" he said. "Don't give it wings, but use it to snuff along the ground!"

"Now, now!" replied the manager with a good-natured laugh.

"It's unheard of!" declared the Suicide: a health resort, a sanatorium, which proposed to freeze him blue and render him totally unfit for human life!

Moss too laughed at the Suicide's indignation and curious

choice of words. "My room is at your service," he said to the manager.

"Yes, of course!" cried the Suicide. "Oh, I'm ashamed of you, you're a boneless louse! Look at him, Herr Svendsen, his room's at your service! But do you think his spots will stand an icy room?"

"I don't have a fire in my stove as it is," protested Moss.

"No, I don't suppose you do, that's what makes you look like that, I dare say it's frost that gave it you. No, I don't have a fire either; but what if it sets in cold tomorrow or the next day?"

"Ha ha ha!"

"Yes, ha ha ha!" mimicked the Suicide. "Damn it, a woman can say things that turn a man sick. A guffaw, do you call that an answer? You're a woman!"

"Let the ladies have my room," repeated Moss.

The manager thanked him and went off.

Silence.

"No, I can't forget it!" exclaimed the Suicide. "I was to wait till a parson and his youngsters left before I could get my room back! Not your room, not the parson's room, but my own room!"

"You forget the three school-teachers."

"Well, what then?"

"Imagine, three nice young ladies on the verge of distress! Have you no chivalry?"

"No!" yelled the Suicide.

"Ha ha ha! Not that you aren't honestly worth a room with a stove, but these sanatorium people can't see that. They haven't even an inkling that you really came here to take your own life."

"Let that be as it may, it's no business of yours!" the Suicide admonished him paternally. "If you think you're in a state to be chivalrous, then be so!"

Moss was put down for the moment; then he said: "The fact is, you've given it up. You intend to live, you've begun to think about the rich widow."

"What rich widow?"

"Fru Ruben, of course."

"I see, Fru Ruben!" The Suicide yawned and grew tired of squabbling; the reaction followed upon his irritation and he fell into moody pondering.

"Yes, she might suit you," Moss went on; "in the prime of life, bulky enough for two, rich, a big business—"

"She's more likely to suit you. What do you know about her riches? Be quiet!"

"That kind of people are always rich."

"Be quiet!"

Moss was silent for a while, then he got up and left. The Suicide watched him go and followed at once, they could not be away from each other for long. They lay on their backs in the sun and talked no more. Oh, how a common misfortune had made these two men cling to each other, two shipwrecked sailors on the same beach! Moss went to sleep. He had put his hat over his face to keep the flies off his sores.

When he awoke, the Suicide was still lying with open eyes. He said: "You went to sleep?"

"Yes. The heat of the sun made me drowsy."

"It's debility. We're wretchedly fed here, nothing but canned stuff. We fall asleep at all hours."

"I hadn't thought of that," replied Moss. "Is it canned stuff they give us?"

"Why the hell don't we ever get that bull?" asked the Suicide all at once. "That's what I should like to know. Haven't they promised us the bull?"

"Ask the manager!"

The Suicide gave a scornful snort: "The manager! No, come on, we'll go straight to the doctor!"

But Moss wouldn't, wasn't up to it, couldn't be bothered—

"There you are again; it's debility and bad feeding; I'm getting more miserable every day. Nobody ought to stay here."

"Are you thinking of leaving?"

"Leaving? Well, I dare say. What makes you ask? I'm not going to leave, don't you believe it. The manager can try to get rid of me till he's black in the face, he can try it on with two parsons! I'll show them!" He had suddenly conceived a violent grudge against this parson whose coming had made him insecure about his own room.

Nor did it make things any better when they went to supper, and the parson with his two little boys was seated, by the irony of fate, or perhaps by the malice of the manager, next to the Suicide. The parson bowed to his neighbour, and the Suicide returned a little nod, a prodigiously thrifty and economical nod. Being oneself an old inhabitant, one had to make a new-comer feel a certain constraint; it would not do to be lavish with one's nods.

The stranger said a few words; the Suicide did not answer him, but Moss on his other side made due and courteous acknowledgment.

Then the stranger gave his name: Oliver. The Suicide paid no attention and called him Jensen.

"Jensen?" queried the stranger.

"Oh, perhaps it's pronounced Nikolaisen?"

The stranger's face was blank with astonishment, and presently he turned to his plate again.

"It's a good thing we've got some assistance in consuming the canned stuff they give us here," the Suicide remarked to him.

The stranger let this pass and bravely did justice to the canned hash; he was hungry.

The Suicide asked: "Did you come over the fells, Herr Pastor?"

The stranger looked up: "Do you mean me? I'm not a pastor, I'm a rector."*

The Suicide, puzzled: "Rector?"

The stranger pulled out his card and presented it; the Suicide read: "Frank Oliver, Ph.D., rector."

"I beg your pardon!" said the Suicide, beaten. "It was that ass of a manager who made a parson of you."

Not that it mattered; the Suicide had once for all taken a dislike to this stranger and he transferred it from the parson to the headmaster; it was, after all, this same person who had tried to make him homeless, and during the Rector's whole stay at Torahus the Suicide found many a good opportunity of showing him his displeasure.

However, poor Rector Oliver did no harm, and if there was not much to be said about him, there was nothing to be said against him either. He was lean with learning and poor living, his coat hung on his shoulders as on a coat-hanger, he had scant hair and scant beard and grey the little there was—all that must be admitted. But that was not the end of him. He must have possessed an intrinsic value which made him hold his head high. He did not conceal it, there was a certain simplicity in his firmly based conceit, he lost no time in bringing out his name and distinctions in order to create respect from the start. Of course it is unlikely that Rector Oliver had attained his highest aim in life; who has? He had attained what many men aspire to utterly in vain; that in itself is an aim. He occupied an important position in the scholastic world and himself entertained an unflinching respect for that position; as did everyone else, without exception. What was his calling and life-work; was it not providing people with culture and refinement or something of that sort? Was he not educating the whole middle class in scholastic civilization? Good. It was due to him if the youth of the country was no longer ignorant, he spread his light abroad; he exterminated

---

*Principal of a college.

illiteracy, and Norway became enlightened.

If Rector Oliver bestirs himself nowadays it is not to run away from anything, nor is it to run after anything; he is what he is, his destiny is closed, his ship has come into port. From now on he lives unharmed year in, year out; he is immutably and durably the same, the law of the land permits him to earn his bread as he does, he is the supreme head of his school; if the Rector says a thing, that thing has been said!

It must have been rather a new experience for him to enter a house with two or three score strangers in it, but it was not many hours before he was known to them, they said good-morning to him, listened attentively to what he said, got up and offered him their chairs; in order to get into the Rector's good graces they even took notice of his little boys and chatted with them by the hour together.

But the Suicide scowled at him. "Do you know what?" he said to Moss; "that parson—that Rector—of course he gave himself out to be a parson simply to get a room. It was cute of him. But he didn't fool me."

At last there was a talk once more of buying Daniel's bull for the sanatorium. "Why now?" asked the Suicide, interfering; "why not before? Just when we've got people in who can live on canned hash—they give us the bull!"

He had quite changed his mind, there was no hurry about the bull. He got up an agitation among the visitors and among the staff to have the purchase postponed; it could wait until the Rector had gone; otherwise how long would a carcass last? Unparalleled greediness and lack of hospitality on the part of this Suicide! Not that anyone minded what he said. "Don't you intend to die anyhow?" asked the manager with a laugh; "then why do you worry so much about the food?"

CHAPTER THE LAST

The bull was bought.

They wouldn't have done it if they had foreseen the consequences, that must be their excuse; they would have been spared much blame and a heavy responsibility if they had let it alone. They could argue about it after the event, quarrel over it, lay the blame on each other—what was done could not be undone. But they could wring their hands and lament.

Oh yes, Daniel could sell his big bull now, a few hundred crowns meant money to the man of Torahus Sæter, Mountain, and Forest, he could find use for them. From his point of view there was much in favour of an immediate deal: a great part of the summer was already gone, the pasture was getting poor, the price was high; besides which Daniel's little bull had grown well in the course of the summer and could now take the place of the big one.

So two men went across to Daniel's sæter to lead the bull home to the sanatorium, the porter and the postman. They had a rope with them, which the porter cunningly bound about the bull's neck and muzzle.

"That's a pretty light rope," said Daniel.

"It's thick enough," replied the porter.

Even before they started, Daniel had his doubts and said: "I wouldn't like to bet you'll get him home."

The porter scoffed and opined that it was not the first bull he'd handled in his time.

And in fact all went well till they were a long way on the road, but then the bull suddenly turned restive, stopped, put his muzzle to the ground, and shook his head. He must have seen that he was on unfamiliar ground, the men too were strange to him and he'd see them to blazes before he'd be led any farther on a clothes-line, a piece of packthread! Patting and kind words made no difference one way or the other, nor did it make any impression on the bull when the postman used a stick on him, he just snorted. So there.

But they couldn't stand there all day, the porter was already cursing freely. "Take and give him a bit of a crack right on the end of his rump," he ordered; "but wait till I've got a good hold. Now!"

But it was no good, the bull stood fast.

The porter yelled fiercely: "No, give him one that is one!"

Oh yes, the postman gave him a proper crack.

Now it was God in heaven save the porter! What happened was an explosion. The postman was left standing in empty space, as he watched the bull bolting off with the porter, bolting straight ahead, off the road, making for rocks and bushes. At first the postman thought this the maddest fun he had ever been in for, the porter followed the bull like a baited hook, now in the air, now on the ground, and across the bog they both sent the mud flying high. The postman was bleating inwardly with laughter. All at once he heard a cry, a wail, and ran after them; the bull, had come to a standstill, a tree had stopped it, and right against the tree stood the porter with one hand caught, held fast by the rope. "Wait a second, I'll cut it!" said the postman, horror-struck, feeling for his knife. "No!" hissed the porter. The man was plucky and fiendish with rage, gnashing his teeth. "You must unhitch it; bring the bight round this way, but don't let the bull go!"

When at last he was set free he trembled from head to foot, his hand was blue and raw, there was blood on some of his fingers. He swung his hand backwards and forwards a few times and said spitefully: "Did I ask you to crack his rump right off?"

The postman could only mutter: "What, right off? No."

"You ass!"

"You ought to have let go the rope," replied the postman.

"I don't let go!" yelled the porter.

"Shut up! Can't you see you're scaring the beast with your noise?"

Though the porter was forced to moderate his voice he was none

CHAPTER THE LAST

the less furious and abused his companion soundly.

People appeared on the road, visitors from the sanatorium who had heard what was to take place and had come out to meet the procession. There were a good many of them, including ladies, including Bertelsen; even Herr Fleming was out again, for the first time since his illness. Oh, maybe it was not all pure natural courage that the porter evinced in not letting go, perhaps there was a touch of vanity in it, he wanted to be a man in the eyes of all these spectators.

"Let's try again!" he said in a loud and ringing voice.

The postman muttered a warning.

"You're an old woman!" exclaimed the porter. "Isn't it a beast for slaughter? Are we going to give in to it? Ha ha."

The bull refused.

"Look at his eyes," said the postman; "they're red."

"That be damned!" replied the porter. "There, hurry up!"

But the bull refused.

"Come here," ordered the porter; "get a good hold of his halter the same as me—no, the other side of course! Let's get back to the road with the brute instead of standing here."

They took up their positions. Meanwhile the bull seemed to be waiting, with his nose to the ground, scowling with his bloodshot eyes and snorting now and then.

The preparations were finished, both had a good purchase with their feet, the porter held fast with one hand and used the other to prick up the bull's hind quarters—a pretty innocent means of driving him on, a pin-prick.

Another explosion, ho! This time the postman didn't laugh, didn't bleat, the ground was jerked from under him; he and his mate were both like baited hooks in the air. Oh, what was the strength of two men against the might of the bull? All at once they both lay on the ground, left behind, flung aside; the porter still held the rope in his hand, he had not let go this time either—bravely done, but the rope had broken.

Yes, and the bull was loose.

There he stands, a beast at liberty, brown all over and shiny, with his mountainous weight resting on his short legs. The immense neck has almost the thickness of the whole body, and the power of a locomotive. The animal is a sight.

It is a sight, but one that is too much for the human beings; the human beings are visitors at the sanatorium, they utter a groan, they are ready to sink on their knees, they are afraid. There is a bewildered panic among them; though the beast is brown and shiny, it radiates chill and danger, the human beings feel they are in a tight place. At the first moment two little boys are the only ones to move, they cannot control their excitement and scramble up a rock to have a good view. And as though a signal had been given, others follow them and scramble up the same rock. Here they recover their breath, the human beings take courage again, they are at a circus, spectators at a circus.

The postman picks himself up and goes over his limbs to find if they are unbroken. The porter, a little dazed, a little shaken, is already examining the rope; he knots it together again and goes after the bull. He is as furious as ever and tries to look as dauntless. A lady stands wringing her gloves for all she is worth and begs him to leave the bull alone; he won't listen to her, but when Bertelsen— Timber-merchant Bertelsen who has such a big share in the sanatorium—also calls to him to wait, the porter stops and asks: "Why am I to wait?"

"Yes, wait a bit," replies Bertelsen; "Fröken d'Espard has gone up to the sæter to fetch Daniel."

No, when the porter hears that, nothing will make him wait, Daniel be blowed, the bull himself be blowed, he's got to reach the sanatorium! He looks for the postman and calls to him; the postman has gone a long way back for his cap, which had fallen off in his career, that cap with the gold braid which was the symbol of his office. The porter waits and calls to him again: "Are you afraid of a bull, a bull-calf? He hasn't even got proper horns, only a pair of warts on his head! You're a nice one!"

"A three-year-old bull's no calf," replies the postman indignantly; "I won't have any more to do with it. Mark that!"

Time passes while they are squabbling and now the bull begins to show temper, he butts at tufts and tree-stumps and gets himself in a fearful mess, he digs the ground with his forefeet and growls like thunder. Suddenly he catches sight of the porter and comes running towards him; oh, he is so huge as he comes on, enormous, and he remembers to sway his flanks; the porter hurriedly takes refuge on the rock with the others, saying: "If that dummy there won't lend a hand I must give it up! Give him a bit more braid on his cap, then perhaps he'll have the pluck!" He shifted all the blame on to the postman.

Daniel arrives on the scene. That Fröken d'Espard, she was a graceless person and not much liked, but a deuce of a girl for presence of mind; once more she had done the only sensible thing and fetched Daniel. He comes with a stout rope in his hand and approaches the bull in a friendly and ingratiating way. With outstretched hand and coaxing words he gives him to understand that he may still expect kind treatment, but the bull only gets wild and tears up the ground with his forefeet. "No, you've offended the beast!" says Daniel indignantly.

"There are enough of us to tether him," proposed the porter. Yes, there were enough of them, no doubt about that, but— And maybe the porter had the pluck. But it couldn't be done. Tether a mad bull! When you've got him rounded up, the worst is still to come.

And there they stand and can't do anything.

"I believe somebody will have to go for Marta," says Daniel; "he knows her best." Marta, that was Daniel's old servant.

Good, somebody goes for Marta. And as nobody else seems inclined and all pretend they don't know the way, it is Fröken d'Espard again; she simply hangs her hat on a tree and steps down from the rock, does Fröken d'Espard, while the others stand looking on and are frightened.

Meanwhile the porter crows a bit over Daniel's not being able to master the bull: "Look there, now, he can't do it either!" But no one would have suspected the porter's courage even if he had said nothing; moreover, it was clear to an unbiased view that he and nobody else had got them into the mess. Hold your tongue, porter!

Bertelsen says: "I'm just thinking whether I shall go back for my rifle and shoot the brute."

"Oh, do!" exclaims the lady who wrings her hands and her gloves.

Bertelsen looks about for a safe descent and seems not to find one; whichever way you go you may meet the furious beast. Fröken Ellingsen takes Bertelsen by the arm and begs him to stay—Marta will soon be here, thank God!

Daniel has another try to get hold of the bull, but after failing again and again, he too climbs up the rock. Now they are all assembled there. The bull goes on with his work, looks up, thunders, and turns to again. It seems no concern of his that a crowd of people is watching him with interest. What now? Shouts from the coppice. More visitors and spectators from the sanatorium, asking if it is safe to come nearer. "No, no, the bull's loose!" replies everybody on the rock, and "Go home again at once, instantly!" shouts Bertelsen, driving them back. These cries seem to confuse the bull, he stands quivering for a moment—and now comes the disaster!

The bull gives a short, unnatural roar, a howl of insanity, and suddenly, as though goaded again, flings himself round and gallops up the rock. A single shriek from every human throat, a wild flight in all directions, and the rock is deserted, the rock is swept clear. Only one lady is left standing, she no longer wrings her gloves, she is paralysed; and now she totters, now she sinks on her knees and falls. The bull takes her by the neck and slings her across the rock like a bundle. Finished!

But there's the porter. The porter wouldn't run away like the others after all, he has climbed into a tree just like a monkey. That devil of a porter, he must have thought of this means of escape the whole time, otherwise he couldn't have been so quick and so cunning. There he sits in his fork of the tree, unafraid. Not even when the bull catches sight of him is he alarmed, not a scrap; but it is only a minute, and then the bull charges the tree, looking as if nothing was too much for him.

Now the porter is done for, he can give himself up for lost, the tree-trunk sways and creaks. He yells down to the beast, cursing it, calling it names, but when he sees that his life is in danger he checks himself and by devious ways arrives at serious reflection and prays God to help him.

The fugitives see his position from a distance and call to him to come; they don't understand that this is impossible, that he has no escape. Now and again there comes a roll of thunder from the bull's throat, the animal wrestles with the tree-trunk and bends it back; Fröken d'Espard's hat falls from its branch, the bull crushes it into the ground, crushes it again, is taken up with crushing it. The hat saves the man. The moment he sees the bull fully occupied with the hat, the porter slips to the ground just like a monkey and runs, runs—

He is saved by a miracle.

He overtakes the others and shouts to them what the bull has done—killed the lady, she's lying there on the rock, on the other side of the rock, perhaps she's dead, but they must look, they must find out—! Oh, the porter is on top again, the fellow has recovered his presence of mind, he asks for help to save the lady. He actually declares that that is all he has come for, nothing else, otherwise he might be sitting quite comfortably in the tree!

Daniel hurries back with him. With noble disregard of danger Bertelsen wants to accompany them, but Fröken Ellingsen dissuades him. "Stay here, wait here!" she says. "I'll be back directly!" With that she runs after the two men. Well done! Perhaps she has a vague idea that her red blouse will call off the bull from the corpse.

And indeed it is not too soon; the bull has bethought himself of his victim, his corpse, and has found it again. He is hard at work completing its destruction when the rescue party arrives. The men set up a shout, they make all the noise they can, but now the beast is working desperately and takes no heed. Until a voice reaches it from the road, a cheerful coaxing voice that the bull knows; it is Marta coming. She has a pail in her hand and goes right up to the maddened beast and offers him the bran mash. That does it. And Daniel is ready with the rope.

VI

A time of trouble and unrest.

It could not be avoided, so lamentable an event must necessarily be discussed at all hours, day after day. How did the whole thing come about? The doctor was run off his feet fetching tonics and restoratives, the porter and the postman could not show themselves without meeting a shower of abuse, Daniel was solemnly asked whether he had any more mad bulls, perhaps one or two in reserve? Was there no decorum about the place, should not the body be decently buried, should not the bull be slaughtered? And the sooner, the better?

Lawyer Robertsen had to leave his office and his business in town and come up to Torahus again as principal director. He worked hard to allay the prevailing dissatisfaction, the patients had got such a scare, what security had they for life and limb at such a place? The porter was a murderer, sure enough; but then there was Daniel, who had kept a mad bull; was he entirely free from blame? And there were the lawyer himself and the doctor, who had built a sanatorium in immediate proximity to a mad bull. What was the meaning of it anyhow, wasn't the monster still alive, wasn't it eating hay at the very moment in the sanatorium's cow-shed?

The Suicide nodded and said prophetically: "The second death!"

Otherwise things were going more or less to the Suicide's liking: the longer the slaughtering was postponed, the less fresh beef would reach the Rector's maw; according to human calculation they would soon have saved the whole bull!

But the lawyer disturbed this computation.

He was closeted with the doctor to discuss the situation. The doctor had been rather uneasy of late: two deaths one after the other, and one of them a great Consul—to be sure they were accidents, but they didn't give the place a good advertisement.

"The sword strikes blindly!" replied the lawyer.

The new batch of visitors had asked for the permanent musician, the doctor told him. They had seen in the papers, they said, that the sanatorium had a regular pianist, and where was he?

The lawyer replied: "Let them see it in the papers; you can't believe everything you see in the papers. Our musician has been given a holiday," he said; "we have sent him abroad to make him greater still. It's very simple, we shall get him back when his studies are completed, as a master. Besides, I've said all along that I respect that young man's ambition. That is well known."

Then the visitors asked for the Princess. She had also been in the papers. Where was she?

"Yes, where is she? The deuce only knows," said the lawyer candidly. "Perhaps she's dead too, or absconded, or arrested; I don't know. She stayed here and we got our bill paid."

The two gentlemen thought it over. "But in any case we have the Count," the lawyer continued.

"The Count!" said the doctor, with a shake of the head. "He's been ill. He's no show specimen."

The lawyer was not at a loss: "And now we've got Rector Oliver!"

"Yes. Oh yes."

"A celebrity, a learned man. I'll go and say how d'ye do to him."

"He's not likely to stay more than the week."

"I'll talk to him," replied the lawyer; "I'll bid him welcome, hope his stay may do him good, ask if he has any objection to my putting him in the papers. That'll do the trick!"

The doctor's courage returned and he laughed at the lawyer's resourcefulness. After all, they were laying their heads together in all innocence, it could harm no one, it was all to the advantage of Torahus Sanatorium.

"I was just wondering whether the Rector and I were not fellow students. I have an idea we were close friends."

The doctor laughed still more.

The lawyer frowned and said seriously: "Anyhow we'll hang on to him till we get somebody else. If he's hard up he can stay here gratis...."

And Rector Oliver and his little boys stayed a second and a third week. The bull was slaughtered at once and turned into meat, the canned stuff was replaced by delicate joints and steaks and a sense of well-being became general. Yes, the Rector was doing well and putting on flesh, he took it easy, read Fröken d'Espard's French novels, and went over their contents with her afterwards; it was an experience for him to meet so cultured a lady, in his own town he had practically no one to exchange ideas with.

But the Suicide gnashed his teeth.

He saw very well that the Rector could not be thrown out; the lady who had given up her room to him was now dead and the Rector was no longer squeezing anyone out. But that did not put an end to the Suicide's ill feeling and vexation at this man's coming here and demanding a room with a stove. Who had sent for him? What reason was there to make a fuss about him? And then the unparalleled appetite of this schoolmaster! The Suicide said to his crony, Anton Moss: "I do all I can to avoid that person, but if it comes to a collision I shan't side-step it!"

So the beginning of it was that one day the Suicide seated himself in the smoking-room and waited. He was waiting for the papers to come from the post office. Very well, the papers came. Now, it was the rule that the Rector, as the most intelligent and proficient reader, was allowed to go through the papers first; all the visitors thought this a reasonable arrangement, but it annoyed the Suicide. When the papers arrived he hastily proceeded to scatter them all over the table and shuffle them up with a lot of old numbers that had been read and reread, while he himself sat down with an English paper that had been taken for Mylady's benefit. Now all was in readiness.

The Rector came in.

The two men fell out at once: the Rector couldn't find the new papers without comparing numbers and dates with the old ones and he asked the Suicide: "What is your number?"

The Suicide replied as though he didn't understand at all: "My number? I haven't a number, I have letters, my name is Magnus."

The Rector continued his search among the papers, saying again and again: "I've never seen anything like it!"

"What is it?" asked the Suicide.

"What is it?" exclaimed the Rector, exasperated. "Why have you gone and jumbled the papers together?"

Then the Suicide put this amazing question: "Did you hit upon that by yourself?"

The Rector said nothing. It must have dawned upon him that he had to deal with a lunatic. He sat down and began to dip into the papers he had already sorted out.

But the lunatic showed no sign of moving; the Rector went through the papers twice and three times, but nothing happened, the lunatic still clutched the English paper in his hands just as if he had guessed that it was that very paper the Rector was waiting for. Yes, for this was the particular day when Rector Oliver was keen on the foreign papers, they were his greatest delight, his hobby from boyhood.

"Couldn't you be so kind as to change papers with me?" he asked in desperation.

No answer.

"You see, I've noticed you're not reading, you don't turn over."

This was speaking plainly, but even this had no effect on the

CHAPTER THE LAST

lunatic.

Fröken d'Espard came into the room with a respectful greeting: "Good-morning, Herr Rector!"

The Rector lost no time in alluding to the papers: they were in the wildest confusion, he couldn't find anything he wanted.

The young lady at once set to work and arranged them, it took her a couple of minutes, she was a handy person and always made herself useful. Then she went over to the Suicide and spoke to him in a low and pleading voice: "Won't you lend me your paper for a moment?" A deuce of a girl that; she was so unpopular among the ladies, but she got her own back, she knew how to please the men. There she stood, full of sweetness; she went up close to the Suicide, breathed on him. "But perhaps you haven't read it?" she said.

"No," he replied, handing her the paper; "you're right, I haven't. I can't read it."

But now the Rector made himself unpleasant, although he had got the paper: "Can't you read it? Why, then you can't read English? But what made you keep the paper all this time? I don't understand it."

The Suicide answered him: "If I told you that my sight was bad and that was why I couldn't read the paper, it would not be true. My eyesight is good enough, it is my friend Anton Moss who is troubled in that way, unfortunately."

"Well, what then?" asked the Rector, bewildered.

"No, that's all. He's got an eruption in his face, it has begun to attack his eyesight."

The Rector gave him up. He threw a questioning glance at Fröken d'Espard. She said: "He knows English all right!"

"No, I don't," he settled it.

The Rector and the lady began to read. But now the learned man had been disturbed in his daily habits and was out of his groove, he could not shake off his annoyance: "Fancy, not knowing English!"

he said to the lady. "Then he can't know any languages. My little boys have already made a very fair beginning at languages."

And the lady replied: "But they have the advantage of being sons of Rector Oliver."

"I'm sure it isn't everybody nowadays that counts it an advantage to be a cultured person and know languages."

They resumed their reading. The Rector, however, had been somewhat mollified by the lady's words, and as he looked at the ignorant man sitting by himself in his corner without a paper, he felt a sort of pity for him. He was a rector, he was a teacher, and must behave accordingly. Of course, it was not every child that was so favoured by circumstances, his own children were more fortunate than others in their birth. He said a few words to this effect and returned to his reading. Fröken d'Espard wrote something, jotted something down on a scrap of paper and passed it to the Rector. Perhaps it was French. "I see," said the Rector with a nod; "that's it," he said. And now it looked as if some light had dawned upon him, he understood more than he did before. He got up and took a chair close to the Suicide and addressed him in a friendly tone: "It just occurred to me—I'm a schoolmaster, as you know—if you like I shall be glad to give you a few lessons in languages while I am here. What do you think of that?"

The Suicide looked at him.

"The Rector is not an impossible man, you mustn't think that. If we were at home, at my own place, I would give you my private instruction for nothing."

The Suicide was not overwhelmed. "I suppose it's not to be taken literally," he said; "there must be some higher meaning in it."

"No, far from it!" replied the Rector, smiling. "There's no catch about it, I shall be glad to teach you what you don't know."

"Those papers you were making all the row about," said the Suicide with sudden rudeness; "that's how we find them every day when

CHAPTER THE LAST

you've done with them—all tossed about as they were just now."

The Rector, beaten: "You don't say so!" He looked helplessly at Fröken d'Espard and asked: "Is it possible, do I leave the papers in such an untidy state? If I do, it is very wrong of me."

Fröken d'Espard excused him to the Suicide: "The Rector is a learned man, you know, he can't be just like the rest of us."

"Oh yes," protested the Rector, "I'll really—it shan't occur again—"

"That lady who died," the Suicide went on, hard as stove; "—you know that you turned her out of her room and made life unbearable for her. She wished herself dead more than once."

"I don't understand that either. What lady?"

"That unmarried lady. She was given a room without a stove and wished herself dead. And then the bull gored her to death."

Fröken d'Espard laughed aloud at the Suicide's story and refused to take it literally; no, now he was going too far with his jokes and his fertile imagination! He himself sat there as solemn and unmerciful as ever, apparently unwilling to abandon his aggressiveness. What was the object of his unamiable attitude? He gained nothing by it, his hearers simply grew more and more tolerant and smiled and agreed with him. At last he got up and went out.

"I see, he's a bit queer; not right in the head? It was a good thing you pointed that out to me. Fancy, *suicidant!*" said the Rector, reading the lady's scrap of paper again. "So that's it!"

"Yes, but perhaps it's only his talk. The doctor doesn't believe in it."

"I treated him nicely, didn't I?"

"You really spoke very kindly to him, Rector, offering him instruction and all."

"Yes, but you heard how it was, he wouldn't accept it, he didn't thank me. No, I know how it is. But what was I going to say?—you see what a good thing it is to know languages! If you had written that in Norwegian he might have chanced to read it himself."

"Yes," the lady agreed, "my French has more than once been useful and a comfort to me."

"But you heard how it was," the Rector went on, disheartened; "he did not care for my instruction. You can't make any headway with people of that sort, I have tried it before! They don't want knowledge, they won't thank you for it."

"So it is!" said the lady, with an exaggerated nod, as though the Rector had hit the nail on the head.

"Oh, I can tell you I've tried it, even with my nearest relations! For instance, I have a brother in my town. He is a blacksmith. An excellent blacksmith and with good enough brains in his own way, but so ignorant and uneducated. We have nothing in common; you can understand that our interests are entirely different, we hardly ever meet. Not that I would say anything against him, far from it, he does not disgrace me, he is doing well, is a man of means and respected by all, but we don't see much of each other. When he was made chairman of the Town Council I sent him my card, but he never thanked me. We have exchanged a few words on one or two occasions; one of which was when he was to assist me with a loan. Well, he did so, but only as he might have assisted anyone else. No particular readiness, rather the reverse; he hesitated. He had taken his children away from school as soon as they were confirmed, though they had talent and I wished them to stay on and rise in the world. No. And then my worthy brother Abel gave me his views, actually preached to me: 'Rise in the world!' he scoffed. What was I working at? At something cold and dead, stone-dead, at teaching children languages and foreign words and all sorts of grand and unnatural things. What did this not cost the children in time and energy year after year? Just as if it was all thrown away, you understand. And you must not imagine he was joking, no, he meant it. I was working on a false and meaningless system, it appeared; I and my colleagues were learned, but blind; the inanity and mental darkness we fostered was not admired even by ourselves. What was I hunting for? A street name in our town, Oliver Street? Oh, I was destined to live in poverty, body and soul, all my life. Poverty of soul, he said!"

The lady brought her hands together with a smack.

"Yes," said the Rector with a smile, "I can assure you I have something to put up with. And this is our chairman, he gets people to listen to him, it's in the Town Council that he has learnt to express himself, and people think there is sound sense in what he says. Well, the next talk I had with him was when I was going to take my doctor's degree and wanted a little assistance again. Once more he utterly failed to understand: 'Doctor's degree, what's that?' he asked; 'I suppose it's some other dead thing you're going in for?' 'No,' I replied, 'it's quite alive, it's research, scholarship, a thing that never dies!' Well, then, what was it, was it anything we didn't know already? And then he began a rigmarole: was it anything with blood in it, artificial manure, messages from the stars, deep-sea fish, music, a cure for blight on roses—he is fond of flowers and has a garden—in short, was it anything at all to do with love and rosy cheeks?—that is the kind of language he has trained himself to use. No, said I in my poverty, standing like a schoolboy in front of my brother the blacksmith; no, it was nothing of that sort, but a philosophical treatise on the *Batrachomyomachia*, it was philological research, discovery, a little of everything, *Margites*, homonyms, and so forth. 'But why?' he asked. 'Why?' I said; 'who can answer a question like that? But don't you understand that if Homer was not the author of this ancient poem it may well have been written by Pigres of Caria?' No, he didn't understand that. 'You're after something that's stone-dead as usual,' he said. Oh, it was all the most absurd futility to him; 'It's money thrown away,' he said as he gave it me. Well, to that I made no reply; I have made it a rule not to enter into discussions with him, it's hopeless. He once returned to the question of calling a street after me in my town, but I replied that there was no necessity, perhaps I should not even have my monument in Christiania itself."

"Oh, but you surely will!" exclaimed Fröken d'Espard.

"Well, posterity must see to that, I don't expect much of my contemporaries. But those were the two occasions on which I have conversed with my brother Abel. Then it happened that the lock of one of my doors was out of order and I telephoned to my brother to come and put it right. I explained that it was evidently a troublesome business, we couldn't get the key to turn. Do you think he came himself? He sent one of his little boys, and it wasn't even the eldest! Well, the boy managed it, he unscrewed the lock and took it to pieces and repaired it—of course, that's just what boys of that class have learnt, to use their hands. But then, you see, my own boys, who have studied languages and mathematics—they had to stand and look on! No, you can't expect delicacy of feeling. In matters of this sort one sees that the whole town takes my brother's part, the blacksmith's part against the Rector's; when they talk about us you hear people say: 'What a difference between two brothers, one of them has sense, the other learning!' And of course it's the learned one who comes second," added the Rector with a smile.

"Evidently!" said Fröken d'Espard, smiling in her turn.

"Ah yes, one does not meet with much appreciation in one's good borne town, it is frequently discouraging!" Presently the Rector nodded several times and said: "Of course his money shall be repaid at the first opportunity."

"Of course."

"It shall really. One of these days it must surely occur to the powers that be that I am worthy of a government pension."

Poor Rector Oliver, he had his grievances too, he was slighted and badly treated. He was so obviously in the right, but his right was set aside for popular and uneducated opinions. Was he to capitulate? His only recourse was to hold his head high, to stand his ground, he might even be excused for exaggerating his little boys' knowledge of languages and mathematics; in reality they knew very little, they wouldn't work, but preferred to haunt their uncle's forge or go in search of adventures. It was not pleasant for the Rector, his efforts did not bear the fruits he looked for.

Herr Fleming walked in, tired and hollow-chested, but smiling and bowing, a consumptive, a patient, a gentleman in his dress. "Good-morning, Fröken!" And then he bowed to the Rector.

"We were sitting here enjoying a little chat," said the lady. "The Rector has been so kind as to tell me a lot of things about his own town."

Herr Fleming took a seat and asked, with a glance at the table: "Any news in the papers today?"

The Rector replied: "Nothing new, I believe. Though I haven't finished reading them yet."

"You see, the Rector was disturbed today by our friend the Suicide," Fröken d'Espard explained. "He sat here and accused the Rector of conspiring with the bull to take that lady's life."

They smiled and pursued the subject of the great fatality, the Rector expressing surprise that the bull, a four-footed beast, had been able to storm the rock. Herr Fleming, with his knowledge of farming, explained it: the animal was horn-footed, it could dig its nails in, so to speak, and as it was so wild and had such terrific speed it scaled the rock in a few seconds.

"Were you on the rock too?"

"No," replied Herr Fleming; "Fröken d'Espard had driven me home before that."

"Yes, you were still too weak, you know," murmured the lady.

"I was so afraid for my boys," said the Rector; "but what could I do? Afterwards, to be sure, I gave them the punishment they deserved. I can only hope they will keep out of danger in future. As far as possible out of danger."

"They were clever boys," replied Fröken d'Espard; "they were the first to climb up the rock and show us the way. But for that it might have been worse. As it was, the casualties were one human life and one lady's hat."

A shadow crossed Herr Fleming's face at her frivolity and he asked: "Shall we go now?"

As she got up, the lady said: "What do you think, Herr Fleming has promised me a new hat! I'm awfully excited about it. All right, let's go!" And she explained to the Rector: "We're going across to Daniel's sæter again, to get curds and cream for Herr Fleming."

Then they went out.

No sooner had they left the sanatorium precincts than they changed their tone. The new tone was silence. People cannot play on the same string for ever, some strings break, sometimes they are worn to a thread. Now there was Fröken d'Espard; she was so ready to talk about everything under the sun, why had she nothing to say just now? Herr Fleming was naturally surprised. He himself was no great talker, no gushing spout, but he liked to be entertained. Now and again he would cut in with a few shrewd and telling words, leaving the others to do the rest, that was his way. But Fröken d'Espard!

And at last she did say a thing which could no longer remain unsaid: that now she supposed this would be her last visit to the sæter with him!

It took effect: Oh? What did she mean? said Herr Fleming. What a surprise! He was quite unprepared. "Are you leaving?" he asked.

Yes, she had received a second summons to the office.

Ah. Herr Fleming grew very thoughtful. "I never even heard of the first one," he said.

"No, why should I—you were still weak—it wasn't a thing to tell you about either—"

Herr Fleming grew even more thoughtful; both were silent.

They were walking in the most glorious weather, Indian summer, with a view of a wide valley far below them, both were young, loving life, and both were silent. Fröken d'Espard had borne a serious mischance with equanimity; a fortnight ago already she had received instructions to return to her employment, but she did not go, she could not very well leave a sick man who needed her company. And a couple of days ago she had received her dismissal.

Her dismissal. She had borne it well; for some mysterious reason she had said nothing to Herr Fleming, and this very morning she had forgotten her own worries and sat listening attentively to Rector Oliver's. That was a girl, she didn't make a howl! But now her money was running short and she had to come out with it.

"How many times do they summon you?" asked Herr Fleming. He hoped perhaps it might be postponed, and guessed: "Three times? Three warnings?"

"No," she replied with a smile; "there won't be anymore. Only this one."

"Ah, then there's no help for it. Are you leaving tomorrow?"

"Yes, tomorrow."

They were silent again. Herr Fleming stopped; it seemed not to be worth his while to go on now.

The lady came to his aid: "What sort of a house is that?" she asked. "It wasn't there before. Let's look."

They came to a little barn in the fields, a shed that Daniel had just put up to take the hay from his outlying meadows; and as it was so fresh with new-mown hay they went in to rest. The shed had no door, the sun shone in upon them through the wide opening, little sparrows flew in and out after midges. Perhaps memories stirred in Herr Fleming's mind, he grew melancholy and full of feeling, he began to talk of his home; it was not a big place, not an estate, properly speaking; not a castle, after all, no, only a farmhouse, nothing wealthy, you see, far from it—

"Now I'm sure you're taking too gloomy a view of it," she comforted him.

Well, perhaps he was taking rather too gloomy a view; at any rate there were some trees, some forest, a scent of hay, a murmuring brook; there was a plank across the brook and on that plank he had lain more than once and fished with a bent pin. Childhood memories and melancholy, sadness, and poetry in a young man who was drifting from one country to another with wounded lungs. He hinted that he ought to go home, but wanted to stay awhile longer in the mountains and try to get well again. At times he had been depressed and doubtful of his cure, but then it was that Fröken d'Espard cheered him up and kindled his hopes. Oh yes, she must not deny it and make light of it, he was grateful to her for all she had done, and did not know how he could have got through the time without her.

That was how he spoke.

She listened to him with delight, their tone became intimate and tender, they were open with each other and smiled and nodded at every word. When he remembered that they were to part on the morrow, his face fell, the corners of his mouth drooped; then she said: "Shan't we go for your curds and cream?"

"No. To tell the truth, nothing matters now."

"Oh, what nonsense! You're not like yourself!"

"No, nothing matters now," he repeated.

Silence. They each followed their own thoughts—perhaps both were thinking the same. Suddenly Fröken d'Espard said helpfully: "Is it me you're troubled about? Don't worry about that. I have money enough to get away from here."

He replied in amazement that, good Lord, it wasn't that! But what, then? No money? He could let her have that. But how was he to get on alone?

Silence. She sat there looking at his thin fingers; his ring seemed as if it would fall off. Those fingers are of no use for anything, perhaps she was thinking, they cannot strike a blow, they cannot make a grasp, no, they are so helpless, they call rather for patting and caressing. She recognized the silk socks on his calves and recalled the fine night-shirt that he changed next day when a drop of coffee as big as a pin's head had fallen on it. Counts were like that, no doubt. Twice he had been a little indiscreet and had shown more kindness than she was prepared to accept, that was so, and then his eyes had had a drawing-on look. Quite right. But that was when he was ill; she could better excuse it now, altogether she had grown more attached to him since that time.

"I don't know what we're to do," she said. "Perhaps I could stay here—"

Her manner was charming and confidential. He asked right out: "Could you give up your place in town?"

"Yes," she replied.

"Then do so! I'll look after all the rest."

This decision put new life into them both, he broke through all rules of propriety and was very friendly, picked the hay from her bosom, brushed it from her knees, stroked, patted, threw his arms around her. Some call it free will—

Afterwards they went to Daniel's. Strange how subdued their joy was now; their voices were hushed, their playfulness was gone, their eyes were on the ground. It was better when they reached the sæter and were received with welcomes and curds and cream; the old housekeeper refused the big sum offered, but accepted it at last with a shake of the hand. Herr Fleming's face expressed satisfaction.

On the way home they came back to the little barn in the fields, and Herr Fleming said: "Let us go in and rest again." The young lady dropped her eyes and followed him. . . .

And from now on they resumed their daily visits to the sæter, for curds and cream and healing for sick lungs. All went well again. Herr Fleming made such visible progress that he began to recover his spirits and a natural complexion; at the same time he showed more interest in everything about him, was inquisitive about news in the papers and flung himself upon the telegrams. The doctor treated him with rehabilitated authority, bowing as soon as he caught sight of him and sweeping the ground with the feather of his hat. And as the doctor made no objection to the sick man's taking wine at his meals, he drank steadily, often a little beyond moderation. It did not matter, however, he was not noisy, but behaved quite nicely, only got a fixed stare and walked as though following a chalk line. Fröken d'Espard kept him company.

But now the remarkable thing occurred that one day Herr Fleming suddenly became uneasy about Fröken d'Espard's reputation; he asked her to get Fröken Ellingsen to join them, then they would be three and the sour old clergymen's daughters would have nothing to say.

Perhaps this was a wise scheme on the part of Herr Fleming, perhaps it was not a scheme at all, but merely a momentary need of a little variety. This companionship, this inseparability, may have begun to oppress him as he grew stronger and was not so dependent on the lady's nursing; latterly indeed she seemed to be getting a bore with her French. Of course he knew the language and understood everything she said, anything else was unthinkable; but he was apt to be irritated when she parleyvooed away nineteen to the dozen and particularly when she put a direct question to him in that lofty language and expected an answer. He then simply left it unanswered, on the plea that he didn't understand French—at which pleasantry everyone smiled.

Fröken d'Espard had accustomed herself more and more to compliance and she accepted his suggestion of a third party in the same way. She was rather taken aback, she was, and pondered what it might mean—why Fröken Ellingsen in particular? She was tall and nice-looking, oh yes, but she had slanting eyes, and was that a great charm? And why a third party at all? Fröken d'Espard raised no objection, she fetched the third party and installed her, but she had her own ideas about it: *she* was no giddy young thing, but faithful to one only, didn't flirt, didn't drink, but passed nearly all her time watching a man drinking—what was there scandalous in that? Only a Count could tell. And anyhow Fröken Ellingsen was not staying much longer at the sanatorium, perhaps only the week. Very well, then, Fröken Ellingsen, come and join us, if you please! A glass of wine? Sweets? Certainly. But if you think you're a beauty, a scrap prettier than I am—no. Besides, you have a way of bursting into tears and making yourself interesting when you're making up stories and stick fast in the middle—

So they were three, and when Fröken Ellingsen's friend Bertelsen joined them, they were four, a party for bezique. They could now occupy a corner of the smoking-room without exciting ill will in any quarter.

It answered well; they mutually regretted not having thought of this before, they clinked each other's glasses and enjoyed themselves. Bertelsen, the timber merchant, was not exactly aristocratic, he was not that; but he was a rich man, had been educated abroad, both at Southampton and Havre, besides which he was almost the owner of Torahus Sanatorium and could assert himself if he pleased. And how was it, hadn't he founded a travelling scholarship, didn't he keep a musician going in Paris? Bertelsen was no disgrace to the party. Moreover, he insisted on paying for the wine in his turn.

Now and again Rector Oliver honoured the party with his presence and took a glass of wine, though he was a man of perfectly regular habits. Cards were then laid aside, the Rector took a chair, sat down, and was given his say. Oh, Rector Oliver was no ordinary philologist, he was a specialist, he had exceptional acquirements. This exhaustively learned man never laughed, he was so stacked with what some would call abnormality as to be blinded to the world that cheers the heart and rejoices the eye. But he had his merits, had been industrious all his life, frugal in his requirements, had never been dissolute, a drinker or a gambler. He had brought up his children in the same frugality: every morning he took his penknife and cut four pieces of equal size from a newspaper; they were for a certain use. The children once asked him why there should be four, neither more nor less, and their father answered: "I require no more, four is enough, and let that be your rule too!"

No, a prodigal and a squanderer he was not, but was always content with cheap tobacco, with the catering his wife provided, and with shiny clothes on his back. The respect that his name commanded was enough for him. Envious colleagues had flung themselves upon his doctor's thesis with considerable eloquence, and, as the conscientious man he was, he had then investigated his whole position. He wavered, but remained standing; he could say to himself: "I had doubts of my own learning, but my many books prove it. And then look at my doctor's thesis, with its two whole pages of bibliography!" His doubts were overcome.

When Rector Oliver came and joined a party, he was at first buttoned up with cocksureness and superior knowledge. He could measure himself, full-measure himself, with almost anybody and when he opened his mouth the others had to keep silence. He made himself intelligible at once, he knew the dictionary meanings of words by heart and never made mistakes, nor used foreign words incorrectly. That in itself was much, among chance sanatorium acquaintances it was a great deal, but it was not all. They could apply to him in case of doubt and get the decision of an authority, that was the culminating point. And he answered so readily, it pleased him to give instruction in "languages," he beamed with satisfaction.

And at the same time it gave him an opportunity of talking about himself, but always in an innocent and becoming way; his pretensions were no more than reasonable.

He now had his doubts about the Suicide: the man must know English after all; the Rector had found him sitting all by himself in the manager's room with a back number of an English paper, and what reason could he have for that?

There was something mysterious about the Suicide, everyone could see that. "Yes," said Fröken d'Espard, "that man is capable of a good deal!" And as they were all agreed in this, Bertelsen had to go one better and exaggerate: "I'm sure he knows more than we think, only he's a bit queer. There's no doubt he speaks French too and the other languages!"

The Rector was alarmed, he regretted his offer to give lessons to the Suicide and didn't see how he was going to make it good again. The Rector was quite nervous about it; the others had to calm him down and get him to understand that he had done nothing wrong. They tried to take him off the subject and fell to chatting of the news of the day, of books, fashions, education, foreign girls' schools; the Rector was in his element once more, he held forth: "Progressing? Certainly we are progressing! There's no comparison possible between past and present. What sanatoriums and country hotels did we have even in my childhood? Now there will soon be one on every mountain. I have a feeling that we have advanced a century, we are beginning to overtake Switzerland. What had we in the way of schools and learning? And what have we now? It is not surprising that we are accounted one of the most progressive nations in the world. We have physicians, clergymen, jurists, and professors who are the envy of many another country, our scientists lose no time in assimilating every fresh discovery among the great nations, we are well abreast of the times. Oh yes, we are progressing. Now here we have two young ladies who, each in her own way, have benefited by the general advance in literary education. One of the most gratifying developments of modern life is this improvement in woman's lot, she can now raise herself in the community to the same level as man and choose her career just as well as he can. It was an error on the part of some jealous critics of mine when they represented me as a man of hidebound habits of thought, a pedant only busied with bygone things. Yes, you may laugh, but they actually did so. There was one in particular, named Reinert, son of the parish clerk in our town, who had difficulty in forgiving my doctor's degree. He and I were schoolfellows and contemporaries at the university, but, you see, I was a little in front of him the whole time and that mortified him. He was an expensive boy, the ruin of his father, and at last the old parish clerk had to borrow money against his next Christmas offertory in order that his smart son might lack nothing. To make a long story short, the boy did not work as he ought to have done; it took him two years longer than me to pass his examination, in spite of his having my example as an incentive. Now he's assistant master in a little west coast town and I don't suppose he'll ever be anything else. But at that time he was envious and bitter enough to attack me. He wrote that I had scraped up two pages of authorities in my doctor's thesis simply and solely to make myself appear learned; most of these authorities had nothing to do with the subject, he said. I replied calmly and to the point, adding that he seemed to be blinded by a private grudge. Then he got a colleague to help him. He was no great shakes either, a radical and a roisterer; it was this man who accused me of old-fashioned pedantry and out-of-date ideas. Me! When I do nothing but provide facilities for the higher education of all. I venture to say that my conscience is of the clearest on this score. I even instituted lectures for my fellow-townsmen; the attempt was unsuccessful, it is true, but that was not my fault. Imagine me standing there and lecturing on a subject taken from the history of the Hellenes: I mention Thucydides.

Whereupon a mad fellow on one of the benches interrupts me with a laugh and asks if I mean Thicksides! Oh—after that I could do nothing more there, the whole of my auditory roared with laughter, I stepped down from my desk and abandoned the rest of the lectures. You see, it was hopeless. But this might have been avoided, mightn't it?—if my hearers had had more schooling; Thucydides, as we know, is not Thicksides. More schooling, more schooling! Therefore I have always, all my life in fact, been a warm advocate of popular education; I should like to see every servant-girl pass her matriculation and become a cultured person. Thus I hold the most advanced opinions on the subject of woman; for instance, let her develop herself, let her be given equal rights, that will be, as a great Englishman has said, a doubling of mankind! And so it ought to be all along the line, schools and courses for great and small, for men and women, schools of every kind, colleges of every kind. And so it will be before long. A woman can now be whatever she pleases, there are swarms of women students, they can become magistrates, physicians, and teachers, we have schools for everything, industrial schools, drawing schools, commercial schools, language courses, seminaries, schools for defectives where even idiots can learn their letters, institutes where cripples without hands can learn a trade with their toes, schools, schools—"

But now that the Rector was well started he was interrupted by a chance circumstance: outside the window the two cronies, the Suicide and Anton Moss, were to be seen sitting in two basket-chairs and apparently shivering with cold. The Rector was the first to notice them; he started back, saying: "Ah, there are those two!" Bertelsen proposed bringing them in and giving them a glass of wine, and Fröken d'Espard fetched them. You see, Fröken d'Espard was the one who could manage a thing of that sort; the rest of the party had a full view of the two friends' surprise at the invitation, saw them talking together, as though one were asking the other what he thought about it; meanwhile Fröken d'Espard stood by, smiling, with her head to one side. Finally all three came in.

Room was made for the newcomers and they were given wine, they were offered cigars, ash-trays were put in their way; but the guests had nothing to say for themselves, not a word. Bertelsen had probably expected to get a little entertainment out of the Suicide, a little of his queer talk, the outcome of his cracked brain, but no. His friend Anton Moss seemed ill at ease in such good company, he tried to hide the rags on his fingers, his sight was bad and he upset his glass. "Never mind that!" said Fröken d'Espard. Everyone was obliging, the Rector most of all; he tried to open a conversation, asking: "I suppose you gentlemen didn't see anything of my little boys while you were outside?"

"Yes, we did," replied the Suicide; "they've gone fishing."

"Of course! Oh, these mountain tarns are so treacherous and full of danger, I have always heard. I have forbidden the boys to go there, but— Were they alone?"

"No, they were with a man who said he was the Sheriff. A young man."

"Of course, they take up with everybody."

Bertelsen said by way of a joke: "The Sheriff—what do our estimable police want here?"

"He asked us who was staying here, and my friend and I gave him a list."

Herr Fleming gave a sudden gasp; when everyone looked at him he stooped and busied himself with his shoe-string under the table. "No, it's nothing this time," he remarked to Fröken d'Espard, who must have feared a fresh hæmorrhage. Oh, but it was something, Herr Fleming was feeling bad, his smile was the smile of a lost man and from now on he relapsed into complete silence. To cheer him up Fröken d'Espard said in a sprightly tone: "Well, Rector, if your boys have the police with them, I'm sure you can be easy in your mind!"

"I'm not easy!" the Rector persisted. He got up and took his leave, repeating that he had forbidden it, strictly forbidden it!

"How wild he was with his youngsters," remarked Bertelsen, when the Rector had gone.

"I'm not surprised," replied Fröken d'Espard. "I'm sure he's a model father."

"A great man!" declared Bertelsen, going one better. "With all his learning and all his knowledge!"

Herr Fleming got up; the two friends seemed to take it as a hint and followed his example, took their leave and went. No, these two were not of much use socially. What about the Suicide? Did he bring any variety with him, any wild humour, any giddy high spirits? Or did he just sit there wrapped up in himself like an exceptionally seductive song-bird? His friend was far more sympathetic, but it was a shame how disfigured that man was with sores and blotches. Bertelsen said he wouldn't dare even to hint at the disease Anton Moss might be suffering from. It had closed up his eyes and given a twist to his mouth.

"Good-morning," said Herr Fleming and went out.

Fröken d'Espard followed. She found Herr Fleming waiting for her, she had again become necessary to him, in the highest degree indispensable to him, he needed her care. Oh yes, there was something, Herr Fleming was visibly perturbed, the mannerly Count now cut a different figure, he was very hard up for a little encouragement.

They went upstairs and into Herr Fleming's room. "It's nothing, only another bad day," he told her.

"You haven't quite got your strength back," she excused him.

"No." And Herr Fleming made a nervous grab at his inside pocket: "You see, if anything should happen, anything at all, one never knows—"

"You've just got to get well again."

"I don't mean that I'm going to die. Well, there's that too. Can you imagine how little I feel inclined to die? I could sell myself into slavery to be allowed to live, I could do a murder to be allowed to live. But it's not that just now. That is to say, it is. I'm talking disconnectedly, but it is that. If I'm suddenly shut up I shall die."

She replied, rather in the dark: "But you're not going to be shut up. What nonsense!"

"I had a warning just now. The fact is, everybody is not my friend, there are some enemies after me from home. Can I be frank with you?"

"Yes!" she shouted with a loud laugh.

Herr Fleming could never have found a better one to confide in; Fröken d'Espard was no little girl who had lost herself in a great forest and couldn't find her way out, no, no. And there she sat.

"I am not an innocent person," he said with a woebegone smile.

Fröken d'Espard replied helpfully: "Nor am I either. No one is."

The road was clear.

It was not a slip, nothing of the kind, it was a premeditated act, he would do the same again. The beginning of it was that death was after him. It was so unexpected and so extraordinarily hard, it was positively not right; he had hæmorrhages and broke down; why should he have hæmorrhages and break down? He had no chance of life unless he made a bold stroke. Did she understand?

She understood.

He made his stroke and made it so cunningly that only a very suspicious auditor could find an innocent clerical error somewhere, a nought, a cipher, nothing. Then he left and came up to the sanatorium. Was this the right place, would he find here what he wanted? He had been up and down, up and down again; God knows, perhaps he had made a mistake. And all the time he had had this hanging over him, night and day, weighing on him, torturing him. It was not for nothing that he asked for news in the papers and nosed into the telegrams. He must beware of doing it too openly, nobody must think it strange, nobody must be on the track of his secret. He was living on a quicksand.

Very well, this did not discourage Fröken d'Espard, that brave little soul, she did not take a gloomy view of it; on the contrary, her view was to a certain extent that of an expert and she excused him with a laugh. And in itself this light-hearted way of taking it was enough to cheer the poor fellow, he no longer felt utterly done for, she shielded him.

And he explained more fully: if his chest were healed and he had got back his strength he would have given himself up and taken his punishment, honest to God he would, as willingly as possible, with a cheerful heart. "Only give me time!" he exclaimed; "let me be in a state to suffer, don't kill me before I've given this cure a chance!"

One or two things still seemed obscure to the lady, and he confessed away like a man: No, of course he was no aristocrat from Finland; he came from the country and the soil, from a little place with a horse and three cows; how much it must mean, then, to him to live in fresh air! But he had stood for six years behind a bank counter, he had not had one happy day there, he was a country lad and knew to a nicety that a bull was a horn-footed animal, the roots of his being still yearned for his home. It was no accident that he had taken to Daniel's sæter, with its little houses, its curds and cream: its bed with sheepskin coverlet; those were the things to make him well again, weren't they?

Yes.

They were to make him well again, confound it! But the idiots couldn't understand that, they only wanted to catch him on the first opportunity. No indeed, he had no lordly notions, he hadn't made for a big hotel in Paris and put up there and squandered the proceeds; he had chosen fresh air, mountains, and open sky. Why, then, had he given himself out as a Count? That was easily understood:

for the sake of the protection it gave, of course. They would be far quicker to suspect an Axelson than a Fleming. "At home we go into the byre twice a day, morning and afternoon; my father is dead, my mother's name is Lisa," he said. "It's a heaven-sent joy to her to hear how well her son is getting on here in the fells; she boasts of me before the other women and was always proud of my getting into a bank. If only she may be allowed to die in time and be spared the catastrophe!"

In truth things did not look too rosy for Fröken d'Espard either, but in spite of that she said: "Well, well, don't take it like that!"

Oh, but he realized quite well that one day he would be caught, it was only a question of time; while they were talking downstairs a word had dropped upon him like a spark.

Herr Fleming now took out his pocket-book in earnest and produced a kind of letter, a thick wad. "I want to be prepared," he said. "This is all money; what am I to do with it? Burn it?"

"You don't mean that!"

"No more I do. But there's no time to get it away, perhaps at this moment there's a man outside watching for me; you understand who I mean."

"I'll hide it," said the lady.

"Ah, will you? Dare you?"

She merely gave a spirited toss of the head and smiled.

"Well, you see, the fact is, you can't feel quite safe either. It occurred to me a few days ago, we've been so much together that suspicion may light on you too. That was the real reason why I got you to bring in Fröken Ellingsen and through her Bertelsen."

Fröken d'Espard snatched the thick envelope from the table and tucked it well in against her bare bosom. "For the present!" she said.

Good! Well, of course he could burn the money, he went on. But it might turn out that he didn't die, that on the contrary he survived his punishment, his ailment was a capricious one, it had been known to take the most extraordinary turns. If he survived being shut up—

Fröken d'Espard nodded; there was no need to say more, she herself would have been glad to find a pot of money after being shut up.

"There's another thing I should like to mention," he said. "So that your acquaintance with me may not damage you too much in the place, I shall of course deny everything. Understand? Deny every word. I shall be sentenced, but I deny all the time. What else can I do? And in reality I haven't committed any crime either, I only wanted to be able to live."

"Of course."

They were so thick, so well agreed in the affair, they never counted the money, no sum was mentioned. When the lady left the room she removed half the burden from Herr Fleming's chest. It had all gone so slick.

A few moments later she knocked again at Herr Fleming's door, came in, and said: "It wasn't the Sheriff who was here; it was only his officer."

Herr Fleming may well have feared she had been putting indiscreet questions to the servants, but she reassured him with a crafty smile: "I asked for the Rector's boys," she said.

"Ah, the Sheriff's officer—what then?"

"The man who ran off with Daniel's sweetheart."

Herr Fleming thought it over: "Sheriff or Sheriff's officer—it's all one, it's only a question of time. Today's Wednesday, I must clear out."

Herr Fleming might have felt safe for that day, the Sheriff's officer had returned from fishing and had already left the sanatorium and gone home; Fröken d'Espard had seen him go. Whatever purpose he may have had in his head had been upset by chance. There was great talk among the visitors about the Sheriff's officer: he had been in the water, he arrived soaking wet from top to toe, even his cap with the gold band and the gold lion was like a wet rag. "What has happened to you?" some of them asked him, among them Fröken d'Espard. "Don't talk about it," he replied; "I had an accident, slipped on a rock and went right in, to the bottom!" He could not conceal the fact that the little boys had rescued him.

Wonderful boys, they had first thrown in a log, but as the Sheriff's officer still lay in the mud at the bottom and didn't come up again, they jumped in and hauled him up into the light of day. Oh, those little devils of boys, incredible scapegraces, adventurous as you like, but real little men! Now they had gone to bed while their clothes were being dried.

Herr Fleming and Fröken d'Espard could breathe again, and they did so, they drank wine, were gay, stretched their legs and sprawled. It was gallows humour.

She made fun of his dread of the Sheriff's officer, an angler who went into the water head first—God help us!

Herr Fleming was for a while infected by her careless humour and joined in tempestuously: "He had to take himself off home this time!"

"Had to sneak home like a wet dog. I saw him!"

"As a matter of fact," he said with a laugh, "there was something genteel and correct about his behaviour. If handcuffs were to be used, his wet ones would have spoilt my shirt cuffs."

"Ha ha ha!" laughed the lady, making the very utmost of the consumptive's gaiety. And when she could do no more she fell back on her usual trick when she wanted to amuse and talked bad French: coffee with "*avec*," a *lit-de-parade* bed.

"You mustn't talk French to me," he said with a smile, making an even cleaner breast of it. "For very good reasons!" he said.

Later in the day, when it was growing dark, he asked her for some of the money back, he would have to use it. On this occasion it was he who had to unhook her blouse at the back, and this led on the instant to a passionate embrace, a frenzy of tenderness, with tears and kisses, half hysterical. Suspense had unnerved them both. If perhaps she had felt a slight disappointment at his being neither a landowner nor a count, she was clever enough to conceal it; indeed, his self-exposure had brought him nearer to her, he still behaved like a gentleman, that was natural to him, and in any case he had a valuable ring and an envelope full of money.

Speaking of the money, he once more gave her instructions to be careful and to burn it in case of emergency.

"Never in this world!" she replied.

They took leave of each other with no ordinary solemnity; he wished it so. They loved one another, kissed one another, and gave one another lifelong promises. Good-night! By the way, she might have had this ring, but it would compromise her. More kisses and more good-nights. And they parted without his having opened the wad of money and taken any out. Perhaps that had only been a pretext.

In the morning she went to his door and listened; his shoes were outside, she knocked gently and waited as usual for him to unlock the door and get back to bed. No. She knocked again. No. Then she tried the door, it was unlocked and she walked in. No one there; otherwise all in order, the bed untouched. Clothes hung on the wall, two trunks stood on the floor with keys in their locks, a hand-bag was gone.

Fröken d'Espard threw a glance round the room and understood what had happened, perhaps indeed she had expected it. The first thing she did was to lock the door and shut herself in; she had often done that before when Herr Fleming was unwell and stayed in bed. When the maid knocked in the course of the forenoon, Fröken d'Espard explained through the crack of the door that Herr Fleming had caught a fresh cold and that meals were to be sent up for both of them as usual. And when the food arrived she took the tray at the door. Now all she had to do was to eat a little on two sets of plates.

For three days she kept this going, locked up at night, slept in her own room, and in the day-time resumed her place in Herr Fleming's. And his shoes continued to stand outside the door.

She sat there thinking all sorts of things; what would be the end of it? She was not down-hearted and actually luxuriated in her fears and her awkward situation; curiously enough she also felt a secret opulent security in the knowledge that a certain wad of notes was in her keeping. For the present she had hidden it in the padded back of a chair, until she could get into the open.

Now if only Herr Fleming could get clean away by train! If only he could get down to the railway in the first place, without dying on his own hands! He was not yet very strong, he was apt to burst into a perspiration; the only hope was that his determination to live would carry him through, a sudden flash of energy in the face of danger. Who could tell?

One day, looking out of the window, she again saw the Sheriff's officer in the grounds of the sanatorium. His clothes were now dry and his cap had been put into shape. Had he come in earnest this time, on official business? He must have received a negative answer; at any rate he left the sanatorium again after he had had dinner. Yes, Fröken d'Espard must have thought; a man confined to his bed is not to be disturbed!

On the third day two things happened: in the first place the postman brought a big round box for Fröken d'Espard; in it was a hat. Oh, it was the hat Herr Fleming had promised her, he had not forgotten! She drew a deep breath and felt safe; this was a proof that he had duly arrived at Christiania; besides which the fact that he could think of such trifles as a lady's hat showed that his situation was not serious for the moment. And so relieved was she and free from care that she actually opened the box on the spot, in this room where she was on guard, and eagerly tried on the new hat in front of the glass. A splendid gift, a treasure, only far too expensive.

The other important event was that Lawyer Robertsen paid another visit to Torahus, the result of which was that Fröken d'Espard was relieved of her vigil. Something must have reached the lawyer's ears through the servants about the repeated visits of the Sheriff's officer and who it was he asked for; the lawyer went straight upstairs and knocked at Herr Fleming's door. Even before the door was opened he announced himself in a friendly shout and asked if he might see the patient.

Fröken d'Espard opened the door. Her mind was made up, she was bold, impudent, and very clever.

The lawyer looked about him, perhaps his surprise was a little put on. He asked with a frown: "But—where is the patient?"

"I don't know," replied the lady, looking him in the face.

"Oh. Well, but who does know?"

"Himself, perhaps," she answered. "Won't you sit down?"

"What does it all mean, has the Count run away?"

The lady could not say. All she knew was that when she came into the room that morning Herr Fleming was not there.

The lawyer asked: "Do you know what he's been up to?"

"No, how should I know? Has he done anything bad?"

"Not that I know of. He's paid his bill and he's not in the sanatorium. Where is he? Has he had a quarrel with you and gone across to Daniel's sæter?"

"We never had quarrels," she replied curtly. "And I'm sure he's not at Daniel's."

"Don't take my joking in bad part," said Lawyer Robertsen abruptly; "I only meant a little tiff."

"We had no little tiffs either. We were not intimate enough for that, we were only chance acquaintances."

"I am much upset over what has happened," explained the lawyer. "Unless he has just gone for a trip and is coming back. Anything irregular damages a place like this, it gets into the papers and is talked about, it gives us a rather bad name."

"Yes."

"You understand, Fröken, don't you?"

"Oh, yes. I had just the same idea, that's why I came in here and locked the door till you arrived."

The lawyer threw a glance at her. Well, it wouldn't do to be a direct accomplice of the lady, so he said: "It is not unlikely that the Sheriff will come here and examine you. However, you need not let that worry you. For that matter, I dare say Herr Fleming will come back; it's a good sign that he's left his baggage behind."

"Yes."

"Meanwhile we must lock up his trunks and wait. If there's anything wrong about him—I don't say that there is, I don't even think it—good God! if I thought Count Fleming had the smallest account unsettled with the police, I'd be the first to give him up. But in my eyes he is a fine and blameless nobleman. On the other hand, he may of course be wanted on some entirely groundless suspicion, and even in this case the sanatorium will unfortunately suffer. I should hate to see him pinched on our premises. Let us wait a bit."

The lawyer had good reasons for his caution. Torahus Sanatorium, this brand-new institution, had already had several strokes of ill luck, first with a couple of compromising deaths, and then with a certain English Princess and Minister's wife whom nobody seemed willing to acknowledge; the sanatorium was not yearning for a fresh shock, this time due to a Finnish Count. The lawyer did not take Fröken d'Espard to task for the possible share she might have had in Herr Fleming's flight, arguments of that kind were foreign to his nature, he was the host here, everyone's guardian as it were, it was his business to find a way out of the mess.

He pondered the matter for a while and said: "You didn't find him here this morning, so he may have had eight hours' start. That's little enough; I should hate to see him brought back here—that is, unless he comes back of his own accord. But let's see: eight hours; the morning train left at six fifteen. I'll wait—always supposing that Herr Fleming doesn't turn up here in the course of the day—I'll wait till tomorrow."

"Yes," the lady agreed.

"That's what I'll do, wait till tomorrow. But do you know what I shall do then, Fröken?" he asked with a resolute air. "I shall go myself to the Sheriff with my information. Then we shan't have him coming here, it will really be far pleasanter for all of us. All things considered, it wouldn't be in the interest of the Sheriff or of the district to disoblige us; we pay heavy taxes here, we provide work locally, we buy the farmers' produce and beasts, we shed a lustre on the whole district."

VII

The Rector and his little boys have left, Bertelsen, the timber merchant, has left, Fröken Ellingsen has left; yes, autumn is coming on, holidays are over for country visitors to the mountains.

Not that the place was empty by any means; many visitors stayed on, people with small private means, clergymen's widows, shopkeepers' wives who were still suffering with their nerves and showed no intention of getting well, a few young votaries of sport who had damaged themselves in the exercise of their calling and had come to be cured—so plenty of people were left. Besides which, visitors sometimes arrived on foot to take the place of those who left the sanatorium; true, they were on their way from one mountain to another, they only stayed the night as a rule and were of no use to the lawyer as an advertisement, but their custom was welcome, the sanatorium made more out of them than out of the monthly patients.

Of the original guests two, the Suicide and his spotty-faced friend, were not to be moved. Perhaps they were looked upon with least favour, one for his inward, the other for his outward condition; but they stuck to the place from faithfulness or defiance.

Nor did they do any particular harm, they didn't make a noise or go in off the deep end, they were insignificant gentry, miserable gentry. Day after day life proved somewhat dull and depressing for those two; they went and read the white placards on the noticeboards, studied the weather reports, played cards in the evening with the manager and the porter, sat at meals with nervous patients who took pills and salts at regular hours. Thus they got through

CHAPTER THE LAST

the day.

But of late the Suicide had taken to outdoor life and rock-climbing for a change, to keep himself fit. That extraordinary man, who seemed to have lived for nothing but his suicide since he was knee-high, was now beginning to change his mind. Was it not so that he had expressly postponed taking his life till he had found a form which would not discredit murder? Even then he had eaten food and put on clothes, oh yes, and he had attended to business; but at that time he had clearly seen the foolishness of all such conduct, oh, he had looked down upon himself and spat upon himself for it. Now this was all changed. Was this the effect of the air of Torahus Sanatorium, or was he penetrated by a new wisdom? He had become more tractable both with himself and with others, he stepped aside when he encountered anyone in a doorway, he began to speak of his suicide with a certain scepticism. When his crony, Anton Moss, chaffed him for this, the Suicide asserted that every standpoint a person adopted was temporary, every opinion transitory.

Excellent. A man saved for himself and others. How alive one might be; nay, how immortal one might be! If one were not exactly a vocalist, one could go up among the rocks and sing loudly and lustily. The only question was how long this bright state of things would last!

"Are you married?" his friend asked him suspiciously.

"Married? No."

"Have you been married?"

"What's that to do with you!" replied the Suicide sharply. "I don't ask you if you have a disease which I decline to mention."

Moss dropped his head. After a while he went on: "Anyhow, you've got over it now, I can see that. And it would be a damned silly thing to shoot oneself for the sake of a woman."

The Suicide seemed taken off his guard. "I haven't asked you what I ought to do," he said.

Silence. A confession seemed on the point of bursting from the Suicide's quivering lips, he was like one caught. "Where did you get that from?" he broke out. "Do you go listening at doors, have you heard from the maids that I talk in my sleep? It shows what one has to look out for!"

This was enough to put the Suicide on his mettle; if he had a secret, he would see that nobody betrayed it. He would take very good care not to be known as a man with a tragic fate, one who had been ruined on the stock exchange or deceived by his wife. Why, then, did he not keep it up, was there really a string loose in him? He began talking again, and his talk was prosiness and philosophy, a little ordinary and factitious bravado: "But all the same you're right, it would be a damned silly thing to shoot oneself for the sake of a woman. Taking one's life to avenge oneself on a woman is only cutting off one's nose to spite one's face. It may give the lady a slight shock at the moment, but in a little while it's all the same to her, she eats and drinks, knows whether her hair's tidy, remembers her lip-stick. A little while longer and she has a feeling of pride at having been found worth a revolver shot, she thinks it makes her interesting that someone has killed himself for her sake, she puts on side about it. Now don't misunderstand me, I'm not talking of any woman in particular, but of women in general."

"Of course!" replied Moss. But this time he must have heard a strange note in his crony's voice. Moss had bad eyes, but good ears; perhaps he was afraid this was going to lead to confessions and sentiment, so he had recourse as usual to a joke, a sneer: Well, it wouldn't do to condemn suicide entirely, not entirely; it had its value both as a deed and as exercise—

"You're an ape," replied the Suicide, scowling at him.

And again there was a breeze between them, they gave each other what they deserved and were spiteful to their hearts' content. But at this kind of sparring Anton Moss was seldom able to hold his own for long, he was outmatched.

"You dropped a nice little sum again last night," he said.

"Yes, and you paid for me!"

"Well, but it annoyed me to see the silly way you played. Losing to the postman—it must be because he has such bright gold braid on his cap. You're fond of losing to the postman."

"That ought not to hurt you. The postman can't afford to lose."

"Oh, is that the reason?"

"No. Once more you're incredibly wanting. That's not the reason at all."

"Wanting? Perhaps you'd like to make me ashamed of being passed over when you were given your fixed idea?"

"At any rate your face is not all there!" exclaimed the Suicide with disgust. "No, and you don't even talk plainly now, your lips are cracked."

"Ha ha ha!" said Moss. He didn't laugh it, he said it, and "What nonsense are you talking!" he said too. But he was knocked out, he had nothing but a miserable answer: "I'm flourishing and putting on flesh, but you're getting more and more weedy and hollow-eyed. It's a strange thing you don't wear a straw hat."

"And then you're always unshaven," the Suicide went on.

Here Moss had to give in, he did not look clean and nice; besides his sores he had a stubbly beard and it put him out of countenance, he avoided people's eyes. He answered: "You have a mind and a sense of humour that make me shudder. You're just about fit for the cattle trade. I can't shave myself anymore, my skin won't stand it. But I clip myself often and that comes to the same thing, close, close, with a small pair of scissors. Anybody else would understand it."

And now it was the Suicide's turn to be on the watch against snivelling: "Well, be quiet, don't let's have any tears!"

"Ha ha ha!" said Moss again.

They both relapsed into silence, both sat blinking and following their own thoughts; now and again they threw up their heads and cleared their throats to appear manly.

"The air's brisk today," said the Suicide; "we shall soon have snow. What was I going to say?—it doesn't matter anyhow, but you seem to claim an understanding of life's mysteries. Do you understand yourself?"

Moss replied: "Myself? No. I shall soon be blind, I understand that."

"It's a damn silly thing to shoot oneself for the sake of a woman, you say. Just so. But if you were an impartial man you would understand what superficial chatter this is. For instance, are husband and wife the only ones concerned? What about the child? Don't misunderstand me, the child in general."

Moss waved him aside with a toss of the head and replied: "I don't know what you're talking about, all you say is so beside the mark. I won't be forced into a discussion with you."

"As you please!" But the Suicide went on, as though something compelled him: "A child, then, boy or girl; we can call it a girl. If she is, say, three months old, you needn't ask me to believe you haven't seen her and thought her wonderful. What does the mother do? What has the mother done three months after? There you are! But the child lies there and holds your finger, holds you fast and won't let you go. Do you think you can get away? I'm speaking generally, of course—"

They were interrupted, somebody came and told them something that had happened during the night: a grisly figure had appeared in the path, Death. This was no first-rate disaster or loss to the world at large, no, and it did not make the Suicide give up his healthful scrambles among the rocks, but it was just enough to make him tick off a fresh death. And indeed it cast a fresh gloom over the place.

CHAPTER THE LAST

Strange that so much could result from one of the sanatorium's chambermaids' having entered an empty room on the first floor and seated herself there all alone.

The matron found her there plunged in darkness and night. The matron went prying dutifully about the house after everybody had gone to bed, striking matches, peering in, and going on again. Well, then she had found the chambermaid sitting with door unlocked as though she had something to do there; she was not crying, nor was she rocking to and fro and humming; on the contrary, she kept as quiet as possible and listened, scarcely venturing to draw her breath.

The matron was so astonished that she only whispered from the doorway: "But—are you sitting here?"

The maid beckoned to the matron to come in. They both listened, listened to sounds of unrest in the visitor's room next door, weeping, plaintive whispering, an audible sorrow. "It's Fröken d'Espard," thought the matron; "I wonder if there's anything the matter with her?" "Has she been at it long?" she whispered to the maid. "Oh yes, a good while this evening. She has gone on like that every evening for the last week. She doesn't eat anything either, and brings up all ordinary food."

The matron went out into the passage, knocked at Fröken d'Espard's door, and asked: "Is there anything the matter with you, Fröken d'Espard?"

"With me?" replied the lady in a bold voice. "No. I was only reading aloud from a French book."

The matron certainly pulled a rather long face in the dark. "I beg your pardon!" The maid was ordered off to bed instantly, this minute!

The next night the maid came back. Oh, she must have heard Norwegian lamentations a little too plainly to have come from a French book, her inquisitive nose had scented out that there was something behind this, she took up her post in the empty room again and let the darkness swallow her up. Then it was that it happened: Fröken d'Espard appeared at the door, clad in white, with a lighted match in her hand—

The maid gave a despairing whine, threw her arm up to her face, and dashed past the lady in the doorway, dashed on down the corridor, on and on. There was a crash and a scream from the back stairs, then nothing more was heard in the darkness. . . .

But this death—casual and unimportant as it was—seemed to have given Fröken d'Espard a scare. This girl from the office and the typewriter could not stand any more shocks just now, she had had enough already; oh, more than enough. There was no more comfort and holiday-making for her at Torahus Sanatorium, she suspected the maids of making remarks about her state of health: that she could not take ordinary food, but demanded outrageous dishes, things that nobody had ever heard of, such as pickled herring on sweet biscuits, or a plate of raw peas. And now it appeared that the maids actually lay in wait in passages and neighbouring rooms to spy on her. It was not to be endured!

She was positively abandoned, deserted, her friend had gone away and left her, she had to bear her burden alone. Her burden—what burden? That a chambermaid had broken her neck? Not at all. As nobody questioned her about this insignificant event she held her tongue about her share in it. Oh yes, she *had* heard a scream as she was reading a French book in bed, but that was all.

She walked into the country to find a safe place for burying a certain wad of notes. Up to now she had faithfully guarded the back of a certain chair which was full of money, and had never had a thought of appropriating any of it to her own use. This was from honesty towards Herr Fleming, magnanimity to her sick friend, perhaps from something else as well, perhaps from love, a hope of meeting him again; there might be so many reasons for it.

It had not escaped her observation that the Suicide had taken to roaming abroad of late, and she wanted to make sure that he was well out of the way when she started on her secret expedition. She found her place; oh, there were plenty of safe places on the mountain, especially on Daniel's side, near the little barn she knew so well—

Yes indeed.

But as she weighed the heavy envelope in her hand it occurred to her to open it and look inside before she buried it under the stone. It was the first time she had thought of doing so, her anxiety after her friend's flight and, later on, certain secret qualms of her own had hitherto left her no time for such curiosity. She found in the envelope a letter, addressed to herself, a deed of gift: the enclosed notes were for her, he had promised her help in return for the loss of her place on his account; he himself had money enough. Only she must observe the greatest caution and burn the money in case of emergency—

Fröken d'Espard put her hand to her forehead, to her eyes, a compelling wind swept through her little head, in the next few minutes all her qualms had marvellously vanished. Hew delicate, how noble, how like a count or whatever he might be! To Fröken d'Espard it was no longer stolen goods that she carried in her bosom, it was a parting gift, a souvenir of a nobleman. She counted the notes, no, she did not count them, but she looked through them, made a rough estimate; they were good notes, big notes, some thousands, not the kind of sums she had been used to type out at the office, no, but some thousands all the same, several thousands, a fortune. And among them were some smaller notes and quite small ones—just as if he wished to save her having to change any for some time to come. He had thought of everything.

After that she sat down to meditate. Had she now any reason to wring her hands and lament at night? Certainly she had, the same reason as before, that was the worst of it. But money is money, and suddenly she seemed struck by a happy thought; she got up, rather explosively, stuffed the wad of money back in her bosom and after a struggle with two or three patent fasteners at the back of her blouse she left the spot.

Perhaps she would have preferred to go straight back to the sanatorium undisturbed, but now Daniel appeared, he caught sight of her, he had a rope in his hand and a skirt, one of Marta's skirts, in which he was going to bring in hay from the little outhouse; yes, and he greeted the lady a long way off, so she had to speak to him. It was quite an occasion, their meeting, Daniel was evidently glad to see her again.

It was so long since he had seen her, he said; he thought she had gone away.

No.

Ah, but what about the Count, where was the Count?

The Count had left. Perhaps he would come back, but just now it was too cold in the mountains for his weak chest.

"Can guess that!" said Daniel with a judicious nod. And so she was alone now, altogether alone? Well, well, it was only for a little while.

Without ceremony she had bent her arm back and pulled open the patent fasteners; she hauled out the wad of notes before Daniel's incredulous eyes, found a ten-crown note, and handed it to him, saying: "That is for you, he asked me to give it you. It's lucky I met you."

"No, no, no," said Daniel, retreating a step or two. "It's not possible! From the Count?"

"From the Count. Oh, he thought of everybody!"

They had quite a long chat about the Count, an excellent man, he never forgot Marta a single day. It was a great pity such a man should have anything wrong with him—

The lady said: "Perhaps you could hook me up at the back, I

can't reach."

He threw down the rope and the skirt and answered: "It's not so sure that I can do a job like that—so fine—"

He managed it, she felt his hands at her back and heard the clipping of the fasteners. Oh yes, he managed it, she noticed that in his innocence he was afraid of being too rough.

They walked together along the path to the hay barn. Fröken d'Espard peeped in, no doubt with thoughts of her own. For she had passed many a good hour in there with her friend, and he had kissed and embraced her. Oh, they had both been in terror of the consequences, that was sure, and just as constantly they had renewed their terrors. No, it was not sport or wagering, it was a chafing in the blood, unavoidable folly and stupidity of the world's oldest pattern, perhaps with something golden in it, love perhaps; it might be so many things at the same time.

"Good-bye," said the lady, leaving Daniel to his hay.

When she came home to the sanatorium she packed her things, collected her French novels and locked them in her trunk, asked for her bill and paid it with some notes she had taken out on purpose. She was rather grand about it; as the bill was made out for one day short she sent it back to be corrected, and she gave very decent tips. It gave a mystic and all-powerful support to feel a wad of notes in her bosom.

The doctor came. If he understood her sudden departure somewhat better than she intended, he was wise enough this time to feign ignorance; but, after all, Doctor Oyen can have known nothing. "You too, Brutussa!" he said chaffingly, and for some reason or other he was pleased with the words and laughed at them. However, he was not surprised at her leaving, it was beginning to get cold in the mountains, he would be glad to get away himself. She hadn't forgotten anything, a book perhaps?

If she had, it wouldn't matter, she would soon be back, she was only going for a little trip to Christiania, leaving her trunk behind.

The doctor was pleasantly surprised: "That's right, Fröken, you'll be heartily welcome! We shall be doubly glad to see you, as one of the faithful, one of our first lot of guests."

The matron came. The same assurances, the same politeness.

As Fröken d'Espard went out carrying her suit-case, she passed through the drawing-room. On purpose. She knew very well that she had never been liked by the other lady visitors and she wished once more to show them how little she cared. They should not think anything bad of her, here she was, let them take a look! Was not the boldest course the safest? She walked through the drawing-room like a procession passing through two ranks of spectators, yes, and she even dug her little finger into her ear as she went. Nobody could show more superiority.

In the train there was nobody who knew her.

The very first day in Christiania she met her familiars from her old office. There were compliments and invitations to visit the bachelor diggings she knew so well. Yes, thanks, she would come, but first she had some things to do in town.

Then she arranged it so that she ran into Bertelsen, the timber merchant. That gentleman had by no means frowned upon her at the sanatorium; on the contrary, he had shown that he appreciated her. And one day when flushed with wine he had even pressed her foot under the table.

She asked after Fröken Ellingsen.

Oh yes, he saw her fairly often, she was quite well. In return he asked after Herr Fleming. But wouldn't it be better to go into a café instead of standing here in the open street?

Yes, thanks, if he would telephone for Fröken Ellingsen.

He promised to do so and they went into a café and had food and drink. Bertelsen reported of Fru Ruben that she had grown much thinner, she could walk now; "Do you remember Fru Ruben? Well, you wouldn't know her again, whether it's sorrow for her husband's death or whatever it may be. But do you remember Mylady, the wife of the English Minister? All lies, I've now heard from Sweden, a dangerous female swindler! But look here, Fröken, shan't we take a taxi, home to my place? It'll be cosier to sit and talk there."

"Yes, if you'll telephone for Fröken Ellingsen."

"Fröken Ellingsen—well, no, she's on duty, she can't get away—"

And now the remarkable thing happened that Fröken d'Espard lost her temper. She was not the least gone on Fröken Ellingsen, but she suddenly turned white in the face with rage because Bertelsen had fooled her. Oh, she was so irritable, it would have taken little or nothing to make her burst out, she was in an unaccustomed state of mind. What—did not Fröken d'Espard understand what he was offering her? She was no schoolgirl. But what he offered was something for which she was now totally unfit, she could have spat upon his taxi-drive. Of course she recovered her temper at once and thanked him for his invitation, but they separated outside the café and went in opposite directions.

In the afternoon she looked up Fröken Ellingsen and found her unchanged, full of romance and poetry and wild stories, her head a tissue of thrilling tales which she meant to write, which she was writing. They would certainly be some good, everybody said so. The only tiresome thing was her oath, she was bound to silence.

Fröken d'Espard would have liked to inquire of this lady, who knew so much from her telegraph instrument, about a certain fugitive, an invalid nobleman, but dared not. Thank God, he could not have been caught yet, perhaps he would get away by one of the transoceanic lines to Australia, to South America—

Would Fröken Ellingsen go with her to a bachelor flat this evening, to the head of her old office?

Yes, thanks. Was Bertelsen going?

Bertelsen—oh yes, they'd get him on the telephone.

Fröken d'Espard fetched her in the evening and they drove to the flat. But no, there was no comfort there either; her old companions were too much as they used to be, but Fröken d'Espard had changed. Good God, what did it interest her to hear how the business was going or that the managing director himself made love to his new typist!

"Does she know French?" asked Fröken d'Espard.

"Well, there's French and French. It's not the same as when you start in, but still—"

Yes, Fröken d'Espard smiled, but after all it was nothing to her. "She got the place through her photograph," said one of the men. That too was nothing to her.

"She's got a rise already."

Nothing, nothing at all; Fröken d'Espard had something else in her head. It was pure instinct of self-preservation and she must not spare herself. Now look at Fröken Ellingsen, how she's enjoying herself! But, then, she's not in the position of having to hurry up and fight for her life. There she sits, tall and handsome, but she doesn't make any show because she's not obliged to. To begin with, the gentlemen are delighted with her appearance, those glances come from a pair of eyes which slant a little and give her a characteristic look, she has the loveliest big mouth, glorious brown hair—all the same, she doesn't let herself go with the others, she takes no part, is not alive. She has become purely mechanical: wind her up and she will romance away, will give the reins to a captive imagination and let it run till it comes to a standstill. But couldn't she tell stories that brought colour into her cheeks and a flash to her eyes? Quite correct; the mechanism became heated. Then it began to grate and jar and then she stopped. After that came tears.

"Dry stick!" thought Fröken d'Espard and said: "Your health, Fröken Ellingsen!"

CHAPTER THE LAST

"Your health!"

Fröken d'Espard was full of her own affairs and divided her attention tentatively among her companions. They were more or less hairless, worn out by standing and writing at a desk, withered in this labour-lacking occupation; the head of the office was worst, that elderly gallant himself made fun of his baldness, stroking it with the palm of his hand and calling attention to it: "A family weakness," he said. Smart fellow, signet-ring on his first finger, passed among his equals for a regular man about town, a rip, and still far from superannuated. Besides, he had cut his coat according to his cloth: two rooms, with a portière between. But for Fröken d'Espard he was not the man, he was too loose, no backbone, no foundation; she gave him up.

"Oughtn't we to telephone?" whispered Fröken Ellingsen.

Telephone? Oh, to Bertelsen—all right. But Fröken d'Espard was taken up with her own business, everything else had to wait. She attached herself to one of the clerks, one of the younger members of the party, a man of ordinary appearance and with all his hair. He was from the country, a peasant, had been seven years in the business, his salary was now ample, but he did not manage to put by anything to speak of. Fröken d'Espard was aware that he speculated a little on his own account; a pushing fellow and smart, peasant to the tips of his finger-nails. He was grateful to his office superior for having included him in the invitation this evening, was careful in his drinking and respectful all the time.

The hours passed. There were sandwiches, snaps, beer, chat, whisky and soda, pipes and cigarettes—no, it wouldn't have bored Fröken d'Espard in other circumstances, but now she had something else to think about. When the coffee and benedictine arrived she could just bring herself to amuse the company with her "Coffee with '*avec*.'"

Fröken Ellingsen whispered again: "Can't we ring up now?"

"Ring up? Yes. But I don't know whether these gentlemen know Bertelsen."

Fröken Ellingsen, crest-fallen: "Bertelsen doesn't like my going out without him."

Oh, but then Fröken d'Espard was ready enough to help and asked aloud: "Do you mind if we telephone for Bertelsen?"

"Bertelsen?"

"Bertelsen & Son, you know. The son."

Everybody knew him, the head of the office knew him. "By all means, the telephone's in there!"

The ladies went behind the portière and started ringing; Bertelsen was not at the office and not at home, he was at some café or other, Fröken Ellingsen grew more and more embarrassed. "Well, you just go in and sit down," said Fröken d'Espard at length; "I'll find him all right!" She pushed Fröken Ellingsen out and called to the clerk, the peasant: "Come here and help me; you were always so clever at the telephone, I remember."

These two then telephoned hither and thither in the semi-darkness of the bedroom and when they were done with that and had found their man Fröken d'Espard began to put in a little work on her own behalf, throwing her arms around the peasant and stroking all his hair. What the devil—he'd never imagined—never expected—

Oh, but she'd been thinking of him all the time.

He was confused and half afraid, the strangeness of the experience made him hold back; he kissed her right enough, but not without suspiciousness. What in the world—Fröken d'Espard, whom the head of the office himself had made eyes at! "No, we must go in to the others," he said.

Yes. But then he knew now that she thought of him, that, to put it plainly, she couldn't forget him. What did he say to that?

Hm. Well, he'd never dreamt of a thing like that, never in all his life. And he was so utterly unworthy of her, a poor man—a wretched

CHAPTER THE LAST

job in an office—no future—

Oh, but she had something of her own. She would say no more, but a little windfall, a legacy from her people in France, a gift from heaven! But as though to leave a loop-hole open she said at last: "You shouldn't have kissed me if you don't care for me. Ugh, I've got such a pain in my head!"

When they rejoined the others the peasant was a good deal flustered; Fröken d'Espard managed it better, perhaps from compulsion; she held her hand to her eyes, crying: "Oh, what a lot of light! Well, we found Bertelsen for you, Fröken Ellingsen, he's coming right away!"

And Bertelsen came, left his party, he said, and came. He was excited and talkative, not a little bemused, he must have been at it in cafés all the afternoon. He instantly made a set at Fröken d'Espard, taking advantage of their acquaintance at the sanatorium. That Count was really nothing for her, a man with one foot in the grave; perhaps he wasn't even a nobleman.

Fröken d'Espard's irritation returned: "No, perhaps he didn't belong to the timber nobility."

But the timber merchant took this piece of rudeness very nicely and disarmed her: It wouldn't do to spit upon timber, upon money, easy circumstances. He for his part had been of some little help to his friends, he also—though he mentioned it himself—kept a scholarship going in Paris, a musician—

"Yes, we know that!" exclaimed Fröken d'Espard, repentant. "It was really most generous of you!"

"Now, don't let's exaggerate," returned Bertelsen; "you're making too much of it."

"Not at all!" And in her ardent desire to be good and kind again she made even more of it: "I know it's not the first time you've been a benefactor."

Bertelsen looked round at the company in feigned surprise and said: "She's raving! Well, I didn't really mean to say a word to the discredit of your Count, Fröken d'Espard; he was an agreeable man, we played cards and drank wine together, he was undoubtedly a gentleman. Only a pity he was so far gone. Are you engaged to him?"

"I? No. What nonsense!"

"Nonsense—very well. But you can turn and twist it any way you like—it's I who love you."

They all laughed at this and took it anything but seriously; only Fröken Ellingsen sat there gloomy and strange and joyless.

Bertelsen talked nineteen to the dozen—about Fru Ruben again, met her the other day, must have gone through a cure, wonderful change. "A rich lady, colossally rich, nice-looking too in her way, lovely eyes, almond eyes. Have you heard about Lawyer Robertsen? Well, he calls himself Rupprecht now; he applied for a royal warrant to change his name to Rupprecht. A fool. Should I ask the King to let me call myself Bertillon? *Jamais!*"

Bertelsen drank more and more; being a strong fellow he could stand a good deal without falling off his chair, but he played the rich man with a lot of noise and did not make entirely for comfort. Fröken d'Espard made no bones about ignoring his talk; she tried to unload some of his attention upon Fröken Ellingsen, but Bertelsen wouldn't rise to it. There, for instance, he took his latch-key off the ring and offered it in his drunkenness to Fröken d'Espard—he was unaccountable.

"Am I to have it?" she asked.

"You're to *earn* it."

"No; why? I don't want it."

Their host came to the rescue: "Wait a moment, let me have the key. I'm sure Herr Bertelsen has a lot of silver in his home."

"Ha ha ha!" they all laughed. But Fröken Ellingsen sat there, tall and handsome, and had nothing to say to it. Had she no shame, did she put up with anything? Invariable—went through life with her

CHAPTER THE LAST

head in the air, heard nothing, saw nothing, untouched and immovable, boring and lovely. There was no doubt she could crochet too and play the piano. Her passion had passed into literature and into gossip on the telegraph-line, into dreams and imaginings. "Dry stick!" thought Fröken d'Espard.

"Your health again, Fröken Ellingsen! You're so silent."

"Your health!"

Bertelsen was not to be beaten, he stuck obstinately to Fröken d'Espard, grew familiar and called her Julie.

Fröken d'Espard suddenly pushed her chair back from the table and said pitilessly: "You keep on treading on the wrong foot, Herr Bertelsen!"

No, use, he was proof against anything.

Fröken d'Espard got up and said to the peasant with the hair: "It's late; come and help me to find a taxi."

The peasant looked at his host, his superior, and went behind the portière again.

Fröken d'Espard was in a sort of hysterics, blazing with hopelessness and itching to be married; she tackled him at once and asked him right out. He found her a nuisance, she disturbed his telephoning and he had to ring again. He succeeded in putting up some sort of defence, saying that he had nothing against her, of course, either as regarded her appearance or anything else. All said and done, he didn't suppose she wanted him either, she'd see—

She guessed she was doing no good and asked curtly: "Did you get the taxi?"

"It'll be here in a moment." And now he seemed to have second thoughts about it: "I don't know what to say, but anyhow it was a stroke of luck for you getting that money, that legacy. I congratulate you with all my heart."

"Thanks," said she. "I'm sure you don't believe me, and it doesn't matter now, but feel here!"

She made him feel the bosom of her blouse and he exclaimed: "Good heavens! Do you carry it about on you? You must put it in the bank at once. How much is it?"

Oh, now the moment had arrived, she didn't hold her tongue and put up with everything. "Ah, if you only knew!" she replied. And suddenly, in a kind of fit, she hissed in his face: "Just wouldn't you like to know, eh? Lick your lips over it! And do you think I'd have kissed you just now if I hadn't been drunk? Go to blazes with you!"

Did she stop there? Oh, her follies were not ended, but being quick-witted and clever she persisted in order to cover her defeat; she smothered him in a torrent of French which he didn't understand, reciting as from a book, gesticulating; he could take it as joke or earnest, but she parleyvooed at him, and she kept it up after she had flung the portière aside and rejoined the others.

The company looked at her in surprise and their host said jokingly to the peasant: "Answer her now, why don't you answer?"

Fröken d'Espard explained: "I've proposed to him, but he won't have me. Are you coming in my taxi, Fröken Ellingsen?" She went up to the host and thanked him, she said good-bye to the others, including the peasant, giving him her hand and saying: "Glad to have met you! Well, are you coming with me, Fröken Ellingsen?"

"Ah—I don't know—"

"Can't you see that Bertelsen's gone to sleep?"

"Yes, but—"

"There's the taxi hooting! Well, thanks, everybody, for a jolly evening!"

But down in the taxi she couldn't put a bold face on it any longer, she began to cry. She drove to her hotel, gave orders to be called at a certain time, and went to bed. Of course there was no question of sleep for hours, her nerves were on edge and she was tortured by fears for the future. Her trip to Christiania seemed to have been in vain, nothing achieved, nothing arrived at, she lay here with a harrowed mind and wept again. What sort of company had she been in? It might well be that she did the peasant with the mop of hair an injustice, but he had given her an impression of greediness, of wanting to get his hands on her money, of trying to find out how much she could offer him. Just so. But afterwards, when the child was there and the money was put into some business or other—what then? Wouldn't he then show the other side of himself?

She was very unhappy, she wept, crooked her fingers like claws and scratched at the coverlet, went through the whole series of her male acquaintance time after time without pausing at any of them. She might have been wedded to Herr Fleming—quite so, but then she would have been mixed up in his affairs; he had evidently wished to save her from a disaster she could avoid. Oh, but if he only knew what he had not saved her from! On top of all the rest her looks had now gone off; she jumped out of bed and went to the glass, she had grown uglier in the last few days, her face was grey and puffy. Better to get away from here in all haste. There wasn't even a forest here, a safe hiding-place for her money, the town was full of people who would watch her when she went to bury it.

In the morning, after an almost sleepless night, it was with a certain relief that she seated herself in the train again. She acted without reflection, her journey had no plan, but she wanted to get away from Christiania again and thought it might be best to make for Torahus Sanatorium once more. Why? God knows. At any rate there was a forest. She allowed herself to be led by her own irresolution, by a reason in things, a latent wisdom.

When she arrived she was not in a mood to renew her triumphs over anyone, for she returned from her trip without accomplishing her errand; the lady visitors might have free play again. Their numbers had thinned, by the way, in these few days; she had not remarked it before, but it struck her now that there were not many people left, the whole place was beginning to look empty. The fresh snow and the cold had come, there was no life, no skiing, not a thing. Here and there on the paths could be seen the footprints of people who had been to look at the weather reports or some fresh notice posted up.

She got her old room again and unpacked her baggage, the cheap French books in yellow covers, once her pride; now they were of less consequence, they did not brighten her spirits, did not help her. And now began her days and nights with the same anguish—

VIII

The doctor had consulted the manager about getting up something for the entertainment of the visitors, something attractive, skiing competitions on the slopes, a skating tournament on one of the mountain tarns. Oh yes, certainly, that should be done. But Manager Svendsen, the old sailor, hadn't much idea of sports on terra firma and had to call in the aid of the postman and the porter. The three men then went to work and chose a suitable skiing slope, and when the ice was firm enough they swept off the snow and made a smooth skating-rink. And here again Lawyer Robertsen showed his thoughtfulness and his gifts as a host: he sent up to the sanatorium several pairs of skis and skates for the free use of the visitors. In a communication which accompanied them and which was posted on a notice-board he jokingly advised his guests to break the skis rather than their necks. The communication was signed: "Rupprecht."

The semi-invalid visitors and patients who had nothing in the world to do began to look on at the performances, and the younger and bolder ones now and then took part in them; only the elderly ladies were debarred from doing so; at the best they could toboggan, but as they were no longer children their toboggans would have to be sledges. "Well, we'll get a proper sledge!" said Manager Svendsen. For the present there was not enough snow for the skis, but there was ice for the skates, black ice five nights old, dangerous only in one place—by the stream which ran down to Daniel's sæter.

The visitors had to provide themselves with outdoor clothes for a hard winter; some preferred to take their departure. So the castle and its two annexes became yet more desolate. The Suicide, as the well-to-do man he was, had had an overcoat and an ulster sent up, but as he couldn't wear both these garments he made over the ulster to Moss, who had nothing of the kind.

"Then why don't you go away?" asked the Suicide.

"I'm going soon," replied Moss.

"So am I."

Neither of them left and perhaps they had their reasons for it: the Suicide had evidently come here so as at any rate not to be at home, what else? So how could he go back?

They went to look at the skaters, that was the kind of thing they had to do. Since Moss's sight had been so bad, he had taken to walking with a stick and got along somehow with it, but he accompanied his friend pretty closely everywhere, even up among the rocks, even, as now, to the rink.

The skaters turned out to be the porter and the postman, now and then they took a lady between them and sailed away with her, and later on they got others to try their luck, a young clergyman's widow or a shopkeeper might screw on skates and stagger off on their own account. The ice was full of little cries and screams, bumps and crashes.

At dusk, when the Suicide and Anton Moss were going home, they met Fröken d'Espard. She had wrapped herself in perhaps all the clothes she possessed, one thing over another, but her calves were badly off for protection.

The two friends bowed. They had taken a fancy to this lady from the day, a few weeks ago, when she had invited them in to wine and cakes in good company.

"It's cold on the ice," remarked the Suicide with a glance at her get-up.

"Yes," she replied, "and I've got no clothes at all, but—"

Moss unbuttoned the ulster and began to pull it off.

"What are you doing?" she cried.
"Won't you have it?"
"No. What in the world—! No, thanks."
"But I'm going home," he protested.
"Well, it doesn't matter. Besides, I'm going back again myself. I am really. No, it was stupid of me, I might have brought winter things with me when I came back from Christiania, but I didn't think of it. Now I've written for a coat and long snow-stockings."

They walked home together. The lady acknowledged right out that she was down on her luck and bored, it was getting lonely and melancholy in the mountains. Would not the gentlemen be leaving soon?

Oh, yes, they thought of leaving. But it wasn't certain that it would be better anywhere else.

No, she agreed. And she added as her own experience that it wasn't any good moping either, it didn't make things any brighter. Did it?

The two friends took it for granted that she missed Herr Fleming, the Count, and guessed that she must be feeling it. Moss dropped his eyes and said to cheer her: "Deuce take moping!"

He looked as if he had least reason to be satisfied; Fröken d'Espard was sorry for him and backed him up in spite of the voice of her own heart: "I'm sure you're right there. It's no use brooding, no use sitting in one's room and groping for one's own eyes. What's the sense of that?"

The Suicide was more critical: "It all depends," he retorted. "One might find a happy issue through long and serious meditation, perhaps. I don't know."

They reached home. These two were not to be despised, their talk was not café-chatter and flirting and there was something in them. In the days that followed, Fröken d'Espard was to be seen more often in their company. Birds of a feather flock together. Since misfortune had come upon her the two cronies were not beneath her notice, they braced her up with a certain pride in their mental attitude and a liveliness in their language, at times they even made her laugh. How stiff-necked they were, though they too had been stricken by fate, each in his own way. Though, as far as that went, the Suicide was anything but mad now. He mad? Not a bit. He could see right through a question and answer it with all reason and logic. Anton Moss was quieter and ill at ease, a sympathetic figure, he would have been good-looking but for the sores on his face and his increasing blindness. There was nothing else wrong with him. Queer lads, the devil was in them; they laid it on rather thick with their witticisms, their gallows humour, but it kept them up. They were not so lucky as to be able to snap their fingers at trouble—oh, God preserve us from musketeers! Were they equal to a bold stroke, could they cut down their sorrows with a sword? If they wanted anything, could they go ahead and buy it, hire it, or steal it? No. Could they hold their own, were they masters of their fate? Did they rejoice in a dangerous situation, did they plunge in and hit about them? No.

No, lost lads they were, each in his own way; even in such things as sleep and appetite they were reduced to shamming. But they were a famous pair of die-hards in keeping their troubles to themselves.

A chance was to throw Fröken d'Espard even more closely into their society.

The Sheriff came; Sheriff's officer he was really, but everybody called him the Sheriff. It was the same young man who had married Daniel's sweetheart, and he came to Torahus Sanatorium once more. He carried a portfolio under his arm to write his report in, he talked to the matron and the manager and wanted to hear more about Herr Fleming.

The matron knew nothing, the manager knew nothing, and what was it anyhow about Herr Fleming?

CHAPTER THE LAST

There seemed to be something wrong with him, he was arrested. God save us!

And now the Sheriff had received orders to look into one or two things connected with his last place of residence, which was Torahus Sanatorium. Lawyer Robertsen had reported on a former occasion that two trunks had been left behind belonging to Herr Fleming; where were they?

The manager went with him up to the attic and they rummaged the trunks; they contained clothes, expensive clothes some of them, silk, but nothing else. The Sheriff locked them again, even putting his seal on the keys, but letting them hang in the trunks. Then he wrote in his report.

However, the two trunks of clothes were nothing compared with a certain considerable sum of money which Herr Fleming was stated to have borrowed or taken from a bank in Finland. Where was the money?

The matron and the manager didn't know. The doctor was sent for and he didn't know either.

Hadn't Herr Fleming deposited anything, put away a few fat thousands in the sanatorium's safe?

No.

The Sheriff wrote.

The doctor was further cross-examined as the distinguished patient's medical man. Not a thing could the doctor disclose beyond what everyone knew, that Herr Fleming was consumptive, was now and then on the way to recovery, but was incautious, caught cold, had relapses, and was obliged to build up fresh improvement with patience and care. At times he was hypochondriacal, at other times excessively hopeful, one thing or the other; he drank a little wine, but this extravagance didn't come to much in money, as the sanatorium's books would show. For that matter, the doctor hadn't even seen the patient during his last cold; it was Fröken d'Espard who usually sat with him and who was the last to see him.

The Sheriff wrote. When he had finished, his next question referred to Fröken d'Espard.

"Shall I fetch her?" asked the matron.

"Is she staying here? Wait a moment. Then I should prefer to be shown straight to her room."

Fröken d'Espard was visibly surprised at a man's knocking and coming in with a portfolio under his arm and a gold band on his cap; nor did he take off his cap until it had produced its effect. It was a moment before she recognized him.

"Excuse me, Fröken, I've come to hear what you know about Herr Fleming, who was staying here recently. I am here officially."

"Herr Fleming—oh—is he dead?"

"No, no. What if he were though? No, it's something else."

Fröken d'Espard had not always stood on safe ground, time had made her very resourceful and smart, oh, she was a heroine for presence of mind. She replied: "It's always unpleasant to hear of a death, that's what I meant."

"You knew the man, I understand; you were the last to see him before he absconded?"

"Absconded?"

"Before he left here, then. Will you answer my question?"

"It depends what you mean by knowing," she said. "Herr Fleming was often ill and I sat with him; to that extent I knew him."

"Not more, not in any other way?" The Sheriff turned over his papers and pretended he had found something: "I have been given the impression that you were with him, so to speak, constantly; is that so? That is what I am told."

Now the lady smiled, rather a pale smile, but she smiled and said: "How often and how much I was with him? I believe I may say daily, but not all day long; we were visitors here at the sanatorium both of us, we talked together."

"You were in his confidence?"

"We talked together. You see, I'm more French than Norwegian, and, Herr Fleming being a man of culture, we talked French," she explained.

"Oh?" said the Sheriff; that checked him a little, impressed him a little. "The French language?"

The lady pointed round at her books: "I read practically nothing but French. Herr Fleming and I talked about the books we read; is that the kind of thing you mean by confidence?"

The Sheriff, huffed: "It is my business to put questions, Fröken. I am here to draw up a report."

The lady: "I shall answer."

"Thank you. The fact is, then, that Herr Fleming has been arrested—"

"What has he done?"

"Well—forgery, embezzlement from a bank, or whatever it turns out to be; a considerable sum is involved. That is how it is. And now 1 should like to ask—you don't happen to know where he's buried this money?"

"I?" The lady laughed loud and shrilly. "Have you felt in his pockets?"

The Sheriff, flushing with offence: "You will do best to answer my question!"

The lady continued to laugh without exactly showing signs of terror; in fact she said: "Excuse me, I can't help laughing. It's so comic."

But now her merriment must have sounded false in his ears, he gathered himself for an onslaught, a coup, and asked curtly: "Now, then, where's the money?"

Oh, there she sat with it on her bare bosom and the door shut! Yes indeed, the wad of money was on her, had almost become one with her, had moulded itself to the shape of her body, had rested for many weeks in that warm spot. Fröken d'Espard was so courageous a heroine, she saw well enough that she was in a tight place, but she did not evacuate the position, no, she took offence at the rudeness of the Sheriff's question, nay, she was very deeply wounded by it, and that ought not to have surprised him. Then with a sudden gesture she flung the key of her trunk before him on the table and sprang up, exclaiming: "There you are, please search my room and my trunk, I shan't interfere!"

And with that she tore open the door and stormed out!

She stormed on through the passage and escaped down the stairs, stormed out into the veranda. There sat the Suicide and Anton Moss. On the way she had dragged open the back of her blouse and got hold of the big envelope; she held it out in the wildest excitement, saying: "The Sheriff's officer's here, he wants to take this! Hide it; it's letters from the Count, from Herr Fleming, only letters—"

Moss was nearest and seized the packet; he could not see much, but he saw that she was being hunted, that her blouse was torn open, her voice sounded full of alarm; he didn't stop to consider, but unbuttoned his ulster and jacket, hid the packet, and buttoned them up again.

"Oh!" she panted, throwing herself into a basket-chair.

"What's up?" asked the Suicide.

"How should I know? Well, it's Herr Fleming, he's supposed to owe some money, he's got hold of some money that doesn't belong to him, what do I know about it? And now he insists, this Sheriff's officer, that I know where he's hidden this money."

"Has he searched you?" asked the Suicide incredulously.

"Yes. That is to say, he wanted to. But he won't get the packet, the letters. Will he, now?"

"No!" said Moss with immense calmness.

The Suicide warmed up in his turn; he put on an invincible air and addressed himself to his friend: "Lend me your stick, Moss. I want to have it by me in case of emergency!"

"Can't spare it," replied Moss. "I'm first!"

"Oh, thanks, thanks!" said the lady, laughing and crying. "I'll do anything you ask in return." In the end she must have been afraid of her own courage; one might be smart, but one couldn't keep it up so long, especially if one were enervated already with sorrow and adversity; no, then one is nothing but a little bird which has to hide in a bush.

And now she had found refuge with two patients, two poor fellows who were in a pretty bad way themselves. They were sitting there because it didn't matter what they did or where they went, nobody troubled about them day or night.

For the moment the Suicide was bellicose: "Where is the fellow?" he asked.

The lady laughed and cried again in gratitude for this indomitable force which could call the police a fellow, and she explained: "He's up in my room. I told him he was at liberty to search the room and my trunk, I gave him the key."

The two friends thought that was capital, brilliant, that was the way to treat the fellow! They didn't put it into words, but they nodded. When the Suicide spoke, it was to express his misgivings at leaving a perfect stranger alone in her room with an unlocked trunk before him. "I think I'll just run up," he said, rising from his chair.

The lady seized him by the arm and begged him not to: "He won't find anything, there's nothing there. No, for heaven's sake, don't!" But she could not deny herself another laugh, a little howl of delight at the Suicide's gorgeous idea of suspecting the police, the very police. Little by little her excitement subsided and her nerves calmed down. She leaned back against the chair cushion to cover the open back of her blouse; the friends thought she would catch her death of cold, she ought to go in; but no, no, she said, she would sit there now till the man came, she wanted to see him off the premises, she wasn't cold! Brilliant again, she had a clear conscience, she didn't run away.

The Sheriff came. He was subdued and peaceable, his coup had not come off. "You misunderstood me, Fröken, you should not have gone away," he said.

Fröken d'Espard looked at him and said nothing.

"Of course I have made no search in your room; you will find the key of your trunk where you put it. I have just been writing down your statement."

Fröken d'Espard said nothing. But she was in a great fright that her friends might speak, that Anton Moss might slap his breast pocket and say: "Here are the Count's letters to the lady, try and take them from me!"

The Suicide could keep silent no longer: "It seems to be a dangerous matter to have lived under the same roof as Count Fleming and talked to him."

The Sheriff, off his guard: "Oh? What?"

"I am one of those who talked to him."

"So am I," said Moss without looking up.

The lady in alarm: "No, stop! Not that!"

The Sheriff asked: "You said Count, was he a Count?"

"Don't you even know that!" returned the Suicide, as though he had never come across such ignorance.

Now, whether the Sheriff believed in the Count or not, he guessed anyhow that he was in hostile company and broke off the interview, saying: "Well, I have finished my business here!" Whereupon he bowed and raised his hand to his cap with the gold band. Then he left.

His exit was so correct that it did much to make his peace with the company. Besides which the man had to win his spurs—Fröken d'Espard had heard this from Daniel—he was trying to get a deputy and be made Sheriff himself, so that his wife Helena might be a fine lady. It all hung together.

As Moss handed back the thick packet he said jokingly, with his eyes on the floor: "Bring it back whenever you like! I've no objection to carrying it, it gives me a feeling of having something in my pocket, of being worth something!" And he smiled at this with his lamentable mouth.

That smile—it affected Fröken d'Espard by its utter hopelessness; she was unstrung by the many emotions she had gone through and at that moment she could have thrown herself upon the tainted man's bosom and caressed him. "Now what can I do for you gentlemen in return?" she asked. But as they were not exactly ladies' men they could find no enormously delicate answer to this, but simply waved it aside as nothing; in fact Moss even murmured in his clumsy way: "It is we who have to thank you!"

After this Fröken d'Espard had many a good chat with the cronies, for, as we know, she was a man's sort, and the men on their part livened her up without knowing it. She wanted to find out about the sores on Anton Moss's face, but he was shy and refused to talk about them; she was prepared to pay for all sorts of cures, but he wouldn't hear of it.

Day after day went by, the two cronies cheered her, that was so, but the days went by all the same, they flew, and for the time being she hadn't any days to spare. In her restless perplexity she sought the society of the two patients in the smoking-room and listened to them wrangling and accusing one another of everything that was bad. They had had some practice, they were incredibly offensive to one another, and never had Fröken d'Espard heard such virulence in the way of chaff. Was it chaff?

There was Moss coolly jeering at the Suicide for still going about and being alive. "Of course you daren't bring it off," he said.

"Give me time to consider it intelligently," replied the Suicide. "I'll try to explain the whole thing to you."

Fröken d'Espard turned red with embarrassment. What was coming next?

Moss went on unabashed: "The fact is, you haven't yet discovered how unnecessary you are, how superfluous you are here on earth."

That must have stung; the Suicide said: "Don't you believe him, Fröken, that's not what I haven't discovered. It's something else. All at once I can't see why I should fly in my own face by quitting life."

"No," she agreed. And she could not understand how Moss could sit there and say such brutal things.

"Oh, is that all, you don't want to fly in your own face? No, you haven't the pluck!"

Silence.

Moss went on roasting him and presented it in a charming and attractive light: supposing he brought it off tonight, he'd wake up tomorrow in heaven with a harp between his knees.

That such things could be said was a riddle to Fröken d'Espard. What was this Suicide made of that he didn't hit back? There he sat laughing quietly, she thought he was far too patient.

But that was only the first round; the next was the Suicide's. Oh, that wretched Anton Moss, he invited spitefulness only too readily.

"Would anyone have thought a blind man had so much gall in him!" said the Suicide.

"I'm not blind," protested Moss.

"You can't see to read."

"Can't I?" Moss got up, intending to fetch a paper from the table to prove how well he could see; he ran against a chair and knocked it down.

The Suicide picked up the chair, saying: "For the sake of the furniture in here I propose that you go out into the yard."

Fröken d'Espard interposed again: "Poor fellow, he can't have seen the chair!"

"No, but I can see to read," declared Moss. "What rot!"

"Look there!" exclaimed the Suicide; "you've torn that beastly rag off your finger. There it is on the floor. No, sit down, man, I'll pick it up, you can't see. There, now stick it on again! You have to be told everything, you're like a baby, you make me sick. And then you go about with that finger hanging on to your hand just as if it was your sweetheart. Cut it off with a pair of scissors!"

"Ha ha ha!" said Moss.

All things considered, the relations between these two men were somewhat complicated. They appeared to fight in order to save themselves from collapsing, and this state of things had developed as though by agreement; one of them had mental trouble, the other a bodily ailment, a skin disease; the youth of both was wrecked.

And what blows they could exchange! The Suicide cried shame upon the other for his appearance, beginning with his clothes: "The back of your jacket's turning rusty in patches, nobody would think it was meant to be all one colour. With your keen eyesight you must have discovered it."

"You do nothing but growl and grumble," retorted Moss; "you're so disgusted with life that nothing seems right to you. It takes a lot of self-forgiveness before you can start abusing everybody else."

The Suicide, cutting him to the quick: "Well, but, my dear man, you're perfectly awful to look at! Don't you think so too, Fröken?"

The lady, terrified: "No, but look here—both of you—"

The. Suicide, direct to Moss: "What if you tried powdering yourself? But perhaps you're too religious for that?"

"Ha ha ha!" said Moss.

Even Fröken d'Espard could not help a slight smile, but at the same time she clapped her hands together and exclaimed: "No, it's too bad; are you both crazy—!"

They wrangled on and on, stopped for a while, and started again. Of course they were unhappy, they were victims of a ferocious fate, their lips were incapable of a kindly jest, of an honest smile. The truth was, no doubt, that they nursed their bitterness so as not to whimper, they gnashed their teeth so as not to burst into tears.

It was characteristic of the two that while the Suicide often tried to drag Fröken d'Espard into the conversation by directly addressing her, Moss never permitted himself this liberty. He sat looking down, stooping low with his terrible face.

But now and then it would happen that the three would talk together as though there were nothing wrong with any of them, they forgot their ills for a while and exchanged question and answer without malice. These occasions were not without significance to Fröken d'Espard, she too had undergone a change, events had made her more taciturn, she had begun to think more seriously. How rapidly everything had evolved: there was Herr Fleming, living here but lately with the respect of all, diamond ring, silk under-clothing, a Count, a free man—and now in prison! Herself, Julie d'Espard, raised out of her poverty at one moment to be plunged at the next into a far deeper abyss! What was she to do, walk here on hot coals with her deed of gift and her riches, tormented at the same time by a secret anguish which she scarcely dared confide to herself? Her personal distress being so serious, she only remembered Herr Fleming now and then, he was slipping farther and farther away from her; she pitied him, wished him luck to escape his punishment or strength to survive it, but she no longer had fidelity and affection to offer him. No one could be surprised at that; she was far from being heartless, but in these days she was just as far from being disposed to love. The Suicide and his friend were fit company for her.

They might be talking of schools and education, and Fröken d'Espard mentioned Rector Oliver. The Suicide made a grimace.

Anton Moss said: "He had two rattling little boys."

"Yes, but the Rector himself?" she asked.

"A man devised by his fellow-creatures," said the Suicide, putting his oar in.

And from now on he was almost the only one who spoke. Bertelsen, the timber merchant, ought to have been present now, as he had been so set on witnessing the outbreaks of a deranged man; yes, he ought to have been here, he would have heard about one or two things between heaven and earth, some of them perhaps quite plain and obvious things, others doubtful and unfamiliar, a little of everything, madness and sound sense: Rector Oliver, a man whose head was crammed with a conglomeration of dictionaries, piping from out of this chaos a helpless cry for his nurse and his milk-bottle! A misguided creature who thought he could develop into a man by means of books—where would the character come in, the personality? What cannot one teach a parrot to repeat, what cannot a man cram from books? But it only makes him a man by virtue of his caste, as Rector Oliver is a philologist by caste, he knows "languages" and nothing else.

Now, Fröken d'Espard found this rather personal and objected from an ordinary high-school point of view: "But you can't call languages a bad thing; I only wish I knew a few more of them."

"Why? What for?" he asked.

"Why? Well, what does one learn languages for? To enlarge one's mind, I suppose, to keep abreast of foreign literature, to make oneself a cultured person."

"I don't even manage to keep abreast of our own literature," he said.

"Oh, our own!" she replied as usual.

He was fired with a sudden zeal, was disagreeable, combative, as though his cause was too good a one to be frittered away: "Languages, foreign people's books—why in the world! We have in the Scandinavian languages a million volumes which we jump over to come to the foreign ones. What if ours are just as good? What if they may be a trifle better, in the first place because they are easier to assimilate? And then this intellectual development which is supposed to result from the study of languages—look at the philologist, the Rector man: ordinary type, fairly indistinguishable from the majority; that is, not exactly worse, which of course was not the assumption either; but in what way is he better? Higher flights, a more refined spirituality; is he profounder in wisdom, more resigned in adversity, happier, more starry-eyed? Alas, what can one expect of him, seeing that he is stuffed inside with rubbish, with words, words, and again words."

"That's pretty severe!"

"No, it's past comprehension, when you think of the esteem he's held in by the multitude. He attracts people's attention, this incredible figure, he's packed his head with dictionaries, he's consolidated his idiocy, so people applaud him and shout: 'Try to manage a couple more dictionaries, only a couple; there, bravo, we'll pay you for it!' And all this is done in order that he may set up a shop, a school, where he can supply the children of men with his rubbish."

"What's the idea then, are there to be no teachers of languages? Are there to be no languages in the schools?"

"Perhaps not, perhaps none at all, what do you think? What if we lose more than we gain by 'languages'? Life is so short, we haven't time for parrotry. This learning languages is not for the rank and file of humanity, it's only for the specially fitted, for those who can't aspire any higher than training themselves as specialists, as translators, interpreters, dragomans. Of course we must except the great linguistic geniuses, the discoverers; we're talking about ourselves, the nodding automatons. We've already begun to doubt the advantage of making each and all learn to play on a piano, but we don't for that reason underrate the musician by the special grace of God. Do we?"

"But what will be left of the school if you take away languages?"

"No, there you're right: what will be left of the drudgery? A few dates that don't matter, of kings and wars; a few gymnastic notions to take the place of useful labour; some mathematical tomfoolery for twelve-year-old brains—there'll be plenty left. What is schooling? Schooling is a mother's daily instruction and a father's daily teaching; book-schooling, on the other hand, is a thing invented, an institution purposely designed to complicate life and make it more irksome from our sixth year until death. For the book, the printed word for all and sundry, fills the world with discontent and disaster, with quantitative culture, civilization."

"Isn't it rather queer that people in general—I mean to say that everybody looks up to the one who has learnt something and most of all to the one who has learnt most, the learned man—?"

"You mean, oughtn't that to make me hesitate? Oh no. Aren't we ready to look up to any mortal thing, to the horse that wins a race, to the day's skiing champion?—in both cases my admiration is mingled with pity for the animal. We get up and give our chair to a lame man, we listen patiently while a stammerer hacks out his fatuities, we open the door for a lady as though she had no hands of her own—"

He checked himself.

"Well, what then?" asked Fröken d'Espard.

"I only mention it," he replied. "There was once a flautist, a virtuoso, who ended by flinging his music on the floor in disgust and blowing soap-bubbles with his flute. Again, I only mention it."

Then he came to a stop. Neither said anything.

Moss broke the silence: "You're in a state of exaltation!" he said.

The Suicide looked at him and blinked his eyes thoughtfully.

"It was thrilling to listen to you, at times it was quite like poetry," said Moss.

The lady replied by a slight smile, but as the Suicide didn't seem to hear even now, Moss made no further attempt to get him to talk, but stood looking out of the window for a while and then went out.

The two were left sitting. Dusk was coming on.

It was as though a change came over them on finding themselves *tête-à-tête*. Fröken d'Espard, the man-magnet, put her head on one side and set herself to think over what he had said; at any rate she gave herself an air of doing so. Now, this man was not exactly mad, and that in itself was something. And from various signs she had drawn the conclusion that he did not deny himself necessary things, but bought what he required—so what could be the matter with him? Had he a business in town or did he live on his means? But, above all, what was it that had gone to smash with him? She herself was one who was interested to find out how an unfortunate could abandon suicide.

She deigned to ask his pardon if she had worried him with her silly objections, she didn't understand these questions, she really hadn't meant—

No, no, no, it was he who ought to apologize! Great heaven, was she trying to make a fool of him?

"I've so often wondered just why you're here," she said boldly and in her casual tone.

"Why I am here—what?"

"Why you are staying so long anyhow. You're not ill, there's nothing the matter with you, the holiday season is over long ago. Excuse me, it's not for the sake of curiosity."

"I suppose I may have my reasons."

"Yes, of course."

"Why are you here yourself?"

She suddenly flung herself forward in her chair, bending her head and shoulders: "O God, O God—yes, you're right, I ought not to have asked!"

"Come, come, it was all right," he said in alarm. "That's to say, it was I who ought not to have asked. Don't let that trouble you."

"You see, I thought—I hoped as you're so clever and on top of things, that you could give me some advice. Yes; that you could show me what to do. I can't tell you what it is. You've helped me once already."

He guessed that she referred to a visit from the Sheriff's officer and a certain packet of letters; he concluded further that she had love troubles on her mind, nothing else.

"We really mustn't lose heart, Fröken!" he said to console her. "We mustn't do that. If we come up against fate there's nothing for us to do but to step aside."

"No. But it's so hard."

"Well, we step aside with more or less politeness, but aside we must go. After all, it's a question whether it's worth taking the whole thing so tragically. With some people it soon rights itself."

"It won't right itself with me, it only gets worse and worse."

"Don't say that!" And to cheer her up he felt constrained to divulge something of his own secret; that would give her something else to think about, a tragedy with a vengeance! Of what consequence was it that a Count took himself off, perhaps only for a short time at that; or even that he had got into a mess over money matters and hadn't paid a lot of little bills as punctually as might be? Wasn't his very name more than good enough, hadn't be a family rolling in money to step in and make the creditors feel ashamed of themselves? Oh, other people had worse troubles!

"Are you in a bad way too?"

"Oh well—not too good exactly, but—"

And this unhappy little lady made the Suicide so affected with his own misery that his lips were a-quiver. He dropped hints that in other circumstances would never have escaped him, her sympathy played him the trick of being sweet to him, he had difficulty in keeping back his tears. Deuce take the girl, she was upsetting the steadfastness he had so laboriously built up in his association with Moss.

Had Fröken d'Espard for her part any hidden intention in sitting here and listening to him? God knows; but she was very depressed, in great perplexity, so that much might be excused her.

When she asked him if he hadn't a home, a wife and children who were waiting for him and writing for him constantly, he brusquely denied it, retorting that it was an extraordinary idea of hers; what did she mean, what could have suggested it to her?

No, she only asked; it was silly of her.

He reacted: Well, he wouldn't exactly call it silly, not at all—

Yes, but she ought to have understood that a man who stayed here so long in the mountains couldn't have left behind any dear ones where he came from.

But listen—what was there to stop him? he protested, firing up. What did we human beings know of one another, couldn't a man abandon both wife and child? He would go so far as to say that perhaps it was precisely for that reason a poor devil might take to the mountains. "I'm not talking of myself," he hastened to add; "but of anyone else you like. I'm only supposing the case."

There was no mistake about it, she got him to open his heart more and more. Taking good care all the time to be talking of anybody hut himself and probably thinking he was well screened, he explained to her why a man might take to the mountains: It might happen to him—happen to anybody you please, that is—that the Devil entered a house and possessed, let us say, a married woman, and then what was the result? The child lies there and is forgotten, the whole house is forgotten by God, the wife doesn't come home for ever so long. Not that he meant to blame her, she might have her reasons for it, an ungovernable temperament for instance, an irrepressible passion, such things have been known; but the child lies there, and it may be as pretty and charming as was ever seen, if it's a little girl then perhaps she has hair and all, that's nothing out of the common. Well, this sort of thing happens not only once, but many times; a winter passes, let us say, then the man can stand it no longer; he clears out. You see! Takes ship for Australia—nobody takes to the mountains for a thing like that. Well, now, if the man is one of the poor, limited sort and not particularly intelligent, he may lose his head, he may have thoughts of taking the matter into his own hands and putting an end to his troubles. That is what may occupy his mind while he's out there in Australia. Well, then let him buy the pistol. Pistol? It may have been bought long ago, may be lying in his possession, cleaned and oiled and loaded. Why doesn't he use it? You see, Fröken, the man may be human, we are all human; the man may even have some roots in life, he may be in love too, in spite of all, and he may be racked with terror lest the child come to grief; should he not live, then, and save it? And so he wavers to and fro. . . .

The Suicide covered himself, saying: "All this I've been told, I can scarcely realize it myself. The child in any case—what in the world can it matter? I've never heard of a man who cared about newborn baby girls. And if I had a creature like that, what should I call her to begin with, what name should I give her? No, many thanks!" he said with gratuitous hardness—

Moss was standing in the doorway.

Moss had no sight, but he had hearing and perception. That miserable Suicide, he must have been dying for sympathy all this time and when he found it he broke down. Moss made no allowance for this; he said: "Excuse me if I'm intruding on a good cry!"

"Cry?" replied the Suicide, beginning to laugh; "your keen sight always spots a thing at once!" Oh, but the Suicide can't have felt too safe, he knew he could expect an extra dose of scorn as soon as he was alone with his crony, so he said: "If I ring and have a full glass put in front of you, I wonder what will happen! Fröken, I suppose I can't offer you anything?"

"No, ever so many thanks!"

No, Fröken d'Espard really had no mind to gossip anymore about other people's sorrows, she had her own. She retired to her room again, lay down on her bed for a while, dipped into a book, couldn't settle down to anything, brooded, sighed, and felt ill. The Suicide was no use to her either, he was hooked already, married, in love even, lucky man! She had thoughts of making another hopeless trip to Christiania; why, she didn't know, but what was there to stay here for? One consolation was left to her in her abandonment: the wad of notes she carried in her bosom. That braced her, that gave her strength to get up when the dinner-bell rang and go down and eat, that put her through the evening—and then came the night.

There was one of the maids whom she got to hook up her back; she came every morning and hurriedly did the job. Her fingers were cold, she pulled and struggled at the blouse as though she could have told something about the lady: that she must be eating too much, that she was putting on flesh. Now, this was by no means true, but the maid had insinuated as much more than once, with a giggle: Was it really possible to get fat on raw peas and pickled herring with biscuits?

Impudent hussy! The lady knew there might be more to come and said to forestall it: "Ugh, I have such bad dreams these nights!"

"I guessed that," replied the maid; "you moan and talk aloud, like."

"It doesn't mean anything."

The maid held her tongue.

"One talks such a lot of rubbish when one has bad dreams; names and figures and sums of money and all sorts of things. But it doesn't mean anything, you know."

The maid held her tongue. What was her idea, did she expect to be paid for agreeing?

CHAPTER THE LAST

When the maid was gone Fröken d'Espard threw open the window and looked out; the air was full of snow, the ground was heaped, the forest powdered over, a rocky knoll close to the sanatorium grounds—"the Peak"—seemed sinking more and more into itself. But it was a still, lost world of snow; in the hushed air came the sound of a report, someone was shooting on the hill, first one shot, then another; it must be Daniel out shooting ptarmigan for the sanatorium. Daniel was a sportsman, Daniel was sound and healthy and had got over his love trouble. She remembered two guns on his wall.

She went down—down to the other visitors and another day. It was a bad thing to be in her shoes.

Oh, but today at last she was to have the plain and simple idea, and it was a mystery it hadn't occurred to her before: she would reply to an advertisement in a paper right before her eyes, would go and stay at a secluded spot, with a kind lady, a lady proficient at the business, three hours from the capital. Then what was there to make a fuss about? She was helped out of her difficulties, absolutely saved! She could afford this little excursion, she had time enough and to spare, there was no longer any hurry, she could go on this side of Christmas or wait till after. Absolutely saved!

After these long, dark days of despair she was now thrilled with joy, she was young and gay once more. Step aside for fate? What a stupid, forlorn maxim that was! She would take fate by the neck and bend it!

"Let me have a tube of vaseline," she said to the doctor.

"What do you want it for?" he asked, liking to have his little joke. "It's dangerous stuff," he said.

And she replied, not to be beaten: "I'm going to make a sandwich of it."

"I can well believe it," he said; "since you take pickled herrings on biscuits."

"And tomorrow I shall want tomatoes on birch-bark."

They both laughed hugely at this crazy idea. The doctor had little to do nowadays, there were so few patients; he was grateful for a chance to gossip and said: "Take a seat, Fröken."

"Haven't time. By the way—what's the matter with Moss's face?"

"Moss? Why, he's leaving soon."

"But what's the matter with him, I ask."

The doctor busied himself with some papers on the table and replied: "Atrophy of the skin. No, you're not going already?"

"Can't you cure him?"

"Why do you ask? Moss is leaving soon."

Fröken d'Espard went up to her room and used her vaseline, she smeared her face with it and began to massage. It was a shame how she had neglected her face the last few weeks, it was limp from the sufferings she had gone through and full of unfamiliar little wrinkles. What a falling off! This must now be put right, after her visit to the kind lady of the advertisement she would need to be good-looking and eligible again. From now on she intended to devote attention to her face daily. "Come in!"

It was the maid again.

The lady looked at her in surprise and said: "But you *have* hooked me up?"

The maid: "Yes, but it's only that I'm leaving. I didn't want to say so this morning, but I'm not going to be here any longer."

"No?"

"I thought that if you were satisfied with what I've done for you, then you'd know how I was and that I haven't said anything about you or anything else."

Was the girl mad? Fröken d'Espard was no longer dejected, she dismissed the maid, shaking with anger, and returned to her massage. So that was what the hussy had meant by her impudence this morning, she wanted to reduce the lady to submission and get an extra tip out of her; what for? Hadn't Fröken d'Espard contributed month by month to the servants' fund? What were things coming to? Oh, the only way was not to let oneself be put down, bluff was what paid! In future she intended to be a trifle exacting, it might be that she would have to speak about one or two things, such as the food and the waiting here at the sanatorium, the scandalous prices charged for washing, the stuffiness of the drawing-room, where the elderly widows of officials exhaled an odour of poverty. She was not going to put up with everything in future, and she had no need to, since a happy means of escape had revealed itself to her; now that she had taken fate by the neck and bent it, she intended to have a good time. Coffee in bed? More than that: Coffee and breakfast in bed. As in her French novels. She was going to treat herself to a little luxury, she was indeed; she owed that to herself after all she had gone through.

And meanwhile she would make herself smart and pretty again. There was no doubt massage was a help.

"Look here, my friends," she said to Moss and the Suicide; "I've been having such pleasant dreams lately that I'm not going to mope anymore. There's always a way out of the difficulty, isn't there?"

"Yes?" replied the friends in surprise.

"Always a way out. Now we'll go bob-sleighing in the snow!" Moss was ready, Moss with his ravaged face was ready; the Suicide, on the other hand, got up rather reluctantly, saying: "We shall get our boots so wet."

"What of it? We'll dry them again."

"And we haven't a proper bob-sleigh."

Moss retorted that, oh yes, they had rigged up a neat little sledge, just big enough, there was no trouble about the bob-sleigh.

"Yes, you're a blooming open-air sportsman!" muttered the Suicide, looking him up and down with disfavour.

They changed their clothes and went out. The air was thick with snow, even the Peak was hardly visible.

All three of them hauled the little sledge uphill, higher up, right to the top, and then coasted down. They dashed on at a terrific pace, the Suicide was steering, the lady sat in the middle, the snow wrapped them in a whirling white darkness, they could only see through a slit of their eyelids—heavens, how good and desperate!

Up again, the sleigh was heavy, but there were three of them to pull. "Devil take moping!" said the lady, swearing with delight. Down again, another flight through the air, the lady had her arms round Moss and sat cosily behind him; it was madness to sail like this, to fly like this, but it was so good.

After a few turns up and down, the Suicide wanted to stop.

"No, why?" she asked.

"I can't do any more. You two can go on!" Was the Suicide tired or was he envious of Moss, sitting in front and being embraced? "We're all human. I can't do any more," he repeated.

"Well, that's a nice, modest thing to say," Moss admitted. "There's no bluster about it. So you're all out?"

The Suicide, with unwonted heat: "I've nothing more to say to you, Moss. When I want to go in, I go in. I can't see any pampering in that. Good-bye!"

It was no use saying any more, the Suicide left them, and the lady and Moss had the sleigh to themselves. They tugged and toiled at it.

When they reached the top he asked doubtfully: "Will you steer?"

No, she couldn't steer, wouldn't steer.

And he was in an utter fix.

"Can't you see? Are you too blind?" she asked anxiously.

He braced himself up: "Blind? Not a bit. It's only that I'm snow-blind."

"I'll keep a look-out and warn you," she reassured him.

CHAPTER THE LAST

So they set off.

But now, as the lady's in front, she can't open her eyes for the driving snow, and Moss is too blind to see the dangers in time; they shoot along as best they can, taking the rough with the smooth; half-way down they fly into the air, the lady screams, they dash into something at a terrific pace, the sleigh cracks up, and they are flung out.

Moss picks himself up, rubs the snow out of his eyes, and looks about him, rocking like a ship in a storm. The sleigh is done for, sure enough, and there's the lady; she doesn't get up, doesn't move, what can be the matter? He takes a look at her and lifts her up, she falls back again. There is blood on her face, her chin's bleeding. He calls to her. No.

He carries her home, and before they get there she comes to her senses again. She is able to walk up the steps, but has to be supported; she has a wound, an ugly wound, her chin is split across.

The doctor is sent for.

IX

So the doctor found a little more to do and sewed the lady up.

He had also had a reply from the hospital saying that Moss could be received; the doctor therefore felt indispensable to himself and others and had important business on his hands.

And it must be said that he was not a hard man, he was sorry for Moss and had kept him longer than he should have done. Whether it was right or wrong of him, Doctor Oyen turned nobody away; he was a kindly man who hated acting harshly and making people unhappy. Besides, the sanatorium wanted all the patients it could get.

He found Moss and prepared him: "Now, my dear Moss, at last I have good news for you."

Moss's scarred face turned pale and dropped: "Ah. Well, well."

"Yes, it's all arranged. And indeed my last application was a very urgent one."

Moss seemed to feel the news as a blow; he said: "Well, well, thank you!" But he was very down about it.

The doctor, to cheer him: "It's far the best thing for you. You'll get good food and drink, the most skillful attention, plenty of companionship, just the same as here. And after a certain time you'll be well again, they'll find a remedy, a serum, science is advancing by leaps and bounds in these days."

"When shall I have to go?" asked the unhappy man.

"When you're ready. Bless me, it's not a question of hours, take your time about packing. And, as I say, science performs miracles in these days, it will discover a serum and you'll be restored to life!"

CHAPTER THE LAST

Moss found his friend the Suicide and sat down by him as though nothing had happened. They had wrangled and fought every day and hour since the unfortunate accident on the bob-sleigh run; they began again now, and strangely enough it was Moss who started the squabble, as though he couldn't do without it.

"Did you get your boots wet?" he asked.

"How do you mean?"

"That day on the bob-sleigh run."

"Be quiet!" replied the Suicide.

"You must admit it was cowardly of you to leave us alone at it."

The Suicide took the bait: "I took myself off because you two wanted to cuddle. It was a disgusting sight!"

"Ha ha ha," said Moss. "And yesterday you wanted to make out that I tried to kill the lady."

"Well, will you tell me what are the rights of it? She came home half dead, and you carried her. She's still in bed."

"No, she's up again and will soon be as well as ever," Moss consoled him.

"At any rate you've disfigured her for life; she'll always have that red line on her face. It isn't everybody who cares as little what their face is like as certain people I could mention."

Moss said nothing.

"It isn't even a straight line, it's an ugly crooked line, because you hadn't eyes to aim with. It's a pitiful business altogether."

Childish drivel, the cronies were in bad form, Moss couldn't pull himself together for the slightest passage of arms today; all he could say was: "Go ahead, I'm coming!"

Then they went across to dinner, and in these short days it was dusk by about four. The Suicide made Moss come for their usual walk up the mountain; by constant use they had trodden a path in the snow and now it was frozen and good going.

They went in single file, the Suicide first, Moss with his stick; he seemed to see nothing. It was a clear afternoon, the full moon shone like a big gold coin lying on blue silk, but there were a few clouds down in the west. "Unsettled" was the weather forecast, a triangle over a square.

Climbing the Peak was nothing to the Suicide, he had trained himself daily by moderate exercise and his muscles were hard, he was getting absurdly healthy. He girded at Moss who was fumbling behind with his stick. "And so you're wearing a fur cap today," he said.

The other explained that he had bought the fur cap of the manager because it was warmer for the ears than a hat. "What business is it of yours anyhow?" he asked.

"What did you give for it?"

"Nothing. I got it for sixty öre. It's good enough for me."

"I wouldn't be seen in it."

"No," replied Moss; "you'll hang yourself with bared head—so as not to disgrace murder."

"You've plenty of gall, though your face is half eaten up!"

Moss fell behind and the Suicide had gone a long way on before noticing that he was alone. He saw Moss waving his stick and called out to him: "It's nothing, only that little gully—stride over it!"

"I'm snow-blind," replied Moss. "Where are you?"

The Suicide had to turn back and exclaimed impatiently: "What are you playing at? You've been here every day, across this little gully."

"Help me a second, lend me your hand!"

The Suicide answered: "I don't like touching you, you must allow that. You've got sores all over!" It was with great reluctance that he helped his companion over the gully.

"I can't make it out," said Moss; "nothing seems to be distinct now, it's all getting so blurred. Isn't that a stone?" he asked, striking it with his stick.

"Of course it is."

"And its colour seems to me grey. I can see that much anyhow."

Perhaps the Suicide himself shrank from believing the worst: "Then you must be blind in a freakish sort of way. Come on now!"

They climbed higher. But the Suicide saw that his companion could not find his direction; he often stepped off the path and fell, picked himself up again and staggered on.

"It's a strange thing," said Moss; "I got left behind down there because I somehow couldn't see."

"Do you see better now?"

"Much better, a great deal better; I was a little snow-blind." But Moss had so many tumbles and now he fell on his face. He excused himself at once: "I just stumbled over something. Of course I can see just as well as before, there's nothing wrong there. This bush, isn't it a young birch, a stunted birch? I can see that anyhow."

"In other words it's an alder, an alder-bush."

"Ha ha ha," said Moss foolishly; "it was alder I meant."

They were now as high up the Peak as they usually went, and sat down, each on a stone, to recover breath. A cloud passed over the moon.

"I can't imagine what I take these walks for," said Moss.

"For the same reason as I do, I should think," replied the Suicide. "For the sake of your health."

"Health—I have all the health I want."

"On the contrary, they say you're in a bad way, that it's a dangerous thing you're afflicted with."

Moss broke into a loud and scornful laugh: "Bosh, doctors' tattle!"

He still put a brave face on it, but after a while he gave up laughing so recklessly. The Suicide smelt a rat from the way Moss fumbled about, trying to find his stick, which he had put down.

"We'd better see about getting home," said the Suicide, rising to his feet.

Moss answered, without getting up: "Why, it's bright moonlight."

"For the moment the moon's gone in."

"Yes, I see that all right. You go on ahead, I'll wait a bit."

"No, then I'll wait too."

They sat on for a while, till the Suicide said: "Come on!"

"What do you want?" asked Moss.

"What do I want? To go home, of course."

"Go on ahead, do you hear! How can you be such a fool? You must see that I can't."

The Suicide reflected: "Well, well, I'm going. But you've got to come too!"

Moss replied: "You've more imagination than I have, it seems."

"Be quiet!" cried the Suicide, taking him by the shoulder. "I must have you with me, I don't see how I can help it."

"It's all right for an inspired person like you; you can walk. Now it's simply pitch-dark to me."

"Rubbish!" the Suicide cut him short. "That is, it's dark to me too, pitch-dark to me too."

"I don't believe it."

"You don't? Then I'll explain it to you in detail as we go along."

He got his companion on to his feet, holding him by the sleeve of his ulster, and thus they started for home. Progress was slow; at last they were back at the gully and there Moss made a false step and sank in to the bottom. It took a good while to pull him out again. After that they sat down to get their breath.

"Don't think too badly of me or be disgusted with me," said Moss; "but I tell you straight out that I can't see. It must be the night."

"No, it must be that you're blind," replied the Suicide.

"Just what I thought!" admitted Moss with a nod. "That shows that I'm right."

The Suicide: "It's really nothing to swagger about."

"Oh yes," replied Moss; "what I thought was perfectly correct, and it's not a thing to deny either. Fair's fair."

"Does the doctor know what's wrong with you?"

"Of course. He told me long ago I should have to leave. He's got a bed at the hospital for me."

"Long ago? Then how is it you haven't left?"

Moss was silent.

"I don't understand why you haven't left."

Moss with rising irritation: "You're incredibly foolish! Why haven't you left yourself? What are you suffering from? You're going to an institution yourself, aren't you? You're insane."

"Not a bit of it!"

"Yes, you are. And what has my disease got to do with you, what are you prying after?"

"I'm not insane, it's only depression, mental sorrows."

"Ha ha ha, say that again! As if some sorrows were bodily ones! You're thinking of hanging yourself, you're going to an asylum. The difference between you and me is that you have to pass an examination for admission and I get off that. You have to show that you're insane *enough*."

Silence.

"I'm tired of lugging you along, but I must get you home," said the Suicide unmercifully, as he pulled his companion after him. They arrived on level ground and stopped again. Moss wiped the perspiration from his forehead with the sleeve of his ulster, he was much exhausted. The Suicide announced: "This is the last time I drag you about, you may as well know it!"

Moss replied: "Yes, because I'm leaving tomorrow."

"That's a good thing!"

They went on again. And as they went the Suicide asked all at once: "As soon as that? Are you going tomorrow?"

"Yes, tomorrow."

"You're in an awful hurry. But it's all the same to me."

Moss made no reply.

"I suppose you haven't thought of how I shall get on? No, I'm sure you haven't."

"You? It's all the same to you," replied Moss.

"Aha, that shows what your religion's like!"

"You'll take your walks here every day and exhibit your incapacity for living. You fancy it's a matter of importance that you should be in a particular place, sitting and blinking and brooding and doing neither good nor evil; but, good Lord, no! you're not producing anything needful by so doing, any gospel, any benefit to mankind, daily bread for a sparrow, or a scrap of fairy-tale for a child—"

"Be quiet! That's word for word what I've said some time and you've learnt by heart."

"Yes, it is. You said it about me."

"There's something petty and mean about you," said the Suicide. "You store up things you hear, things that other people throw off; you go harping on them all the time: suicide disgraces murder; that's one of your cuckoo-cries. It's a good thing you're leaving, I'm tired of you long ago. Naturally one may sometimes think of murder rather than suicide. I've heard of a man who wanted to shoot his wife—whom he was in love with, by the way, but we can talk about that another time. Well, of course, he meant to shoot himself afterwards."

"Then there'd be an end of *that* story."

"No, then there was the child. They had a child, I was told."

The two walked on in silence for a while. Then Moss said: "No, it's not good for us mortals!"

This little concession finished the Suicide, but he cleared his throat and plucked up heart to reject it: "What do you know about it! Be quiet with you, you can't even talk plainly."

Again they were silent for a while. Moss fell flat on his face and got covered with snow.

"Can't you see anything at all?" asked the Suicide.

"Yes, a little. But I'm very snow-blind."

"Are you incurable?"

"I?" yelled Moss, halting. And all at once his gameness seemed to snap, he leaned forward heavily as though his whole body would say yes. In another instant he pulled himself up again and answered: "Is it your idea that we're not to get home tonight?"

Before they reached the sanatorium Moss asked with a groan: "Is it much farther?"

"No. Can't you even see the lights?"

"Yes, of course I can see the lights. I only asked."

Now the Suicide halted and said in a voice unlike his own: "If you could—I'm only saying if you could—you know—"

"What is it?"

"What is it?" mimicked the Suicide curtly and savagely. "You might guess that yourself. I was only going to say that for my part, I don't know. It's possible you'd find it a help; it never helped me to pray to God. I don't advise you one way or the other."

"Pray to God?" repeated Moss, out of his reckoning.

The Suicide, furiously: "What then? Do you think you're too big for that?"

Moss must have heard that his friend's bravery was assumed, that he was near despair; Moss himself caught the emotion and could say nothing in reply.

The Suicide continued: "I have heard of some people who were made happier by it. Who died more peacefully."

"Shut up!" wailed Moss.

And now the Suicide was at pains to cover up his weakness and be a man again; he snatched at the first joke that occurred to him: he had never succeeded in getting God to spend a couple of minutes with him; no, He never descended upon him through a trap-door in the roof—

In the morning the news got about that Moss was leaving, even Fröken d'Espard heard of it and sent for him—whatever she can have wanted with him. Fröken d'Espard herself was down on her luck and disfigured, indeed she was, but she sincerely pitied the unhappy Moss and wished to show him all the kindness she could. Moss seemed to have misgivings; he groped his way into the lady's room and stood there feeling responsible for her accident on the bob-sleigh run. The sight of him brought tears into her eyes, these last few months had altered his face beyond recognition; she took his hand and led him to a chair. No, he was not to blame; how could he imagine anything so silly? On the contrary, she would thank him for the time they had spent together at the sanatorium: "I have often thought about you; I think it's such a shame you should suffer like this. But surely somebody must be able to find a cure for you, don't you think so? You're so young and so plucky, you'll get over it all right."

"I hear it was a very bad cut you got," replied Moss.

"It isn't a bad cut at all, look for yourself!"

"Yes, I see. Right across the chin. Yes, it was very unfortunate."

Doubtless the lady had no objection to his sitting there weighed down by guilt, and for that very reason it was a pleasure to her to console him and put him on his feet: "Hush! you're not to care about anything but getting well again. What nonsense, that little rose-pink scar doesn't show at all! Now, look here, you must take this and keep it—put it in your pocket. You're not to thank me!"

"What is it?" asked Moss. "Is it money?"

"No, hardly any, I tell you!" she cried in a fervour of excitement.

"You'll be doing me a pleasure—"

"Thanks," he said; "I have no use for money."

"But it might be a help. Look here, it isn't much—"

"But I have no use for it, Fröken!"

"I don't understand you," she said, disappointed.

Moss, in a gloomy voice: "I am one of those who are publicly provided for. I'm to have a place at the public charge."

"Oh?" she asked innocently. "What sort of a place? A situation?"

"Yes, an easy situation. All I've got to do is to carry a rattle and call out: 'Unclean—unclean!'"

The lady stared at him in panic and whispered: "Are you—?" She checked herself.

Moss nodded, got up, and felt his way out of the room.

But the one who found it most difficult to say good-bye to Moss was assuredly the Suicide. He too tried to slip some money into the blind man's pocket, but on being foiled he abused him at great length. It was no trifle in the way of recrimination and insult that he heaped upon him: "I can't imagine what God wanted with a man like you here on earth. And if I call you a man, it's only so as not to go too far, but it doesn't express what I really feel."

"Go ahead!" said Moss.

"No, I won't be bothered to go ahead," replied the Suicide, but went on all the same. Oh, he was wound up and talked away, he knew no moderation, made himself hoarse with his exaggerations: "As I have said all the time, you're full of gall, gall and spitefulness and obstinacy. It wouldn't surprise me if you were tickled to death at the idea of quitting a world you can no longer see, while the rest of us are doomed to stop here amid the beauties of nature. That would be like you. Where is it you're being taken to now? It depends on what you've done; God knows if they won't drive you straight off to jail."

Moss, grimly: "Is that intended as a feeble hint of something to my disadvantage?"

"As you please—precisely as you please!"

"Because if so, we must fight!" declared Moss, brandishing his fists, all covered with rags.

"Tomfoolery! And I won't have another word to say to you. There was a grand ape lost in you. But you needn't think I don't understand you; you're as ridiculously simple as a child and your highfalutin's all a trick. How could it hurt you to have a shilling or two, in your pocket when you get there?"

"I have all I need in my pocket."

"Oh yes, and you buy a worn-out fur cap for sixty öre—"

"You envy me the warmth of it, that's what's the matter!"

"Bosh! Your stoicism is forced, you comfort yourself with a trumpery show of stubbornness like that; oh yes, you're a great man in your own eyes. I should prefer to call you a miserable wretch; you're full of vanity, you are. How do I know that? By your being so misguided, so childish, as to stand here insisting all the time on your hardihood. Do you think I don't see through you? It's all pretence and bravado. . . ."

The postman, who was to drive him, called from outside the window and Moss groped his way out, the Suicide helping him. At the last moment the Suicide went so far as to offer his hand, but Moss didn't see it and just said good-bye at random. Oh, he couldn't find anything better or more forcible than "Good-bye, Suicide Magnus!" Was that anything? Really the Suicide had been more equal to the occasion and with his abuse had helped his friend capitally over the moment of parting.

On the steps stood the matron wishing Moss a good journey and a happy recovery. The doctor was by the sledge, talking in low tones to Moss and helping to pack him in; aloud he said: "Keep up

CHAPTER THE LAST

your spirits, Antonius, remember what I said!"

"Yes, thanks," replied Moss. And as it was snowing a little it may have been a wretched little snow-flake or two that he wiped from his eyes.

So Moss was driven away, in the manager's fur cap and the Suicide's ulster—away to his living grave. No wonder he had flinched so long from leaving Torahus and life....

And then all was more or less in order again.

But now there was Fröken d'Espard.

She was well again, she was up, yes, on her feet, eating a little, sleeping a little, chatting now and then with the doctor. But she was far from being in a good humour, that line across the chin was no ornament. She asked the doctor if he thought it would go after a time, and "Oh yes," replied the Doctor, "it'll go." Meanwhile the lady massaged her face with vaseline and the tips of her fingers.

But one day—

It began with her waking after a good sleep, and as it was Sunday she put on her best clothes. It was a clear day; directly after lunch she walked out along the snow-covered paths and got some colour into her cheeks, after that she read the papers and then went up to her room. The young lady took a brighter view of things than she had done for a long time.

She went down to dinner, and as it was Sunday the food was a little better than usual, ptarmigan and currant mash. So few visitors were left that they all sat at the same table, the doctor as host at the head, then all the clergymen's widows and small tradesmen with their wives, and at the far end the matron.

Suddenly Fröken d'Espard jumped up from her chair.

"What is it?" asked the doctor, asked the boarders. No answer. "What is it, Fröken?" No. The doctor got up and was going to her, but she hurried past him, slamming the doors, stamping, holding her hand to her mouth.

"Toothache!" said the doctor with a smile, and got the boarders to go on with their ptarmigan.

Fröken d'Espard dashed up to her room. Her hand was shaking, but she found the shot in her mouth and found the tooth, alas, a broken tooth, a front tooth, good looks—O God! and she ran to the glass and saw the black hole, the terrible hole. Just at that moment she could do nothing, but after a while, as she experimented before the glass with different ways of smiling and opening her mouth to laugh, an ungovernable rage took hold of her and she broke into a storm of cursing. Her little hands became claw-like and she tore at the air with them. And, dear me, what else could be expected? Of what avail was now her face massage and all the attention she bestowed on the rose-pink scar upon her chin? Of what avail indeed was her whole plan, with the lady of the advertisement and the prospect of a good match to follow? All had crumbled into dust!

Wasn't it she who was going to take fate by the neck and bend it? And wasn't this a devilish trick to deal blow after blow at her face, of all places? With her appearance spoilt she was now perfectly hopeless, and what was she going to do? As she grew calmer she seemed to find some consolation again in the thick wad of notes she carried in her bosom, there was a certain support in that, as long as she had it she would be neither hungry nor homeless. She examined the tooth in her hand and saw that it was half decayed to begin with, it had been only a question of time when it would break, and now a shot from Daniel's gun had done the work of a hard crust or a piece of bone. When her hysterical rage had subsided she tried how she was to smile and laugh in future with her ruined mouth. A comfortless rehearsal.

In the course of the day she thought over every possibility: another trip to Christiania, or a surrender of everything, or a journey to Finland; nothing brought her peace, all the good solutions

CHAPTER THE LAST

faded out of sight, she was left to darkness and despair. One night she lay awake, but the morning found her with a clenched and resolute expression on her face. There was nothing grand in the plans she had laid; oh, it was neither a count nor a millionaire she had use for now, but she had arrived at some settlement with herself.

She entered the smoking-room and collected a few old newspapers, which she tucked under her arm; then she turned her steps to the forest.

It may not have been so terribly right and proper that she should make for Daniel's sæter just now in search of sympathy for toothache and other troubles, but there was an excuse for her and no doubt she knew what she was doing. It was certainly no worse than many another course she might have hit upon. Daniel was a man with a good deal of understanding, he had been exposed to one thing and another in the course of his life, had lost both his father's farm and his sweetheart, he knew the value of care and curds and cream and a stout heart. It was Monday today, Daniel would be hard at work with something or other.

Quite right, she found Daniel half-way, by the little barn in the wood; he had come to fetch hay again, and as the going was good he drew the hay on a sledge. A stroke of luck perhaps, a notable omen, that he should meet her just here, half-way.

They exchanged greetings, pleased as usual to see each other again, it was so long since, Fröken was quite a stranger.

She brought out her pretext and handed him the newspapers; they might do to while away an evening hour, mightn't they?

He thanked her with an air of positive delight. Reading was the jolliest thing he knew, he'd thought of taking a paper himself, but it hadn't come to that yet, said the hypocrite, and likely enough he could scarcely read.

He could have papers every day from the sanatorium; she'd be glad to bring them. After the visitors had done with them they were burnt anyhow.

Burnt?

Burnt, she nodded. Newspapers in all languages!

He'd never heard the like! But they could afford anything over at the castle, they were so rich. "Look at me now," he said, "here I go on, I'm still my own horse."

"Ah yes, that can't be very nice," she replied.

Oh well, he couldn't complain. He'd get a horse as easy as anything, he had credit and a good name among folk, he could go down to the village this very day and hour and get a horse.

That was splendid.

This very day and hour. But he would wait till the spring.

"There's one very good thing about you, Daniel; you're always in such capital spirits."

"Dear bless you!" he exclaimed, cheered by her words; "I have my hands, I have house and home and cows, I sell a bull now and again, I shoot hares and ptarmigan. By the spring I'll have a horse, then I'll plough up the bogs here and sow them."

Then she seized this good opportunity of showing him her mouth, how one of his shots had broken one of her teeth; yes, that was a charming thing to do, wasn't he ashamed?

He threw up his arms in horror and distress, but as she took it so nicely and didn't cry or reproach him, he plucked up heart: Honestly, it hardly showed at all, it didn't make any difference really, she was just as pretty and charming as ever—

"Oh, heavens, charming? Look here! I've got this too since I saw you. A pretty scar, isn't it?"

She had to tell him the whole story of the bob-sleigh accident and presently Daniel nodded, saying: "You ought to have had me to steer!"

"Yes, that's so."

"Next time you just send for me, I'll come with both myself and the sledge."

Already his resourcefulness and cheery talk was making her smile and look comforted; she took him confidentially by the arm and asked: "Doesn't it look frightful when I smile?"

"How? That little gap in your teeth? I'll go bail I wouldn't have seen it if you hadn't told me yourself. It's nothing of a hole."

"Ha ha ha!"

"And, besides, I'm sure you're just as good to kiss as you were before," he said, getting above himself.

"Oh, you!" she said, making a slap at him.

They sat down inside the barn, and there was sunshine, and a whole wall of dust to hide them like a curtain; it was as though it had all been arranged and intended. And when he kissed her she didn't forget to squeal a little and say: "No, how horrid you are!"

"Ay, words can't express it!" he replied.

She got up and looked back at him: if he had a good wash he'd be a nice-looking lad, his big mouth was not so bad. "Now you'll have to brush the hay off me," she said.

"Yes, if you'll give me another kiss."

She smiled invitingly and replied: "Afterwards, perhaps."

But he didn't brush her, he reached up for her arm and tried to drag her down to him again. This didn't come off; no, he was overdoing it, she wanted a little time. This young fellow, he seemed to be a regular dog, he'd have to be put back a bit. In spite of the setback to her appearance she would have to risk making herself rather hard to come at and keeping him in his place.

She stepped out of the barn and shook her dress, and to earn his reward he followed her and brushed her. Then all at once he stopped brushing.

"No, no, you're not to take it!" she cried. "There now! Ah, but you shouldn't have taken it. I'd promised you, but you shouldn't have taken it, I'd have given it you myself."

"It isn't too late to give me one yourself."

"Oh, you're too greedy—there you are! But I shall bring some more papers tomorrow. Oh dear, I have such a toothache, I'm in such pain, Daniel!"

"Ay, toothache's no good," he agreed; "I've had it twice. Marta, she's always got toothache, she'll go about with it for weeks without saying anything; I for my part could never get used to toothache."

"Ah, and if you'd had all the other troubles I have."

"Oh, blow them! There's a cure for all other troubles. But toothache—!"

"It's the worst thing you know?"

"Yes, it is."

She reckoned up other ills, sorrows, sleeplessness, fate in general. It didn't take with him. What was he made of, did he never feel unhappy? Yes, about a year ago. But life, the constant struggle, the anguish? No, he had no idea of such outside things.

He tried to get her back into the barn, but she ignored him. Why, sure, he was hot stuff, she could see that; he stared at her without blinking, she dropped her eyes, and when she looked up again his gaze was still rooted on her. At that moment he knew only one thing: that she was sweet and softly made, that she was full of charm and yielding of body. He enjoyed her in advance, he was heated up like an oven. This strength of his desire was in fact the virtue of his vice.

She went a few steps and withdrew from him half in alarm; something cannibalistic had come over him, his gestures were so coming-on, his nostrils went in and out, his white teeth shone, his stomach began to heave.

"There, now I must go," she said.

"No!" he protested. Oh, but it was no use, the lady was now a good way off and he grasped that she was going in earnest. "Don't go, don't go!" he called.

She answered with a wave of the hand.

"Won't you ever come again?"

"Yes, tomorrow. I've promised you some more papers, you know—"

The morning after.

Again it may not have been right and proper to go back to the barn, but she knew what she was doing. Otherwise why should she have tried the ground the day before? Fröken d'Espard had not many expedients to choose from.

There she goes, a human being like the rest of us, a wanderer in the earth, a little girl, ah me! a life gone astray, a flying seed. She was fairly undejected in her walk, taking care not to step outside the path and get snow in her boots. For that matter the weather was fine and sunny as the day before, she had the packet of papers under her arm, she knew what awaited her at the barn, and there she went. Some call it free will.

There was no sign of a sledge with him today, and perhaps this was because he didn't want to empty the barn of hay, or whatever may have been his idea. He was rather better dressed and had washed himself right well.

As he didn't want to risk another failure like that of yesterday he proceeded with caution, oh, so gently, dodging round the outskirts; it was actually she and not he who was the first to go into the barn and sit down. But he may come too, she says, if he'll be a good boy! And, oh yes, he will most decidedly be that!

They talked about the papers, she pointed to a story here and there that she advised him to read, and "Yes, that'll be fun!" he answered. To be sure, he was keeping himself well in hand, she had given him a lesson, he carried it so far that she had to hint of going home again, and even then he didn't put his arm around her. He was not quite himself, he talked too much and gave off a lot of twaddle, put on airs and made himself jocular; so she cut him short and faltered out: "I felt so sorry for you yesterday—leaving you like that. I'll do it now—what you asked me, I mean—"

"A kiss?"

"Yes—what you wanted. I was sorry for you—"

Afterwards all tension was relaxed and she collapsed in tears. It was more than she could bear; no, this little girl had been tortured for many weeks by a secret misfortune, her strength was gone, she burst into sobs, she got up and leaned against the wall of the barn, trembling.

He was dismayed, couldn't make it out at all, he had no experience of hysterics and asked what was the matter. He patted her and spoke kindly: "There, there, what are you crying for?"

"Here I am how—ling!" she sobbed. It ended in a sort of laugh, laughter and tears.

He got her down into the hay again, and they sat so long billing and cooing that his wildness reawakened and she yielded once more.

Devil of a fellow! He discussed her, expressed his opinion of her: she was tiptop, God's truth, not to be beat! He was, to put it mildly, a bit hard to please when it came to anything fleshly, so to speak; but anything like her—!

"Can't you keep quiet?" she cried, hiding her face.

No, he wouldn't keep quiet; this unlooked-for adventure with a town lady, a fine lady, had turned his head, let loose his tongue, and he went on bragging about her. Not that he wasn't pleased with himself too, bursting with professional pride.

"Can't you see that this may turn out badly?" she asked.

Badly? Well, of course—but, oh no, she mustn't think about that. And what made her think it might turn out badly?

"The consequences!" she said, as though overwhelmed. "The consequences!"

CHAPTER THE LAST

He was all frivolity and refused to consider this properly: "Now you must be good and not worry yourself!" he comforted her. "I assure you there's no sense in that. My goodness, if you should get into trouble! My two strong hands would be no use then. But I tell you, we're just like feathers floating in the air, we're carried wherever God pleases. There's nothing to be done about that. I wouldn't for all I'm worth that you should come to any harm, and so you're not to go racking your brains over nothing, please—"

Foolishness and disconnected twaddle. She herself didn't seem inclined to discuss it either, but she thought it wise to mention it at once, to nail it down, so that it might not come as a surprise later on. Again she was all foresight. Nor was his idle talk devoid of a certain consolation, the lady needed his kindness, his cheerful outlook had a healthy effect, his shoulders were good and broad. He could surely take her up in his arms like a child and carry her home to his hut. In any case he was something to lean on.

"Very well, then I'll be calm if you say that," she declared. "If you'll help me," she said.

"Oh, I—! But I'll do all you wish, depend upon it! Nothing shall happen to you, I'll see to that!"

"Yes, you must, Daniel. I have nobody but you—"

"Well, I never! You're to come to me and not to any other living soul, whether it's bob-sleighing or anything else."

No, this was taking the wrong turn, he was thinking too thoughtlessly, so to speak; she broke off for today and said good-bye. For the present she could allow herself a rest, she had made a step in advance, now she would sleep—eat and sleep. What had happened? Complete conquest achieved, with complete success. In a week or two another little step forward!

She went home with a mind easier than when she had gone out; relieved of a pressure that had long weighed on her. This little girl, she had not surrendered, but had put up the best fight she could, had planned, arranged, taken her own line in defiance of fate. What she might achieve by this manœuvre would not be undeserved. . . .

Day after day went by; the rest she had secured for herself did her good, her complexion improved, before she fell asleep at night she lay looking up into the darkness with her soul in a restful light. Daniel had no eye for her dilapidations, she might ignore that side of the matter; every time he met her he seemed more and more enraptured with what was left of Julie d'Espard. And for that matter she was no ruin, far from it, her figure was as faultless as ever and she could have that wretched front tooth crowned, so many had had to do that. . . .

Lawyer Rupprecht was expected at the sanatorium. The manager and the matron wished to make a few preparations, to tidy up the place within and without, have the paths swept, and, above all, lay in food, fresh food—a conspiracy headed by the Suicide had lately brought renewed complaints against the canned stuff.

The matron demanded fish, fresh trout. The manager was no fisherman, he was an old sailor, in addition to which he was now the manager, a man in authority; he went to Daniel about it. Daniel chopped a hole in the ice of the mountain tarn and stood there fishing all day long, and there it was that Fröken d'Espard sought him out and announced her sinister tidings: Now unfortunately there was trouble, no doubt about it, in fact she had known it from the very first. Didn't he remember her saying so?

What was Daniel to answer? Hm. That's it. I see.

Each time Daniel had pulled up his line it had brought some water with it, and this water had frozen to ice and made the approach to the hole slippery and dangerous. He warned her not to come too near. "O my God, what does it matter!" she cried. "The best thing would be if you'd push me down into the hole and have done with it!"

He put down his fishing-tackle, came over to her, took her in his arms, and set her down a little way off. As he did so he gave her a highly necessary kiss.

"God bless you!" she whispered amidst smiles and tears, and put her arms around his neck.

He himself was happy at having thought of this trick which had had so cordial an effect on her; he swaggered hugely, saying: "That's how we take a little thing like that!"

"Ah, it's all very well for you to say so. But what am I to do?"

"Don't cry, don't cry! We'll put it right!"

"Ah, thanks! I'm so glad you're going to help me!"

"Help you? Didn't I say, come to me? We're sure to find some way when there's two of us. Here I am on the ice earning money day after day and not small money either—"

"Money," she said; "I have a little of that too."

He started. Ah yes, he had seen it, seen a thick wad of money on her a few weeks ago, and now he came to think of it he had even felt it against his chest when he held her in his arms. "Then what's the matter?" he asked aloud.

"Well—nothing," she admitted, falling in with his view.

"Take care of your health!" he called after her as she went. "Don't get snow in your boots!"

It had turned out very well, Daniel was a trump, he was just like one of the fine French gentlemen in her books, a Monsieur without spot or blemish, his very offhandedness was appealing. She often went over to him on the ice and had a chat, sometimes she found him at a new hole he had had to cut, and finally he moved right up to the farthest tarn and went steadily on with his fishing. Oh, to be sure, it was no big catch he brought home, but to Daniel, whose scale was a modest one, it represented a day's wage. His spirits never failed: it would run to coffee for Marta, he said, and that was fine earnings for a winter's day! The lady asked how much he got for each fish, but he couldn't say, it was not a little, depended on the size, the weight, it meant a good bit of coffee and sugar for every fish, and even then he could put a little by. Altogether he was jocular and boastful: what he had to see to was to get his outgoings more or less to cover his incomings and not the other way about!

At this time the female boarders at the sanatorium had something on hand, they met in conclave and held discussions, a cawing rookery; one of the ladies had a pencil and wrote things down on a piece of paper. Every time Fröken d'Espard appeared there was silence.

This was of no consequence to Fröken Julie d'Espard, oh, a matter of complete indifference; she was a lady who could affect not to see the whole congregation! But after a while it was boring to be left outside, she tried to make advances, offered French books to anyone who would borrow them, but without success. Existence became dull, became lonely, human beings no more than rooks can endure to be alone. She had Daniel on the ice, but it was a long, cold walk up to the farthest tarn; the Suicide was less entertaining since his crony had left, the unhappy Suicide had again begun to mope and had given up his climbs among the rocks. Nor was he ever to be seen on the skittle-alley now.

The lawyer's arrival was therefore cheering to the lady. He was so easy and good-natured, so helpful, and as Fröken d'Espard was one of the first batch of visitors he paid special attention to her, to the envy and annoyance of the others.

The lawyer was able to tell her a little about Herr Fleming, and some of it was new to the lady: that he had got no farther than Christiania when he was stopped, and that, being consumptive, he was privileged to be detained in a hospital while the question of his extradition was being decided. He paid his own expenses, however, and was a gentleman all over. The curious thing was that the Finnish authorities themselves did not seem altogether in earnest

CHAPTER THE LAST

in dealing with the forger, it was they who had requested that the patient be given good treatment and nursing. "God knows who he may turn out to be and what wrong he may have done!" said the lawyer. "Perhaps nothing wrong, perhaps it's only a misunderstanding which may be cleared up. We don't know, you and I."

"No."

"No. What should we at a sanatorium know about our guests? We don't cross-examine them, we take them for what they give themselves out to be. They swarm to us from east and west, they leave us again, where they go we don't know, most of them are lost to us, life closes over them again. At a sanatorium they come and go, a stay here is not a lifetime, we provide them with rest and recreation, some of them with health and life, but they are only here for a limited time. Perhaps we have once or twice had adventurers under our roof; what of it? We are not the police. Sometimes a piece of news reaches us, a paragraph in a paper reminds us of some person or other whom we saw here. Do you remember the Princess?"

"Yes."

"The English Minister's lady, I mean. Well, now it is whispered that she was neither a Lady nor a Princess. She is said to be exposed. That does not concern us. She was here with interpreter and maid for such and such a time, she did no harm to the place, our bill was paid. That it was actually Fru Ruben who happened to pay it is her affair and not ours; if Fru Ruben paid she must have known what she was about. By the way, Fru Ruben has got much thinner."

"So I have heard."

"Much thinner, much lighter on her feet, considerably improved in looks, it's a pleasure to see it. I shouldn't be surprised if it was due to the after-effects of her stay here at Torahus. I feel reborn myself every time I come here. Don't you find this a healthful place too?"

"Yes."

"Though you haven't exactly lost flesh, I can't say that; you've rather put on a little."

Fröken d'Espard, turning crimson: "I'm just the same as I was."

"But perhaps a little fuller, a mere trifle, of course. And that is as it should be: reduction for the corpulent and increase of weight for the slight. I expect it's the water here that does it, I must really have it analysed. Oh, there's so much I ought to get done; now there's the flag. Imagine, we've had no flag here all this time, it's one of the things I forgot when we were starting. We have two flagstaffs, one on the roof and one away from the building, but no flag. But for Christmas we must have a flag. By the way, I've invited Rector Oliver here for Christmas. You got on quite well with Rector Oliver?"

"Yes."

"I've invited him to spend the Christmas holidays here. I don't want to lose him, a national celebrity, a great name. When he went home in the autumn he wrote a very laudatory article about our place, this home of healing among the fells, and about our work here. It appeared in a local paper, but now I should like to get him to write something in one of the big dailies, and I'm sure that would please himself better."

The lady remarked: "We had a visit from the Sheriff's officer some time ago. He came to interrogate us."

"About Herr Fleming, yes. I heard about it afterwards, you know; it was unfortunate I was not on the spot to prevent it. I hope he behaved with consideration? He could hardly do anything else! I intend, by the way, to look up the Sheriff again and ask that our guests be left in peace."

"Since you mention Herr Fleming—he's not dead, is he? He's still alive?"

"I hope so," replied the lawyer, as easy and good-natured as ever, even to the absent forger. "I haven't heard anything, but I certainly hope Herr Fleming has derived benefit from his stay here and has improved in health. Herr Fleming was an extremely amiable and sympathetic young man, aristocratic and refined, a pattern of manners; if he comes back Torahus Sanatorium will be open to him again. Generally speaking, we have been fortunate in all our guests, good people all of them, whom it would be a pleasure to get back. As regards the Princess, she was by no means a bad advertisement for us; she too will be welcome again if she cares to come. What an air, what a carriage! I don't know whether you think much of such things, but I must say they impress me, call me a fool if you like!"

"I think a good deal of them too," said the lady.

"Naturally. Since you are French. Oh yes, the Princess was good enough. She talked to the doctor and to me and to all of us as though we were her domestics. It does one no harm to be given a little lesson in the ways of princesses. Doctor Oyen asked if he ought to put on gloves to visit her, but I considered that would be overdoing it; he might perhaps have occasion to feel her pulse and then his gloves would be in the way. No, one mustn't be servile, we have our self-respect. But I regret to this day that we had no flag when she came."

Oh yes, in Lawyer Rupprecht there spoke now and then a rather childish man, he had learnt a few follies, a little snobbery, some naïve gentility from the circle in which he moved; but what he possessed before was of greater value: his kind-heartedness, his obligingness, his excellent qualities as a host. Nor was he devoid of natural tact; thus he behaved as though he had not even seen the damage to Fröken d'Espard's face. When at last she called his attention to it, Lawyer Rupprecht bent forward to see better and said: "Now you mention it—!"

"Oh," she said with a laugh, "why all this delicacy?"

"Yes, now you mention it! I don't see quite so well as I used, but when you point to it, of course I notice it. That scar makes no difference, not a scrap of difference; you have the advantage that now you needn't wear patches."

"Yes," she said with a smile; "I shall certainly have to give up patches."

"A scratch like that is by no means unbecoming. How did you get it?"

When he heard all about the accident on the bob-sleigh run he was instantly full of ideas for avoiding its recurrence. The run should be cleared of stumps and stones by summer, and before Christmas he would have more snow dumped on it, he would have posts set up on each side of the run, everything should be done. "Well, now Christmas is not far off," he said: "you'll be staying, won't you, Fröken?"

"I believe so."

"But I hope so! You are one of our most cherished ones. I'm coming up myself, several more are coming, I've spoken to lots of people. And now we shall sweep the snow off the first tarn and make a fine skating-rink before the new visitors arrive. I'm pretty sure we'll have something fine to show them. Altogether we're going to make something big and unique of Torahus, there shall be no trouble spared so long as I'm director of the establishment. The next thing is electric light. That shall come. By the spring we'll bring up furniture and fit up all the rest of our rooms. Do you think that will end it? No, then we shall have to build. The sanatorium turns out to be too small, we must extend it. It's quite a little universe to have to look after—"

X

A big parcel arrived for the Suicide—Anton Moss sent back his ulster. An accompanying letter said there would be no danger in wearing it again as it had been disinfected. Many thanks for the loan.

Now, Moss hadn't written this letter himself, but he had certainly dictated it, his expressions were easily recognizable; it was a strange letter, full of sneers, advising the Suicide to get married again or take to missionary work.

"He's gone mad!" said the Suicide.

Oddly enough the Suicide was deeply offended at his old crony's sarcasm, it goaded him to unseemly utterances and rejoinders, just as in the days when they had wrangled away by the hour. He got hold of Fröken d'Espard and asked her to listen to the answer he was going to send to this impudent letter, point by point. It was no trifles that this blind man, this corpse, should get in reply, and he would really write it too, said the Suicide, in black and white, said he, by God he would, he'd send this scurvy dog the kind of letter he deserved, he should not have the last word. Fröken d'Espard begged him if possible to soften a sentence here and there, but he wouldn't hear of it, he even found more scurrilous names for the pestiferous fellow, laughing with inward scorn as he repeated them. The Suicide actually carried it so far as to sit over his letter for a couple of days, and after accomplishing a glorious draft his resentment was still so great that he took to scrambling among the rocks again out of sheer defiance. The remark that he ought to get married "again" seemed to be what hurt him most: "What does that hooligan know about my being married or not?" he cried. "I never told him a word! Are you for a walk, Fröken? If you don't mind, I'll go a little way with you, I'm going up to the Peak."

Yes, Fröken d'Espard was going to see Daniel again at his fishing. She had stopped her visits for a few days, so as not to make them too frequent, but the other ladies at the sanatorium still ostracized her and she was forced to go back to the ice.

Oh, those infamous other ladies! It turned out to be needlework they were plotting about, a piece of embroidery in many colours on green felt. Fröken d'Espard happened inadvertently to see it one day in the room of one of the ladies: the maid who was doing the room stood there with the door open, spreading it out and admiring it. Fröken d'Espard's quick eye took it all in in a long glance: they had got up a sewing-bee over a table-cloth, the lady with the pencil had jotted down so much for green felt, so much for silk, satin for lining, fringes to go round. That was the reason they sat by turns in each other's rooms of late, sewing and having extra coffee and reading aloud while it lasted.

Fröken d'Espard was once more the lady who could not help smiling at the whole congregation; so this was the delightful entertainment from which the other ladies had excluded her! Not that Fröken d'Espard was any hand at embroidery, she could not ply a needle, had really never learnt to; she had learnt other things, typewriting, French, she had enlarged her mind. Oh, but in this environment, in such nondescript company, she had of course no use for her accomplishments; here feminine handiwork counted for more than she was accustomed to; she was a modern lady.

When the lawyer left, Fröken d'Espard was again reduced to Daniel's conversation, and indeed this was what necessarily interested her most just then. What was it coming to? How did the land lie? No direct question and no answer, nothing decided. Would she take him? How could she tell? Well, of course that must have been her idea; what else, after all there had been between them? She was by no means out of love with him altogether, she might quite well grow fond of him some day, he had attractive qualities and did not look badly. Besides, had she any choice? A small farmer was now good enough for her.

The lady walked past the nearest tarn, where the male staff of the sanatorium and some men from the village were just then at work clearing the snow in an immense ring round the whole tarn to make a skating-track. These men from the village, by the way, were rather badly behaved, they were mostly young fellows; they nudged each other, sniggering and whispering as she went past. This was not exactly amusing, but on reaching Daniel she felt safe, he was still the same, manly and helpful; when he heard that the lads from the village had been ill-mannered he wanted instantly to leave his fishing and go down to them. "It's all the riff-raff that hang about the store," he said; "I bet it's them. So you don't want me to go and talk to them? All right. Well, anyhow I can get Helmer to do that."

Helmer—who was that?

Helmer, that was a lad he'd known since they were both kids, a first-rate fellow, his best friend. Daniel told her with a little laugh that Helmer had even stopped him setting fire to a house one time; ay, that was just when he'd been jilted so shamefully a couple of years ago and she'd taken another, taken the Sheriff's officer. And then Daniel had had a drop too much one day and wanted to pay her out and burn her, house and all. And if it hadn't been for Helmer, God knows—

"Could you have done it?" asked the lady.

"Yes," said Daniel. Perhaps it was mainly boasting, but he said yes. And he went on: "Remember what she had done; why should she fool me? Didn't I come from a farm just the same as she? But it don't matter now," said Daniel with a nod; "I don't care about her anymore!"

They had quite a talk about this, and the lady understood that his half-jocular, half-serious words had, as it were, a false bottom to them and that from now on he cared for her and no one else. Good. She asked in an offhand way what he would do now if she fell into his hole in the ice? Again he threw down his fishing-tackle and seized her and carried her away and kissed her with great thoroughness. Yes, he was really a proper man, she could rest safely upon this chest, which was as broad as a door. "Oh, but, Daniel," she said, with a smile and a whimper, "if you had a scrap of love for me you'd propose to me now!"

"What—?"

On seeing his astonishment she drew back at once, afraid of having spoilt it all; it must be said that she was a little hurt too. "Ha ha ha!" she laughed; "it's only my way. Good heavens, did you think I meant it? It was *en l'air.* Ooh! no, you don't understand French! How shall I put it?"

"I'm to do that, I'm to propose to you?" asked Daniel. "Well, what would you answer?"

"Ah—that depends. I don't know."

"I mean, just in a general sort of way?"

The lady answered: "I suppose I should say that we ought both to think about it."

Silence.

"I'd never have thought you would," said Daniel, nicely. "And I don't believe it yet."

"Why not? There's been that between us which can't be undone."

Now he pricked up his ears in earnest and asked straight out: "Well, what's the idea, is it your idea to take me? But it can't be, can it?"

Silence.

"No, there you see!" he said, shaking his head with an awkward laugh.

CHAPTER THE LAST

Then she clinched it: "Yes, I'll take you. We can do nothing else now, you know. I'll take you. And you've got to do something too, you've got to take me. You really must, Daniel, after the state you've got me in."

Well, after all, he didn't seem to have reflected on it, to have realized the possibility, and there he was! The result was another outburst of wordy hilarity; as once before, he was flurried and talked a lot of rubbish: she was again a lady to beat all, the stunningest young lady that ever stepped. He'd never expected anything like this, couldn't possibly have imagined such a thing, it was too much—

"Hush!" she said. "I shan't be any use to you, I can't milk."

"I'll do that."

"But I can help you to give the animals hay."

"No, I'll do that. God bless you, you're not coming into service!"

"Oh, you'd soon get tired of having me only for show."

"But what about Marta? I never do a hand's turn on the farm in winter, Marta does all that. But now I'm going to ask you one thing all the same: have you thought over this, are you in earnest about it?"

She explained once more that they could do nothing else.

He dropped his chin on his chest and meditated, smiling and shaking his head, overpowered by the idea. Ah, if this came off they'd get a nice surprise down in the village, he guessed, Helena and the others. This was evidently his chief thought, the triumph over his neighbours. And now he hadn't talked half enough about Helena and started again with racy turns and queer expressions: didn't he come from a farm too and weren't his folks just as good as hers? Good-bye and good luck to her! Hadn't they had a kindness for each other ever since they were children? He should think so, exactly the same as marriage and plighted troth. There hadn't been any lack of kisses either, and pleasant handling on his part many a time, Fröken mustn't think that; the only thing was that he couldn't stomach her taking another man. And if Daniel had done what he ought that time, he'd have burnt her up and slain every hair of her head. Yes. There wouldn't have been enough ashes left of her to fill a pint pot. No.

"Hush!" said the lady, trying to calm his passion; "now we mustn't think of anybody but ourselves."

"Ay, but won't it be a bit of news, pretty near what you might call the greatest of miracles?" Daniel laughed and smacked his fists together in the air.

The lady didn't always know where she had him; he struck her as thoughtless and flighty, but at the same time he was staunch enough of purpose and steady at his work, a mixture of good and bad like other people. When he offered to leave his fishing for today and carry her home to the sæter and keep her right away, he was naturally a Monsieur after her own heart. "We mustn't lose our heads," she admonished him; "but there's something in what you say."

She should have the new cottage, he went on persuasively, the whole new cottage, he and Marta would never put foot inside it, she should have curds and cream and meat and potatoes and eggs—

As she walked home to the sanatorium she thought once more that all had gone well, and if not exactly overjoyed, she was content, she had an even mind, was saved, on top again. He had called out to her as she was going: "But—you, there, Fröken—what was I going to say? Just let me ask you one thing: is this positively your act and deed?" This was at least the third time he had asked the question and received her assurance. What else should she have answered? She was sensible enough to see the advantage of finding a refuge in Torahus Sæter, she was tumbled and shop-soiled, a young man offered her a home and such family life as he knew; that must be all she could expect at present. But of course it was mainly from necessity that she accepted. . . .

CHAPTER THE LAST

Christmas came and on Christmas eve all the sanatorium's boarders were assembled. There was no Christmas-tree, as there were no children, and presents were out of the question in this fortuitous assemblage; however, the men visitors had subscribed to buy a brooch for the matron, a nice one in coloured enamel with a gilt edge. The doctor rose at the end of the supper-table and made a speech, expressing the thanks of the matron for the precious jewel which the gentlemen—married and unmarried admirers or, should he say, suitors—had fastened upon her bosom. Then he passed on to express his own thanks to the ladies for a present so great and unexpected that he could not find words for it! The doctor was really moved, it was a moment or two before he could continue, and his eyes were moist. Such an extraordinary mark of friendliness on the part of the fair ladies could only fill him with pride and gratitude—while at the same time it naturally made all the gentlemen sitting here green with envy. This gift, the creation of art and good taste, the result of the infinite industry of many sweet little hands, now brightened his existence; it was a cloth without equal, it made an altar of his table and a sanctuary of his room. "Ladies, I thank you from an overflowing heart!" After that he spoke of Christmas and proposed the toast of all the guests who had had the courage and the sound sense to pass the winter here among the mountains. He wished them all pleasure and profit of it!

So that was the destination of the table-cloth, it was the doctor who was to have it. Fröken d'Espard could afford to smile once more as she sat there, yes, and she could dispense with the doctor's soul-stirring thanks for the present. To her there seemed to be something far-fetched about it all, for Doctor Oyen was not generally so highly esteemed by the visitors, he was kind and fussy and well-meaning, but was not held in any great respect; it must have been the clergymen's widows who had got Christmas on the brain and insisted on giving a Christmas present, even if it was to the doctor. Of course it was very nice that he should be pleased and touched by it, positively he had tears in his eyes when he thanked them for the altar-cloth for his sanctuary.

After supper the mail was distributed, an inundation of picture postcards, some Christmas numbers, here and there a book. Among the rest was a roll with French stamps and a Paris postmark: it was a present for the sanatorium, a "Torahus March," composed by the pianist Selmer Eyde. Splendid! The young artist had not forgotten Torahus amid the glories of the great city! A lady music-teacher was taken to the piano to play the march, but she soon had to give up and ask for time to practise it. Instead she played two Christmas hymns, which were sung by the whole company. Afterwards, when coffee and cakes, wine and sweets, were handed round, it became more and more Christmasy and the doctor made another speech, this time on behalf of the homes all over the country, the gleaming windows of house and cottage, the children's happy eyes, the mothers—"the mothers, ladies and gentlemen, who in this sweet yuletide are busy from morning to night and often perhaps from night to morning again. Let us drink to the homes and the mothers."

Very well, they drank, a tender chord was touched, the mothers nodded their thanks.

And an hour later the solemnity was at an end and Christmas eve dissolved; the doctor was very strict about the nervous patients' getting to bed in good time and the others, the night-birds, conforming to the rules posted in the hall. The Suicide, the manager and a small tradesman were therefore going across to the annex to play nap.

As the Suicide passed her, Fröken d'Espard said: "Well, Herr Magnus, happy Christmas!"

It was only a word in passing, but the Suicide answered curtly: "What makes you say that?"

Evidently she had not said anything to please him, and she tried

CHAPTER THE LAST

again: "Did you get many Christmas cards?"

"Fröken—did you get many yourself?"

"No. Only two."

"Who should I get Christmas cards from?" asked the Suicide. "I don't know of anybody."

"I beg your pardon!"

The Suicide, penitently: "No, look here—! Well, we can talk about that another time. You go on," he said to the other card-players, "I'll come in a minute. No, I didn't get any Christmas cards, but I didn't expect any either. It's a lot of bosh. All I regret is that I myself happened to send off one of these idiotic greetings, it was the stupidest thing I could have thought of—just imagine, to Moss, to a stinker like that!"

"Oh, to Moss."

"You're surprised. But hadn't he sent me the ulster with an abominable letter?"

"And you sent him a reply to his letter?"

"No, I sent a card. I bought it down at the store. It might have been a blown-out candle or a man with a long nose, that would have been very suitable; but what it had on it was nothing less ridiculous than a squirrel. I didn't choose the card; I just took what was there. But think of it, a squirrel, anything so strikingly absurd! Now you know the way a squirrel sits, with its tail curling up its back, sitting in a sort of ball. It couldn't have been worse if I'd sent him a little red house in the snow or an infant Jesus. A squirrel—did you ever hear of anything so innocent?"

"Don't you think," said the lady, "that he'll fall to wondering about the squirrel? That will pass the time for him. You know, he's blind and all alone."

"What? Yes, you'll see it'll give him something to think about. That's not so bad, he must want some work for his rotten head. A squirrel, he'll say, what can it mean? Look here, Fröken, shan't we put on some things and go out in the moonlight?"

"But aren't they waiting for you in the annex?"

"No. They can get the postman and the porter."

They went out into the moonlight.

"The more I think of it, the more I see what a lot of good he'll get out of that squirrel," said the Suicide. "Thank you, Fröken, for putting me on to it; you spotted at once that there was something desperate in it. He'll ask somebody with eyes in his head what there is on the card. A squirrel! they'll say. Then he'll be filled with darkness and mystification, I can see his face—"

The Suicide continued to hold forth. The lady remarked: "He has so much darkness already. It was a good thing you didn't send an answer to his letter."

"Who told you I'm not going to send it?" asked the Suicide sharply. "He shall get it all right, I'm busy on it now. Oh, then I ought not to send it? Will you tell me why he is to have the last word?"

They strolled on in the moonlight, the paths were now well swept, so that they could walk side by side. Once or twice the lady uttered a reminder that they would have to go in and go to bed, but the Suicide answered that he didn't consider twelve or two o'clock too late, often enough it might be four or five before it was late for him, he was sleeping worse again now. Oh, when all was said and done, the Suicide's inward wrath and stiff upper lip were of no great account; he was grateful to the lady for consenting to walk with him and shorten his life an hour or so, it brought him so much the nearer to death, it seemed. He entertained her with mournful reflections on the world and existence; it was waste of time for him to be hanging on here, he had reached the north side of life, his heart danced no more, no, and even his clothes wouldn't last any longer. All at once he turned to the lady and asked, rather incomprehensibly: "What about you?"

"How do you mean—?"

"Why, don't you think you're wasting your time here?"

"Yes, that's possible. However, I'm leaving here after Christmas."

"No—after Christmas, at once?" he exclaimed. It seemed to strike him that he would be left alone, and that hurt him. And the Suicide, who had got out of the habit of talking and arguing since Moss had left, warmed up and grew chatty: "That's unexpected news, unpleasant news. Are you going far? Of course it's no business of mine, but are you sure you'll find it better anywhere else? I'm not sure of that, and that's why I'm staying here. Don't you think that, after all, it makes no difference where we human beings are? That's my opinion. Now look at the full moon, we think it's pretty, but it's so useless and nonsensical, it just stands there wasting itself. So it is with everything and with us all, we perish whichever way we turn. But you know: This night a Saviour is born unto you. I don't say that by way of bombast, it's quite possible that there is something in that side of the question too, I mean as to the Saviour and salvation—salvation from the existence that has been given us without our asking, salvation from a life that we've been bounced into without the slightest wish on our part. O God, how mysterious it all is, though I don't say it's entirely incredible on that account; some people, you know, can believe just because it's absurd. Here we are, led with a rope round our neck to our destruction, and we go willingly, but dead against our own interest. We hear about the wise scheme of existence, but as to seeing it, perceiving it—no. I don't know which is the right way to take it, some men are serious and wouldn't think of making fun of life. But there we go along the road. We are led without a stop, whatever part of us time and old age do not completely destroy, they at any rate render unrecognizable. When we have travelled for a time, we travel awhile longer, then we go on for one day more, after that a night, and finally in the grey dawn of the next morning the hour has come and we are killed, killed in earnest and for good. That is the romance of Life, with Death as chapter the last. It is so mysterious, the whole thing. So when all's said and done we were only a mine waiting for its spark, and after the bang we lie still, stiller than stillness itself, we are dead. We try to struggle against it while there is yet time, we travel hither and thither seeking to escape, we come here to the sanatorium, but this place seems to be under a ban, a house of death where one after another succumbs and is laid in a coffin. Very well, then we run away—as you are doing, Fröken—we try some other place—as if that were any use at all! A hue and cry is raised after us, we are on the muster, we may change our garrison, but not our War Lord. Ah but, good God, how we kick against it! When Death comes in at the door we get up on tiptoe and hiss at him, and when he takes us in his arms there's not a bit of nonsense between us, we fight. Of course it's not very long before we're down, and then we look rather blue here and there. Then we're buried in the ground. What for? Why, so as to make it healthier to die for those who are left. But we ourselves lie there with maggots in our eyes, much too dead to brush them away. Isn't that how it is? And yet that's only half of it. We're talking about what Death can accomplish when he just goes stalking around and picking here and there, but that doesn't always satisfy him; in wars, earthquakes, epidemics, he appears in his majesty with thumb turned permanently down, Death wading in lives—"

A sound swung up to them from the village, of church bells; some young and zealous clergyman had thought of giving his parishioners a pious surprise. The sound was distant, now and again it died away altogether, but when a breath of wind came it brought a series of loud peals. It had an unaccustomed charm—Christmas-night service in all innocence, in all poverty.

The Suicide gave a start, he seemed to be touched, but was not the man to show it, not for the world would he give himself away.

CHAPTER THE LAST

To Fröken d'Espard it came as a welcome interruption, she gave a shiver and said: "Fancy, it's twelve o'clock! No, I must go in now!"

The Suicide simply would not show that he was moved, it was out of the question, he had to keep up his chat; but all the same there was a change in his tone as he went on: "For all that, Death is not so bad either, it doesn't always mean blood, nor need one be eaten up, it may leave one practically untouched, only a little black and blue from the tussle, and what more can you ask? It's above all among the rich and mighty that Death is such a big affair; poor people object to him less, they will often invoke him: Come along with Death, with Chapter the Last!"

"Yes," said the lady, "that is so. Good-night, Herr Magnus!"

"Oh, you're going in. Pardon me, Fröken," he murmured, pausing at the door; "the whole thing is, you see, that one might have expected a little card by the post, you understand, as it's Christmas eve, just a little sign. Don't you agree?"

"Yes, oh yes," she replied.

"They might have remembered it, I think. If I send a card because it's Christmas eve, they might send an answer. But no. It doesn't matter, I'm not accusing anybody. Of course it's easy to forget a trifle like that when one's at home and has one's house and all to look after."

Fröken d'Espard pricked up her ears and asked: "Did you only send one card, the one to Moss?"

"No, I sent one more," the Suicide confessed. "But you mustn't think there was any meaning in it, just a picture of a flower or two."

"But surely you can't very well get an answer to that before New Year?"

"I've thought of that," he replied. "But why should it come as an answer to mine? Why couldn't her card be sent off just as soon as mine? No, it's been forgotten, that's the truth. Or should you imagine it was omitted on purpose?"

"That can't be very likely."

"No. And I think it's not impossible there may be a New Year's card. Generally speaking, I consider New Year's cards more tasteful and appropriate than Christmas cards. I don't know whether you agree?"

"Yes, I'm sure you're right."

"Am I not? Christmas cards are a lot of nonsense, nothing else. They are all right for children, but for grown-ups—"

After the lady had gone in, the Suicide stayed a long while out on the steps. The church bells had ceased, he heard nothing, only the murmuring breeze from the mountain. The full moon shone down upon him; the despondency of his first days at the sanatorium had again come over his face and his whole attitude, a look of brooding and suffering. . . .

The day after Christmas came Lawyer Rupprecht with some other visitors, among them an engineer; next day came Rector Oliver, Bertelsen the timber merchant, Fru Ruben, and Fröken Ellingsen; afterwards a few strangers arrived with skis and skates. It was no big rush, perhaps half a score of people added to the company, no more. The lawyer thought that others might be expected; in any case Torahus was a new place, it was too much to ask that it should be full the first Christmas.

The new flag was flown and the "Torahus March" was played for the benefit of Bertelsen, the Mæcenas who had enabled a young artist to produce this work. Beyond that, Bertelsen had made a definite pretext for visiting the sanatorium: he was going to investigate the conditions for installing electric light. What had he to do with that? Nothing. It was self-importance more than anything else on the part of the young capitalist to meddle with this affair, since the lawyer had brought an engineer with him to make a survey of the water-power available.

There was something aggressive about Bertelsen when he came to Torahus, he wanted rather too much to own the whole place; besides which he said straight out that he came here chiefly in order to take out in food some of the money he had sunk in the establishment. And by the same token he refused to pay the bill for his former stay.

One day the lawyer was obliged gently to disabuse him of his error: "I am not aware of your having any claims against us. You're mistaken there. What you have is a block of shares in the establishment."

"Well, will you buy them?" asked Bertelsen.

No; the lawyer replied, as was the truth, that he was not in a position to do that. But he didn't consider it impossible that he might be able to relieve him of the shares later on.

"Ah, but now?"

"No, not now. Why just now? You're not in need of the money?"

Bertelsen, with a frown on his brow and otherwise bursting with riches: "No, thank God!"

The deuce could tell what it meant, but Bertelsen was not an exceptionally agreeable gentleman whom it was a real pleasure to have as a boarder, and that was the opinion of all at the sanatorium. He might actually sit there and speak disparagingly of his own "Torahus March" and wish he had never spent the money on the travelling scholarship. "This place is costing me a lot too much!" he would say. When everybody knew that his business was a big and solid one, full of money, it didn't look well to regret a few thousands spent on supporting an artist abroad. What could be the reason? One of the small tradesmen among the visitors—Ruud was his name—was, strangely enough, no longer so sure about the financial position of the house of Bertelsen & Son: "I know old Bertelsen," he said, "a safe and steady old fellow; but what the son may be I don't know, he won't acknowledge me or nod to me even, though he knows well enough that I might have come down hard on his father many years ago, but didn't. I have heard," said shopkeeper Ruud, "that young Bertelsen's last huge timber deal has damaged the firm's credit."

"But, then, the firm has received value?" somebody suggested.

"That's not so sure," replied the shopkeeper. "It depends in the first place on whether the young man hasn't made a bad bargain, and in the second on the state of the market. Of course if England starts another war in some part of the world the price of timber will go up, and then Bertelsen & Son may come out all right. Perhaps they may do that anyhow, I can't tell. At any rate it would be a sad thing if that big concern were handicapped in its operations or even had to cut them down; they have saw-mills, a furniture factory, and pulp mills in two places. It's to be hoped they're not threatened with disaster," concluded Ruud; "it means daily bread to a lot of people."

There was nothing to be gathered from young Bertelsen, he held his head as high as ever, his petty remarks about the scholarship and the shares in the sanatorium must have been due to transient ill humour. But he was not liked, there were certainly not a few who would have been glad to see him shaken up. He was not exactly bad-looking, nor was he stupid, but there was so remarkably little that was attractive either in his appearance or in his behaviour. The way he treated Fröken Ellingsen was alone enough to repel one. Was he engaged to her or was he not? The old boarders of the first batch well remembered how from the very beginning he had appropriated the best-looking of the ladies and went for walks with her under the greenwood tree and all that—now he seemed scarcely to notice her existence, though no fault could be found with her devotion. Often and often she gave up a pleasant chat and delicate overtures on the part of the other gentlemen simply for Bertelsen's benefit, but apparently it made no impression on him. He pretended to be busily engaged with the affairs of the sanatorium, and, to be sure, he poked his nose in wherever there was a crack; but at the same time he found leisure to pay a good deal of attention to a certain other lady at the sanatorium. Who was this other lady; perhaps Fröken d'Espard, to whom at one time he had paid court? No, not Fröken d'Espard, not a bit of it, she didn't seem to be his sort any longer, whether on account of her damaged face or for some other reason. No, it was none other than Fru Ruben who occupied his attention. Fröken Ellingsen would find him sitting with Fru Ruben in unexpected places with morning tea and cakes in front of them, and then the elder lady would call to her, a little put out, a little embarrassed, and say: "It's a good thing you came, Fröken Ellingsen; we've been sitting here." "I couldn't find you," Bertelsen was forced to say. "Where were you? Will you ring for another cup?"

Not that Fru Ruben stole away into corners with the young business man and tried to make a conquest of him; on the contrary, flirting was not in her nature. And, by the way, what induced Fru Ruben to return to this spot, where her husband, the Consul, had met with a strange and mysterious death? Was she drawn by that terrible event, like a moth flitting about a candle? In any case she had asked to be given her old room, just as though she meant to abandon herself once more to her grief. She had reduced her bulk enormously, it was a marvel how she had got rid of her corpulence; her figure was now quite neat and well laced. Her face, on the other hand, had not grown younger, it had rather acquired a flabby and unwholesome look. When the Suicide saw her again for the first time he said to Fröken d'Espard: "But—what *does* she look like?" "How do you mean?" asked the lady. "So deflated. She looks as if she'd had a puncture."

Well, anyhow Fru Ruben had the same deep and lovely almond eyes as of old.

And if she was back in her old room, going through the tragedy of her husband again and again all night long, was it strange that in the day-time she should take up with what company was available? Bertelsen and she had interests in common, both belonged to the business world and might have many subjects to discuss. She probably did not care for him personally, very few people did, but he was a well-known man in town and had youth and good health on his side, he smoked good cigars too and was not one of those who stain their fingers with cigarettes. Bertelsen for his part might have reasons of his own for preferring Fru Ruben's society to that of other women; her skin had sagged into little pouches and underneath it she was positively emaciated, in fact she appeared to be underfed—all that might be granted. But perhaps Bertelsen was not out for rosebuds just now, he might have taken a fancy to the lady's practical sense, and business ability, not to mention her money; God knows.

So they sat together and chatted, and now and then Fröken Ellingsen joined them and made three.

"You were going to tell me about the Princess when you were interrupted," said Bertelsen.

Fru Ruben was not unwilling to begin again; it was of "Mylady" she was talking: "Well, as I was saying, I lent her money on the ring, it came to a big sum in the end, but I wouldn't have minded that if only I could have kept the ring—"

"Couldn't you keep it?"

"It's not here!" said the lady, holding out her dark hands.

"But where is it? Stolen?"

"It's gone. Not that I worry about it, what is it to me?"

Silence.

"Yes, it was a disgraceful affair," Fru Ruben went on. "I wanted to help the lady and even had a disagreement with my husband about it. I believed all the things she told me about her husband, about a packet of letters she made play with, about a poultry farm she wanted to have; but I'm sure it was all swindling and forgery.

CHAPTER THE LAST

The ring, you say? Well, if she didn't actually take it back, steal it back! I won't deny that it was chiefly the ring that made me do it all; a glorious ring, I've never seen such water, a singularly fine stone, I saw that at once, God knows where she got it from. And that ring she brought me and wanted to borrow money on it. I had plenty of rings already, but not that one. She didn't give it me, she pawned it. I was to raise money on it for her. 'All right!' said I and gave her all I had. But that wasn't enough, she had to have a certain sum. 'Well,' I told her, 'I'm afraid my husband won't buy me a ring for as much as that.' 'Then give him these letters,' she said; 'he'll know more about them; they ought to be worth a million in your little Norwegian money, get me ten thousand, twenty thousand!' 'I'll speak to my husband,' I replied. 'At once?' she insisted. 'Very well, at once; I'll telegraph for him.' I wore the ring, I took off two other rings to give it a worthy place by itself and I kept it on at night. But as I told you, I was not so awfully keen on the ring, you mustn't think that. My husband came, sure enough, and he seemed to think I had rings enough already, which was true; but what was worse, he was suspicious about the letters and refused to take any action as Consul. If I had only been warned by him then, but I wouldn't listen. He read the letters and examined them and shook his head, we talked it over till late at night, in the end he was tired and went to bed; as I was going to do the same I heard a thud; it was his head striking against the end of the bedstead—he lay still, he was dead."

"A stroke," said Bertelsen with a nod.

"Yes, a stroke. There was I. Of course I had to gather my wits and be sensible about it: my husband had grown a bull neck, the stroke was bound to come sooner or later, that it happened just now could not be helped. And I had the ring; of course it hadn't become the apple of my eye by any means, but I wore it every night for safety's sake. What happened then? I paid the lady's bills for herself and maid and we left the sanatorium, they stayed with me in Christiania, I paid for a lot of her shopping, paid and paid, but then it was a lovely ring and I wanted it for my own. Well, but at last I had to give the lady to understand that it couldn't go on for ever. 'No, no,' she said; 'but then there are the letters!' 'But I haven't a notion how to handle these letters,' said I, 'and my husband's dead.' Oh, but the letters were worth a million and they were written by the English politician and Minister So-and-so. Well, I still didn't doubt this, but I couldn't turn them into money for her. I dealt quite fairly with the lady—the swindler—I went to a couple of jewellers and had the ring valued; they thought I could go a little further and a little further yet, it was a valuable antique ring. Finally I said stop, I wouldn't pay out any more money. No, the lady thought that was not unreasonable. And now comes the climax, you'll see how I was let in: one morning while I was washing I was called to the telephone, it was Fru Stern; I threw on a few clothes and went down, leaving my rings lying on the bedside table. There was nobody on the telephone. I ring up Fru Stern; no, she hasn't called me; I ring up the exchange, they can't tell me anything. But all this calling up took time and when I get back to my bedroom the ring is gone from the table. The ring is gone! The other rings are still there, but not that one. Had I taken it down to the telephone? I go down again and look. It's not there. Up again and look—no. Then my head began to swim, I called for the lady and she came; she listened to me sympathetically and smiled when I asked her if she had taken the ring. 'You're joking!' she said. But perhaps her maid, the interpreter, might have found it, I suggested. Well, the lady instantly called for Mary, but it turned out that the maid wasn't even in the house, she had gone out shopping."

"Exactly what I thought!" exclaimed Fröken Ellingsen. She had followed the story with intense interest, it was quite in her line, that of detective stories and flights of fancy, she was at home there, had dealt with the same thing more than once. "Of course they were in collusion; it was the maid who rang you up from somewhere in town," she said.

Fru Ruben nodded: "That was it, no doubt. But the ring was lost."

Bertelsen asked: "What did you do then?"

"Do? I'd learnt a little wisdom by then, I turned the swindlers out of my house."

"What became of them?"

"How should I know! I suppose they went somewhere else and did some more swindling."

"It's the most impudent thing I've ever heard! Didn't you go to the police?"

"No. I'm not a sleuth. Besides, I should hate to be mixed up in a scandal."

Silence.

"Hm!" said Fröken Ellingsen, asserting herself; "I could tell you a good deal about these two ladies, only I'm bound by my oath."

Bertelsen listened to her disdainfully and replied: "Yes but you can't get back the ring, and all the rest's of no consequence."

Fröken Ellingsen, full of secret information about Grand Dukes and other notables, remarked: "I'm not so sure that the facts I could give might not lead to something. But I must be mute."

"No," said Fru Ruben suddenly; "the only thing would be for the sanatorium to refund me what I paid for the ladies here."

Bertelsen, rather taken back: "I wonder?"

"That would be the only thing."

"But that wouldn't cover it, would it?"

"That's just it. Yes, it would be about a third of the whole. And the other two-thirds I made sure of before I turned the ladies out of doors."

"How?" asked Bertelsen.

"I took back the goods they had bought in Christiania."

"Well done! And they submitted to that?"

"They had to. Oh, they were very thick-skinned. Imagine a lady who quite openly, without any show of concealment, steals a ring from my bedside—a lady like that hasn't much delicacy in her. She understood well enough that I knew who had taken the ring, but she disregarded that entirely, she stood and faced it out and didn't sink into the ground."

"The whole thing's like a fairy-tale!"

Fru Ruben asked: "Don't you think the sanatorium ought to meet me?"

"Yes, I'll manage that," replied Bertelsen with decision.

"Will you?" Fru Ruben smiled gratefully. "Well, I thought I would mention it to you, as you have so much to say here. And don't you agree, if Torahus Sanatorium takes in that kind of 'Princesses' they ought to see that the other visitors don't suffer by it?"

"I'll manage it," repeated Bertelsen. He looked at his watch, got up, and excused himself: he had to go on a "survey," he said, up to the two tarns to investigate the prospects of electric light. "We must make something of this place, you know," he announced; "it's going to cost some money, but we can't help that!"

But Bertelsen might just as well have stayed quietly with the ladies; it appeared that the lawyer, the doctor, and the engineer had gone off without him—at which he was both surprised and offended. And be sure he would pay the lawyer out for it one of these days....

At dinner-time the sanatorium had a scare: the Suicide was missing. He didn't come to table, nor was he to be found hanging in any of the lofts; the doctor, who had stood out all the time that it would not end tragically, was no longer so sure; after dinner he took some men with him and searched the forest. That devil of a Suicide had probably devised something intricate; quite likely he had shot himself and then burrowed into a snow-drift.

CHAPTER THE LAST

They searched and called, wading in snow, cursing and threatening, they kept it up till dusk, they ransacked his room for the tenth time: there were his things, clothes hanging on the wall, a few books, a couple of historical works lying on the table—so he had not run away, and where could he be?

Then Fröken d'Espard had the idea of telephoning to the railway station. Oh, that extraordinary Fröken d'Espard, she had her wits about her; quite right, Suicide Magnus had left by the morning train.

When Fröken d'Espard had thus been the means of restoring calm, they all thanked her in their hearts and even those ladies who had boycotted her before were not far from feeling a shade of regret; in any case she had saved all the patients from a sleepless night. Rector Oliver said straight out that his nerves could not have stood a case of hanging in the forest so near the sanatorium. "You see, we intellectuals are not constituted just like everyone else," he said; "we have our nerves, the others have theirs. Our long years of study have affected us, our nerves have been refined to the highest pitch and are therefore not very robust."

"But you are looking well, Rector," Fröken d'Espard complimented him.

"I am not ill," he replied, "only run down—as my brother the blacksmith says. Others might call it hypersensitized, but my brother says run down. He has a language of his own, you know."

"And how are things going in your home town, Rector?"

"Oh, they're going. That is to say, as things *can* go in a small town. Conditions are not very favourable for us who have to maintain the intellectual *niveau* to the best of our ability, for all higher interests are absent; I have succeeded in inducing the club to subscribe to a couple of foreign newspapers, that is all."

A change must have come over Fröken d'Espard, the Rector's life and experiences in his home town did not interest her so absorbingly as on his previous visit; no, the fact that his club took foreign papers left her pretty cold. Had the crazy Suicide Magnus infected her the other day with his disrespectful words about philological studies and culture? She was not as she had been, perhaps she was blunted; she was to be the wife of a small farmer.

But now the Rector had once had her willing ear, she had spoilt him, and therefore he continued to initiate her into anything and everything connected with his town. With smiling condescension he told her of the town's steamship *Fia*, how when the *Fia* came in to the quay with her flag at half-mast for a sailor who had been washed overboard, there was a great stir among the whole congregation; but it would make no impression on the same congregation if the world's greatest scholar were borne to his grave. "Now it is the fact that the sailor has dependents in the town, which is more, Heaven knows, than any scholar among us has; the circumstances do not admit of it. What people want is an Italian with a hurdy-gurdy and a monkey, or, better still, a merry-go-round out on the common! It is weary work under such conditions, passive resistance everywhere. Last autumn when I came home from my vacation some of our gunboats lay out in the bay and there was to be a dinner and a ball in honour of the officers. Strictly speaking, of course, it was the chairman of the Town Council who should have given this dinner, but the chairman, my worthy brother Abel, presumably felt that he lacked something of what we others possess, and so it was Scheldrup Johnsen, the Consul, who gave the dinner. This scandalous disgrace might have been avoided. I rang up my brother and placed my own spacious apartment at his disposal, my wife would undertake the dinner, and I offered to make the speech. My brother's answer was to stand there and fill the telephone with his laughter. 'You're just the same as ever!' he said. 'Yes, thank God!' I replied. 'You haven't learnt to blow your own nose yet,' he said. That was the kind of language he used. So I rang off. What do you think of it, Fröken? I offered my services and was met in that fashion! Well," added the Rector with a nod, "there was a sequel to it; at the next elections the state of feeling had changed and my worthy brother the blacksmith was only re-elected chairman by the skin of his teeth. Another little incident of that kind—and Scheldrup Johnsen will take his place!"

"Fancy!" said Fröken d'Espard.

"Yes, I can assure you," said the Rector impressively; "that will be the result. I know the state of affairs well enough for that." The Rector nodded again with a decided air.

Fröken d'Espard made a movement as though to go.

But the Rector was full of his subject; he could not forget the great event and set off again: "No, if my brother had had his way there would have been no dinner and certainly no ball. But the better-class families of the town would never have allowed that. It was therefore a fortunate thing that we had a man like the Consul in our midst. He is not exactly a man of college education, he is not that; but in any case he is a man with a knowledge of languages and a certain polish, and moreover he is a rich man."

"Yes," said the lady.

"It was a good thing we had him to fall back upon on that occasion. The electors evidently thought the same: without the Consul we should have been the laughing-stock of the officers, and that was clear to everybody. Oh, when all's said and done, people do feel a longing to rise above their surroundings, even those at the bottom will sigh for the heights. My brother the blacksmith may succeed for a while in getting the lower classes to jeer at us who have spent our whole lives and our whole strength in study and teaching, but when it's a question of a public function, or of a literary reference, or of answering a foreign letter, then they are forced to come to us. I have experienced several cases of the kind. And so it is doubly annoying when one of our own set turns against us. It happened not long ago that a well-known Swedish Professor—I won't mention his name—did his best to destroy all the respect for culture and scholarship which we others had laboriously built up in the course of generations. What satisfaction it could have given him I am unable to guess. Children ought not to sit learning lessons from their sixth to their twentieth year and beyond it, that is not what they need in order to become real human beings, he wrote. Well, if so I don't know what they do need, I don't grasp it at all. Do you?"

"No," said the lady.

"There, you see! He thought too that our school-books were too big and too full of matter, the children had to grind so hard that at last they knew nothing. Did you ever hear such a thing? Isn't the very contrary the fact, that the more one grinds, the more one knows? He spoke disparagingly of popular scientific lectures, of people's colleges that is, and by implication of the general spread of enlightenment. It was the immense scientific and technical advances of the last century that were responsible for our superstitious respect for all that goes by the name of science, he wrote. He did not shrink from writing: 'our superstitious respect'! No, what children ought to do, concluded the Professor, was to work, instead of learning a lot of dead stuff by heart. As though learning by heart was not work! Heavens, how I have worked at learning by heart!" the Rector ejaculated with feeling. "The Professor is profoundly mistaken. Is not the course of development precisely in the direction of more schooling, more and more subjects both for boys and girls? And is this one man on the other side more likely to be right than all the rest of us who stand on this side? But he has received his answer. Should you like to hear how it came about?"

"If it doesn't bore you, Rector—"

"Doesn't bore me in the least. Well, now you shall hear! I don't know whether you remember that some time ago there was a sharp discussion in the papers about the higher education of women. Now you know where I stand with regard to this question: mine is the liberal and humanitarian standpoint that woman has just as much right to a masculine education as man himself. Articles appeared for and against, until I thought I could no longer refrain from taking part, it might be expected of me, I have a name, you see. Very well then, I took up my pen. I did not mince matters, my article was very decided: 'Schooling and again schooling!' I said. Voices had been raised for more manual labour and less schooling; this was nothing but the delusions of demagogues. I would not say anything in depreciation of manual labour; women, for instance, ought to learn gardening; but the verbs 'to cook,' 'to sew,' 'to dance,' and 'to play' had now become the main verbs for the majority of them and this makes them superficial and flighty. All honour to the hand and the work of the hand, but the mind before all! 'I will say no more at present about these four verbs,' I wrote, 'but I consider that the education of young ladies is now threatened. We are not speaking here of those who matriculate and work their way through the University and enter the various professions: it is the others I am thinking of. What are these others to learn in order to educate themselves for the duties of a mother, for conducting a house and home? The mind before all!' I repeated with good effect. 'They are to receive a complete education in languages, in literature, art, the history of civilization, and the rhythmical basis of music. Why? Because otherwise they will stand abashed in the presence of foreigners. The girls of the present day have a great desire for foreign travel and facilities for gratifying it, but they often lack the necessary acquirements for turning their stay abroad to good account.' Those were the main points of my article; of course this resume is very incomplete; thus, it was full of well-directed thrusts at the Swedish Professor, which I hope gave him food for reflection. In any case I have this satisfaction, that so far as I know he has not attempted to answer me to this day."

Silence.

"Well, what do you think, Fröken?"

"Oh," she said; "it's so difficult for me—I understand so little about it—"

"That is very nicely answered," said the Rector. "If everyone would answer like that the decision would be left to us who have worked on the question for thirty years and ought to know best about it. You have, I may say, practical experience of the matter, and yet you cannot gainsay us. Am I not right?—you possess at this moment something in advance of our ladies in general, you have an advantage in that you have been to school and learnt French. Should you have derived any benefit from your stay in France if you had not known the language? Oh, one can never have too much school or too much grind, it's not possible to grind so hard that you know nothing in the end, the Swedish Professor was wrong."

Silence.

"You didn't bring the little boys with you this time, Rector?" she asked.

"No. You see, they were here in the autumn and it won't do to spoil them. They've got to stick to their lessons like good boys and get on in the world. Unfortunately they are not so studiously inclined as I was at their age, but no doubt that will come right in time."

These were not very good days for Fröken d'Espard; it was Christmas, but a joyless one, she didn't belong anywhere now, she was uprooted. The sanatorium itself lacked any air of home; last year's flowers still stood there, not dead, but wilted and cheerless, the big plant in the drawing-room was grey with dust and its shoots had been clipped. Her sense of domestic comfort was doubtless not very highly developed, but she had a certain instinct like other people; she took upon herself to tidy the newspapers in the smoking-room and she always kept a branch of spruce above the looking-glass

CHAPTER THE LAST

in her own room. And of course she had her yellow French novels, but the walls were bare of any decoration but her clothes.

She could not sit in her room the whole time, and where else was she to go? To the Rector and again to the Rector? Oh well, yes. He was no worse than other bores. There were not many new visitors, the lawyer was wrong in saying that more and more might be expected; all his advertisements of winter sports, ski-runs, and skating-rinks had only brought a few youngsters with plus fours and up-to-date slang, and, by the way, a young journalist who was going to do a series of articles on Christmas in the mountains. Nobody was any good to Fröken d'Espard, Bertelsen paid no attention to her, Fru Ruben she had never cottoned to, Fröken Ellingsen had slipped away. So there was nothing left but the sæter and Daniel.

Fröken d'Espard had looked in at her sweetheart's on Christmas eve and had given Daniel a big bank-note, and Marta, his housekeeper, a smaller one, and they were both hugely delighted, uproariously delighted; they were going to buy splendid presents with the money. Daniel's busy brain went to work at once: he was going to buy a horse for his present. That was just what he'd do. He'd go down to the village directly after Christmas and have a look at a nice little three-year-old that his good friend Helmer had in his stable. Oh, Daniel had his own idea in buying a horse in the middle of winter, he'd get it cheap, as the farms were generally short of fodder, but Daniel had plenty of it since he had sold the big bull.

When Fröken d'Espard paid another visit to the sæter in the middle of the holidays, Daniel was away, sure enough, on horse-dealing business, he had been at it for some days and still he had not finished haggling. That was the way with horse-dealing. The lady could not stay and wait for him, she went back to the sanatorium and Rector Oliver.

The doctor, the lawyer, and the engineer were returning from their expedition; the doctor swept the ground with the feather of his hat and was tremendously excited: "We'll have some light, won't we, engineer? Light in every window of Torahus, in every pane. When we stand up on the Peak, we shall look down into a heaven on earth, crammed full of stars!" The doctor was irrepressible in his generosity.

"Unfortunately I shan't be here so very much longer," replied Fröken d'Espard. "So there will be no electric light in my time."

"What—are you going to desert us?" asked the lawyer. "I should be sorry for that."

"We shall all be sorry," said the doctor.

Rector Oliver nodded agreement.

"I can't afford it in the long run," she explained; "I'm leaving after New Year."

"Back to Christiania or—?"

"No, to Daniel's. To the sæter."

Speechlessness all round.

"Can you stay there?" asked the doctor.

"Why not?" she replied. "I'm to have his new cottage to myself and a superabundance of food."

The lawyer was the first to recover himself: "Well, well, Fröken, at any rate we shall still have you here on the mountain. And we shall welcome you back whenever you want a change!"

Bertelsen had joined them. Away in a corner sat shopkeeper Ruud looking at a paper; maybe he didn't trouble about what the others were saying, maybe he listened to every word; Ruud was such a silent and thoughtful man. Bertelsen was sour about these gentlemen having gone up to the mountain tarns without him, as though he had no interests in the place which wanted watching. Where would they get the money from for electric light? he asked ominously.

"We shall find a way," the lawyer assured him. "You will help, others will help. The scheme won't fail for want of a little money."

"I'm not going to help anymore," said Bertelsen; "I've had enough of it. I've had a travelling scholarship foisted on me here, which cost me a lot of money, and I've had to take over a big block of shares. I'm not going to do any more."

The lawyer, in a restrained and friendly tone: "That's a pity. Then you don't want to dispose of your shares?"

"Don't I, by Jove! Find me a buyer!"

The lawyer asked in a drawling voice: "Have you the scrip here?"

"Here? No," replied Bertelsen, rather surprised at the lawyer's tone. "But I don't suppose there's any buyer here either."

"Well, you mustn't assume that offhand."

"Oh," said Bertelsen, badly put down. "All right," he said. "But of course I haven't the scrip here. My fire-proof safe is full of papers that I can't carry about with me."

"But you can ask to have the scrip sent here."

"Oh yes," said Bertelsen, "I can do that of course. But there can't be such an awful hurry, I'm here to keep Christmas."

During this little conversation shopkeeper Ruud had been sitting in his corner hidden behind his paper; now he gave a little cough, folded the paper neatly, and left the smoking-room.

"Is it he who wants to take over the shares?" asked Bertelsen, pointing with his head. "Have you had an offer from him?"

The lawyer replied pleasantly and evasively that contingently—contingently, he said—he would buy the shares on commission. More than that he did not say, and thus he did not deny that he was buying for the little shopkeeper Ruud, who had been sitting in his corner; so insignificant, so quiet, and so stuffed with savings.

But Bertelsen had made no progress. The worst of it was that now he had lost his hold on the sanatorium and on Lawyer Rupprecht; he could no longer bring any pressure to bear on Fru Ruben's behalf. He took the lawyer aside and laid the question before him in all friendliness, lowering his note, and asked that indulgence might be shown to Fru Ruben. The lawyer listened to him, was all the time a host, an old acquaintance, almost a friend. Was he to compensate the visitors for being let in by sharpers? He was afraid it would not do to carry on a health resort on those lines. "No, Herr Bertelsen, you must excuse me!"

Bertelsen saw that all was lost, he would have to appear before Fru Ruben as a man who had nothing to say in the place. This seemed to cross him badly just now, as though it upset his plans.

The lawyer sat thinking and allowed his refusal to take effect; he thought for a long time and blinked his eyes. Then he spoke again: "No, if we ran the sanatorium on those lines, where should we be? It would be another matter if Fru Ruben could make it up to us in one way or another, that might be worth considering. Is she very anxious to have these expenses refunded?"

Bertelsen replied that of course Fru Consul Ruben was a very wealthy lady, it was not a question of this trifling sum. On the other hand it could easily be understood that she was vexed at having lost that ring, and her object in asking to have her expenses refunded was to re-establish the *status quo* in herself, in her own heart, to put herself back to the time when she had never set eyes on the ring.

"That is a very acute analysis," said the lawyer; "what you say deserves consideration. Should you suppose that the lady would be willing to grant an interview?"

"An interview—?"

"She has grown so nice and thin, she is a lily, a beauty. Might we not suppose that this change is due to her former stay at Torahus Sanatorium?"

Bertelsen sat speechless.

"I mean, might it not be due to the after-effects of her stay here? That they led to this reduction in her which has made her a young girl again?"

"I don't know," said Bertelsen.

CHAPTER THE LAST

"No. But I don't consider it impossible. And neither Doctor Oyen here nor any other doctor I have spoken to considers it impossible."

Here perhaps Bertelsen glimpsed a means of escape. "I'll ask her," he said.

"Do. Tell her at the same time that we think it is the water here which has this effect—the water in conjunction with the air and the life here, our cure taken as a whole, which operates in this beneficial manner. Tell her that; she is a sensible lady and won't think it unreasonable."

"But what if it is not the case? If for instance she has simply starved herself thin?"

"You think that then there would be no basis for an interview? But if Fru Ruben has starved herself thin, others can also avail themselves of this auxiliary remedy, in addition to the water here. I cannot see that that affects the case very much. And even if the sanatorium had nothing at all to do with her renewal of youth, her interview will be a good advertisement for a beautiful health resort among the mountains. That in itself is meritorious. But as a matter of fact we can show some miraculous cures: Rector Oliver's nerves, Suicide Magnus's mental condition, Count Fleming's lungs, and so on; if we may now add Fru Ruben's reduction it may benefit other sufferers."

"Who would interview her?"

"We have here for the moment a gentleman who writes for three papers, one in Christiania, one in Stockholm, and one in Copenhagen, three big papers."

"I'll speak to her," said Bertelsen.

"Say that contingently it will be a pleasure to the sanatorium to oblige Fru Ruben and make her forget that positively shocking affair of the female sharpers."

XI

The people crawled and crawled, some this way, others that. Sometimes they crawled in company, sometimes they collided and neither would give way. But occasionally they crawled over each other's corpses. Could it be otherwise? Were they not human?

Lawyer Rupprecht desired no man's ruin. If through an accidental circumstance he might be said to have won a victory over Bertelsen, the timber merchant, he had no wish to triumph over him; on the contrary, he tried to smooth over the fact that the other had lost. Out with your shares—quite so; but he did not exult at having to treat a guest in this downright manner, nor did he rub his hands and laugh.

Shopkeeper Ruud came and asked what was happening about the shares?

The lawyer knew no more than Ruud himself had overheard in the smoking-room.

The shopkeeper thought it suspicious that Bertelsen had shilly-shallied about producing the shares. Perhaps he couldn't lay his hands on them.

How?

They might be deposited as security; young Bertelsen might have raised money on them.

The lawyer hoped it hadn't come to that with the firm of Bertelsen & Son.

Such a man was the lawyer, easy and good-natured, a conciliatory soul. He preferred to see the guests in his boarding-house at unity and not crawling over each other's corpses.

Nor was shopkeeper Ruud specially keen on getting possession of those shares. Ruud was not such a bad type of man, he was no criminal, no devil, oh, far from it. He walked with his eyes on the floor and if he saw a pin lying on the carpet he placed it conspicuously on the table in front of its owner. He was a man with a neatly trimmed grey beard, wore a freemason's ring on his finger, and was sufficiently well off to be honest. What did he want with the shares? For one thing his worldly fortune enabled him to slap his breast pocket a little when occasion arose, to take down the insolence of young Bertelsen, who would not acknowledge him or nod to him though he was so worthy of respect. On the other hand he had nothing but good wishes for his father, for old Bertelsen, who had once come to Ruud to ask a little favour and had been granted it.

Such a man was shopkeeper Ruud.

But Lawyer Rupprecht was cock of the walk, his kindness won all hearts. He got up a little gathering with eatables and drinkables in the drawing-room and invited everyone who passed to come in and sit down. It was Christmas and holiday time, he said; no cause for moping. He got the music-mistress to play the "Torahus March" and afterwards he proposed the health of the absent pianist; he had once been connected with this place and he played like a god, but he was tormented by a longing to go abroad—a thing the lawyer had always respected, but unfortunately without having it in his power to gratify. Then appeared the man who had both the means and the open mind, and thus the young artist was saved, transported far away over land and sea. For this great and good deed the lawyer would raise his glass in honour of Herr Bertelsen!

Everyone stood up, bowed, and drank.

Now, what was Lawyer Rupprecht's idea in hitting upon this?

Nothing, he meant no harm, he wanted to give Bertelsen a moment's pleasure, a gleam of festivity. It was Christmas and holiday time and Bertelsen was a guest, moreover he had been taken down.

On the same day the lawyer found occasion to pay some attention to Fröken d'Espard: "It's a pity you want to leave us, Fröken. You are one of the first batch and we have all become much attached to you."

The lady smiled.

"But I suppose there's no help for it, you're going, it's settled?"

"Yes."

"Otherwise I would have made you a proposal: you were saying that it's too expensive for you in the long run, but the sanatorium might remedy this if you wished."

"Thank you, but I think I must—as you say, it's settled—"

"Ah yes," said the lawyer, with a smile; "young people will fly. But you'll be welcome back to the nest any time!"

He went about talking to all the visitors, made his rounds, looked into stables and cow-house, talked to the staff. Here again the lawyer was easy and pleasant to deal with. There came, for instance, Manager Svendsen with a positively comic question on his mind: what else could it be called, when he came and asked to be given the title of—Director?

"Director?" queried the lawyer. And he gave Manager Svendsen a look, but remembered at that moment that it was Christmas and holiday time and the old sailor's head might be a little confused.

"You see," said Svendsen, "they come here and ask if I'm the director. No, I answer them. Well, where is the director? they ask. And then I'm stumped."

"I see," said the lawyer and thought it over. "But what do people want the director for?"

"I don't know. But now the thing is that the porter, he's full director of the cow-house, and the postman, he's got gold braid on his cap."

"Yes, you're quite right. But I don't know—no, I don't think you

CHAPTER THE LAST

ought to be a director, Svendsen. I don't think so. But you know that anyhow you're the man who can talk English and who's been all over the world and you come next after the doctor here."

"Well, I only wanted to ask," said Svendsen curtly, making as though to go. Perhaps he was a little offended.

But as the lawyer did not want to hurt him he went so far as to add: "You see, Svendsen, you're the one who's manager of the whole place and it's a man like that the visitors want. If you were made director, where should we find a capable manager? Have you thought of that?"

Such a man was the lawyer.

He came to terms with Fru Ruben. It was all settled, she agreed to be interviewed and was refunded the money she had spent on Mylady. And really the interview was very correct and delicately put, with only a hint or two about the Torahus water and its marvellous reducing properties; there were no bold assertions, only a few quiet words in the course of conversation with a journalist, with the press. All was in order, Fru Ruben was satisfied, Bertelsen was satisfied, the lawyer showed no dissatisfaction. Oh, his amiability as proprietor and host was a godsend. Nor did he scold the Suicide on his return for the scare he had given the sanatorium by his disappearance; no, Lawyer Rupprecht was friendly, with a smile in his eyes, and told him to go in and get something to eat at once: "How long have you been on the journey? From this morning? And walked all the way from the station? I'll give orders for some hot food for you this moment!"

So now the Suicide had turned up again. He had completely disappeared a few days ago, that could not be denied, but now he came back on the last day of the old year to begin a new year in the mountains tomorrow. He was silent and dejected, he hid himself from the others, turned his back to escape their greetings; he somehow seemed ashamed of himself. It was a long time since he had been so dismal, it reminded them of his first appearance at the sanatorium, when he brooded dolefully and contemplated suicide. As though wishing to put himself straight and show a certain dignity in his downfall, he went at once to his room and shaved, and placed a reddish aster, which looked as if it had spent some time in his pocket, into his buttonhole, where its death agonies were prolonged. Then he went down to his meal. He apologized to the maid for coming at an irregular time.

His meal was not a long one and he might have made it even shorter if the doctor had not come and sat down opposite him. The doctor did not abuse him any more than the lawyer, it was not his way; he tried on the contrary to be entertaining, telling him that now the electric light was to be installed in the sanatorium.

"Oh," said the Suicide.

An ocean of light, a conflagration. They would be able to sit up on the Peak and read their letters by it.

"Yes," said the Suicide.

"Oh, Herr Magnus, I'm sure it interests you more than you care to admit!"

"It does not interest me."

"And this evening we shall be able to welcome the New Year with a 'Torahus March,'" said the doctor, continuing his catalogue.

Silence.

"Do you know that by the summer we shall have to build? Isn't that well done? We've already burst the walls of this new place and have to extend it. We're not only fitting up the unfinished rooms, we have to build. It was found in the autumn that we haven't room enough."

Silence.

"Did you notice that we've got a flag?"

"Yes."

"Altogether, we're getting on, we shall be the leading sanatorium. We're going to widen the road to the station and make it a motor road. We shall attract the big business men, people with their own horses and servants, rich people, the sort that reserve a suite of rooms in advance."

"You're arranging to live a long time, I see," said the Suicide gloomily.

The doctor was scarcely prepared for so obtrusive an utterance; he repeated, "Live a long time? Well, what else can I do? But for that matter—whether we live a long or a short time, we must make what we can out of life."

"Who said so?"

"I say so myself. Our work is not thrown away. When we die others will come after us."

"Who will die in their turn, yes."

"Quite right, who will die in their turn. That is the way of it."

"But what is the whole thing for?"

"It's the system, it's life, it's the way things are."

"No, the whole thing's death," said the Suicide.

The doctor agreed to this too, so as not to irritate the man in his distress, but he smiled and hum'd and ha'd as though he really knew a great deal better.

"Where is it to end?" the Suicide went on. "When is it to end? Why doesn't this eternal destruction ever stop? For it's not getting any better. Then what's the meaning of it? Continuity of ferocity?"

He had finished his meal and was going, but the doctor detained him. The resulting conversation might have been shorter if the doctor had not answered now and then. "Your trip has done you no good," he said.

"What do you know about that?"

"I infer it as a physician."

"Physician!" sneered the Suicide. "How are their digestions here in the hospital?"

"You have come back much more poorly than you went away. You'd have done much better to stay with us."

"Have you a good sale for salts?"

"Look here," said the doctor, "you must really be like the rest of us, Herr Magnus, healthy as we are, happy as we are. There's no use at all in moping. Take a glass and pull yourself up again! Why, you were getting so fit and spry lately, what is it you've come up against since you went away?"

"Life," said the Suicide. "What you call life."

"Life!" repeated the doctor. "Let life pass for what it is. Life is rich, splendid, we ought to rejoice in life and let the evil thereof be sufficient unto the day."

"And so on. I've heard that a few times before. Have you ever pulled up and considered for a moment? You may have seen the terror and the ruin of it in another, in his face, in his eyes, but have you had them in your own bosom? Have you stood in the midst of a lake and cried out?"

"I haven't even had the time, I have work to do, I'm active in my own line—"

"Yes, we're all active, each in his own line, you in yours, I in mine; God, how active we are! But it leads us all sooner or later to certain death. The only one who doesn't remember this is the happy fool. He believes himself superior for forgetting it."

"But what does it lead to if we remember it?"

"To death."

"And if we forget it?"

"To death."

"Well, then—?"

"So the result is that one man has an additional foolish happiness—which another man doesn't envy him."

The doctor considered for a moment and said: "He has the happiness of enduring life. That is not so foolish."

The Suicide ignored him: "The system, you said just now. When have you seen that 'the system' stimulated and encouraged us if we were trying to do good? No, at best this same 'system' was precisely as it always is, blind, implacable, and impassive."

"Well but, good Lord—!" the doctor began, but stopped short.

"Physician, you said. You build, you extend the hospital, why? Here we come from the east and from the west, some of us from great distances, we are full of prayers and supplications, we are all in search of healing, but none of us is helped, Death overtakes us all."

At this the doctor could not resist smiling and saying in his airy way: "That sounded almost like a text from the Bible—the east and the west—"

And instantly the Suicide bristled up and was again very downright: "Has the physician put up many fresh notices since I've been away? Visitors are requested to walk as noiselessly as possible after ten p.m. so as not to disturb the bedridden victims of Life! Visitors are requested to be careful of fire and to extinguish lamps and candles so as not to burn alive the half-dead!"

"Ha ha ha!" laughed the doctor rather insincerely. "But now listen to what this same physician is going to do: he's going down to the ice at the hour of midnight to try a new pair of skates. That's what he's going to do. He thinks he can't inaugurate the new year in a happier and more healthy way. You ought to come too! There'll be a little moonlight."

"There's a notice in the hall saying that I ought to be in bed by ten o'clock."

"The physician will give you a dispensation on New Year's eve."

The Suicide went to his room, lay down, and slept or pretended to sleep till the supper bell summoned him to the festive board. Then he dressed in all haste and went down.

There was a full house, all dressed in their best; the Suicide had his aster in his buttonhole, rather the worse for wear.

At supper the doctor again made a speech, that untiring man thanked all those present for a good old year and wished each and all a still better new one! There was nothing else to say, those were the right words and nobody could say them better than Doctor Oyen. He had luck with him. As of course he was bound to show off a little and be funny, he remarked in conclusion, to the amusement of the visitors, that the director, Herr Rupprecht, would undoubtedly have made a better speech, one need only look at his hands to see what rotund and comfortable words he would have poured out over them. But they were to lose all that, for the doctor thought more of the visitors than of the director's vanity; now they would have the music, the "Torahus March" and other items, and finally the distribution of New Year's cards, of which there was a whole pile he said.

They assembled in the drawing-room for coffee and cakes, the music-mistress played, and all joined in singing the New Year hymn. Then the mail was brought in.

Oh, it was not a very big mail, but it was none the less welcome for that; cordial little messages from the outside world, a bundle of cards and letters which the matron had collected and now dealt out. The doctor got a couple of cards, shopkeeper Ruud a letter, Fru Ruben five cards, Fröken d'Espard nothing. "Herr Magnus!" called the matron. Everyone looked up. The Suicide came forward. A card. He looked at it inquisitively as it was handed to him, then examined the edge, to see if there weren't two, and retired with a frown to a corner, where he sat down. The rest of the cards were for the servants, several for each of the maids, some of them belated Christmas greetings from America. And then the matron was left with empty hands.

There was much chatting, followed by more music, after which the visiting engineer recited poetry. He did it well and was asked for more and again more; he recited till he was empty and had to take

CHAPTER THE LAST

to card tricks instead. They were surprised he had not gone on the stage, and he replied that he had thought of doing so, but—Silence. "Ah, but a capable engineer is not to be despised!" said Lawyer Rupprecht, smoothing it over.

Finally they all went to their rooms.

It might be ten o'clock, a respectable bedtime. Fröken d'Espard went out with the Suicide. "We did the same on Christmas eve," she said, making a little conversation to cure his depression.

It was about half-moon, but the sky was overcast and there was little light; they went no farther than the first seat and sat down there. Perhaps she was rather curious to hear about his trip, where he had been and how it had gone with him, but he spoke of other things, of the enlarging of the sanatorium, of Rector Oliver, whom he still despised, and of Fröken d'Espard herself. He appeared to take a great interest in her, though he did not question her closely; she was a companion in suffering, there was evidently something wrong with her, with her too. When she told him of her own accord that she was going to move over to Daniel's sæter, he nodded and showed satisfaction: she might have done worse, he opined.

"No, the sanatorium's too dear for me in the long run," she said. "I shall have the whole of Daniel's new cottage to myself."

"You're right, it is dear. I too had thoughts of giving up this place and going somewhere else, but—"

"But it didn't come off?"

"No. My whole trip was in vain."

Silence.

"But," she began, "the next trip may lead to something, mayn't it? I don't know, but aren't you taking too gloomy a view of—well, of yourself and everything?"

He surprised her by suddenly becoming communicative. No one could draw him out as she could; her sympathy, her appeal, the little bent head listening, made him candid: "What I really thought of was to go home and fire a shot or two. That was what I intended. But as I stood outside the window I changed my mind."

"I see," she said, but could find no other answer.

"Then I bought some asters, but of course I didn't send them either."

"I don't know," she replied cautiously; "but perhaps you ought to have sent them."

"No. One hasn't the heart to do anything, either good or evil."

"I noticed that you got a New Year's greeting."

"Yes," he said.

"There, you see! So no doubt it was an answer to your Christmas card?"

Silence.

"It began a year ago. Or—I don't remember, but about a year. At first I didn't believe it. It seems pretty mean to believe a thing of that sort, and for six months I wouldn't believe it," said the Suicide. And now he seemed to want to explain the whole story, to make a clean breast of it, but he was only partly successful; his opening was a long, disconnected rigmarole, he wanted to make a confession, but was too much overcome and talked in scraps—the lady could not help yawning. What did he say? He made a habit of keeping out of their way, he said, of letting them have the field to themselves, he said. False tactics, he had discovered. He went home and took to his bed instead of obtruding himself. What did he achieve by that? To go home and take to one's bed is not the easiest thing in the world; he changed his mind and went after them, but for the sake of appearances he could not trot and so lost sight of them: At home he hung a map of the world on the wall and lay in bed looking at it; he concocted various mathematical problems and tried to solve them; he read books, counted up the pattern of the carpet. One evening he was told that the little one was ill. . . . The Suicide reflected for a moment and asked: "How long did I say it was since it began?"

CHAPTER THE LAST

"A year," answered Fröken d'Espard.

"I meant two years. It's no use disguising it, there was a child. Well, then, they come and tell me the little one is ill. What had that to do with me? I go in and look at her, had scarcely seen her before—a tiny little girl, six months. Gripes and screaming, nothing more. 'Hot flannels on her stomach!' said I. There she lay, a little face, little hands, a charming little work of art, touching, I'm ashamed to say; but what had she to do with me? And in fact I must tell you it was over two years since it began; it's no use disguising that any longer. 'Take two flannels and put some oil on them,' I say; 'warm one of them while the other is on.' We keep on at this and it succeeds, she quiets down, with only a spasm now and then, and at last she falls asleep. It was as though I saw her for the first time and I stood there awhile; in some way or other she got hold of my hand and held fast to a finger; ridiculous, after all I had nothing to do with her. She's not been christened, I say to myself, and what name can you give to a creature like that? It was now so still that I chanced to hear some sounds from the next room, a whispering, a glass that was knocked over and smashed. I looked at the nurse and she looked at me—no, they weren't the nurse's guests. 'Now you'll know what to do another time,' I say to her; 'hot flannels and oil, then it'll pass off.' I went back to my room, but I was no longer in doubt that I had been called in to the child in order to be put up to a very different matter. I lay for a little while, reading and thinking, put out the lamp and thought again. I had not grown listless and blunted in those six months; on the contrary, I was tense and excitable, quick to clench my fists. Then I heard a crash at the back of the house. The nurse appeared again. 'Something's happened,' she said in a scared voice; 'somebody fell, it's in the backstairs.' I had a pocket torch by my bedside to see the time by at night; I snatched up this torch and went out. Just so, he was not dead and not stunned either, but he was limp as a rag, he was drunk. I turned the light on him and saw the state he was in; he could do nothing, he lay on the floor smiling at me. 'Out with you!' I said, found his hat for him and helped him through the door. When I came up again, somebody was sitting in my room in the dark; I heard her mumbling something or other, there was no light and I switched it on. Exactly as I thought—she was unsteady too, not excessively so, but rather fuddled and maudlin; she smelt of wine. What did she want? Why—to excuse herself! She had heard the child crying plainly enough, but she didn't dare come in, her head was so muddled, she had had too much. It should never occur again, never. But I mustn't get any ideas into my head, I mustn't on any account believe the worst; when he wanted to, she had answered: "No, go away with you, I can see who you are, I know you and you're not my husband!' She sat there and told me this; she was fully dressed, while I was only in my dressing-gown, and she actually asked me to go back to bed and not catch cold. Time after time she declared that none of this should happen anymore, good God, no! What was I to say to all this? Nothing was incredible, I could only fume and blaze and she could only excuse herself and beg for mercy. Of course it ended as so many times before; she stayed with me, and in the morning it was all forgotten."

"Ah, that was wrong, that was wrong!" said Fröken d'Espard, as though it had happened to herself.

"Now, don't misunderstand me," the Suicide cautioned her; "there was no malice in the case. Malice? Not by any means. People always take a wrong view of these things and that's so stupid. It was not for the sake of hurting me that she went wrong; she simply yielded, it was more tempting to yield than to resist. Another thing was that he was an old friend of hers, not a drunkard at all or anything particularly bad, simply a big, good-looking man, but not very intelligent. No doubt they were to have married, only I got in the way, I was better off and could offer a home. Did I know about this? Of course I knew about it, I forced myself on her; one does that sort of thing, one is only human. Put all that together, if you please. But they had no reason for causing me pain, nor did that occur to them. If I had been out of the way it would have been so much better, but there I was and I myself was without malice. Take all that into consideration. But now, on the other hand, put yourself in my place: could I go any farther, hadn't I waited six months, refusing to believe it? What would have happened that evening if the child hadn't cried and disturbed them? Everything was arranged; could not they have come to a tacit agreement? This thought—this suspicion—soon leads one to the child. I began by talking of a year, but I couldn't keep that up, I couldn't disguise the fact that it was two years since it began and more than two years; so it began early, very early—and then what had the child to do with me? A question far more serious than any other."

The Suicide paused.

Fröken d'Espard tried to comfort him: "No, you mustn't believe it. It's not done so early, I'm sure of that."

"You don't say so?" he asked with interest.

"It takes not one, but two or three years for such a thing to happen; it only happens when perhaps people have got sick and tired of each other—I mean, of themselves, sick and tired of themselves. Haven't you asked her?"

"No. Only hinted. What kind of truth could I expect from that quarter? Well, but let's follow it up: what happens then?"

"How?"

"No, you won't go into it. You treat it as a familiar, everyday affair and don't think it worth discussing."

"How it happens, do you mean? I don't understand you. One is human, as you say; one gets tired of oneself and throws oneself away. That is liable to happen, isn't it?"

"Precisely my own opinion. But how does it take place? The positions? Do they struggle a little? Is it in the dark?"

Fröken d'Espard tried to see his face in the dark. She said nothing. She could not believe her ears.

Then he gave it up and asked no more.

The lady gathered her cloak about her; he dropped into an attitude of collapse to mark his wretchedness if she abandoned him. He spoke with his chin in his chest: "Well, I don't get anything out of her, though I chase her from room to room and question her."

"I really wouldn't do that in your place—chase her."

"No. She says too that I'm just mad. But it was my way of going to work that was mad, I was too easily satisfied. I was more stupid than all the beasts of the field. After the six months of disbelief came all the months of belief, one day I was forced to believe it. Thought I was anyway. I kept awake more, there were weeks when I only slept while we were both sitting in the same room; I followed them, found them out and could prove it! Thought I could. Once? What is once! I don't make an ass of myself for so little. Many times, I tell him!" cried the Suicide, suddenly flaring up; "every time I cared to follow them! They didn't feel the shamefulness of it, the infamy of it, they looked me in the face as they came out of cafés and theatres. I thought: as they treat this so much as a matter of course, it must seem right and proper to them, otherwise I don't understand it! Exactly as I thought—she told me right out that it was this man and nobody else, that it always had been him and that I had parted them! My tactics were wrong again: I replied. Actually replied, stood there and defended myself! I said that if she had opened her heart to me in time I should have left her in peace! This in itself was no lie, but I ought just to have held my tongue. It made the game too easy for her: she replied that she had given me to understand all the time how it was with her, but I would not or could not hear! I'm sure this wasn't a lie either, it was very credible. So there I was."

"Had you no thoughts of divorce?"

"No doubt we had, the idea occurred to us vaguely now and

then. I for my part did not think much about it, but perhaps she was braver, I don't know, I heard nothing. When I thought of it I only came to the conclusion that divorce does not by any means solve the problem, it merely unties a knot. What did she want with divorce? She could get on without it, and she said nothing. I myself hadn't enough courage and manliness to demand it. One is contemptible, one is human. I imagine that she leaves me, taking everything belonging to her; so that there isn't even a little blouse left hanging on the wall. I open the drawers, they are empty; I look at the dressing-table, there isn't a veil or a pair of gloves lying there. If I buy another little diamond ring and leave it there it will not be fetched. No; no divorce! There wouldn't even be a scent left in there, not even a little breath or a dropped word—no, a bare, deserted room. Would that be better than now? Besides, in my abasement I was not excluded from her, her door was by no means barred against me, the ring moved her to tears and embraces—I ought to have sunk into the ground, but I feasted on the moment and wept myself. One is contemptible. Afterwards we both went to look at the child. The next day everything was forgotten."

Fröken d'Espard shook her head.

"Everything was forgotten. It might have been different, all might have been well."

"Ah, dear me; yes," she said sadly; "there are so many things which should have been different!"

"You are right again. It is not impossible that if I myself had been different, had looked differently and behaved better, she might have come back or perhaps never have gone away. There's all that. But put yourself in my place once more; what about me? I existed and there I stood. If my worthlessness was obvious, that of the others was not invisible either, I could point to it and prove it. It has now lasted over two years."

"What will you do?" asked the lady, almost in a whisper.

"Nothing," he replied; "I am no use either for good or evil. I went in to Christiania to settle it and make an end of it once for all, but gave it up. At any rate it's a warm little house for the child, I thought, it gets the sun all the forenoon. Not that I met anyone or went in, but there were lights in the windows in the evening, only my own room was dark, they respect my having locked it up. There was no noise going on, no dancing or shouting."

"No, that would be a little too much!"

"I appreciate it, I don't ask for much now. I'm grateful too that she doesn't open my room and use it; by not doing so she makes me a little less homeless, I have that room in town."

"It's horribly uncomfortable for you," she said with feeling.

It seemed to dawn on him that he had been talking a long time and must have shown too much emotion; he changed his tone all at once and rose to his feet. "It's late, I'm sure you're cold; excuse 1 me for forgetting myself like this!"

"You have nothing to apologize for."

"Thank you. Oh, but my story can't have any interest for you. For that matter, my lot is not so bad as a good many other people's; I'm not the worst off, I have many happy days."

"I hope so!"

"Come along, Fröken, it's late!"

As they went in she repeated: "Yes! I sincerely hope so. That you have many happy days, I mean. And, dear me, everything may come right perhaps, don't you think?"

"Oh no. Well, you never can tell."

"You had a card—"

"Yes, I had a card. Who do you think it was from? Moss?"

"No, perhaps not from Moss. Perhaps it was much better than that!"

"It was from myself," said the Suicide.

In the light of the hall lamp she saw his care-worn face; she kept her eyes on him. He took the card out of his pocket and showed it to her: the Castle of Akershus, with "Happy New Year" and his own initials underneath. He stood there with quivering lips.

"I bought it when I was in town," he said. "I knew well enough there would be no other card for me and that didn't worry me. It was not for my own sake I sent it, I don't care about such things; it was for the other visitors, to let them see that I got it. Well, now you must go to bed, Fröken; good-night!" He turned hastily and went out again into the winter night. . . .

In the morning the place hummed with a report, an obscure and ominous report. It began early, when the maid took in the doctor's coffee; she came out again flabbergasted and announced it to the other maids, from them it reached some of the boarders, Lawyer Rupprecht got up instantly and started on a round of the sanatorium. What had happened? Something uncanny and mysterious, and that on New Year's Day.

The lawyer came across Manager Svendsen just as he was going to hoist the flag and stopped him, saying: "Wait now, don't hoist the flag just yet! Have you seen the doctor?"

No, the manager hadn't seen the doctor this morning. "There's a lamp still burning in the office, isn't he there?"

"No. But let's have another look."

The doctor was not there.

From the office they went to the doctor's bedroom; he wasn't there either. So God knew where he was. And New Year's Day and all.

Several of the boarders had hurriedly dressed and now took part in the search. It leaked out that the doctor had intended to try a new pair of skates on the tarn the night before; some of the men ran off to the rink to investigate. They met a lady; it was Fröken Ellingsen, who had forestalled them and was already on her way back from the ice; she carried a stake in her hand. They asked her if she had seen the doctor, but she had not; she shook her head with a mournful air and said: "But I have found out something: there are several holes in the ice, fishing holes, one of them is open now."

"Well—what do you mean—?"

"Open," she nodded. "It happened last night."

"Is it possible that he's— What do you say?"

They ran on to see the open hole, and Fröken Ellingsen pursued her way homewards. She was very thoughtful; oh yes, Fröken Ellingsen was deeply preoccupied, this open hole in the ice was a ready-made English "short story," a nocturnal tragedy, she knew what she knew!

She collected several of the visitors about her, since she came from the fatal spot and had the latest news; her voice was hushed and very effective, she induced her hearers to fear the worst. "If only there hasn't been an accident!" said the lawyer. "The hole is open, you say?"

"Open. The ice that had formed over it was broken during the night. The edges are not yet joined."

"It's these fishing holes of Daniel's," said the manager.

"Wasn't there moonlight last night?" asked someone.

"No," said the manager. "And what did he want to go on the ice in the dark for? Which of the holes was it, Fröken?"

"The one nearest the stream. By the outlet."

"Just where the ice was weakest. We had put a post to warn people."

"Here's your post," said Fröken Ellingsen. "It was lying on the ice and I brought it with me."

"Why?" asked Bertelsen.

She answered him—him and no one else, and perhaps all her talk was intended simply to get him to listen: "It may be necessary to have it examined."

CHAPTER THE LAST

"The pole?" queried Bertelsen in extreme astonishment.

"Well, don't let's stand here talking any longer," interrupted the lawyer. "Take your men with you, Svendsen, and break up the ice. Good God, if there's been an accident!"

"I should like to have a few words with you in your room," Fröken Ellingsen said to him. "Perhaps you will be kind enough to come too, Bertelsen."

The young lady had something on her mind, there was no doubt of that, she had an unusually preoccupied look. The lawyer led the way to his room. "Please take a seat, Fröken. You wished to tell me something?"

Fröken Ellingsen had her say, she gave a more detailed account of her discoveries, talked till a flush came into her cheeks. Bertelsen, who was used to her precious stories, tried to appear indifferent, but gave it up in the face of her profound earnestness: "It is established that the sky was overcast and there was no moonlight; I myself have examined the hole, it is big enough to swallow up a man who came sweeping towards it on skates. But I don't say on that account that an accident has happened."

"No, no. But what do you say?" asked Bertelsen impatiently.

She turned to him: "You asked why I brought this stick with me. I brought it because perhaps it ought to be chemically examined. There is something resembling blood on it."

"Blood?" said the men.

They were shown some reddish spots on the bark and did not know what to believe. Yes, it was undoubtedly blood, but Bertelsen asked: "Well, but what if it is blood?"

"Then the stake may have been used as a weapon."

"An assault, you think?" guessed the lawyer. "No, that's not likely!"

The lady was silent. There was no trace of a pose in her, she was wrestling with a problem, making the most of it; they could see that she was busy with her thoughts.

"Who in the world should attack the doctor? The kindest man in the place, everybody's friend."

"Someone or other might have done it."

The lawyer asked: "Are you thinking of anyone in particular?"

"Yes," she replied, "I am thinking of someone in particular."

"Whom?"

"I am disinclined to mention names in the present state of the case. But if it is to go no farther—"

"Of course not!" exclaimed both men, listening intently.

Fröken Ellingsen, in a deep, calm voice: "I do not say it is he, but I am thinking of the man we call the Suicide. I have my reasons for indicating him."

Silence. Her earnestness had its effect, the men looked at her and weighed her words.

"Why should he do it?" asked Bertelsen.

"An insane person—if he is insane—is capable of all sorts of things."

"Yes," said the lawyer; "I must agree with you there, Fröken. You mentioned that you had reasons for indicating him?"

"There is circumstantial evidence," she replied. "I heard him talking to Fröken d'Espard down in the hall last night. It was past twelve o'clock. When they had said good-night to each other Fröken d'Espard came upstairs alone. The Suicide went out again."

"What were they talking about?"

"Oh, that doesn't give us any hint. It was about a postcard or something of the sort. But the Suicide went out again into the night."

"Yes," said the men; "there's no denying it sounds rather queer. And you're quite positive about it?"

The lady merely gave a nod. "However," she said, "the strongest piece of evidence is still to come: I have just returned from the skating-rink. What does that imply? It implies that I was before anyone else, I was the first on the road and the first on the spot. There I found—I found—"

"What did you find?"

"This!" she said, almost in a whisper, holding up the Suicide's aster.

Nobody spoke, the men were too busy with their thoughts. After waiting awhile Fröken Ellingsen said: "I suppose you recognize it? You remember whose buttonhole it adorned yesterday evening?"

Yes, they remembered.

"I found it on the ice, a little way from the hole. It was dropped last night."

The men both agreed that they had seen this miserable aster in the Suicide's buttonhole; Bertelsen remembered in particular the moment when the Suicide came forward into the lamplight to receive a card from the matron; he had then had a clear view of this withered flower.

"There can be no difference of opinion as to its being the same aster," said the lawyer. "So far all is clear. I must really express my admiration for you, Fröken Ellingsen, for your ability in following up the clues—your perspicacity—"

"She?" exclaimed Bertelsen, going one better. "I assure you, she's a regular detective. Give her a scrap of thread or a spat-out cigarette butt and she'll trace out a whole crime."

Fröken Ellingsen swelled with pride, an appreciation from that quarter was almost more than she could bear; she leaned forward to conceal her emotion. "In any case," she said, plunging again into the story, "in any case the Suicide must have been the last who saw the doctor. He must be able to give some information."

The tension showed signs of wearing off as the discussion proceeded; an assault appeared so unlikely, so impossible, to the two men. But one could never tell, and it seemed certain that there was blood on the stake. Fröken Ellingsen was asked to approach the Suicide subtly—a task, said the lawyer, which could not be placed in better hands. But even when the meeting was at an end and they separated, the lawyer could not abandon all hope of finding his partner; he gave orders to a maid whom he met in the passage to look once more in the doctor's room, though he himself had searched it several times. "Look under the bed too," he said.

The lawyer himself went down to the ice.

Fröken Ellingsen's interview with the Suicide led to nothing, he had not seen the doctor. He had been out last night, he told her, till long after midnight, it might have been two o'clock when he came in; he had been down on the ice too, as the doctor had asked him, but he must have come too late, the doctor had left the rink.

"Did you see a stake down there by the outlet?" she asked.

"A stake? No. Why do you ask that?"

"It looks as if it had blood on it."

"Oh," said the Suicide, without interest. "All the same I can't see the doctor making away with himself. He's a scatter-brain."

"I found that flower you had in your buttonhole yesterday—I found it on the ice this morning."

"Oh," said the Suicide again. "Well, it wasn't anything to keep, it was done for."

No, there was really nothing to be dragged out of the Suicide; that is to say, he told his whole story without making any mystery of it. Finally he paid no particular attention to what the lady said, merely repeating once or twice that no doubt the doctor would turn up again.

Dinner-time came, the boarders assembled, but they ate in silence. A long, depressing New Year's Day, without flag, without music, laughter, or rejoicing, perhaps a heavy financial loss for the sanatorium. In the course of the afternoon things looked a trifle brighter, Manager Svendsen and his men had broken up the ice from the fishing hole as far as the outlet of the stream, but had found no corpse. So the doctor was not in the tarn. This discovery must have delighted everyone in the place, it surely delighted Fröken Ellingsen too, but she had taken refuge in her room, where she lay on her bed and wept. Oh, that big, good-looking Fröken Ellingsen with her jejune detective stories and her strained imagination, she could not put up with a loss now, it would have been such a blessing for her to have triumphed this time; she was not stupid, she saw well enough how the wind blew: her fate was shortly to be decided. Where was Bertelsen sitting at this moment, entertaining another lady for all he was worth? Why was this so? If her evidence had held good she might have had a hope, but the evidence seemed to miss fire. For the Suicide made no secret of his nocturnal ramble, the dropped aster meant nothing to him, and when Lawyer Rupprecht returned from the rink he said to her: "It must be fishes' blood on your stake, there's a lot of blood round the hole where Daniel has been cutting up fish." And to that Fröken Ellingsen had only been able to reply that yes, possibly it was only fishes' blood, that could be decided by analysis if necessary. No, she was surely beaten; that was why she now lay weeping and did not show herself at the dinner-table.

But although it was pretty certain that the doctor was not drowned, they had not succeeded in finding him, and where could he be? They were just making arrangements for a search-party when the sanatorium experienced a great sensation: a bell rang from an out-of-the-way room, a tiny little hole which was unoccupied and had no stove, it had no proper bed either, but only a camp-bed with a canvas bottom; that was where the ring came from. When the maid went there to solve the mystery she found him, found the doctor, Doctor Oyen. "What—?" she screamed. "Be quiet!" he said from the camp-bed; "go and fetch the lawyer!" The maid went, but she had the impression that the doctor had gone mad, his eyes were bloodshot.

The lawyer raised both arms to heaven as he came in and was

about to put some necessary questions, but checked himself; the doctor did not look as if he could give an account of himself. "Are you lying here?" was all the lawyer said, and the doctor replied: "I must be moved!" He lay there shivering with his overcoat spread over him, he was ill. There were pools of water on the floor from his drenched clothes and boots, a pair of skates had been flung down, there was no fire, no stove even, the light struggled in through a dirty, curtainless window, all was dismal and miserable, and there he lay. "The porter's a strong man, he can carry me," he said. "We'll carry you in the bed," said the lawyer. "No," replied the other, "then everybody will see me. The porter can carry me by the backstairs."

Very well, he was carried, first to his dispensary, where he gave himself a dose, then to his bedroom. That meant two journeys across the yard, but the porter carried him. A fire was lighted in his stove, he was given warm bedclothes, warm bottles, and warm drinks; he was feeling better, he said.

The lawyer questioned him forbearingly, trying to arrive at an explanation; It was a rather disconnected one, but it proved sure enough that the doctor was a scatter-brain. Of course he had run right into the fishing hole, but instead of dashing off home without delay and putting himself properly to bed in his own warm room, he tried to hide himself in that little cell of a place, not wishing to have it known that he had been in the water. The feather-brained soul, he didn't want to scare the visitors; perhaps at the same time he was trying to prove to himself that he—the physician—could take a ducking on a winter's night without its doing him the slightest harm. In this he was mistaken, he could not stand it. When the lawyer hinted that there had been uneasiness in the sanatorium the doctor was much upset. "What did the visitors say?" he asked; "did they laugh?" He had made for the little empty room on purpose not to be found, he explained, and of course he had intended to get up early that morning when the water had run out of his clothes and go to his own room, but he had not been able to, he was poorly, very poorly—

Altogether he seemed to think himself disgraced by the accident of the night before.

"I can't make it out at all!" the lawyer confessed at last with a shake of the head.

"It all came from its being so dark and no moon," said the doctor.

That was undoubtedly his genuine belief. But more probably it all came from his never having learnt this unusual situation, which he therefore did not know how to deal with. He had studied away his personality in medicine, there was nothing much left of him, he thought no doubt his idea was a good one. A boy, a child that had passed examinations. He might have shown a little more form, this man, God help us, he might really have had a spark of existence, have been something, somebody. He had thought out this big baby trick of hiding his silly ducking in an attic. A healthy uninstructed ape would have thought differently.

Now he would go to sleep, he said. But wasn't the room very cold?

The lawyer looked at the thermometer: "It's over seventy. You must have fever."

The doctor: "If it's over seventy it's not cold. Now I'm going to sleep for a bit. I'll get up for supper."

The lawyer was glad that his partner was at any rate comfortably settled; he spread the news wherever he went, with as much explanation as was necessary, and gave orders to hoist the flag. It was already past midday, but after all it was New Year's Day.

Strangely enough it proved difficult to revive people's spirits. There was no longer any reason for pulling a long face, but a certain dismal hush had fallen upon the boarders and they could not shake it off: Somebody came in from outside and said that Svendsen had a bother with the flag; he had got it half up and then it stuck; now he couldn't get it up or down! This episode made the atmosphere of the drawing-room yet more gloomy, it gave a kind of solemn feeling, perhaps it meant something, a flag at half-mast. "Haul it down!" the lawyer shouted from the veranda. "I can't get it down!" the manager yelled back. "Then lower the flagstaff!" This was done, and now the flagstaff was left lying bare and flat upon the snow and was not raised again.

No wonder the lawyer was annoyed. He appealed to Rector Oliver and complained of the way things were going, but Rector Oliver was not to be roused, his vocation was not to comfort and amuse, his vocation was to instruct, and it so happened that he was left without pupils, without listeners; even Fröken d'Espard had deserted him and seemed occupied with her own affairs. Hum and ha, said Rector Oliver. Well, but how in the world did it come about, asked the lawyer, that a palace full of people lay as though spellbound? Had it never happened before that a flag-halyard slipped off the block and stuck fast? What was there mystical about it? It was not very likely that a sign was sent from heaven to tell them that Doctor Oyen had gone and given himself a cold, was it?

"It is entirely unthinkable," said the Rector Oliver.

The lawyer asked the engineer to do something to cheer the visitors. The engineer didn't say no, he had acted before and knew how to do it: he thought of games, he mimicked actors, got some of the young people to join him in blind-man's-buff, and even admitted a knowledge of nigger songs. Indeed, the engineer did not spare himself and especially in the blind-man's-buff he went great lengths, dancing and carrying on with elaborate idiocy and ending in a grand burlesque of lamentation over an imaginary misfortune—all with his eyes blindfolded. The correspondent for three papers said straight out that a great actor had been lost in the engineer and he was going to say as much in his next article. But everyone was not like the correspondent, the other spectators were dull and listless, whatever may have been the matter with them; they wouldn't go skiing or skating either, they just sat there. Nothing happened, nothing was levelled with the ground, no, but a mute horror pervaded the place, as though presaging a misdeed.

It was rumoured that Doctor Oyen was worse and the lawyer telephoned for the doctor from the village, the district physician. It was difficult to telephone without someone's hearing it and perhaps the lawyer was rather incautious: "If only it doesn't turn out to be typhus!" he said. These words were passed on and soon they were all over the house. Several of the visitors thought of breaking off their stay and going home the very next day—a big financial loss to the sanatorium. Shopkeeper Ruud stole upstairs and packed his handbag.

The district physician arrived. Inflammation of the lungs. He ordered drugs and mixtures and went away again. When he came back next day, the patient was worse. On the third day he died.

What a New Year!

Of course the Suicide was not going to let this good opportunity pass without remark, he nodded and opined that they had not seen the end of it yet. "Death is getting life at a cheap figure," he said; "the next one of us is booked already!" For a day or two he went out of his way to diffuse his uncanny pessimism among the boarders, always alluding to himself and the others as "the survivors."

Many of the visitors left, the correspondent, shopkeeper Ruud, the engineer, and the young people of both sexes. They had nothing to stay for, they were in the midst of life and were not interested in seeing Doctor Oyen's coffin arrive, to be packed with a corpse and sent off again by rail. Shopkeeper Ruud made no secret of the fact that he had other things to look after, he could spare no more time away from his business. He said to the lawyer: "And with regard to those shares, I've now ascertained that they've been lodged as security, Bertelsen can't sell them!" "Have they?" replied the lawyer, unwilling to discuss the matter. "But you can redeem the shares from the bank at the figure we mentioned," Ruud went on—"that is, if you keep the sanatorium's fire-policy paid up promptly."

Oh, shopkeeper Ruud had his eyes about him, the lawyer can't have longed to be more closely associated with him. What advantage was there in having this man instead of Bertelsen interfering with the management of the sanatorium? No, thanks. Besides, Bertelsen had now been properly put down, the lawyer did not wish to humiliate him.

Rector Oliver did not leave, nor did Bertelsen and the two ladies, Ruben and Ellingsen; Lawyer Rupprecht himself, the director, could not desert his beloved Torahus before the place was in full swing again, at present he was busy telegraphing and telephoning for a new physician and making his choice among the applicants.

The next one to fall ill was Fru Ruben. Curious that this lady had managed to keep alive at all, she ate nothing, drank nothing, but kept going on scraps of food and pills; she must have had great powers of resistance. What kind of pills were they? Mysterious pills, she got them from London and concealed them carefully after taking each dose. One of the old maids of the sanatorium had seen the very same pill-boxes in "Mylady's" room, so apparently the intimacy between Fru Ruben and the Englishwoman took more than one form.

Poor Fru Ruben, she fell ill and collapsed—whatever may have been the reason, perhaps it was that contrary to habit she had eaten her fill on New Year's eve. She lay there with a good deal of pain and with a strange look in her deep and lovely eyes; she was in a bad way, but she wouldn't hear of the district physician; not at all, she would be up again tomorrow, she said. Oh, but that didn't come off; she kept her bed and was in a bad way, but she wouldn't give up. She had two pairs of pointed-toed boots sent her on approval; they were patent leather with cloth tops and she can't have had much hope of getting her queer splay-feet into them, but they could stand there and look as if they were just her size. They stood there on the dressing-table when the new doctor came.

For now the new doctor came, the sanatorium physician, and it made a little excitement at Torahus. The boarders got a sight of him at the dinner-table; he was short-sighted, very tall and thin; and when he bent over his plate it was as though he was stretching his head over a balcony to look down into the street. He had a pleasant smile and a shrewd and determined air. He was young in the profession, but was not to be made light of; his father had been a doctor before him, he was born in medicine.

When he came into Fru Ruben's room he bowed politely, introduced himself, and said: "Is that the sort of boots you wear here in the mountains?" He caught sight of the pill-box, which betrayed itself under the pillow; he pulled it out, read the label, smelt the pills, and said: "Why are you taking this?"

Fru Ruben would have liked to snatch the box from him; she replied with vexation: "I don't take them—or hardly ever—"

Without ceremony the doctor got up and locked the door, threw back the bedclothes, and said: "Turn over a moment!" When he had finished his examination he asked: "Have you any more of these boxes?"

"I don't know. No, I'm sure I haven't. Why?"

"I'm not a chemist, but I don't think these pills improve your appetite exactly."

"I eat all l can," she replied.

"No doubt. But you ought to eat more, you mustn't take a dislike to food," said the doctor, putting the pill-box in his pocket.

XII

The doctor introduced himself to all the visitors, one after another, and inquired about their complaints. Bertelsen had nothing the matter with him, but he was staying on and asked anxiously after Fru Ruben. The widow and he had come there together, he explained, and he couldn't very well leave again without her. This was said in the hearing of Fröken Ellingsen; she gave him a look, not that that made any impression on Bertelsen, not a scrap. "I thought it was I who came here with you," she said, jesting in deadly earnest.

"And why are you here, Fröken?" asked the doctor.

"There's nothing wrong with me. I'm leaving tomorrow, for that matter."

"Of course I'm not simply staying here to wait for Fru Ruben," Bertelsen then said. "As you know, Fröken, I'm not altogether uninterested in Torahus Sanatorium, I have one or two things to look after here."

Next day Fröken Ellingsen left, alone. She must have grasped the hopelessness of waiting any longer.

"I shall be along by return," said Bertelsen; "I've only to arrange about the new buildings for the spring."

For some reason or other Bertelsen had been allowed to come in that morning to see Fru Ruben; he had sympathized and consoled her and hinted that she did not bear her sufferings alone. The widow had begun to take a little nourishment and was already sleeping better, she could talk cheerfully to Bertelsen and joke and make herself pleasant; they had a good time together. When he came out of her room he was in high spirits. He found Fröken Ellingsen's pocket-handkerchief lying at his feet, snow-white and unused, he picked it up and handed it to her: "Look here what I've found, your handkerchief, with your monogram. It's so white and innocent, it doesn't look as if it had been dropped in my way on purpose."

"What, on purpose—?"

"My little joke, Fröken! Well, you're ready to start. Let me see you into the sledge. Give my regards to town!"

She was so helpless, perhaps she had really dropped her handkerchief outside Fru Ruben's door on purpose, not being able to think of anything better when she heard Bertelsen's voice in there. Naturally it cost her an effort to take such a decisive leave of Bertelsen today, once for all; on the other hand, what possibility was there of its ever coming to anything? Was she not aware of his boredom, his indifference? And so this episode of her life had ended just as abruptly and jejunely as her detective stories. Fröken Ellingsen was a big, good-looking woman and she just missed being something; she had feeling and imagination, but made no profit of either: her feeling she frittered away like a fool, and her imagination she took out in fictions and delusions. She could not keep a hold of Bertelsen and at the last she had to give him up. What else was there for her to do? She would have bored the life out of him, a little bit every day and a little bit every night....

In the course of his rounds the doctor arrived at the Suicide. Perhaps he had been given some information about this eccentric and shaped his conduct accordingly; perhaps too he had heard something of his story in Christiania, God knows.

The Suicide met him with his most insolent air, saying: "Well, I suppose you've come here to choose a site for a burial-ground?"

The doctor said: "Hard winter. You're the only one who wears sensible clothes, I see."

"It must cost a good deal to send off the corpses from here," the

Suicide went on. "I can show you a place where we survivors can be put into the ground."

"If you have time I'd like to see the place at once,'" said the doctor.

They went there and then. But the Suicide was evidently not prepared to be taken at his word, he was uncertain of the direction, dodged this way and that, came to a halt in the forest, and said: "You know, it's all bosh your following me about. Let's go back!" The Suicide was offended and went on: "Assumed determination on your part, that's all it was!"

The doctor looked at him and let him talk.

"I see, you're looking at me and making an examination of me. Let's go home, I said!"

On the way home the doctor asked: "How long have you been here?"

"From the dawn of creation. From the day the sanatorium opened."

"And what are you waiting for such a long time in the mountains?"

"I'm not waiting a long time, it's quite untrue to say I'm waiting here a long time. What do you want here yourself?"

Silence.

The Suicide went on: "I didn't ask for the sake of being disagreeable, but to raise the question. Death works faultlessly here without your assistance."

"What makes you keep blowing on that hand of yours?"

"Have you noticed it? Assumed sagacity! Well, I blow on it to keep it thawed.

"If you'll come into my room you shall have a whisky and soda," said the doctor.

The Suicide, taken aback: "What? Thanks, I will!"

When they sat in the consulting-room, each with his glass, the

Suicide became more mannerly and began to talk sensibly. The doctor asked him a few questions about the sanatorium and its inmates and received many evasive answers. Suddenly the Suicide held out his hand and said: "You wanted to know why I was blowing on it? Look at it, what do you make of that sore?"

The doctor: "It isn't a sore to start with."

"What is it then?"

"Nothing."

The Suicide: "I suggest that it's leprosy."

The doctor smiled: "Rubbish! You've just dug a hole in the skin."

"Can I have something for it?"

"Yes, you shall have another whisky."

The Suicide seemed relieved that his sore was nothing and with the second whisky he grew more cheerful than he had been for a long time. The doctor told anecdotes, he was so young in the profession that he still stored up in his mind any out-of-the-way occurrences in his practice. He had a story, for instance, of being sent for to a woman who had had a hiding and was bruised and battered about the seat.

"Oh?" said the Suicide.

"She was a young married woman, pretty too and rather frivolous. The husband was present when I examined her; he explained how it had come about and showed me the cane he had used."

"Was it the husband who—?"

"Who had thrashed her, yes. She was getting too strong for him, she wanted to do as she pleased, treated him as a dummy and took a lover."

The Suicide, suspiciously: "What have that man and his wife to do with me?"

"How do you mean?"

"Why are you telling me this?"

"It was a droll case. I had to cure the woman's back, but the husband cured her strength. No, you're quite right; what have the couple to do with us? But as I was saying—"

Silence.

"It's not without interest, all the same," the Suicide suggested. "He cured her, you say?"

"Radically! I've kept my eye on these people since; they live happily, they have had two children since then. They go out together on Sundays."

"Splendid!" exclaimed the Suicide. "Good luck to them!"

"I've had one or two experiences like that," said the doctor, as though to himself. "Without them a doctor's visits would be boring."

The Suicide proved to be no longer supercilious, he was now inquisitive and naïve: "I can't get that man and his wife out of my head; what kind of people were they?"

"Working-class people, the man's a blacksmith."

"Oh, is that it?" said the Suicide, disappointed. "A blacksmith and his wife."

"What then? Of course a cane is not an appropriate remedy in every class of life; one has to choose remedies according to the individual case, sometimes flowers are indicated."

"Anybody may be troubled with an excess of strength in his home," suggested the Suicide, looking at the walls and up at the ceiling.

The doctor replied absently, as though lost in his memories: "That's so. I was nearly using the cane myself once."

The Suicide, eagerly: "Are you married?"

"No"; the doctor smiled and said no more.

But the Suicide was impatient and questioned him with his eyes.

The doctor said: "No, it was my housekeeper. Not an ordinary blacksmith's wife, let me tell you, though to be sure she was a girl of the people, rather crazy like the other, but with many good qualities."

"Only a housekeeper!" said the Suicide, disappointed again.

"She was young and pretty, a lovely figure, played the piano and guitar, an admirable musician."

"Yes, but all the same—!"

"I was in love with her."

"Ah," said the Suicide, "that alters the case. And it was her you were tempted to take the cane to?"

"After flowers had failed, yes. And after other presents had failed too. One must have recourse to something, mustn't one?"

"I know nothing about it."

"No, perhaps not. But in a dilemma of this sort one has recourse to something. No, it would be quite another thing if it were one's wife, your wife, my wife, a person of one's own class, she would probably listen to reason. But a housekeeper! I suppose you're not married either?" asked the doctor.

"I? *Married?*"

"No, I understood as much."

"I'd have to be pretty crazy for that!" said the Suicide.

The doctor concurred to a certain extent and they discussed the point further, but both agreed that sometimes it was difficult to avoid being married.

"Well, but how did you come off with the girl in the end?" asked the Suicide. "Did you get what you wanted without the cane?"

"No," replied the doctor, "I haven't succeeded—yet. I did another thing instead: I came here. I took the post of doctor here."

Long silence of amazement.

"That's very interesting!" the Suicide nodded. "But what if your coming here doesn't help you either?"

The doctor, with decision: "Then I shall do as the blacksmith!"

His conversation with the doctor seemed to have had an effect on the Suicide, he thought it over and laughed to himself now and then. But it was not many days before a reaction set in and he was once more the brooding, snappish creature he had been. He went to look for Fröken d'Espard, but was unlucky enough to find her in the smoking-room in company with Rector Oliver and there was no way of avoiding a chat with him. As an opening he said, by way of being pleasant: "My respects to the College!"

The others were unused to his jocular tone and made no reply.

"I went to see our new doctor a couple of days, ago about this sore," he said to Fröken d'Espard.

"Did he give you anything for it?" she asked.

"Yes, two whiskies."

"Two *what?*"

"Whiskies. He prescribes rather odd medicines, sometimes cane."

"Cantharides, I expect you mean," suggested the Rector. "But that is not an unusual medicine."

The Suicide scorned to answer him.

"But occasionally he prescribes flowers. He's an original man."

The Rector still tried to be friendly and remarked: "Yes, flowers may doubtless be beneficial in some cases, flowers for the sick."

The Suicide scorned him again.

The lady nodded and said: "Yes, that's certain."

"What is it that's certain?" asked the Suicide. "That flowers are beneficial? Couldn't one just as well send buttons, mother-of-pearl buttons, horn buttons, tin buttons?"

Laughter.

The Rector recovered some of his dignity and would talk no more nonsense: "Well, tomorrow I proceed to terminate my stay here."

Fröken d'Espard: "Oh—so soon as that!"

"Tomorrow I depart. When are you leaving, Fröken?"

"One of these days, very soon."

"And you, young man?"

To this direct question the Suicide answered with reluctance: "I am not leaving."

"Indeed? Then you have absolutely no duties to call you?"

"But you have, I understand?"

"I have. You won't deny that, I hope?" asked the Rector with a smile. "We teachers have our schools to attend to, where to the best of our ability we impart to others what we ourselves have learnt."

"Don't believe him, Fröken," said the Suicide. "It's not so innocent as all that."

Fröken d'Espard was evidently embarrassed at being dragged into it and tried to be peacemaker: "Oh, but schooling is innocent, isn't it?"

"Schooling means going against Nature, turning the pupil into a side-track which runs in quite a different direction from the primary one. Schooling means following this side-track right out into the desert."

The Rector was amused at this, as was only to be expected. "To think that I had always believed I had got out of the desert!" he said.

"Yes," the lady laughed and agreed with him. "No, you must be reasonable, Herr Magnus; remember that the Rector is a great scholar, a *Doctor!*"

"I'm sure the Rector feels that he's a great success," replied the Suicide carelessly. "All rectors must feel like that, otherwise they would never be able to face their classes."

"Oh, we don't find that a torture, it's our delight."

Silence.

"So you're leaving too, Fröken?" said the Suicide. "Ah well, we are vagabonds in the earth, we wander this way and that, some of us stick at a sanatorium. Now I've been out with the doctor to choose a burial-ground for us survivors."

To this incomprehensible language there was no reply.

"Perhaps I did not understand you, sir," said the Rector in his most mealy-mouthed way; "is it our work in the class-room which displeases you?"

Silence.

"The Rector's asking a question," prompted the lady.

"A rector acts in good faith," said the Suicide; "his school teaches the children every kind of knowledge in every kind of branch. And one day the children come out again, after a long, long time they come out again; ay, but they went in as foals and calves. It is impossible for them to remember all they have learnt, and if they did remember it, it is of no importance. They forget what is the western boundary of Lake Oyern, they forget that the carrot plant may have no calyx. 'School' was originally a leisure time, a pastime for grown-up people, now it has become a hell for children. When they escape from this hell they are old, some of them are bald, some are half blind, but some never get out. Children should not be sent to school."

"Amusing, quite amusing!" said the Rector.

Fröken d'Espard asked: "But, dear me, how would people get on in later life without schooling?"

"Schooling doesn't make a man of anybody. In later years, when one's personality is properly established, there might be a talk of just as much schooling as is necessary."

"And even then the minimum?" queried the Rector, getting up to put an end to the conversation; he had had enough. Actually Rector Oliver might here have put in his word and triumphed, he had every advantage on his side, he knew languages and was a learned specialist, a famous man. But Rector Oliver could not discuss pure idiocy, it was a waste of time. But as he was going, some devil must have possessed the Suicide, he turned and addressed the Rector: "I see that my views interest you."

"No, I can't say they do," replied the Rector coldly. "Oh yes, it's no good denying it."

"Indeed? It is true that I have encountered your—what shall I call it?—absurdities before, among my nearest relations even, but not in such an extravagant form, not so utterly preposterous. Unfortunately it is the fact that there are people who take pride in being ignorant, in knowing nothing, no geography, no languages. No indeed, your views do not interest me. Unless as curiosities, as very wild, very mistaken—what shall I call it?—"

"Never mind, I can imagine the rest," interrupted the Suicide, ironically coming to his aid.

"It's like that Swedish Professor I was telling you about," said the Rector, turning to Fröken d'Espard. "And yet I really replied to his fallacies and refuted them point by point. But it seems to be no use. There are things on this earth against which even the gods fight in vain."

The Suicide seemed to consider the Rector's sneers very attractive, very charming in fact. "You spoke of the earth," he said, "the globe. Your infants' school undoubtedly attaches great importance to the earth's angles of inclination, but unfortunately people tread the earth without remembering these angles. Your children are taught about languages and art, about ships and stars, money and wars, about electricity, calories, mathematics, trees, and languages. And languages. But nothing of all this has any real content, you can only use it to establish a formal condition, a set way of living, it is a mechanical training without ethical value. But now what about the indwelling personality, the soul, one's very nature? Our personality is not rich in proportion to what we have learnt from books; on the contrary, it is rich in the degree in which we have been able to dispense with book-learning. That which is inherent in us is our very self, our ego."

It must have been the Rector's impatience which made the Suicide worse and worse, he seemed to enjoy the twitches of the learned man's face, and said: "I noticed that the University had its eye on you last year."

"How?"

"In appointing you censor."

"Ha ha!" Rector Oliver laughed for once in a way. "Yes, the University actually had its eye on me last year, for the Censorship, ha ha! Dear me, you are a delightful young man!"

The Suicide said: "If I'd been in your place I wouldn't have accepted this post of children's executioner. A censor is nothing but a fixed high-water mark of scholastic plodding, he sits there and asks what the Italians called this or that two thousand years ago. The little automatic machine stands and faces him: the censor inserts in the slot a question of the required weight, and then he begins to buzz and the wheels go round. And so he passes his examination. A man of your name and reputation, an officer of scholarship, ought not to lend himself to such work."

"Now, now," interposed Fröken d'Espard, again trying to keep the peace; "the joke's gone far enough!"

But the Rector seemed suspicious and all he would say was: "Whether joke or earnest it doesn't affect me one way or the other."

At that moment a maid came in with a message for Fröken d'Espard that there was a man waiting outside who wished to speak to her, Daniel from the sæter.

A twitch passed over her face as she got up and went out. The Rector also rose and left the room.

Daniel was standing at the foot of the steps with his little sledge; he did not take off his cap, but simply said in a friendly and familiar tone: "Good-day! How about it—I thought I might fetch you now?"

"Fetch me?"

"Fetch your things. Aren't you coming?"

CHAPTER THE LAST

O God, what a loud voice he had, the boy, the fellow! She stole a glance at the front of the house; of course there were boarders at all the windows, even Fru Ruben had got on to her feet and was staring out.

"Of course I'm coming," said Fröken d'Espard. "You see, I haven't packed."

"I can wait," said Daniel.

After all, he was kind and he was the one she was taking and all. "We shall have to leave it till tomorrow, my good Daniel," she said.

"Ay, ay," said Daniel. "I was bringing a calf here, so I thought I might fetch you at the same time. You ought to see that calf now, it's a fine calf, it's in the byre, come on and I'll show it you!"

"No, not now. I've got something to do just now."

"Ay, ay. But it's an extra fine calf, he says so too, the porter."

"I'll get ready to come tomorrow," said the lady.

She went in again. This visit was not amusing; she was glad to find the Suicide still sitting in the smoking-room, she wanted somebody.

"That was Daniel, he wanted to fetch my trunk," she said simply, as was the truth. "But I can't vanish all of a sudden, can I?"

"Daniel naturally wants to get you as soon as possible, he's thinking of the money for your board."

"Yes, you're right."

"Daniel has his concerns, we others have ours. Daniel is not badly off, I should say, he belongs here, lives here on the mountain, works here, lives and dies here when his time comes. It might be a good thing to be as out of the world as he is, God knows; he hasn't any need to run away. Perhaps he isn't even troubled with love."

"I'm sure he isn't."

"Devilish lucky man!"

"Do you say that?"

"Not from my own experience," the Suicide hastened to reply.

"The only thing human beings ought to care for is joy in life, thankfulness for life; but you don't get that through love. On the contrary, love is a scourge."

"Very often it is, no doubt."

"A man like Moss, for instance—I just happen to call him to mind, but he's not a case in point, he has other troubles, we each have our own."

"Did you ever send an answer to that letter of Moss's?" she asked.

"That impudent letter? No. No, I haven't sent one, not yet. But he shall have his answer, he may count upon that. Why should he have the last word?"

"No, But he was a very unhappy man."

"I don't know," said the Suicide reflectively. "Perhaps he was unhappy." All at once he laughed to himself and shook his head: "But that squirrel I sent him must have given him something to think about, I'm pretty sure of that!" But just as suddenly as he had brightened up, the Suicide now relapsed into despondency and gloom. "Do you see this sore?" he said, and it was the same sore he had shown the doctor. This ridiculous abrasion, this scratch, occupied his thoughts, he picked at it and blew on it incessantly and did not give it a chance to heal. "What am I to do with this?" he asked.

"I don't think it's anything. What did the doctor say?"

"The doctor, that ass! You see, there's an imminent danger that it's infection."

"Oh no!"

"Imminent danger. I had my ulster returned to me and I'm sure it hadn't been properly disinfected. And then, you know, I had that scurvy letter from him. What a pig, what a blowfly! Didn't he go about here breathing our air and talking to us and eating at the same table? He ought to be shot. And into the bargain he's had the impertinence to send me another letter."

"Another letter?"

"Another letter, came a day or two ago."

"You never told me that."

"Of course I didn't open the letter, didn't touch it."

"Haven't you read it?"

"The doctor read it. What do you think there was in it? Not a word of truth, nothing but a lot of lies: he says he's not leprous at all, it turns out to be a mistake, he says."

Fröken d'Espard: "Well, I never heard such a thing!"

"All an imposture, you see. He says too that he's recovered a little sight, he can see to walk."

The lady exclaimed: "It's a good thing something's coming right again in this world!"

That was not the only surprise Fröken d'Espard was to experience that afternoon. One of the ladies came to her room, two ladies in fact, but one of them waited outside in the passage. These ladies, who had formerly ostracized her, now approached her with an application: would she not buy this table-cloth?

Fröken d'Espard was speechless.

Well, the fact of the matter was that they had offered it to Fru Ruben, but she hadn't cared for it, she didn't like the pattern; oh, that Fru Ruben, she was no judge of anything but money! So Fru Ruben had referred them to Fröken d'Espard: she was going to move to a sæter and perhaps she might have a use for the cloth.

It was Doctor Oyen's table-cloth, his Christmas present from the ladies, for which he had made a speech of thanks, almost shedding tears of joy.

Ah, possibly it came as something of a surprise—?

"Yes," replied Fröken d'Espard; "that is, perhaps it's not so strange after all—"

No, it wasn't really. For the ladies had taken so much trouble with the cloth and had gone to some expense over it. And indeed it accomplished its mission and rejoiced the doctor's heart as was intended. But now Doctor Oyen was dead, and soon his relations would come and fetch his belongings and divide them. That would be a nice thing! Certainly none of the ladies cared to make Doctor Oyen's relations a present, therefore they had taken back the table-cloth.

This reasoning was so obvious that Fröken d'Espard allowed herself to be convinced; she took the cloth in her hands, spread it out, and looked at it; probably she was a little flattered too that the ladies had come to her and no one else.

"No," continued the saleswoman, "it would have been another matter if the table-cloth could have accompanied its owner in his coffin and been buried with him."

"How much do you want for the cloth?" asked Fröken d'Espard.

The lady called in her companion from the passage, and this was the secretary of the sewing party, the one who had noted down the prices of felt, silk, and fringes. The two ladies consulted together, the secretary pointing out that as there were many of them to share the price, it would not come to very much for each one.

Fröken d'Espard bought the table-cloth.

So quickly was Doctor Oyen's memory effaced. Doctor Oyen left no empty space behind him, he had been of too small importance, people were already crawling over his corpse. And now if it should turn out that he had given a wrong diagnosis in the case of Anton Moss, why—ah, it may have been an injustice to forget this well-disposed man so rapidly, but it was an injustice that he deserved. There was something ignorant about Oyen, something unsuspecting, he was like a fish on dry land. But he too had made the journey hither, the journey to earth, and the journey back again.

CHAPTER THE LAST

Next morning Rector Oliver took his departure for home, and by the same train travelled Fru Ruben, Bertelsen, and the lawyer. Fru Ruben was now much better, she ate and slept, had a more healthy colour, and had filled out a little under her flaccid skin. She had recovered her health and her looks. It was a wonder how this remarkable lady could transform herself in so short a time without breaking down. Good stock, tough stock.

Late in the afternoon Fröken d'Espard paid her bill and walked across in all privacy to Torahus Sæter. She preferred to arrive in the evening, at dusk. She did not chirp or shout for joy; on the contrary, she was rather bashful and self-conscious about her proceeding, but her eyes were dry. Of course she had got into a mess, but latterly she had borne her fate without falling on her knees or uttering cries of distress, tears and prayers had proved of no avail, she would make no further attempt to set a divine machinery going. Directing her steps downward? Oh yes, but she took the downward course with spirit unhumbled. She carried the famous table-cloth under her arm, intending to spread it on the table without delay and light, as it were, a torch in Daniel's new cottage. Wasn't that rather a good idea? She had to smile—perhaps to avoid crying. Oh, seen with wet eyes her fate might indeed have appeared more gloomy.

The last few weeks at the sanatorium had not been comfortable ones for her. She resorted to various tricks with herself, padded herself here and laced herself there, hopped downstairs like a wagtail, showed a laughing, carefree face to all—let the other ladies, the dragons, just dare to look at her suspiciously! But it was fagging to be everlastingly on the alert and she lost by it in other directions. She never exerted her sex appeal now, she no longer attempted to conceal the yawning gap in her teeth, her young body was deformed, it would not do to be isolated in the middle of a room as a cynosure.

And yesterday Daniel had come. He might easily have spoilt

all, he might, and it gave her satisfaction to reflect that she had not shown a sign of anger on meeting him. He had turned up there like any other lover and put her to shame by sending for her and bringing faces to all the windows—really she had steered a middle course between friendliness and strangeness and called him "my dear Daniel" as if he were merely a neighbour.

These and similar thoughts were in her head as she walked, no longer serious or depressed. At the little barn in the forest Daniel came forward and stood before her: "I almost thought you'd come about this time, so I went to meet you," he said. He had his sledge with him and intended to fetch her trunk at once. "What have you got under your arm?" he asked for the sake of saying something.

"Wouldn't you like to know!" she answered.

Her playfulness gave him courage to feel the parcel and peep into it. Suddenly he took her in his arms and carried her into the barn—

"What a fellow! Go away, are you crazy!"

But it was not unpleasant to be lifted up for a moment from the earth and one's tribulations.

She entered upon her new life at the sæter without much preparation, nor did she let her surprise at the unfamiliar surroundings overcome her. No antics, no attitudes, she just took a sound sleep and slept on till late the next morning. There was no denying it, she had reached a kind of heaven.

She threw a glance around her at the few things the room contained: besides her trunk, the bed, a table, and a couple of three-legged stools; over by the stove a white dish with a beaded border; that was the washing-basin. A droll set of furniture, but perfectly clean and not inappropriate, sæter fashion. And there was a solid stillness about the house; Daniel was out of doors no doubt, and if Marta was by her kitchen fire, she made no audible movement.

CHAPTER THE LAST

As Fröken d'Espard was washing herself in the beaded basin, she noticed that a drop of water hissed as it splashed the stove—so the fire had been lighted, yes, the room was warm. Oh, that Marta, she would thank her very particularly for this kindness on her first morning.

Daniel came in view outside the window and she beckoned him in. "Daniel," she said, "what must you think of me, not getting up till now!"

"What should you be doing up? I'd like to see you take another spell in bed," said Daniel. "Have you slept well?"

"Like a stone."

"You see, we've tried to make it as nice as we could for you," said Daniel; "we've put in all these different things that you might need." He looked proudly round, as though the room contained an incredible quantity of furniture and things, and—he told her—if there was anything else she wanted she must just let him know!

A queer lad, a son of the soil, naïve and unenlightened, but not unsympathetic, she was rather touched by him and contrived it so that he kissed her. "I'm fond of you and I must have you," he said in a nice, genuine way. "Yes, I suppose you must," she answered. And again she thought that if this Daniel were properly washed he was not too bad.

"Well, this is your place now," he said.

"How do you mean?"

"Your home. Torahus Sæter, Mountain, and Forest. Do you feel at home here?"

She smiled and replied that she had not had much experience of it yet. "Ask me in a year's time!"

Food was brought in to her and she ate more than she had believed possible; it was not canned stuff, but mountain food, cured meat. "How much am I to pay a month?" she asked. It slipped out of her mouth and showed how little she realized her new position as mistress of the place.

Daniel treated it as a joke: "Ha ha, yes, you may well ask!" And Marta, who seemed thoroughly initiated into the state of affairs, smiled in a quiet way.

They went out to the byre, which was tiny and warm; cows and sheep turned their heads and looked at them. "This bullock here will be a big fellow by autumn," said Daniel, patting the beast. "He's got a different kind of temper to that murderer last summer, you can creep underneath his belly."

They passed on to the horse. Daniel boasted loudly of this little three-year-old, a mare of positively human sagacity and great strength, there was no limit to the loads she could draw. "Look how bright her eyes are, you can see yourself in them. Poor filly, you shall have your bit of bread presently!" Having said this he checked himself all at once: "Stay here, Fröken, wait a moment while I run for a bit of bread, I won't fool her, poor thing!" He was away for a moment and came back with a loaf, which he gave to the mare bit by bit.

"You give her some too, Fröken," he said.

"Julie," she corrected.

"Give her this and feel how soft her muzzle is."

Not till they were outside did he get the name: "Julie, you say, your name's Julie? An extra fine name, there's nobody hereabouts that's called that."

They went round and he showed her everything; finally he opened a chest, saying: "Here are sheets. Here's food. And, by the way, here's wool. Thanks be to God, we have a few things up here in the mountains too; here's wool for you!"

"Yes, I see it."

He showed her his two guns on the wall and explained that one was a shot-gun and the other a rifle; he showed her rolls of stuff, homespun and white linen for underclothes. "Julie," he said; "I can't forget it, it sounds almost like velvet to say it."

CHAPTER THE LAST

"In French we call it *Julie*," she said.*

"What a lot you know!" he replied, wagging his head. "It's you who got me the horse too."

"Oh, you'd have got a horse all right without me."

"Oh, ay, I'm good for a horse and more. But it helped a lot when I showed them the money."

Thus Julie d'Espard entered upon her future.

---

*Daniel's pronunciation would be something like "Yoolia."

XIII

For some weeks things went well and they might have continued to go well, but something came to upset them. However, they did not go badly after all. Fröken d'Espard lived a life of idleness, she only stopped short of coffee in bed. Having nothing to stay up for, she went early to bed, and, having done that, she rose with the early bird. Perhaps there was something abnormal in this getting up at six instead of eleven, but after a while she felt rather proud of it, as though in a way it was a pretty foolhardy thing to do. And Marta sang her praises loudly and declared that she would make a first-rate sæter wife in time.

For the present she took little part in any household work but the washing of clothes. She put on one of Marta's skirts and washed her own underclothes, her handkerchiefs, collars, and blouses. Washing-days were not the most tedious days of the week for her; on the contrary, she had many a sorely needed gossip with Marta over the wash-tubs.

"He's as good a lad as can be," said Marta; "I've known him since the time he was born, it was a shame of Helena to break it off with him."

Strangely enough, Julie d'Espard had turned against Helena by degrees, she didn't like her, she was even beginning to be jealous of her. From what she heard, Helena had not yet shown any sign of a coming child, though she had been married to the Sheriff's officer a sufficiently long time; so there she was, still going about like a young girl and had lost none of her prettiness—how widely different from another poor creature! "Is she pretty, Helena?" she asked.

CHAPTER THE LAST

"Oh, yes indeed," replied Marta; "bright and beautiful, a farmer's daughter."

"Is she tall?"

"Yes, tall too."

Fröken d'Espard was impelled to seek out Daniel. At this time he was wearing a white woollen jacket with a blue border; Marta had knitted it, and the jacket was bleached, pure white, and it suited Daniel so nicely.

"Look here, Daniel," said Fröken d'Espard; "isn't it time we got married?"

"Just so!" replied Daniel. "I've been thinking that a long time, only I didn't like to say anything. When did you have a mind to get it done?"

"You must say that."

"Well, it's Easter next week, and the banns take three Sundays. But there's seven weeks between Easter and Whitsun, so we've plenty of time. Just you write now for your certificates, then we'll be ready."

"You look so well in that nice new jacket," she said.

"Do you think so? It's my own wool. We have fine wool at Torahus!"

"And so soft," she said, feeling it.

"You shall have a jacket of the same sort!"

"Oh, but wouldn't you rather have given it to Helena?"

"Helena?" queried Daniel in surprise.

"Isn't that the name of the girl you were to have had? I don't pretend to know."

"Helena—I never think about her. Hey, she's no more than that to me!"

But there was Fröken d'Espard, with not a trace of her good looks left, toothless and disfigured and out of shape. She must have felt insecure, and she tried to draw him: "What is she like? Can't I see her some day? Did you kiss her often?"

"Never a bit!" he said. "How's this—what are you asking for? I never took much pains over her or went down on my knees to get her up here; I just talked about it casual-like. I come of just as good folks as she, farmer's son and a good hand at my job, I've got my own farm and land, I've got chests and barrels full of stuff, as you've seen for yourself. And when the time comes, I've got my own plans that Helena knows nothing about; no, thank you, she can mind herself now...."

He reassured the lady at great length and brought in many fair and honest words to the effect that she—Julie—was the one God had appointed to make him happy. Of course it was a question of vanity, he could not now wish for any other, both in his own eyes and in those of his neighbours she far outweighed the farmer's daughter. She was a fine lady and had all sorts of accomplishments with her brain and her hands.

Indeed, Fröken d'Espard's jealousy was uncalled-for, quite uncalled-for. Daniel had taken a fancy to get married and thrived on it, if he was too much inclined to hang about the skirts of his lady he must be excused on account of his feelings; apart from that he was companionable in daily intercourse.

"The storekeeper showed me some white curtains for your windows, but I didn't bring them," he said.

"Go and buy them, I'll give you the money," she said. "Get some thick ones too, that nobody can see through."

"Ah, for your lying-in?"

Yes, she made no secret of that, they were for her lying-in. "And get a looking-glass too," she said; "rather a big one for the wall. I've only got a hand-glass."

"Well, just you let me know if there's anything you want," replied Daniel. "You've only got to mention it," he said. . . .

At Easter the sanatorium filled up again and now and then some

CHAPTER THE LAST

of the boarders strolled over to the sæter. Perhaps they had heard of this young lady, this town lady, who had taken up her abode there, and wanted to see her; but in vain, she did not show herself. She could now stand behind her own new curtains and watch the inquisitive holiday folk, idlers, and ski-runners; none of them belonged to the first batch, she saw none that she knew.

But one day Fröken Ellingsen appeared, she came straight into the new cottage and said how d'ye do; the same Fröken Ellingsen as of old, nicely dressed, tall, and ladylike, handsome. This was a surprise. Fröken d'Espard was not sorry to see her, she came, so to speak, from her own country and people, from the old world which was now so strange and far away.

"Is Bertelsen with you?" she blurted out. Oh, she had grown so downright and ill-bred, she regretted her question immediately.

Fröken Ellingsen made no faces. "No," she replied quietly and without a sigh; "he's engaged to Fru Ruben, you know."

"You don't say so—!"

"Haven't you seen it announced in the papers?"

"What papers should I see here?"

Silence.

"Yes, that was the end of it!" said Fröken Ellingsen.

"Well, I never—! Why, it's not so long since her husband died!"

"No. And God knows what were the real facts about his death."

"What do you mean?"

"I mean nothing," said Fröken Ellingsen, but she looked as if she had crime and chloroform in her mind. "One day perhaps I shall show that lady—!"

Fröken d'Espard: "Yes, but Bertelsen's worse."

"Oh, Bertelsen—no, it was the lady who was so crazy to get married." Fröken Ellingsen nodded several times and added: "But some day I shall—!"

"Wasn't it Bertelsen who threw you over?"

"Yes," replied Fröken Ellingsen mournfully. But her emotion did not suggest any great sorrow.

"Do you know what?" exclaimed Fröken d'Espard; "you were too good for him!"

They argued this for a while and there was much to be said on the point; Fröken Ellingsen, however, did not agree, no, she was not too good, not at all. And finally in answer to a direct question she admitted that Bertelsen had never proposed to her.

That altered the case, of course. Had he simply had her on hand so as not to be without a lady?

"No," said Fröken Ellingsen, again anxious to do him justice; "he could really have had any lady he liked, no trouble there, the son in Bertelsen & Son, a millionaire house. But he liked to have me to go about with him," she said.

"I should let him go to blazes!" said Fröken d'Espard with strong partisanship.

Fröken Ellingsen was so well balanced, she was not precipitate and she did not send anyone to blazes; on the other hand she prophesied no good of Fru Ruben. "Just wait!" she said threateningly; "she hasn't finished with me yet!"

"What will you do?"

"Oh, nothing," she said, passing it off. "I shall get over it all right, I have my own interests to live for, my work and my writing. When I come off duty I go home and enjoy myself thoroughly. It is as though my room were filled with people."

The same follies in that handsome head! Fröken Ellingsen, that calm person with the extravagant imagination, likely enough she had been conceived in narcosis, in an after-intoxication, which made her what she was, a topsy-turvy nature, sexually indifferent, tiresome and barren.

"If you don't read any papers you can't have seen either that I'm publishing a collection?" she asked.

"A collection? No."

"My experiences. It's been in the papers. Sketches or whatever you like to call them, stories. They are founded on facts."

"Fancy!"

"Everyone who's read them says they're interesting. I have only to finish them, they say."

"I can't understand how you manage it."

"No, that's what they all say. But, you see, in the first place it's a gift. One has to have a turn for it. And then it's a matter of practice."

"My goodness, yes! You must have practice," exclaimed Fröken d'Espard. "I can see that only from reading French. It won't do for me to forget the language, will it?"

"I've been writing for ten years," said Fröken Ellingsen. "I shall publish my first collection on my anniversary."

And maybe her chief reason for calling was to bring this news; she talked about it as long as Fröken d'Espard would listen to her. That the papers had mentioned it evidently made more impression on her than anything she had previously experienced, more than the loss of Bertelsen. Only when she was on the point of leaving did it occur to her that she was to invite Fröken d'Espard to the sanatorium.

"To the sanatorium—I?"

Some distinguished visitors had arrived and perhaps they would prefer to talk French, a Consul-General and his wife, with two grown-up daughters.

"I can't come," replied Fröken d'Espard helplessly.

"Why not?" asked Fröken Ellingsen, without comprehension. "It's the director who asks you, Lawyer Rupprecht."

Fröken d'Espard thought it over and asked if there were many visitors?

Yes, a crowd, more than there had ever been. A strange thing too, there were so many immensely fat people among them, where-ever one went one could hardly get along for fat stomachs. Of course the ski-runners were thin and blue, but the others—it was disgusting to see them. Fröken d'Espard's old chief at the office in town was there too.

"Andresen?" cried Fröken d'Espard.

"Yes, and a lot more fat people, ladies and gentlemen."

It must have been the interview with Fru Ruben that had filled the sanatorium. These unfortunate people wanted to try a stay at Torahus to get rid of their fat, the water there was so remarkable, they had been told, a safe cure, coupled with a first-class medical treatment which transformed people in a short time.

"So Andresen's there, is he?" said Fröken d'Espard. She did not reflect any longer, it couldn't occur to her to reflect any longer—she replied: "Will you just tell the lawyer that I'm unable to come?"

On leaving, Fröken Ellingsen said good-bye without a smile, without any feeling, and added: "I'll send you some of the papers it has been in."

Fröken d'Espard: "Don't say I'm unable to come, but that I'm engaged. Not 'unable,' remember."

The two ladies took leave of one another, each occupied with her own affairs.

No, of course Fröken d'Espard could no longer show herself at the sanatorium, especially as her old chief was staying there, it was not to be thought of, she would have to miss this good opportunity of meeting civilized people and talking French. It was not amusing, but, strictly speaking, she could not put it on to Daniel, it was fate; and when she went to find Daniel she did not let any of her ill humour fall upon him. She simply told him what had happened and that she had had to decline the invitation.

"You ought to go!" he said.

"You can't mean that! In the state you've got me into?"

"What does that matter?" said Daniel with levity.

CHAPTER THE LAST

It was of no use arguing with him, he had his own view of the matter, which was different from hers. Besides which, he was busy and full of what he was doing. He sat in the kitchen cutting out a pair of leather braces, and that in spite of its being Easter-time. He did not interrupt his work, but went on measuring and marking carefully. He said proudly: "Leather from my own cows!"

"What's it to be?"

"Braces."

"*That!*" she exclaimed in amazement.

She probably remembered a certain other pair of braces, of silk and elastic, dainty and refined, Herr Fleming's braces. But Daniel may have thought for his part that, as everyone knew, braces had to be made of leather all through if they were to last. As he sat there measuring exactly and cutting out these braces, she began to laugh to herself, and Daniel gave her a questioning look. It was good, thick leather, cowhide, well tanned, it wasn't cheap leather, so it was nothing to laugh at. His hands were not clean, but they were strong and steady, there was protection in them. And at the same time he could do many a neat job with knife and gouge with these very hands. He showed her a wooden skimmer of his own workmanship, with a little carving at the end of the handle; he showed her the meal tub hanging on the wall, which he had ornamented with a well-executed rearing horse on the back piece. He had a gift inherited from the past, from the days when a carpenter was a craftsman and an artist, of more account than a public servant.

Daniel was very busy, he settled down to his braces again and tested the leather time after time before using the knife. He chattered all the while, explaining that the whole strap must be of good, even quality, especially where the buttonholes were to come. Daniel was the same today as yesterday, frugal and industrious, content with what he had, proud of what he had. He worked after his fashion even during his Sunday leisure, contriving this and that, casting about, putting things to rights, knocking in a nail where it was wanted or binding withies for a hurdle. He didn't chuck his things about and let them take their chance; on the contrary, he was careful and close-fisted, by nature and training. He was no great connoisseur of crystal and porcelain, and when, once in a while, a plate got smashed in the kitchen he shook his head ever so long over the destruction that had been wrought.

Julie d'Espard vegetated; she sewed a little too at times, whatever it might have been; she hid her work as soon as anyone came near, no doubt because she was such a bad hand with needle and thread. The rest of the time she hovered between her room and the kitchen, lay on her bed for a while, or sat by Daniel's side when he was doing a bit of carpentry. Now and then she read one of her French novels aloud to him, to his huge delight; he sat looking at her with a smile of amazement all over his face. She rattled it off, as he didn't understand a word it was no great matter whether she read correctly, only he mustn't get the idea that she had to spell it out. "But here's something," she might say; "you must be able to understand this, Daniel, where he tells her he loves her!" "Ah, they carry on the same way down there then!" he would answer. "My goodness, yes; you can't imagine how finely these Frenchmen know how to put it!"

But now it was getting on towards spring, the days were lengthening, the midday sunshine was white and keen and hurt the eyes, Marta spread out woollens to bleach. It was in accordance with the place, the season, and a well-regulated life to bleach woollen clothes in the early spring sunshine and get them properly finished. Time went on and the sun began to give some warmth, the ice on the tarns turned blue and brittle at the edge, the snow thawed on the roads, and the hens waded in slush and got rheumatism.

It might have been a time for reviving hopes and bright thoughts, but spring in the mountains did not seem to do Julie d'Espard any good, she grew restless, slept badly, ate less than usual, and lost her self-confidence. What was the matter with her, hadn't she a cosy and peaceful and positively delightful existence? No. And she complained to Daniel, who couldn't make it out at all.

"Oughtn't I to go and put up the banns?" he asked.

"Yes," she replied; "if it is to be, you may as well—"

"I'll do it now; we've got the certificates. Just let me have a bit of a wash!"

When he had finished making himself tidy she said: "No, let it be, wait a bit!"

"What's that—?"

"Wait a bit, don't be in such a hurry."

"Well, I never heard the like!"

"Can't you let it wait a bit?" she cried with irritation.

Daniel took it humorously: "Waste of a wash, I call it—middle of the week and all!"

But waiting did not improve matters, an oppression weighed upon the lady and made her gloomy and impatient. She showed an inclination to be alone, left her cottage and stole away to the woods and sat on a rock moping. It was too bad altogether! She dreaded the coming of bedtime, the last few nights had been full of dreams and horrors: for Doctor Oyen came night after night and claimed his table-cloth. She woke in an agony of fear, with her heart beating wildly. Julie d'Espard had always been plucky and resolute in a tight place, now she had become weak and miserable, she dared not light the lamp, dared not raise her hands from the bed-clothes; and indeed a spectre, a corpse, was not the same thing as an insect.

She whimpered and made fresh complaint to Daniel.

"What's the matter?" he asked. "Isn't there any water in the brook?"

"Water?" she repeated.

"And wood at the very door. Good air, warm room, meat and

eggs. You'll hear the cuckoo any minute."

"Oh, you're past bearing—talk, talk—"

"What's wrong with you then?"

"I don't know."

"No more do I."

"I have such horrid dreams every night."

"Let me stay with you," said Daniel. "Then you'll sleep like a stone again!"

"One for me and two for yourself!" she jeered.

Daniel proposed once more to put up the banns and get the wedding done with, and she nodded and thought the time had come for it. But had she the strength? She was weak and down, scarcely felt equal to walking that long way to the church and back. Daniel offered to borrow a cart of Helmer and harness the three-year-old, she'd be able to pull her—oh, bless you, yes, if you weighed a ton! But the lady was down-hearted and asked him to wait a little while yet, she must surely be better soon....

Daniel put the certificates in his pocket and made for the village; he met friends and acquaintances, had a drop of drink, and then went straight to the parson on his own account. At any rate it would do no harm to have his banns asked in church, he had waited long enough for the moment when he would give the neighbourhood a surprise. Of course he had been dropping hints for a good while about being engaged, but he had never said anything definite; now it should come from the parson himself! He couldn't be acting against the lady's wishes, Julie's wishes, since she could fix the time for the wedding herself when she was in better spirits again.

He arranged things with the parson. He also arranged with Helmer about the cart, and the end of it was that Helmer, who had been with him all day, accompanied him home to the sæter. By that time they were both a little merry; they had a bottle with them besides, and Daniel in his vanity wanted to show off the lady—Julie, that is—and where was she?

Marta thought she was not far away.

They waited in the kitchen for a while, but Daniel proposed that they should go into the new cottage when the lady came home. She could only be sitting on a rock in the woods as usual,

At last Helmer hinted that he would have to be going. Couldn't Daniel show him the new cottage at once? He hadn't seen it since it was being built.

They fortified themselves with another dram and went into the new cottage.

Very snug it was in there, with curtains and looking-glass and French books and a many-coloured table-cloth; Helmer said it was grand.

"Ay, I've tried to make it as fine as I could," said Daniel. And in his slightly exalted state he began to use fine language and applied the word "excellent" to more than one thing. And Helmer was impressed.

Daniel said: "Look at that table-cloth! She makes that kind of thing herself, it's nothing to her."

Helmer examined it closely without touching it.

"Just you take hold of it," said Daniel; "you needn't be afraid! Look at me now, I take hold of everything there is in here, and why not, I should like to know?" He put on a bold air, made free with her books, and scornfully kicked aside a stool. "I don't mind what I do," he said; "she won't bite."

"You're a lucky man, I'm sure, Daniel!" said Helmer.

Daniel nodded and agreed. "She's called by the name of Julie," he said, looking proudly at his friend. "I forget what she calls it in French."

"An extra fine trunk that," declared Helmer approvingly; "brass-bound this way and that!"

But Daniel made still more of it: "Ay, and I wouldn't like to say what's inside; you may be sure it's full of fine things, clothes and outlandish notions from town. If she'd only been in I'd have got her to show you the lot."

"Does she treat you kindly?" asked Helmer.

"Kindly? She's like a child, I do anything I like with her. She's a good creature, gives you anything you like to ask. 'Go and buy a horse, go and buy this thing and that, I'll give you the money!' she says."

"*Has* she got money?" asked Helmer excitedly.

"Money? You don't know her, so it's not so strange for you to ask, but I've seen her take a roll of notes out of the bosom of her dress and you haven't. If you'd seen that roll you wouldn't have asked. For it was the biggest roll I've seen in all my days."

"It's what I was saying, you're a lucky man!" Helmer repeated, full of amazement over the fantastic tale. "I'd have liked to see her close to."

Daniel: "Ah, perhaps you think she's an ugly old woman that nobody would take? Ho ho, now I'll tell you a little thing, Helmer, and that is, at Easter they sent after her from the sanatorium. Yes. It was full of visitors and fine gentlemen who sent a message that they wanted to have her to talk to. Yes. But she didn't so much as stir. Come on, we'll go out and shout for her!"

They went out and Daniel shouted, and in a little while she came out of the wood.

"You were such a long time, I was beginning to get afraid," said Daniel.

Marvellous how it is with young people! She remembered having seen Helmer among a crowd of others sweeping snow from the skating-rink last winter, and now she answered his greeting and even showed him a friendly look from the first; Daniel might well be pleased.

"You've brought a visitor with you, I see," she said.

CHAPTER THE LAST

"Helmer. He's been with me all the time; we went to the parson and put up the banns. Helmer's promised me his cart; and now he wanted badly to see you."

"Me—see me? Heavens, what crazy notions you boys do get!"

"You just be quiet, I couldn't help it, he wouldn't go till he'd seen you."

Whether she was flattered or not, she certainly smiled very nicely and without showing the gap in her teeth. It was a stroke of luck too that she had her outdoor clothes on, with a big cloak that went from her chin down to her ankles and hid her deformity.

"We were in your room for a minute," Daniel confessed; "Helmer wanted to see the new cottage."

"I see," she replied, still in a good humour; "so now he's seen me and the cottage both."

Helmer with becoming modesty said nothing.

"Has Marta given Helmer some coffee?" she asked, in her new part of sæter wife.

Daniel answered: "No. But he's had something better than that—we had a drop in a bottle."

"Oho, so you're out on the spree! Yes, you're nice boys, both of you!"

"It wasn't very much of a spree," replied Helmer laughing, but he turned red all over his face.

The light was fading, and evening was drawing on; they chatted for a while, she did not ask Helmer in—no, for then she would have had to take off her cloak and she would not do that.

As Helmer was going, Daniel said: "Come again soon, look us up, this is where we live!"

"Yes," the lady joined in and gave him a nod.

Perhaps Daniel was expecting a bad quarter of an hour for having put up the banns without his young woman's consent, and when she asked him to come in he took out a cigar which he had in readiness. But it passed off very mildly, the young woman showed no marked displeasure, though she asked him caustically if he meant to get married by himself too. Here it was that Daniel began wetting his cigar, moistening it well with spittle. "It won't do any harm to have our banns asked," he said; "the wedding can come afterwards whenever you like to fix it."

After all, he was right there, she was mollified and questioned him inquisitively about what the clergyman had said and whether he had entered her French name correctly.

Oh yes, the parson had been surprised and had asked if she belonged to the nobility.

She wanted to know why he was smearing his cigar like that.

Didn't she know? A cigar ought always to be wetted outside and it was best to roll it a bit between the hands, or else it didn't last any time. He'd bought this cigar and brought it home so that he could sit and puff smoke for her.

"Well, then you'd better light it!" she said.

Daniel puffed good cigar smoke into the room, and Julie d'Espard sniffed it contentedly. They went together into the kitchen and had supper, and as the lady was afraid of the dark and troubled with gloomy thoughts she got Daniel to join her again in the new cottage. And that night she had a real quiet sleep, with Daniel to look after her.

No sooner was Monday come than Daniel was off to the village again. He ran by fits and starts, he was in a hurry and greatly excited: now the die was cast, the banns had been given out from the pulpit, and what did the neighbours say? Oh, the neighbours were surely speechless, and they had good reason to be.

He went to the store, where there were always a number of people, acquaintances and friends who would be able to tell him something; he pretended he had important business and made his way to

CHAPTER THE LAST

the counter. When folk saw who it was, they drew back and let him pass, never before had he been held in such esteem. And he took it like a grown-up man and was very dignified. Then a hand came out to congratulate him, then another, and finally every hand in the place. Daniel enjoyed his fame and swelled with pride. A woman said: "I always said there was something great in store for you, Daniel; you come of good folk, your mother and I were the same age and we went to be confirmed together; ah well, now she's at rest!"

There were people assembled here from every quarter, they all congratulated him alike, it was clear that the whole neighbourhood knew that he had made a catch. It had made an immense impression in church that the parson had said *Fröken* Julie d'Espard; Daniel could see too that Helmer had been to the fore, talking big about the new cottage and the lady since his visit to the sæter.

Without there being any special call for it Daniel went straight from the store to the Sheriff's: he would pay some little tax or whatever it was; in his inmost heart he must have thought he would show himself to Helena and crow over her. Oh, these young people and their lively hearts! It was not enough to be the owner of a sæter and to have cattle and a sweetheart and food for the day, something else asserted itself in him and craved nourishment. Even the boy from the smoky cabin had his inner life to cherish, oh, a powerful and complicated life whose claims had to be met. Vanity? If you like. Imperiousness, love, triumph? If you like. Helena had once slighted him—

She did not appear, she did not come running up and look at him with tears of repentance; not a bit, she was not to be seen. That was the devil, but let her go and good luck to her!

He paid his tax in the office and pocketed the Sheriff's officer's receipt as if it was nothing, as if he lighted his cigar with papers of that kind, nodded formally, and for once in a way said adieu instead of good-bye. And he didn't so much as cast a glance about him as he left the Sheriff's officer's.

Finished.

But now it was that something happened: he met her in the forest, met Helena, she was walking towards him, came up close and nodded. Both stopped, both blushed. And then they actually entered upon a discussion, with queer arguments and queer language, on one side and the other. No doubt she too, the wife of the Sheriff's officer, had her own inner life, and it was quiet and somewhat restricted, but none the less valid and important to her. She went straight to the point and congratulated him with a shake of the hand. "Yes, it was a great surprise," she then said; "and if it hadn't been the parson that said it we shouldn't have believed it," she said.

"Perhaps I ought to have asked you first?" he snapped. She was nothing to him now, nothing at all, and what made him blush just now was only natural agitation at meeting her.

His reply gave her a set-back: "It's a long time since I've seen you," she remarked.

Daniel seemed to trace sorrow and regret in her words and replied firmly: "Yes, it's a long time since you took yourself off."

"Oh," she said with a smile of humility, "I didn't go so far away either, I live in the village."

"I dare say. But I don't come down to the village except on business. And I hadn't any more business with you."

"No, I suppose that's so."

"Ay, it is so and it's going to be so!" said Daniel. Oh, he was pretty stiff, no sugary sweetness about him, he'd answer her, he'd let her know—

But now she on her side seemed to have gone as far as she meant to go; she asked all at once: "What kind of a swell young woman is that you've got hold of?"

Daniel, pale with fury: "What do you know about her? Isn't it enough for me to know?"

CHAPTER THE LAST

"Ah, but do you know?"

"When I want to know more about her I'll come to you," he said, making as though he would walk on. "You've got your nose into everything since you've been a Sheriff's wife!"

"It's the Sheriff's business to examine all sorts of people," she replied. "You can't get away from that."

"Oh," he said scornfully, "then I expect he's examined her too?"

"Yes, he has that," she answered.

Daniel opened his mouth and stared at her; she too was pale and her lips quivered slightly. Perhaps a thought or two crossed his brain: So the Sheriff had examined the lady—Julie—when could that have been? He knew nothing about this, he had not been present—or he'd have made a Sheriff of him, a mighty small Sheriff—

"I thought I'd let you know that," said Helena.

"Oh, you thought that, did you? And what did he examine her about, eh? Isn't she what she gives herself out for? Would you like to see her certificates?" he asked, unbuttoning his coat; "vaccination certificate, baptism certificate, confirmation certificate? I've got them on me."

"It isn't that!" said Helena.

What wonder that he began to swear, that he sent both her and her Sheriff's officer to the deuce and advised her to go home and leave decent people in peace. Had she become as common as that since her marriage, did she intend to persecute him on top of all the rest—? There he checked himself; a certain look of soreness and suffering in her face made him think he understood her better: she was jealous of the lady, she could not bear his getting over his sorrow and caring for another and wanting to get married; he ought rather to have sat at home and died of a broken heart for a Helena girl he couldn't get! He'd like to see himself! No, far from it, he'd make her properly sore—

"You can just leave her alone," he said with great emphasis.

"She's the only woman I've ever cared for, I'd have you to understand that."

"Oh," said Helena; "I see," said she. "I'm not worrying about her either, you needn't think that; but if she happens to have been examined and cross-questioned about some money that had gone astray—that's not worrying about her, is it?"

"Some money? What money's that? Did she take it?"

"I don't say so."

At that moment Helena had the upper hand, Daniel had felt a little stab of uneasiness: What now? Money gone astray, an envelope full of money—? He said: "It's only some gossip that your husband has raked up!"

"Do you think so? He hasn't raked anything up. He had orders to examine her and he did so. She had been sweethearts or whatever it was with a Finn and this Finn had stolen a lot of money from a bank. So he was arrested, but he only had a few hundred crowns on him. Now where was that money?"

"Do you mean to say the lady—Julie, that is—?"

"No, I don't say so. My husband doesn't say so either."

Daniel answered fiercely, though he now had his misgivings: "Your husband doesn't say so either, no. And he'd better not!"

"But he says that she—that this young lady of yours knows a good deal more about that money than she will admit. That's what he says."

Daniel, reflectively: "I'll ask her."

Pause.

"I just thought I'd let you know," said Helena again.

"She's a good and truthful person, I'll ask her," Daniel repeated. "No, she wasn't sweethearts with that man, he was a great Count and it's all lies that he had taken money from a bank. He had a great big castle at home, you should have seen the ring on his finger, ay, you could have bought half the neighbourhood, farms and all, for that ring! But the Count, he was a sick man and had consumption and bleeding of the lungs; and the lady, she sat with him and gave him medicines and drops, and of course he gave her good money for that, big money, and he was well able to do it. She's told me all about it. They used to come and see me at the sæter and have curds and cream, and sometimes the Count would lie down and sleep an hour or so on my bed and be all the better for it when he went back to the sanatorium. I know them so well, every scrap about them, the Count and her, she told me everything the very first day and that was long before she came to stay with me, for I never knew her in those days. That's how it is from beginning to end, there's nothing for you and your husband to make up stories about," Daniel concluded.

He nodded and left her.

Now Helena was in tears and called after him: "Daniel!"

"What is it?"

She came after him in a few hesitating steps, stopped again, used her handkerchief, and was silent.

"Was there anything?"

"No," she said. "It was only that I felt so sorry for you."

"Don't you ever worry about me!"

"No. But if that's the way of it and she's got a lot of money, you'll know now where it comes from."

Daniel reflected a moment: "Has she got a lot of money? That's more than I know."

"Helmer said so when he'd been to see you."

Daniel, shamed and furious: "Ah, that's it. But just you remember what I told you—you're too fond of poking your nose into everything and I won't talk to you anymore—"

He walked home full of thought. There was no doubt he'd have to have a serious talk with his sweetheart right away, there was no getting out of it.

It turned out otherwise than he imagined.

When he came home Marta was out. He looked cautiously into the new cottage: there was the lady, lying on her bed, with face distraught and a wild look in her eyes. What was the matter, she couldn't have been brought to bed already? No, she had been bitten by an adder. An adder—where? Here! She showed him her hand and arm with the blue mark on it; Marta had bound it up, her fingers were white and dead from the tightness of the bandage, and now Marta had run off to the sanatorium to fetch the doctor.

"I shall suck out the wound!" he said.

But it was too late, though he opened the wound again with a needle and sucked as hard as he could; there was nothing to be done till the doctor arrived. This was a nice state of things, the lady was beside herself, she was beginning to scream. The fright had given her a shock. When the doctor had done his work and poulticed the hand he said at last that she must be undressed and put properly to bed—for several reasons, he said. "O God, what is it?" she asked. "Don't go!"

He did not go, he stayed the little while till it was all over. There hadn't even been time to send Daniel to the sanatorium to telephone for professional assistance, it was a miracle how quickly it was done, an adder had managed the whole thing.

When the doctor had finished and came out to the steps, he found Daniel there, pale and anxious, asking: "She's over it already, isn't she? How's it going to be?"

"Well," replied the doctor, "it came on very suddenly. But now we shall see—"

"Is there any danger?"

"There's always liable to be danger when it's before the time."

"Yes, and so long before the time! But the child's screaming anyhow," said Daniel. "Is it a boy?"

The doctor nodded and said: "Well, I'll call again this evening.

CHAPTER THE LAST

That old servant of yours is capable enough, but I'll telephone for a nurse all the same."

He did scream sure enough, the child, the boy; Daniel thought he didn't do it badly either and he wanted to say as much to the mother. Might he come in? The child stopped screaming, the mother had quieted it, and Daniel was allowed in.

"Hey, there's a fellow that can screech!" he said rather foolishly.

"Yes, but he's so small, he was born so much too soon!" came a voice from the bed.

Poor little Julie d'Espard, she lay there and had her secrets to hide. It was not easy for her, but she was smart and had her wits about her. And then she had stitched together a lot of little garments on the quiet in the last few weeks and was not entirely unprepared, but as she was fairly idiotic with her needle and thread the little shirts were not very grand. And why should they be? They were of fine material all the same, some of them were actually made up from silk blouses, soft as air. And, besides, Marta had plenty of coarser stuff for the outside wrappings, even to a brand-new, snow-white woollen shawl.

Daniel looked about and tried to be funny. "Has he gone again?" he asked.

"Who?"

"The child, the boy. I'll swear I heard crying."

That made the young mother smile, she threw back a corner of the coverlet and disclosed the marvel. "He came so much too soon," she said and laid great stress on this.

"Hey," said Daniel, "he's not a bit small, I see, you needn't think that. I was much smaller myself when I was born, wasn't I, Marta?"

Marta evaded the question and said: "Well, God be praised, he's a well-formed child!"

The mother had calmed down, she no longer had a thought of the adder sting; if she had had her own way she would have torn off the poultice at once—it kept her from holding the child properly, she said. She was well enough now to give a calm account of how she had been bitten: she was sitting as usual on a rock, and the sun was shining and made her sleepy. Then she felt something cold on her hand and gave a start; at that instant the snake glided away, but almost immediately she felt she had been stung and ran home.

"It's beastly with those adders," said Daniel. "I got one in my breeches-pocket one year when I was lying asleep on the ground."

"Did you kill it?"

"No, kill it! And that's what vexes me to this very day. Funny little fingers he's got, let me look once more. You see, he can move them!"

"Now you must go," said Marta.

But there was still the money and the Count, and later in the week he broached the matter to her. It began by her saying she would rather have been married before the child was born—oh, it was too bad happening as it did, but Daniel thought it was all the same. On the other hand, he said, there was another matter, and as far as that went he would just mention it and not give it another thought: it was about the Count, him of the curds and cream; was he a scoundrel?

"The Count—how do you mean? No, no, he was good enough!"

"Ah. But, then, he had stolen some money and been arrested?"

The lady thought a moment: it might well be that he was a scoundrel, she didn't know, she was not so well acquainted with him—

"What had you to do with him?"

"I? Nothing. *Rien du tout*."

"Well, but what do you know about the money he'd stolen, have you got it?"

"*I?*" screamed the lady. "Are you mad?"

"No, I was sure you hadn't," said Daniel.

CHAPTER THE LAST

"I have the money he gave me—well, yes, there was some money and I have that. Didn't I tell you about it?"

"Yes, I'm sure you said something. But if it was rather a lot of money oughtn't you to have handed it over to the Sheriff?"

"What? Not if I know it!"

"Didn't he come and examine you?"

"The Sheriff? Certainly. Didn't I tell you that too?"

"I believe you said something about it."

"He examined everybody at the sanatorium and me too. What makes you ask all these questions?"

"They will have it at the Sheriff's that you know more about the Count and his money than you let on."

"I think everybody's gone mad," said the lady. "What should I know? For that matter the Count hasn't stolen any money and he hasn't been properly arrested either, the lawyer told me that at the sanatorium. The police made a mistake and they sent him to hospital instead because he had consumption. You can ask the lawyer yourself!"

Daniel could not have been more powerfully convinced, his own belief and confidence were confirmed and he went away completely satisfied with the lady's account of the matter. Hey, Helena was not going to succeed in plunging him headlong into a new situation. Poor Helena all the same, she was surely in despair at losing him, likely enough she'd come up to the tarn one day and drown herself. But anyhow he couldn't look on at that in cold blood, he'd have to rescue her—

Now the snow came sliding off the roofs and lay thawing in the roads, dirty and innocent, day after day. Dull thuds were heard among the houses as the wet snow collapsed, more and more bare ground was to be seen on the hill-side and up to the Peak. Then just before Whitsuntide there came a storm and rain, and it was good to be indoors and have enough food and drink for oneself and one's beasts; it lasted for a night, with roars and peals of thunder on high, and this gigantic hullabaloo kept on till four o'clock in the morning, then heaven and earth gradually quieted down. And when the day came it was spring.

And what a spring it was in the mountains! It did not come like a thing that had been well thought out, but like a marvellous idea, hasty and wild, suddenly thrown out. Marta divested herself of a number of garments.

When Fröken d'Espard was up and out again, it was all quite strange to her: the wide world stretched below her down to the village, utterly different from what it had been, all green and rich and sunny, buds were bursting in the woods around the sæter, grass sprouted already on the balks of the cornfields, and there was a strong scent of earth. It did not take her many days to get perfectly well again and she carried the child out with her and sat on the doorstep giving it the breast, while Daniel sat by her side.

"If only he wasn't so small," she said, underlining it again; "if only we can keep him alive! Didn't the doctor say he came too soon?"

"I think he said something about it."

"There, you see! It was many weeks too soon, you know yourself when it was we met!" Oh, but Fröken d'Espard had good reason to be grateful to the adder, she would never have hit upon a better excuse of her own accord.

"He's not small," Daniel insisted, proud of the child. "It's only a fancy of yours," he said.

Everything in order, not a note of discord in the little family. Was not the boy thriving? Were there quarrels over him from morning to night? Never. Next time Daniel went down to the village he bought the little fellow a handkerchief with animals on it and gave it him in all kindness. So what was wrong? Nothing. A merciful blindness had fallen upon Daniel, he looked upon himself and his belongings without vision; his demands were few, his family life was made up of lies, but his contentment was great and good.

And indeed Fröken d'Espard did him justice, he was by no means to be despised; if only everything could remain as it was now, it would be all right. She sat there with the child and grew sound and well again, Daniel should not hear an angry word from her: "Daniel, don't you think we shall be allowed to keep him? Perhaps we haven't deserved it, but still!" She felt very courageous and rehabilitated: "If they were to send for me from the sanatorium today, I'd just take the child on my arm and go!" she said.

Family life made up of lies? Oh yes—a lie may contain beautiful truths. If Life did not make the lie necessary it would not exist.

The wedding was put off again and again, but not from a disinclination on either side; it was the fault of circumstances, not of the lady. For how could she take the child with her to church? To make it a laughing-stock by showing it in public on such an occasion was not to be thought of! But could she leave it at home while it was still so small? Impossible. Marta couldn't give it the breast. What was to be done?

When summer was wearing on, it was Marta at any rate who went off and got the child christened, for, as things were, the young mother could not face the eyes of the congregation.

XIV

All might have gone well.

Holiday time again, on the road up to the sanatorium, people were to be seen once more, driving and walking, holiday-makers who wanted to get fit—and stout people who wanted to be reduced. The manager and the matron received them, the doctor came when he was called, there was excellent order and regularity about this health resort, with its placards and weather reports and servants everywhere, and the director himself, Lawyer Rupprecht, was satisfied.

Work for the new electric plant had been in hand for some weeks, but of course it was delayed as such work always is and was going on slowly; difficulties had occurred, rocks had to be blasted, with thundering reports, and due consideration had to be shown to the patients between certain hours. "But electric light we will have!" said the lawyer. "And a tremendous water-supply," said he.

Carts came up loaded with food, loaded with furniture and fittings for the rooms that were still unused, loaded with building materials for the new additions which were to make the castle about double its original size, cart-loads of iron and cement, planks, mattresses, big mirrors, stoves, rolls of wall-paper.

Then one day a gentleman came up from the station—ah, then he came—

He drove, though he had not much baggage, only an elegant suitcase, and he was elegantly dressed, though his clothes were not very new. He had a diamond ring on his finger and a small diamond in his tie-pin. Helmer drove him.

CHAPTER THE LAST

The gentleman alighted by the big veranda, walked past a number of visitors, greeted the matron in a friendly way, and said: "I should like to have my old room again if possible, I've been here before, my name is Fleming."

The matron, rather taken aback: "I don't know—is it Herr Fleming—?"

The man smiled and nodded.

"Well—your room—let me see—"

The manager came up, bowed, and took the gentleman's suitcase. They went in, and as they passed through the smoking-room the matron said: "It's Herr Fleming!" Lawyer Rupprecht came up and there was a great scene of recognition: "No, what a surprise!" he cried. "I hope you are well, Count? Didn't you recognize the Count?" he asked the matron.

Herr Fleming put in: "It's not to be wondered at, I've grown a beard since I was here."

"I should have known you among a thousand! What can we do about a room for Count Fleming?"

It appeared that his old room was occupied, but that could be arranged, the lawyer would arrange that. He was brilliant as a host, rang for the waitress, ordered port, and offered his guest a glass, calling him Count all the time so that the other visitors might hear. A great fuss he made.

And all was arranged, Herr Fleming got his old room, and the manager brought down his trunks from the attic. The keys were hanging in a sealed envelope, Herr Fleming broke the seal as carelessly as if it had been his own and not the Sheriff's; one would have thought it a pretty dangerous proceeding to break the police seal, but no, it didn't seem so.

The manager said insinuatingly: "It was only that Sheriff's officer fellow who was here and put his wax on it."

Herr Fleming replied: "There was really no necessity to do so;

I'm sure there's nobody here at the sanatorium who would have meddled with my trunks while I was away."

He washed and titivated himself as elaborately as ever and then went down and mixed with the visitors, some few of whom knew him; presently he took a seat in the veranda next to the Suicide and offered him a cigarette.

The Suicide refused it. He had another of his sombre fits, had sunk into himself, and scarcely looked up; he was blowing at a sore hand he had and didn't say a word.

"There seem to be a good many visitors here," said Herr Fleming.

The Suicide, suddenly: "Yes, a lot of stupid creatures. The fat ones come here to lose flesh, and God knows they succeed; we live on Torahus water and canned stuff."

Herr Fleming smiled, he knew the Suicide's discontented tone of old. "And the thin?" he asked.

"The thin live in hope."

Pause.

To Herr Fleming's remark: "You have been a faithful supporter of Torahus," the Suicide replied: "I stay here so as not to be anywhere else!" But when Herr Fleming tried to go on and start a little conversation, the other did not answer him, he had said all he had to say.

There was a crowd of people around them—no, they were not particularly stupid creatures to look at, but they were misshapen in one way or another, some with leanness, others with fat, deformed barrels on legs, overworked schoolmistresses and clerks with the long, thin limbs of insects. There might be very shapely heads among them, with kind, incapable eyes. One lady was expatiating on the big concern in which she was employed, the kind of bills she sometimes had to make out, for thousands, for huge sums in Danish eggs and Danish hams alone. And it looked as if her lean listeners had no objection to hearing about all this good food.

Herr Fleming got up and bowed to Rector Oliver—he had to give everyone his name, on account of his new beard. The elderly schoolmaster was exactly the same as before, in the same clothes, with the same worn, grey face, patiently instructing all those he talked to. There was something hopeless about the man's immutability, he did not seem even to have changed his black tie, his hands were just as long and bony, his boots just as lasting. A durable figure at Torahus.

"*Voilà un homme!*" was his greeting to Herr Fleming. "You know who said that? It was Napoleon on meeting Goethe!" The Rector explained that he had not yet found anyone to talk to, not that he meant to imply that all these visitors were devoid of interests, far from it, only he had not found any kindred spirits. He made one exception: "The engineer in charge of the electricity works, he has the makings of a great actor. You really must meet him!"

The Rector was very pleased at having met Herr Fleming; here was a man he could talk to and make himself understood, a man with good manners and a sense of refinement: he asked after the Rector's family, his bright little boys. Yes, they were with him again this time, flying about everywhere, goodness knew where they might be at that moment! The Rector was not altogether satisfied with his boys, they were far from showing the same fondness and capacity for learning as he had had at their age, and what was he to do with them? Of course they knew something, it would be an irreparable disgrace if they did not, sons of the Rector, children of the town's shining light, if he said it himself; but they were backward in languages, in grammar—extraordinary, the subject the Rector himself had found easiest of all! But give them a boat, or send them into town and you'd soon find them in a blacksmith's forge or on top of a house that was being built!

"That's the way with all boys," said Herr Fleming with a smile.

"But I won't have it so, they have to study and learn and get on!" The Rector went into it at some length and had a good talk, Herr Fleming was so pleasant to converse with, so polite, so intelligent, he bowed to one's better knowledge.

Herr Fleming asked: "Don't you find it a nuisance, Rector, with so many strangers about you, such a crowd of people?"

"A little. Yes, to be frank, I do. You see, we can't all be on the same level, so one has to accommodate oneself to another, all along the line, and that may be rather tiresome. But on the whole I am satisfied. The place is excellent."

Oh, Rector Oliver was not a difficult man to please, he had been accustomed to frugality and poverty all his days, he ate the food that was given him and did not expect to get his shoes polished. Now he seemed to have developed a taste for spending his holidays gratis at this big sanatorium and he would continue to do so as long as he could. He counted up that this was his third visit; he was comfortable here, so why should he go anywhere else? He did not change.

When Herr Fleming was through with his greetings of old acquaintances he took to strolling in the forest. The little hay barn was in its old place and there was fresh hay in it, Daniel's sæter looked as peaceful and pleasant as ever; he did not go right up to the houses, but discovered that there were new curtains to the windows of the new cottage.

One day he saw Fröken d'Espard sitting with the child on the doorstep.

Whether she had expected him or he had unconsciously given a little nod, she got up at once and took the child in; a moment later she came out again and went towards him.

Their meeting was in the forest, it was secret, and a long time since the last. They both blushed, God knows, perhaps from suspense—perhaps from something else. They shook hands and for the moment had not much to say to each other. He saw the gap in her teeth, but at the same time he saw that she tried to conceal it; he pointed to the scar on her chin and said: "Have you hurt yourself badly?"

"That was a long time ago, last winter. You're looking well; you're not coughing now?"

"No. Did you know it was me standing here?"

"I guessed it. Oh, there's no magic about it, I heard from Helmer that you had come, the man who drove you."

Herr Fleming nodded and said: "He gave me some information too."

"Ah," she said with a sigh; "well, well, then you know how things are!"

Pause.

"You're looking well, but rather strange. Why have you grown a beard?"

"It's because—well, you see, I've fallen away rather, I don't want you to be disappointed, but I'm much emaciated. So I thought I could come here and put on flesh again, I remembered Torahus and the sæter and the curds and cream. Besides, I thought that if I showed myself with a beard to the man here, Daniel or whatever his name is, I might for certain reasons pass as somebody else."

"He would have known you at once. Both he and Marta would have known you."

"Yes, I suppose it was a childish idea. Let us talk about you."

"No, not about me. You see what I am like!" And so as to get it over she said abruptly: "Look here, I've lost a tooth too."

"Well, what of it?"

"It isn't very pretty anyhow."

He said with a smile: "It wouldn't have been prettier if you'd got a fang instead. Now let's hear: you're going to be married, aren't you?"

Pause.

"I've had the child," she said.

"The child—ah—"

"His name is Julius. A big child, I can tell you, a fine child. He said it must be named after me."

"Who said so?"

"Daniel."

Pause. They were both busy with their own thoughts.

"And so you're going to be married," he said dreamily.

"Tell me, now," she said; "are you well again, strong again?"

"I'm hanging together. I may tell you, I had certain hopes of Torahus again, but now I don't know, it's all changed—"

"You'll recover sure enough, you'll see. You had so much agitation the last time you were here, at the end, I mean, and that didn't do you any good. But it was all nonsense, I've been told."

"All nonsense. I went into hospital in Christiania and was quite comfortable. Oh, I'm tough and my illness is a capricious illness, the sea voyage home to Finland healed me completely and I had no more hæmorrhage. It was a grand voyage too, the Kattegat, the Baltic, change of air, I couldn't have hit upon a better medicine."

"Yes, but when you got home to Finland—?" she asked, perhaps with thoughts of prison and confinement.

No change, he declared. Well, of course there was a good deal of change, his mother had sold the farm, he could no longer go home and live there—

Had she sold the farm?

Yes, what else was she to do? He could not take it over, he was ill. So she sold it, turned it into money.

And where was his mother now?

Well, you see, she was old—she got inflammation of the lungs—

Pause.

"How sad!" said the lady.

"Don't let's talk about that, it happened before I came home, it happened while I was in hospital in Christiania, I only heard of it by letter. I don't think it was inflammation of the lungs, by the way; she had something wrong with her heart, I couldn't bear to hear the details, perhaps it was a stroke."

He took her hand, with a feeble pressure, a mere nothing regarded as indiscretion; Daniel's grip was of a very different kind. But this frail and lean clerk's hand made its impression on her, it was thin-skinned, warm from a slight fever, pleasant to hold, it sent a thrill through her. She had so long been storing up homesickness for an earlier life and surroundings that she suddenly yielded to it and put her arm round his neck. This put heart into him again, he grew bolder, kissed her, and was affectionate.

"We must be rather careful," said she; "he may come this way."

"How—?"

"Daniel. He's up at the tarns catching fish for the sanatorium, but he may come home this way."

This discouraged him again and made him silent.

"It's quite strange to be sitting with you again," she said. "How long is it since?"

"I don't know, I don't like to think of it. It's a long time."

She observed him from the side. He was right about having lost flesh, his temples were sunk, his nails were blue; God knows, perhaps he had gone through a lot of hardship and been handed his food in a tin mug through a grating. He didn't look very rich either, he wore his diamond ring and the rest of his finery, was dressed in the good clothes out of his trunks, but his bearing seemed to have deteriorated, as though he had no comfortable resources to lean back upon.

All at once she noticed something: "That's not—is that the same ring?"

"Certainly," he replied, holding it up and letting it flash in the sun.

"It doesn't seem to me to sparkle as it used."

"It's full of dust, that's all, dust from the journey. Anyhow I don't mean to wear a ring anymore," he said, putting it in his waistcoat-pocket.

"Thank you," she said, "for everything, all the money—"

He shook his head deprecatingly and asked with a smile: "Did you manage to keep it?"

"Rather!"

"You didn't have to burn it?"

"Not much! On the other hand, I've spent a little, spent some—on Daniel and myself, for a horse and various things for the house—"

"Well, we won't talk about that."

"Won't you have some of it back, some ready money?"

"How? No!" he said.

"Some at any rate, a little?"

He shook his head. "But everything is so changed, I don't know what's to become of me now. I came back because you were here and because I was comfortable here, well looked after with nursing and attention, I got curds and cream at the sæter here, and a good sleep with a sheepskin rug over me. I saw you every day, I've been longing for you, nothing else was in my mind."

"You can see me every day again," she said.

"But how could that be managed?"

"I'll come to the sanatorium whenever you like. He doesn't object to that."

He shook his head again. "It won't be the same thing. Didn't you tell me you were going to be married?"

She hesitated. "Yes."

"There, you see! Then how can you come and see me? No, it's all over!"

He was silent, both were silent, then he continued: "Ready money, did you say? Well, apart from some emergency, you and I were to share it, I thought it might give us a start with something or other. That's what I wanted to come and talk to you about. But now it's all over, circumstances are changed, you don't care for me anymore."

"Yes, I do; don't talk like that, I do care for you."

"Not in that way."

"Yes, in that way. But what was I to do? I was alone, I was rather desperate too, there was the child coming, I had to make a move, had to look about for a home."

"Yes, I see."

Long silence, they both thought it over.

"Circumstances," he said dreamily, "circumstances prevented my being all I ought to have been for you—"

"On the contrary!" she interrupted, comforting him; "you were all you ought to be and more, you were splendid! How would it have gone with me if you hadn't put me in a position to live without employment?"

"Ah well, that's all right!"

"Why, you'd stuffed my dress full of money, you don't know what it meant to me."

"Good! But circumstances prevented my being able to take you with me. Perhaps you would have gone with me then?"

"Yes."

"There, you see! But now you can't."

"Now I'll have to go," she said, getting up; "the little one may wake and I shan't be there."

"May I come here again?" he asked.

"Well," she reflected, "yes—"

"Or can you come to me?"

"Perhaps."

"For I should very much like to talk to you and hear about everything—"

She came now and then to the sanatorium, generally early in the morning; she was up at six and caught him in bed; this happened once or twice, then it raised scandal at the sanatorium. Servant-girls are easily scandalized at such things when they themselves are not concerned. One morning early when she was trying to slip in and had got as far as the passage, Fröken d'Espard ran into the director, Lawyer Rupprecht.

He greeted her with a smile all over his face and rejoiced to see her again: "It's an eternity since I saw you, Fröken, and it wasn't very nice of you to desert us entirely, what have we done to you? This way, Fröken, you must have some coffee, I don't intend to let you go till you have told me how you are getting on. There, let's sit here! I expect you wish to see Herr Fleming? He's not up, he's not such an early bird as you and I, but we can send him a message; meanwhile we'll drink our coffee, you must want it. Lovise, will you please bring coffee for Fröken d'Espard and me. And then go up and knock gently at the Count's door and say a young lady is waiting for him downstairs—"

So that gave a check to their meetings.

Julie d'Espard then broke the news to Daniel and Marta that the Count was back at the sanatorium; they remembered the fine, rich Count, didn't they? Well, now he'd come back and he wanted curds and cream.

Daniel smiled with pleasure at this news, and Marta in a flurry began to make herself tidy. "But I'll tell you this," she insisted, "that now he'll have to have his meals in the new cottage, for the kitchen's not fit to be seen!"

And it appeared that the lady had strong objections to letting him come into the new cottage, but she had to give in.

So the Count came, and he came every day and had curds and cream and put on weight, no doubt about it, he was filling out again. The whole thing might have gone better if it had been fair play instead of cheating; they often went so far as to draw the thick curtains before the windows of the new cottage so that nothing could be seen from outside, and this they did on account of the sun. Afterwards, when Herr Fleming had had his meal and left his big two-crown piece on the table, and the child was asleep, the lady would walk part of the way home with him, and occasionally she accompanied him as far as the sanatorium and spent a little time among the visitors.

She met the Suicide and got him to talk; yes, Fröken d'Espard got him to be communicative and chatty: "I hear two of our maids have been taken ill," he said cheerily enough. "You may be glad you're not living here any longer, Fröken."

"Oh, how's that?"

"They're new maids, just come from the village, they were not used to the food here and it made them ill, they say one of them is absolutely at chapter the last. Well, what can you expect, this canned stuff is unadulterated poison. Can't Daniel sell us another bull?"

"I don't know," replied the lady with a smile.

"It would positively save our lives!"

"You're not looking poorly, Herr Magnus."

"I brace myself up, but I'm far from the man I was. If I eat it's without appetite, if I sit down on a chair it's not because I mean to; I just collapse into it. I pass my evenings playing 'snap' with the servants. What do you think of that?"

"My dear Herr Magnus, we must all of us make the best we can of things."

"Where do you find that written?"

"I don't know. In the Book of Fate."

"Do you see him over there?" asked the Suicide, indicating someone with a glance. "The Rector, the book-mountebank—*he's* making the best he can of things. He knows 'languages' and he's nothing. He takes the greatest pains to steep himself in his school-book learning and gets it up mechanically so that he may pass it on mechanically to children; he sees nothing ridiculous in this, he doesn't ask: 'Is this a life?' On the contrary, when he gets up from performing his 'duty' he has quite an egregious idea of himself, he has once again learnt a little more and can once again pass on his learning to others. *He* makes the best he can of things. He reads foreign papers in the club at home and people bow to him in the street and he's content. That is his life. He hasn't even a respect for the great masters of language, he has no eye for them, doesn't suspect their existence—the seers, the sifters of peoples and periods—"

"Have you heard from our friend Moss?" asked Fröken d'Espard.

"Moss, that swindler! Look here, what he's done to me," said the Suicide, holding out his sore hand. "It won't heal, I've tried burning it out, but it's no good, he's infected me. And that's the man who gave himself out to be religious in a way! But I have a letter that I'm going to send him soon, I'll show him—"

"Does he write sometimes?" she asked. "Or is he dead?"

"He—dead? To be sure he writes. Not that I ever touch his letters myself, it's the doctor who reads them, but he writes and writes, there's no shame in him. He can see better and better, he says, and the last letter he wrote himself."

"No—!" she exclaimed with the greatest astonishment.

"Ah, so you believe in him too?" asked the Suicide in a hurt tone. "But what if he did write it himself—you needn't think the lines were straight and neat, I could have written as well with a handkerchief over my eyes. However, that's not the worst of it by any means: he's trying to make us believe that it was simply barber's itch he had on his face. What do you think of that?"

"I don't understand anything about it."

"Even admitting that it was barber's itch on the face itself, what about the rest of his body, could he have barber's itch there too?"

"Well, but had he sores on the rest of his body?"

"I don't know, I expect he had, he was a dirty beast altogether, covered with boils and ulcers. I don't consider it impossible that he might begin to see better when his eyes were properly cleaned out; but then how will you explain his infecting me with the ulster?"

"Let me have another look at your sore," she asked.

"Leave it alone," replied the Suicide, warning her off; "there's no doubt about that sore."

"What does the doctor say to it?"

"The doctor!" scoffed the Suicide; "he'd better take a dose of salts! Wasn't Doctor Oyen a doctor too?—and he said Moss had leprosy."

You couldn't do anything with him. Fröken d'Espard leaned forward and asked: "Have you heard from home?"

"What makes you ask that? Be quiet!"

"Excuse me, but I meant about the little one, the child, have you heard anything about it?"

"Why should I hear anything about it? I don't even know what her name is, I'm here and she's there. What have I to do with her anyway?"

"It's very sad."

"I intend to go in to Christiania one of these days and settle the whole question. There shan't be any doubt left, even if it means murder and suicide and destruction for all of us! I don't care!" And after these ferocious words the Suicide added: "Be so kind, Fröken, as to ask Daniel if he hasn't a bull to sell us, it's a question of life and death!"

Daniel began to talk about the wedding.

Well—yes, Julie was ready whenever he liked. But was he going to be married in a woollen jersey?

He hadn't thought of that, but perhaps she was right; he had a Sunday suit too, but he supposed he'd have to have new clothes for such a solemn occasion. A confounded nuisance, there was no chance of getting anything made before Whitsun.

The wedding was put off.

After Whitsuntide he was at her again. And again she didn't say no—she did not, but she was backward in offering him money for his outfit. Strange, Daniel must have entertained a hope of it, for until now she had always said: "Go and buy this and that, here's the money!" He had been spoilt and couldn't quite understand her close-fistedness now. He withdrew, a little hurt, and did not mention the wedding again for a long time.

And meanwhile Herr Fleming came to the new cottage, and Fröken d'Espard walked back with him to the sanatorium. This went on for a great part of the summer. But one day when she was just going off with him again, Daniel appeared at the door of the kitchen and called her back: "He's awake again, I hear!"

"Awake?"

"Julius. He's crying, I hear him."

Well, then she turned and let Herr Fleming go away alone; but she came back rather reluctantly, rather as a matter of duty, saying: "That's strange, he was sleeping so soundly!"

Daniel followed her into the new cottage as though to see if the boy was really awake—and he was not, he was sound asleep.

"What's the meaning of this?" she said.

Daniel stammered, Daniel himself was mightily surprised; he had so plainly heard the boy crying, what was he to think of it? Was he fey? Oh, in Heaven's name, he surely wasn't fey?

They discussed this for a while and she was not quite satisfied, but let it pass; however, when Daniel began to be tender and loving she saw the hang of it and put him off, resisted him, but without success. What a fellow! Had he no shame? Not likely she'd have come back if she'd known! She dared not carry her indignation too far either, but only scolded him half in jest and smacked at him; he was so beside himself, so utterly unbridled, she was almost afraid of him—he had growled. Daniel was a stout fellow, he was rude and violent, but irresistible, oh yes, his faults were not without their good points. Besides, his visits to the new cottage had been greatly restricted of late, she was no longer afraid of the dark, it was the season of long daylight, when she didn't want his protection at night. So he had been shut out, as it were.

"Well, now you can go, ogre!" she said.

She began to consider him impartially: if nothing had intervened, perhaps she would now be married to him and installed as a housewife at Torahus Sæter. Daniel was not to be despised, he ate with thoroughness and performed his work like a man. Last winter when he came home from the forest with a gash in his foot, he first sat down to his dinner, but when the blood ran over the floor it did not escape his observation that he had this wound, his gaping boot was leaking blood. "It's only a toe!" he said. And he tied the toe up in a rag and treated it like a piece of furniture.

Although he was such a hard case he had not proved dangerous, he didn't throw knives about, he was kind to beasts and men. He might act with violence, as this afternoon; what of it? No doubt it was partly a question of vanity, and perhaps he had suffered rather too long from jealousy, God knows. But in the ordinary way he was quiet enough, and ashamed of his impetuosity when the fit was past.

How did he take it when he fell off the roof of the barn in the spring? The barn belonging to the sæter was no sky-scraper on the top side, but on the lower side it rested on an ungodly high wall with a road below it, and it was just here that Daniel had his tumble. Perhaps Julie was not altogether blameless in the matter: he was lying up on the ridge of the roof mending a leak, she called up to him and he had to turn round to hear what it was. Then it happened, and she stood below and looked on. He had no time to take any infinite care of himself; no, she saw well enough that he did not come down from heaven in the usual graceful way, descending upon a cloud, but in a knot into which he had tied his body in flight, a spiral with one shoulder advanced. He did not yell, the one who yelled was the lady. He picked himself up from the ground and seemed to be thinking: "What the devil's all this?" He stared incredulously up in the air, his face perfectly stiff with boundless bewilderment. Only after a while was there a little the matter with him. "Have you hurt yourself much, Daniel?" she asked. "I don't think so," he replied, "but I must give a groan or two for the look of the thing!"

Fröken d'Espard's thoughts travelled on.

Now the other, a man sick from his youth, but so delicate and considerate, full of tender entreaties, lifting her up by his language and his sentiments. He needed help and solicitude, but he deserved it; if he was not a Count, he might have been, with his bearing, his handsome smile, patent-leather shoes, silk underclothes, a diamond ring in his waistcoat-pocket—

And he was her first love.

How had it begun? O God, she didn't know, it began with nothing at all: it was one evening at the sanatorium, he just moved his chair a little nearer hers and sat there; perhaps it was his breath or perhaps the scent of his hair, but it released a source within her, it trickled all through her. What is falling in love? She blushed inwardly and smiled, he laid his hand on the back of her chair and it was like an embrace; another moment and she would have made herself ridiculous and swooned away. Then he had shown himself the gentleman and said: "It's cold here, I'm going to get my coat." He was away longer than he need have been and she followed him and said: "Yes, it's cold, I think I'd rather go in."

This led to a little more every day, more confidences, more advances, it led to bezique, love, nursing, and crisis.

That was a long time ago now, many months ago, she had had

to make her arrangements without him. Time had intervened. Oh, but the source had not run dry in her, it was not choked up, it flowed again, a trickle—

It cut her to the heart that he had had to go through so much and that even now he was not quite the great man and himself again. Silk underclothing, oh yes, but it was no longer rich and new. It was also rather remarkable that he was more and more liable to forget the big two-crown piece for his curds and cream; what could be the meaning of that? Julie had to step in behind his back and hand Marta two crowns for him out of her own money....

Daniel came in again and he must have been meditating in the mean time, he had something on his mind. "I shall go down to the village tomorrow evening and order the clothes," he said.

"All right," she answered.

And as she said no more he added: "I was just thinking, is there anything I can do for you while I'm about it?"

"No."

"I can get them on trust," he said.

"Yes, I suppose you can," she replied.

Daniel went out again.

Could it be called delicate and genteel of him only to speak of his own clothes? Would not she want clothes too? If she had her rights she would want a silk dress, white shoes, many yards of veil, and a train which the bridesmaids would carry. His thoughts were earthy as usual. In her novels there was always a honeymoon trip, she wouldn't get that; there were flowers and wine and speeches, she wouldn't get those. She would have a farthing wedding. Helmer would be the only one present. For how could she ask Herr Fleming?

It all began to look impossible to her. She did not give up the idea of the wedding, she regarded it as a matter of form which was better settled and done with. What might come afterwards must be left to Fate. According to her French novels she was quite at liberty to sin against marriage, so long as she did not sin against love. Enough of that. And as to her own trousseau, she could write for it, no difficulty there. But could she go to the altar right in front of the nose of him who had a better right both to her and to the child? Granted that her virtue had shed its blossoms, but in default of an altogether blameless past she might still behave like a well-bred woman, what else had she taken the trouble to learn French for? She couldn't let a man sit in the window of the sanatorium and watch her going to church with another. For that matter—why make such a great fuss about a wedding? In some places one went to the mayor, in others to a consulate.

At night she locked her door so as not to run any risk.

In the morning Herr Fleming came and asked: "Have I come too early?"

"No." And she added: "Daniel has gone to the village."

"Two things have happened to me," he began, and told her his story: "The Sheriff came yesterday and offered to break the seals on my trunks. 1 said that I had really wished to save him the trouble and so I had broken the seals myself. He didn't like that much and said that he thought he was the one to do that. I showed him some papers from the authorities at home, countersigned by the authorities in Christiania, according to which I could naturally dispose freely of my own trunks. Yes, that agreed with the papers he himself had received, said the Sheriff, but all the same it was he who ought to have broken the seals. I dare say he was right in a way and I replied by begging his pardon: I had not been able to wait. After that he was quite amenable, he admitted that it was some days since he had received his papers and that he ought to have come sooner, but had not had time. We were quite good friends. And that about the money, he said, that was all nonsense, the money I had was mine, the bank had made a mistake. Of course, I said, I was good for the money I had borrowed from the bank and I had repaid it. The Sheriff advised me to claim damages for the injury that had been done me."

Herr Fleming paused. Why did he tell the lady these things? He must have had his reasons, no doubt he wished to clear himself in her eyes and wipe out the impression of his needlessly frank confession before he took to flight last autumn. He had embezzled no money, he had borrowed it. What was more, he had paid it back.

Of course Fröken d'Espard made as though his communication delighted her and raised a heavy burden from her mind, but she can hardly have deplored his misdeed very seriously; from an early age she herself had had to get out of many a tight place in various ways and by all sorts of means, and she knew what it was like. She said: "There, you see! I knew very well you were exaggerating."

"Perhaps I did exaggerate a little, I didn't want to minimize it. Of course my action was irregular: I was ill and had hæmorrhage and didn't want to die; how could I wait for the directors of the bank to grant me a loan? I took it. That's the whole story. But now, you see, I'm perfectly free and cleared, and now I've come to you."

She avoided going into this and asked: "And what is the other thing that happened to you?"

"The other thing is that I've just seen the doctor. He has examined me and finds that I'm well on the way to recovery, one lung healed, the other in process of healing. But I shall have to be careful."

"Splendid!"

"Yes. And now's the time when I need you more than ever."

Ah—well, but what could she say?

Pause.

Doubtless she had no great objection to being sought after by two instead of one, but there would have to be a decision some time. So she asked boldly: "Could you agree to my marrying Daniel?"

Herr Fleming, in a toneless voice: "Well—what do you think

yourself?"

"Ah, but you—?"

He thought it over: "There has been so much between us, I thought you couldn't very well desert me."

"No," she agreed. "But can I desert the other any better?"

"I don't know."

"Our banns have been asked already," she said.

They had more to say about it, he was very gloomy and wanted to go again, she saw him part of the way home, but they had gone no farther than the little barn when they stopped, and both were in despair. They had taken so long that she had to go back to the child, but to console him at parting she threw her arms about his neck and kissed him, sobbing: "You know very well who it is I love and want, but it's so difficult; he won't let me go, I'm sure."

"Then there is only one way for us both."

"No, none of that talk, we'll find something, let's think it over!"

They parted and went in opposite directions.

A minute later Daniel got up from the hay in the barn and came out; he didn't take the trouble to brush the hay off him, but went as he was, ran, caught up the lady, and stopped her.

He was pale and out of breath, but he didn't say much, didn't fly into a rage and abuse her, but she was much alarmed and looked at him in a paralysed way; his eyes, his tightly shut mouth, were full of meaning.

"Do you come this way from the village?" she asked.

"I haven't been to the village, I've come from the hay barn," he replied.

She saw that well enough, but affected surprise. As he used neither his fists nor his teeth she recovered herself and was able to consider the situation; strictly speaking, she had done nothing but stand outside a barn and show kindness to a sick man.

"Oh, you've come from the barn. Then I suppose you heard

what we were saying?"

"Yes."

"He's a sick man, I had to humour him."

"You're to stop it!" said Daniel, and nodded.

"Stop it—how do you mean? Certainly, as far as I'm concerned. He can go away again. I don't know."

She took it cleverly and Daniel seemed relieved at her words: "Yes, he can go away again!" he said.

No, Daniel was not dangerous. After all, it was not so strange that he should be displeased, but if he clenched his lips and turned down his thumbs it didn't mean that any doomed victim was to die. When she walked on he walked with her and no longer held her back. She assumed the offensive: "I can't forget your lying in the hay," she said. "Fancy, eavesdropping like that!"

Evidently he did not understand this, it must be town talk or book talk. The fact was, his hitting upon this showed that he was no blockhead, she couldn't fool him, nobody could fool him! He answered with a self-satisfied air: "I'll just let you know that you have to get up early in the morning if you want to fool me and Daniel!"

Well, she was somewhat offended that he had no confidence in her and found it necessary to dog her steps, and she gave expression to her feelings in the following sharp rebuke: "And I'll just let you know that you're to stop spying. I won't have it. And you won't get anywhere with it!"

"Perhaps not! But where were you thinking of getting?" he asked, clenching his lips again.

She was tied, her banns had been asked in church and that was enough for Daniel, that was why he could speak as he did, he felt safe. But the very fact that she was caught in a snare made her flutter: was it not possible to undo what had been done? She would discuss this with Herr Fleming.

Things went on as usual; Herr Fleming came for his curds and cream, and Daniel put up with it or pretended not to notice it; but Fröken d'Espard prudently ceased her visits to the sanatorium and was no longer defiant.

One day Daniel said: "Now I say he's to go."

"Oh," said she.

"Will you tell him or shall I?"

"I'll tell him if you like," she replied. "But I don't think it'll be any good."

"I'll see that it's some good," said he.

She took this for his customary boasting and asked: "What harm are we doing, what is it you're growling about? He comes here and takes his curds and cream to get well again."

"He's not coming here anymore."

"Oh, then I have nothing to say in this house? It's a good thing to know that!"

Daniel shouted: "Yes, you have a say! But he's to go!"

"You can't turn a visitor out of the sanatorium."

"You don't know that. I've been talking to somebody, 1 can report him to the Sheriff."

"Ha ha ha," she laughed; "what for? God, how stupid you are!"

By this time Daniel didn't care if he put things pretty plainly to her and he said: "He stole that money from a bank, I don't care what you say. And you're hiding it."

"That old yarn!" she retorted. "You should just see his papers with the crown and the stamp and all on them! The police have had to beg his pardon, the Prime Minister of Finland has had to give him back all his property and his castle and all the money. Be quiet with you, you don't know what you're talking about!"

"You'll see!" he muttered threateningly. "And the Sheriff was there searching for the money and you had it—"

She got up and opened her trunk, took out the envelope of

money, and showed it to him; oh, that fat envelope full of banknotes! "Here it is," she said; "ask the Sheriff to come and he can see it too, I'll count it out to him. It was the Count's money, but he gave it to me, now it's mine. Go away and be ashamed of yourself!" She threw the packet back into her trunk, slammed the lid, and locked it.

Daniel, much more tamely: "According to what the authorities think, that money was not rightly come by, I don't care what you say. And it was you who had it when the Sheriff was searching for it. And it's still here at Torahus Sæter—"

"—Mountain, and Forest," she added scornfully; "Torahus Sæter, Mountain, and Forest. The money!" she cried, "yes, wouldn't you like to get your fingers into it?"

This brought him down properly; knocked a hole in him, he even showed some signs of sniffling. After all, she was right, she had seen through him and he was annoyed at having said things that recoiled on himself. He didn't know that he'd ever been to her trunk and taken anything of hers, he said in self-pity—

She never said he had!

The Lord had provided for him up to now without her money and vouchsafed him his daily bread according to his needs, and the Lord would surely not cast him off in the future—

And so forth.

Just the kind of talk that was wanted to soften her and affect her in her turn. "Look here," she cried, "don't let's quarrel!" And when this girl, this deuce of a woman, put her arm round his waist and cuddled up to him, how could he help relenting? He explained himself: he seemed to have made a hash of what he wanted to say, he hadn't intended to mention the money, but only to hint that this Count had a very corrupting influence and led her into suspicion and trouble with the police and all sorts of misery—

Very well. But now that was all going to be forgotten. Not a word more!

It was the first time they had abused each other so grossly, and she had put him well in his place, but perhaps this would not be the end of it, the scene would repeat itself. She seriously considered her position, it was not secure.

She might have said: "Go and get your wedding clothes, Daniel; look, here's the money!" Of course such a move would have re-established her position entirely, but how long would it have been before he came again? She was no fool, this Julie d'Espard, she had her wits about her. And hadn't it come to this, that she had been obliged to take over the payment for his curds and cream every time? "Why, what nonsense it is that you should pay for a drop of sour milk," she had said to Herr Fleming, "I believe I have something to say in this house, you are my guest!"

She had to say this, she was forced to it. He was evidently no longer rich, the farm that had been turned into money had perhaps gone to cover his defalcation, how did she know? And now a couple of days ago he had brought his bill from the sanatorium and asked her to "advance it in the mean time"; what could that mean but one thing? Good, she had advanced the money, advanced it liberally. But how long would it be before the next bill came?

She was really no fool, she could not continue to "advance" money to two men, she had to make a choice.

Herr Fleming might be right in saying that the remains of the money might be used to start something with. And that would put her back at a stroke into the life and the world from which she had been pushed out. It could not be denied that she was homesick for it; a sæter was not the place for her, she was living here on the borderland between two classes of society, a ridiculous and insufferable daily life, a borrowed life in which she had tried to induce herself to take root. Could it be done? One day when she was washing her hands in the kitchen Marta in all innocence threw her a sack to dry

CHAPTER THE LAST

them on.

She had to make a choice. Assuredly Herr Fleming was no hero, no, no, he was no hero, but all the same it was he who sent a thrill through her when he smiled and when he put his hand on the back of her chair. How queer it all was! A hero, he? Lord save us, a worn-out young man, not clever, not remarkable in any way, nothing much in himself, just an ordinary, rather petty young man—as all the people of this world are ordinary and petty. But Herr Fleming was a gentlemanly person, he raised her a couple of degrees, he had a manner. When he came with his bill from the sanatorium he actually had gloves on, rather worn gloves, but fit to be seen, in which he held the bill as he asked her to settle it.

The result of her meditations was that she recommenced a practice she had long dropped: she began to massage her face again for the sake of her looks.

"Look here," she said to Daniel; "I believe I'll ask you something: couldn't it be broken off between us?"

Daniel stared at her: "Hey?"

"Between you and me—that we broke it off, I mean—?"

To begin with he thought she was joking, and he was the kind of man who had no objection to a good joke, an altogether irresistible joke. But when it dawned on him that she spoke in earnest his face grew rather long and grey and he began to fumble at his chest, unbuttoning and buttoning his knitted waistcoat. She saw that she would have a hard job with him and said: "Don't let's quarrel, Daniel; come, we'll go up to the wood and sit there!"

They went, ay, Daniel went with her, being a little dazed, a little knocked off his perch, he offered no resistance.

"Don't you think it could be managed?"

No, he thought it as impossible as anything could be. And he shook his head and laughed, so impossible was it.

"Did you ever see anything like it?" she said; "here I've brought my purse out with me to the wood, I must be out of my senses!" She opened and looked into it; oh, it was not the envelope, it was only her purse, but it turned out that there was a good deal of money in it, including some notes. Would he be so kind as to keep it for her, she might lose it in the heather—

It was an artful offer and showed the shrewdness of the girl; but contrary to expectation he refused it. It had evidently aroused his suspicions, he looked at her searchingly and even moved to another tuft.

She burst out laughing and said boldly; "No, there's nothing to be afraid of! I meant you could take care of it till we went in, but I dare say I can look after it myself."

"So you thought we could break it off?" he asked.

"Yes, it's no good going on as we are now. I've thought it over."

"We can't break it off!" he said weightily.

She reflected a moment. "Well—why not, exactly?"

He then produced a reason which was absolutely incomprehensible to her, the town girl: he pointed out that he was a farmer's son.

"What then?" she asked innocently.

"Well, it's all the same if you don't understand," he said. "But I'd have you to know that I'm not just so-and-so from town. That kind of thing won't answer with me!"

This little turn in the wood proved a failure from her point of view; though they debated the matter awhile longer, it was Daniel who broke off the discussion and got up to go. "You're not to speak of it anymore!" he said.

This only increased the tension, the prospect of an amicable parting was closed. But now she began to flutter in earnest, opposition made her furious, she grew feverish, exaggerated to herself her love for Herr Fleming, and wept because she could not have him.

The postman from the sanatorium brought her a note: a party of very grand Americans had arrived, who shook their heads at Man-

CHAPTER THE LAST

ager Svendsen's English and would prefer to talk French—could Fröken d'Espard give the sanatorium the pleasure of her company? It may not have been the director's, Lawyer Rupprecht's own idea, but he had signed the note, with kind regards and "Yours very truly."

Daniel could not say no to this invitation, as he had shown himself so liberal in the past, but he asked her not to stay away too long, on account of the child. Cheerful herself, she wished to cheer him: "Now you mustn't go suspecting me of anything, Daniel, I'll be as quick as I can. And, besides, the Count's gone away, I've heard."

Daniel, promptly: "Has the Count gone?"

"I heard it said that he'd gone."

"I just want you to know," exclaimed Daniel impetuously, "that I don't suspect you with any soul in the place. Who should it be? The manager, the porter, the postman?—no. And what about the visitors?—him they call the Suicide perhaps?—ha ha ha! You just go and stay as long as you like!"

The first person she met in the grounds of the sanatorium was the Suicide. He was better dressed than usual, dressed for a journey, and had a stick in his hand. He said: "One of those maids I told you about is dead."

"Is she dead?" repeated Fröken d'Espard without interest.

"Died yesterday, I hear. Well, that's the way of it, Fröken; we are vagabonds, we wander up to the health resort in the mountains and that's the end of us."

"That was a sad thing."

"Very sad. A healthy girl, fresh from the village, and to succumb like that. I'm certain she'd swallowed some filth that she couldn't digest. I put it down exclusively to the food here."

"The food," repeated the lady, with no more interest than before.

"Of course, it attacked her digestion, cholera. The other maid's still alive, but nobody knows for how long."

Fröken d'Espard: "Has a party of Americans arrived?"

"No."

"Or French perhaps—they talk French?"

"I don't think so, I haven't heard of it. No, we haven't so much news here, only an occasional death, one day's much the same as another. A couple of tourists come on their way across the mountains, a family comes to enjoy a week of 'high life,' that's all. But I nearly forgot to tell you—the engineer in charge of the electricity works is dead."

"What—?"

"An accident. I've been saying all the time that this rock-blasting was dangerous, but they don't pay any attention to danger at this place. A piece of rock fell on him and crushed him."

"When did it happen?"

"This morning, I hear. The first charge that was fired."

So many people had died here that one was now getting accustomed to it, deaths were losing their interests, but the Suicide still kept count of them. He ostentatiously dwelt on the girl from the village, because her death was due to the food and nothing else; she was forgotten by the rest because the engineer died immediately after and took the wind out of her sails. "The engineer," said the Suicide; "oh yes, he counts, he makes one more. But his death was due to an accident which might have happened anywhere. It's worse with the other one! How about it, can Daniel let us have a bull?"

"No, he won't sell before the autumn."

"Then we'll have to try to get eatable food from somewhere else. We can't sit here and get our death."

"Are you going away somewhere?" she asked.

"No. Only running up to Christiania."

XV

The flag hung at half-mast, there was great commotion at the sanatorium, which was full of people since the holidays had begun, they bustled hither and thither. The lawyer came across Fröken d'Espard when she had gone no farther than the passage; he was everywhere, very busy and very tragic.

"Good-day, Fröken d'Espard! You might have seen us in a happier hour, you'll find nothing but sorrow and despair today."

"So I hear. Two deaths."

"I can't bear to speak of it. He was an extraordinarily able man, we had got used to having him here, he was indispensable. Found something to amuse the visitors every evening, he was the soul of the place, engineer here and engineer there—according to all the best judges there was a great actor lost in him. And to end like this!"

"What was l going say—"

"You wanted to see Herr Fleming; I expect he's in his room. I'll send a message."

"And the American family?"

"Which?"

"The American family that wanted to talk French?"

"Oh, ah, yes. Well, they're coming, we expect them one of these days, perhaps more than one family, several families, whole parties. Of course everything will go on as usual, the cure and the life of the place, though a death like that of the engineer—I was just telephoning for another man to take charge of the work."

"So that family has not come?"

"Lovise!" called the lawyer; "will you go up and tell the Count that Fröken d'Espard is here already and is waiting for him. This way, Fröken, please take a seat in the reading-room. Excuse my being so busy!"

Herr Fleming came down and they went into the forest so as to be alone. He was full of the engineer's death and began talking of it; it was the lady who said: "Just so, but now about ourselves!"

"Yes, ourselves! We must think of something."

"You mustn't come to the sæter anymore," she said; "I'm afraid for you."

"Did he say so?"

"Yes."

"Really, you know, I don't come on his account," said Herr Fleming with a superior air; "I go right past him to see you. Doesn't he understand that?"

"That's just what he does understand, and he won't have it any longer."

"What shall we do then?"

"He insists on your going away."

Herr Fleming, with dignity: "I shall not go away."

"I told him you had gone."

Silence. Both sat there feeling as if they were barred in.

"We must clear out," he said.

The lady was more sensible, she saw the impossibility of this plan and said: "I've thought of that too, but he would catch us before we were half-way to the station. The child—"

"The child, of course, take the child with you!"

"It would have to be carried, it's too small, it can't be left alone for a moment. No, let's be serious: can't it be broken off—in proper form—?"

"Well," he suggested, "the Sheriff was very friendly, perhaps he would help—"

She cut him short: "No, not the Sheriff. Look here, you must go to the parson. The Sheriff, what could he do? But the parson—I'm sure I've heard that it can be managed; you must lodge a protest against my marrying another, you're the child's father and I'm its mother. I'll write a statement to that effect."

"I'll do it," he said.

She showed her sense again and was not sure that this plan was free from danger either. Perhaps the law would support them, but the other party, Daniel, what would he do?

Herr Fleming was weak in body, but he was no coward, he was not deterred by what Daniel might think of doing: "I suppose he'll listen to reason," he said.

The lady doubted this, she had already tried it.

"Well, then let him do what he likes!"

"You're not afraid?" she asked. "But he's capable of doing something desperate."

He put this aside with a little toss of the head without boasting, without showing off; his cool, dignified manner gave her confidence. And when he took her hand and said: "The main thing is that you will—that you will have me!" then the die was cast, she wavered no longer, never could she be housewife at a sæter.

They went back to the sanatorium and sat in the smoking-room; the idea was that she should stay to dinner, as Daniel had shown himself liberal and given her as much time as she liked to take. Meanwhile, she herself was perhaps not altogether without renown among the new visitors, they put their heads together when she came in and looked her up and down; God knows, perhaps she was not without notoriety even. There was no doubt Herr Fleming, the Count, enjoyed the highest esteem and kept her head above water, and that without him she would have been looked upon as nothing or perhaps shown out.

Fröken d'Espard revenged herself by regarding strangers and acquaintances alike with some condescension, she could do that very well when she liked. What were these fat people here for, these beer-barrels, these deformities? They were ill, they were patients every one; she, Fröken d'Espard, had no need of the Torahus water to keep herself in shape. As Herr Fleming had excused himself from talking French she could not show them who she really was, but then Rector Oliver sought her out before all others and thus her table became a centre. There were many visitors at the other little tables, but they forgot to read their papers and simply sat and listened.

And at dinner the doctor joined them, the new doctor, who would not let anyone treat him superciliously; yes, and he held out his hand to Fröken d'Espard and greeted her and chatted with her a good while: she was quite well, she had had no ill effects of the adder's bite? No, to be sure. But she must beware of adders—next time in similar circumstances! The doctor passed on, but he had done his work, she was positively in a position to triumph. She looked so well too, she took wine and was witty, was tender, exerted her attraction. There was a group of ladies sitting at a table close by; they seemed envious of her.

The lawyer ran his eye over the tables and missed the Suicide, where was Herr Magnus? No answer. One of the maids was sent up to his room to look; he was not there. Fröken d'Espard supplied the information that she had met Herr Magnus that morning, that he was dressed for travelling, and that he had hinted at taking a run up to Christiania.

"I've always said so," exclaimed the lawyer, "you're indispensable here, Fröken d'Espard! May I drink with you!"

More triumph and more envy.

But the meal was not a particularly cheerful one, the whole sanatorium bore marks of sorrow. The lawyer would indicate the engineer's empty seat and shake his head, everyone spoke in hushed tones; on the other hand the lawyer, as host, could but feel grateful to Fröken d'Espard for livening things up a little; she was not going to be kept under by the ladies at the next table.

After dinner they went into an unfrequented room, where she wrote her document. She was very business-like and declared straight out that it was Herr Fleming who was the father of her child. She was also aware that they would require a statement from the doctor that the child was not prematurely born, and she went and got this. Oh, it went swimmingly, she was splendid, she was topping; in the end she coolly went up to Herr Fleming's room with him, as though she had been given—or had taken—a dispensation. Perhaps she was also a trifle under the influence of the wine.

Herr Fleming walked towards home with her.

They had not gone far before they met two of the sanatorium ladies who had already taken a walk after dinner. Herr Fleming bowed politely and they passed on. "Lord, how jealous they are over you!" said Fröken d'Espard, scenting no danger.

At the little barn she said good-bye to Herr Fleming. They agreed that he should go to the parson next day, but she was still business-like and pointed out various things that he was to put forward. "Now do your best," said she; "good-bye!"

A few paces separated them when suddenly Daniel burst out of the barn. "Now the devil take you—!" he yelled, and in a second his heavy hand was on Herr Fleming's shoulder. Daniel's face was bloodless, Herr Fleming turned pale too, Daniel began to foam and hiss: "Now get out of this! What are you doing here? You're to go away at once and never set your foot here again, do you hear what I tell you?"

"Gently now—!" began Herr Fleming.

Daniel did not take it gently, he roared like a bull and gave Herr Fleming a shaking; the lady ran up, she heard a storm of curses and savage threats: "I'll twist you into a knot, I'll spit a bullet through your skull!" After that Herr Fleming could do nothing but go. Daniel stood and watched him, jumped up, smacked his fists together in the air, and called after him: "Off with you at once, this very day! Mind that!"

He turned round and looked at the lady, evidently very well pleased with his performance. "Just let him come back!" he said.

So he didn't strike her or bite her, he talked to her like a human being, and she took heart again: "A sick man," she said with disapproval.

"You said he'd gone away?" he questioned her grimly.

"And you've been spying again," she replied; but she dared do no less than pick the hay off him, she knew by experience that contact was the best thing.

He shook her off, he did so; but then he relented and explained that he hadn't meant to spy on her at all; only he was told something, he got a kind of message—

"Yes, two ladies came tale-bearing, I know all about that, we met them."

"I believe I'll do something to him!" he said.

Suddenly the lady exclaimed: "Well, well—I beg your pardon!"

A remarkable thing for her to say, something quite unheard-of, and it amazed him so that all he could say was: "No, now you must make haste home to the child! Marta's given him some milk, but—"

"I beg your pardon!" she repeated as they went along.

Nothing more was said till they were sitting at home again, but she had by no means abandoned her cause: "He told me to ask you if you wouldn't like to build some more, a big house with lots of rooms."

"Build?"

"So that you could take boarders and earn money like the others?"

Daniel, utterly bewildered: "Have you two made this up between you?"

"Well, if you did he'd help with the money."

"There's only one thing I know," said Daniel reflectively; "and that is that he's to go."

"Well, then he would go."

This was all incomprehensible to Daniel, he tried to guess his way: "I see, then he'd do this for you?"

"Yes."

"And afterwards he'd go away?"

"Yes."

"And you'd like us to take in boarders here?"

"Yes," she replied; "that is to say, the idea was that I should go away with him."

"What?" shrieked Daniel.

"That you should give me up, you understand. There's no need to shout so loud."

Daniel raised his arms above his head and let them drop: "I believe you've gone mad, both of you!"

"I don't know that you can say that," she replied, sticking to her point. "You can always get another when you have a regular little sanatorium running here. Then you'll be a great man."

He jumped up and stood before her, crouching and furious. For an instant it looked as if he would throw himself upon her, then he said: "I thought I'd warned you never to speak of this again!"

"Yes," she said.

He stood motionless for a while and then went out of the pause.

He took a turn, she saw him go past the window and over to the stream; after a while he came back again and walked straight into the room.

"Shall we say that we'll go and get married on Tuesday next week?" he asked.

She can have seen no escape and had ceased to care what happened, whether he hit or bit or killed her. "We can say that if you like," she answered callously; "but it won't come to anything!"

He had tried being serious, he had tried rage, threats, and oaths and had made no impression; now he was dumb and at a loss. He sat down on a stool and hid his face in his hands.

"You must understand," she said, "that this is getting impossible for all of us."

"What am I to understand?" he asked. "It's me it's impossible for."

She didn't think it was so terribly bad for him, it had happened before that people had been engaged and had broken it off.

But hadn't she any sense, didn't she understand anything? He had been made a fool of once before, it must not happen again; what would everybody say? He came of good people, he didn't deserve that she should think for a moment of putting such a shame on him.

As he took it in this way, with sighing and sorrow, she considered that she had advanced a hair's breadth and was unwilling to provoke him further, but of course she might have retorted. Good people, a farmer's son—she showed no appreciation of these arguments. If anyone was entitled to speak of good birth, proud birth, it was surely she, Julie *née* d'Espard. And indeed the clergyman had taken her for the aristocrat she was.

"You see," he said, "I've had a plan all along. We can get back the farm, what do you think of that?"

"What farm?"

"My father's farm. We can get it back as soon as we can afford it. Then we'll move down into the village, it'll be better for you."

"No," she replied, "that's not it!" However, there was something in his announcement that caught her attention and she asked, with no more than ordinary interest: "When will you be able to afford it?"

"That depends; the udal rights don't expire for another twenty years, so we have lots of time. And I can tell you, we're going ahead every day!"

She: "Then why in the world didn't you sell the sæter for the sanatorium? You'd have got a lump of money all at once."

At this Daniel gave a crooked smile: "No, no, I wasn't such a fool! A lump of money, I dare say, but how much money? Not much. Do you know what Helmer's father got for his sæter for the sanatorium? A few hundred crowns. Perhaps I'd have got more, but it wasn't a few hundred crowns I wanted, it was many times that. And when I'd sold the sæter, how should I have got the rest? No, thanks, I wasn't going to be made a fool of! Here I go working myself up as time goes on, I sell beasts and skins and wool, soon I'll be selling butter, just you wait! And the sæter's still here, it hasn't been thrown away, it's going up in value year by year."

"I don't understand these things and I don't care about them either," she said. But as she was no fool she had her own thoughts on the subject; wasn't he perhaps counting on her money in these plans of his?

"Oh yes, we'll be down in the village one day!" he comforted her. "A grand farm, with woodland, Utby's the name of it, rich clay soil, there's a mill too,"

Frøken d'Espard, irritated: "I don't care about it, I tell you!"

"Oh yes, yes, you must think about it, Julie, just you start thinking about it right away! It's a big farm, I'll work it up, you shall have a good home and Julius'll be able to say he comes from that farm."

"Julius," she said thoughtfully; "no, he doesn't come from there!"

"Think it over," he asked her, patting her hand; "be happy now and say yes!"

She started back in alarm at his tenderness, fearing it might end in violence again. "Go away!" she said.

He rose and went to the door: "Tuesday next week then, that'll suit well! Don't say no!"

She was left to her meditations. No, her building proposals had not moved him, her business-like little head had lost again. Ah, breaking off this engagement was certainly the last thing in his mind; what would the neighbours say? She knew him; he had taken a little drink and boasted a little, had dropped hints of money in the background, and had let it be understood that Helena would be made to suffer exquisite regrets, and finally he had got the parson to put up the banns—it was not possible for him to draw back now. What was it he was talking about, he wanted to get back his father's farm? He was certainly speaking the truth, this was the idea that had been at the bottom of all his industrious plodding at the sæter; he meant to work his way up. Then it was that she had crossed his path, he knew that she had a lot of money hidden away, this money might perhaps redeem his father's farm at one stroke—

No, he would not draw back.

Daniel was bursting with sorrow and indignation; she kept him at arm's length, he might not touch her. Then why should he smarten himself up, walk on tiptoe, knock at her door before entering? Why should he put on other clothes on Sundays? He lapsed and became careless of his person. They were equals in ignorance, in undevelopment, but in barbarism, in unwashedness, she was his inferior. He might have gone on making himself tidy for her sake, been on his best behaviour and smoked a cigar at her now and again, but what was the use? His advances were met with savage looks: Go away!

The work of the sæter had been neglected of late; Daniel would drop what he was doing in the middle of working hours and let potatoes and turnips take care of themselves. He went down to the village.

Well now, if he had put up the banns on his own account, he could order the marriage service too!

In the clergyman's study he was told another story: he was met

CHAPTER THE LAST

with the information that an objection had just been raised to the wedding, a gentleman of the name of Fleming had asserted his right to the bride.

Daniel, with a long face: "Ah, so that's it—"

And therefore the clergyman could not very well—

"Yes, but that was only monkey tricks those two had hit upon!"

"Indeed?" said the clergyman. Well, but it wouldn't do; the situation would have to be cleared up.

No, it was all clear enough, the only thing wanting was the wedding. "Dear bless you," said Daniel, "why, it was all settled until this stranger turned up and started to talk her out of it, then they both went crazy and wanted to have it broken off."

"Yes," said the clergyman, shaking his head.

"Yes," said Daniel too. "And for all that the man's a weakling with one foot in the grave and spitting blood and he's been in the hands of the police and all. It was about some money they said he'd taken."

"No, there was some sort of misunderstanding, he showed me papers about it, that affair is in order."

"Ah," said Daniel; "all right," he said and was silent for a moment. "But now the thing is that our banns have been asked!"

"Yes," said the clergyman, again with a shake of the head.

"And then we've got the child."

"Yes, the child—well, there seems to be something wrong there too."

"Something wrong—?"

"This Fleming says that he is the father of the child."

"What?" cried Daniel, sitting with open mouth.

The clergyman was struck by the good faith, the unfeigned astonishment, with which he was faced. There was something unpleasant, something distinctly unsavoury, about the whole business, but his sympathy went to the lad Daniel. "I can't tell how it all hangs together," said he, "but your name is entered in the register as the father." He opened the book and ran his finger down the entries.

Daniel recovered himself: "Yes, it's me that's the father, they can't get over that. Why, he was away, he was out of the country. I never heard such nonsense!"

"But he asserts that the child was conceived before he left the sanatorium. And that agrees as to time."

"Time—yes, I dare say, but the child came too soon."

"Hm. No, I wonder if you're not making a mistake?" asked the clergyman mildly. "He produced to me a declaration from the sanatorium doctor that the child was born after full gestation."

"It's not possible! He's written that declaration himself! She was bitten by an adder and brought to bed too soon."

"Yes, a day or so, the paper said, or perhaps a few days. But the child was fully mature."

Daniel sat for a while in utter bewilderment, then he exclaimed: "Yes, but the mother must know, mustn't she?"

"Yes, she ought to."

"Yes. And she tells me all the time that I'm the father. I've never heard anything else. And she said the same in the room at home for the god-parents to hear."

The clergyman shook his head: "In any case, she asserts now that this Fleming is the father. He brought with him a statement from her too."

Silence.

"Well, they've gone crazy!" said Daniel blankly.

The clergyman would have liked to help him, but could not: "It is unfortunate for you that the mother was not present when the child was registered; it may be that when brought to book she disavows your statement."

"Ah, but she won't," replied Daniel; "it's not possible, just you let me have a talk with her!"

"Ah well, perhaps it will straighten itself, let us hope so. It is not pleasant for you, I see that very well. And in any case it is you and no one else who are registered as the father in my book."

Daniel went to the door: "So you can't marry us now, sir?"

"Hm. No, not immediately, Daniel, we must have the situation cleared up. But now try to talk it over with her, and with him too if you can; then perhaps it will arrange itself. Let us hope so!"

"But then you won't marry the other one either?"

"No. And I told him as much. But indeed he did not ask me to."

Daniel looked in at the store and made his purchases; he was very moody, bought the few things he remembered for the housekeeping, perhaps forgot others which were more important, moved like a sleep-walker, answered at cross-purposes. On his way home he went over the matter thoroughly, now and again he stopped and stared at the road; then he turned and went back to the store.

No, storming and threats didn't get him anywhere, it was a different thing if he could do something—something for her—to the best of his means. He turned to the counter and asked to see some ribbons: "What's the price of this?" He looked at a wider one: "What's the price of this? All right—a yard!"

Not that she was likely to accept it, she would probably throw it into a corner. Perhaps he'd be cunning and say it was meant for little Julius?

The lady was not at home, but Marta thought she would be back soon.

Daniel went into the new cottage. As ill luck would have it the child was asleep, otherwise he could have tricked it out a little, with a smart ribbon round its neck. Not his child? Bosh, we'll have a bone to pick about that! "Julius!" he called. No, he was asleep. Daniel took the ribbon out of its paper and held it up at full length; it was blue and very pretty, he tried to tie it on top of the mirror and couldn't get it to sit properly. He could have told himself how to make a bow with long ends, it was stupid of him. And, sure enough, when he had bungled it properly, he had to get Marta in to help him. But there hung the blue decoration at last.

"Did she say she wanted it there?" asked Marta.

And Daniel answered: "Yes, I understood so."

"She can't be long coming now," said Marta and went out again.

But the lady did not come. Daniel dodged in and out, humming to himself for Marta's benefit, went to the wood-shed and to the stream, and finally in desperation went off and hoed his little potato patch. This did not take long and it made his muscles easy and supple, he could have carried his whole family on his arm. Then he wandered into the wood, along the little path to the sanatorium.

His visit to the parson had given him a good set-back, he didn't mean to spy, but simply to go and meet her, and he whistled softly to show his peaceable disposition, and perhaps at the same time to give warning of his approach. He could imagine why she had gone out: she had sent an emissary to the parson and now wanted to hear the result. "Oh, little Julie, there won't be any result so long as there's a spark of life in me and Daniel!"

He met her long before he had reached the hay barn; she was alone. "Have you been out for a walk?" he said peaceably.

"Yes, to the sanatorium," she replied, defiantly.

She must have thought another fight was coming, as she cried: "Good God, am I not allowed to move?"

"Then you've had some bad news, I guess," he said, still more peaceably. He was keeping himself well in hand.

"No, I've had good news!"

"Has the Count left?"

"Go and ask him!"

Daniel said nothing for a moment, then: "Aren't you afraid this will end badly one day?"

"What should end badly?"

"Everything. I hear that you want to take the child from me too?"

"The child—from you?" She checked herself at this ambiguous exclamation, judging it inadvisable to speak out at the moment—there was such a deep peace in Daniel's manner, such a sinister peace. "Is Julius awake?" she asked.

"I might give you a word of warning," he went on; "but I've warned you before and it's no use, I'm not going to do it again. And you needn't imagine I'm going to put up with your monkeying with that fellow, the Finn, the Count. And if you think you're going to get the child, let me just tell you that it's me and nobody else that's down in the parson's book, so you won't do any good there either. And it's you and me that's had our banns asked in church."

Now if it had not been that Daniel's voice shook so queerly, she would probably have scoffed at him and treated it as his usual bragging. For she was in possession of facts and evidence and could have given an incontrovertible explanation of everything, but she dared not do this just now, it would have to wait. "I see, you've been to the parson," was all she said.

He announced in conclusion: "I shan't warn you again. Mind that!"

"Oh!" she sneered, "I'm so tired of this kind of talk!"

The days went by, the Tuesday appointed for the wedding was past and gone and there was no change, Fröken d'Espard continued to massage her face, she also took little walks in the forest, sometimes she had Julius with her. As far as Daniel could make out she met no one in the forest.

What was she up to? Was she waiting for something to turn up, or was she trying to tire Daniel out? It was not a good time for her either, she was exhausted by her difficulties, sleepless and furious. It was Daniel's opposition that enraged her; had he let her go, perhaps she would not have gone, God knows; perhaps she'd have gone for a little while and come back, God knows again. His immovability made her mad, she wept hysterically and ground her teeth. She was chained to him, nothing less.

Daniel took to going more often to the village. No, he didn't buy any more ribbon, that yard he brought home one day had made no difference one way or the other, it hung there over the mirror in the new cottage and was blue and pretty, but it was getting fly-blown; the lady never mentioned it, had not said thank-you for it.

On the other hand Daniel went down to the village to meet acquaintances and associate with folk. That was what he did there. He was bowed down and had little to say; what had become of his triumph over the neighbours? Even little Julius they were trying to steal from him. Oh, but Daniel saw very well that on this all-important point he would have to stand firm: it was he who was registered as the father, with the lady's full agreement in the presence of Marta and the god-parents at the cottage. She couldn't get away from that, could she?

His friends were rather reserved; it must have leaked out that all was not as it should be at Torahus Sæter, Daniel himself was changed.

"When are you to be married, Daniel?" one of them might ask.

And Daniel would reply: "Well, you know, I can't say."

"Oh, you can't say?"

"There's always some hitch or other: either the time won't suit, or we haven't any clothes fine enough—always something cropping up."

"That's a strange thing to hear!"

"Oh, I don't know," Daniel would reply. "You see, it's not like any other girl that's to be a bride; Julie, she must have a gown specially for it, with lots of ribbons and beads."

His friends laughed at this and made fun of him.

"I said that for a joke," said Daniel, retrieving himself. "Women, they must have it their way, that's what I meant. But then there's me, I can't very well go to the altar in what I'm sitting in here, and these are pretty near the best clothes I've got."

"Are you so short of clothes?:'

"Yes, I am that."

"That's easily mended!"

Daniel: "I was to have gone and got measured for a suit, but then there was Whit and holidays and all, and there hasn't been a blessed chance to get anything made."

"Well, no harm meant!" his friends said to that. And they sat in the back parlour at the store and ordered beer and drank themselves rather happy and noisy, exchanged forgiveness of sins with each other for any careless remarks they might have dropped when fuddled, and got rid of all misunderstandings. But there was no doubt his friends had heard something of Daniel's distress, he was getting to be talked about once more.

"I wanted to have a word or two with you, Helmer," he said.

Very well, they left the room and strolled along towards Helmer's home. And what Daniel had to say was that probably he'd be shooting somebody one day.

"Hey? H—no, you mustn't do that!" said Helmer, laughing and shaking his head.

"Yes, if I'm forced to it."

"Who might it be?"

"Well, never you mind; but I dare say you've heard."

"No, what have I heard? Well, well, I may have heard one thing or another, but— And what do you think they'll come and do to you afterwards? They'll come and take you."

"I don't care."

"Now, you've got to come to your senses and not make an ass of yourself!" said Helmer. "And that's all I'll ask of you!" he said. "It isn't the first time either; there was one year you wanted to burn up Helena and I got you to drop it."

"Well, as to that—"

"I won't listen to any more, do you hear? And now you'll just come inside and get a drop of hot coffee and pull yourself together."

Daniel went in with him and had some coffee and was a trifle less down-hearted for the time being. As he was going he collapsed again, Helmer went out with him, and Daniel asked: "Do you remember what she said on the day of the christening—that the child was mine?"

"That the child was yours, yes—?"

"'Carry your child nicely, Daniel,' she said. And 'Don't squeeze your child, Daniel,' she said. That was in the new cottage at home. You heard her, didn't you?"

"I'm ready to take my oath to it!"

"Yes. And now I'll go straight home and have a talk to her and get it cleared up. Time's getting on, I'll have to make haste!"

Helmer exhorted him once more to be sensible and let him go. He did not see his friend again till a couple of weeks later, and then everything was changed, everything had gone to ruin. . . .

When Daniel came home he went straight into the new cottage. "I'm already a laughing-stock down in the village," he said.

"Oh," said the lady.

"Now I want to hear what day you can go with me and get married."

A thing that had never happened before happened now; oh, she was so harassed, so pulled down—she began to cry. "I want to go home," she burst out; "I want to go a way from here, home! What have I to do here? God help me, there's nobody, not a soul, no shops, not a window to look into, no streets, no ships at the quayside, in the evenings it's dark, nobody drives past here, no, there's nothing—"

She wept hysterically and asked if he thought there was any

CHAPTER THE LAST

sense in it. "You haven't even seen the Aker River," she said; "it's full of boats, I used to row there with the little boys, we took boats without asking leave, ha ha. Be kind now, Daniel, this is no good, I don't know, but it's getting impossible. Married? Can't you see what a mistake you've made? He's waiting for me and we're going away together, and you keep saying 'married, married'! You look as if you didn't understand it, but the Count's waiting, I tell you, I'm in love with him, I've kept his money for him all the time. But we shall help you too—"

"Now be quiet and let me say just two words," said Daniel; "what day will you go with me and get married?"

"Married—?"

"Yes, that's all I want to know."

"Ah, but I shall take the child and run off with it!" she cried with shining eyes. "You can't run after me if I have the child, we shall fall down and hurt ourselves, Julius will hurt himself—"

Daniel stamped on the floor and shouted: "Be quiet!"

"I beg your pardon!" she said.

Daniel: "You're altogether beside yourself and I won't talk to you anymore. And now there's only one single thing I'll warn you about: that you're not to go to the sanatorium anymore before we're married, do you understand? And you're not to meet a single person in the wood before we're married. No. And that's all the warning I'll give you."

She seemed to be thinking this over, or thinking of something else. Suddenly she turned to him, tender and insinuating: "Forgive me, Daniel, for everything! I haven't been as I ought, you're perfectly right there. And I've driven you away and all and wouldn't have anything to do with you. But now I don't know—I should like to make it up to you in the way you like, if you'll let me. Do be kind now, Daniel! And I'll be nicer with you—come now!"

Oh, she must have thought she would damp his rage and make

him duller and more amenable afterwards. She was in a tight place, an uncommonly tight place.

He caught his breath and turned his head to the window, perhaps his bashfulness was aroused. In the same tone and just as persistently as before he asked her: "Now for the last time, shall we say next Tuesday, or—?"

She gave him up and simply sat looking at her lap.

"For I've had enough of all this gossiping about me in the neighbourhood," he declared. "I'm not a beggarly tramp, I'm from Utby, and everybody knows me. Now what do you say about Tuesday?"

She, not knowing what to say: "I'll go and tell him."

"No!" screamed Daniel. "Haven't I just told you that you're not to go there anymore?"

"Go and tell him that he must leave—that's all I meant—"

Daniel: "I've told him that, there's no need to tell him again, he knows it. God, yes, I let him know!"

From now on she gave up answering and said nothing. He remarked that the clothes she had were fine enough and that he himself could borrow a suit of Helmer; he reminded her that she must get back the papers she had sent to the parson, the declarations, all the cock-and-bull stories. She made no further reply.

The morning after.

Certainly she must speak to Herr Fleming, naturally she must—to warn him, to get him to be careful, for now the danger was greater than ever: Daniel was like a mad bull, nothing less.

She got ready to go; where Daniel was she didn't know, perhaps he was down in the village; Marta must be seeing to the beasts, there was no one in the kitchen.

Of course she must go. She had ventured it before, many times before, and could not shirk it now that the need was greater than it had ever been. That would look nice. After all, what harm was there in it? She wanted to prevent any harm's being done, a hot-headed assault, a catastrophe; how could she tell? An educated person would be grateful to her for averting an evil deed, a man of Herr Fleming's sort would give her credit for it; but what could she expect of Daniel? Oh, he was so wild, so desperate; if he came, perhaps he would throttle her. What did the husband do in that delightful French novel when he came home and found his wife's lover in the bedroom? First he bowed, then he held a lamp to light the lover downstairs. "Take care!" he cautioned him; "there's one rickety step; don't fall on your face, monsieur!" What grace, what polish, the behaviour of a man of the world! Ought not Daniel to have learnt something of this?

She had got over her frightful depression of the day before and was able to think; besides which it was a fine day, the path was dry, birds were singing, and there was a scent of leaves. She walked with brisk and easy steps, but she could not be long away from Julius.

A little beyond the barn she met Herr Fleming, as though he had guessed that she was coming. He tried to get her to turn, but she would not, she dared not: "No, perhaps he's after you, he means mischief!" Rather than that Herr Fleming should encroach on Daniel's domain she was self-sacrificing enough to take the risk of straying too far from it. They walked a little nearer to the sanatorium and then sat down in the heather.

She told him what she had heard: Daniel had been to see the clergyman. He came back from the village yesterday, savage and determined; he had again been the victim of gossip and he wouldn't bear it! She broke off to ask Herr Fleming: "Can you understand why he makes so much of what the neighbours think?"

Oh yes, Herr Fleming could understand that, it was like that among country folk, they all knew each other.

"And his being a farmer's son?"

"Yes, of course, they think a lot of that, they're proud of it, it's the same at home. A farmer's son has to pay more attention to public opinion than other people."

"Just as if he were a nobleman!" she said with a smile.

Herr Fleming nodded: "If a farmer's son goes to the bad it's enough to bring honourable parents to their grave—unhappily."

"Why do you say unhappily?—Well," she said, breaking off, "what are we to do? He wants to be married on Tuesday."

"It can't be done, after my protest."

"Ah, but this time Daniel won't stop at words. I'm afraid of him now."

Herr Fleming suggested that they had better clear out and perhaps leave the child behind for a time.

"No," she answered with a shake of the head.

"Only a short time, only till we have settled down and started to make a living."

"No, no, it won't do. You can't have seen him properly, can't have looked at Julius properly, have you?"

"A stunning child!"

"What was that?" she said all at once. "I thought I heard something."

They both looked around them—no, nothing. Presently she said: "I've been wondering if one day when I'm out with the child in my arms I could steal right over to the sanatorium?"

"To the sanatorium, eh—?"

"And stay there. I mean, that we could all three be there?"

Herr Fleming reflected: Director Rupprecht was a capital fellow, possibly he would allow it. No doubt he would.

"We should surely be safe there," she said; "nobody could get us out. We might stay there for a time."

"But it would be terrible for you—the servants, the visitors; terrible for you with the child, I mean—"

"Oh yes. I've thought of that. But I should have to put up with it."

CHAPTER THE LAST

Herr Fleming, brightening up: "I'll speak to the director!"

They discussed it further: it was a possibility in the midst of impossibilities, but he pitied her for the ordeal she would have to go through.

"Now I must go," she said, getting up. "I've come here without leave."

He also rose: "I'll go with you."

At that instant Julie went pale and stood as though turned to stone: there sat Daniel, above the path, on a little mound, half hidden by brushwood. Then Herr Fleming caught sight of him, and a tense look came into his face.

Suddenly Julie called out: "Daniel, I only came to tell him that, now I'll run home!"

No answer. Daniel was squatting on his haunches and staring at them, crouching like a beast of prey about to spring.

Then Julie d'Espard broke down and another paroxysm came on: "Oh, are you there, Daniel?" she cried in a wild burst of weeping. "I've told him he must go away, but he won't, you're both so mad after me, he won't leave me, do you hear? And now I'll—one day when you're not there—I'll take Julius with me—Julius with me—"

It sounded as if she were spelling it out.

"Let me go back with you," said Herr Fleming.

"No, no!" she cried; "you must look after yourself!"

Daniel did not take his eyes off them; with an imperceptible gliding motion he changed his position and came down on his right knee, then he felt with his hand for something on the ground, the next instant he had the rifle levelled.

Julie threw herself down in the heather with a scream.

"There, there—don't take on like that!" Herr Fleming tried to calm her.

"Lie down!" he heard her say. But he did not forget his dignity and showed no fear, he was in no hurry, cut no capers. Oh, very likely Daniel wouldn't have done it after all, perhaps he wouldn't have done what he did, if he had not been irritated by the fellow's calmness: there he was, caught in this clandestine meeting, and he stood there in the most mendacious fashion giving himself airs over it.

When the shot rang out it was a second or two before Herr Fleming dropped. His fingers twitched slightly, he drew one knee up a little and then lay still.

The next thing Julie d'Espard was aware of was that Daniel came down from the mound striding towards her; she heard rather than saw him, as the heather scraped against his boots. Terror seized her, she started up on her elbow and asked: "What are you going to do?" She saw that his eyes sought her and the corpse by turns, his face was unrecognizable, she saw that his lips moved, and perhaps he was saying something, "What are you going to do to me, I say?" she whimpered. As he did not answer she jumped up and began to run. The last she saw of him was that he stood watching to see if the dead man would move.

She had run off in the direction of the sanatorium. On coming to herself she stopped and considered for a moment; then she made a wide detour through the wood, home to the sæter.

Daniel was left looking at his work, perhaps with a trace of curiosity, of surprise. He too was human, he had left off going on all fours and tearing his enemy to pieces, he had learnt to shoot instead. Oh no, he was nothing great, no hero, he was as human beings are.

XVI

An investigation followed, taking of depositions and examination of witnesses, the neighbourhood bubbled over with stories, timid people bolted their doors at night; what else could be expected? At the same time some men, supposed to be police, were sent out to find Daniel; oh yes, they searched the woods around the sæter and finally they went in a posse into the forest and looked under every bush; but Daniel was on the mountain, and they probably knew it. "Let him be!" they may have thought, with ill-concealed sympathy for the unhappy man; "he'll come of his own accord one of these days, he's not such a bad fellow, it's Daniel Utby; do you think we don't know him?" So they may have thought. Besides, God knows, it might be dangerous to go too near him just now. He was not to be trifled with, the monster, wasn't it a fact that he'd meant to burn up Helena one time?

Fröken d'Espard gave what evidence she could about the event, but her memory was not of the best, her head was in a turmoil, and as to the all-important details of the catastrophe itself her memory failed her altogether. The Sheriff's officer did his best to cross-question her and write in his report, but no. For he had begun by saying that the question was whether it was premeditated murder, as in that case it would involve the death penalty—ah, and this gave the lady a good deal to think about and caused her to lose her memory for a long time at a stretch. Moreover this Fröken d'Espard was a deuce of a lady, the Sheriff's officer had examined her once before and got nothing out of her.

"Now, what were the actual circumstances of the crime?"

She didn't know. She had lost consciousness at an early stage, and when she came to herself again, she didn't notice anything in particular, she simply got up and ran. Could anybody wonder?

"What had Daniel said?"

"Not a word."

"Didn't he give any warning?"

"Yes, he shouted."

"Well, then he must have said something?"

"But he didn't say a word. He just shouted a warning."

"Had Daniel ever threatened to shoot Herr Fleming?"

Not that she had heard.

"Never used threats to him? Never at all?"

"No. Only asked him to go away."

"That morning—did he take his rifle with him in order to shoot Herr Fleming?"

"Did he?"

"It's for me to ask!" said the Sheriff's officer.

The lady looked him in the face and retorted: "I can't answer what I don't know."

"But what do you think? What impression had you?"

Fröken d'Espard reflected rapidly: "He told me he was going out shooting."

The Sheriff's officer hurriedly referred to his report and pointed out: "But you said before that you hadn't spoken to him."

The lady: "He said it the evening before."

"That he was going shooting in the morning?"

"Yes."

"But with a rifle? And at this time of year? What was he going to shoot with a rifle?"

The lady was silent, she put her hand to her forehead, she did not know everything in this world, so she made no answer. And, indeed, was she not completely flabbergasted with all she had gone through lately, as she had every right to be? She looked helplessly at Marta.

When it came to Marta's turn she was able to depose that it was reindeer Daniel meant to shoot. That was what he used his rifle for. Wild reindeer on the mountain.

The lady recovered her voice: "Yes, of course, reindeer, that's what he said!"

"It's not the season," said the Sheriff's officer.

From Marta's answer it appeared that Daniel never paid much attention to the season.

The Sheriff's officer: "Then you mean to say he was going to shoot reindeer in the close season?"

Marta hesitated a moment and then answered with great emphasis: "Yes, Daniel shot all sorts, and he shot all the year round."

"It's against the law!" the Sheriff's officer announced. . . .

Yes indeed, many things are against the law, shooting people is also against the law. When Daniel was sighted high up on the mountain, and men crawled cautiously up towards him and beckoned and tried their blandishments on him, and he called down that he'd make a corpse of anyone who came nearer—why, that too was against the law. So the men crawled down again and let him be.

But this did not satisfy the Sheriff's officer and he armed his men with guns and let them try again; but this did not lead to anything either, though they tried to get round the crazy lad and ring him in; but no, they couldn't come near enough, his gun carried farther than theirs. Oh, they did everything possible.

Then it was that Daniel was king of Torahus Mountain; faith, nobody came near him.

But one morning he saw two specks approaching him from the side, two little boys, they were coming from "the Peak," yes, and they carried a white handkerchief on a pole—oh, they brought a flag of truce, they wanted to parley with the outlaw, with the robber chieftain. Daniel had read no books and this was meaningless to him; but there was nothing to shoot at, two little boys, good Lord! And they came nearer.

Daniel first threw a scouting glance around him, then he laid down his rifle so as not to scare them. And they came right up to him. Well, they were rather pale and breathing heavily, but the one who carried the flag came first and the other had a parcel which he held out at arm's length, saying: "For you, please!"

Daniel, surprised: "What is it?"

"A little food," was the reply; "some lunch."

"We took it off the table," explained the other.

"Where do you come from?"

"We're staying at the sanatorium."

"At the sanatorium? And you've come up here?"

"Yes, we planned it last night. It's only a bit of food, a few sandwiches."

Daniel opened the packet and began to eat, turning his face from them as he did so. He sniffled once or twice, touched by their charity in spite of his being a hard case.

"Does anybody know you were coming here?" he asked.

No, nobody knew.

"You mustn't tell anybody either," he said.

They talked for a while longer, he found out how old they were and that their father's name was Rector Oliver; he too was at the sanatorium. During the whole conversation Daniel turned away from them and sniffled now and again. When he had finished the food he turned round and took both boys by the hand, saying: "Thanks for the meal!"

"It wasn't anything, they said; "it was too little, we'll bring some more tomorrow."

Daniel, with sudden fierceness: "No, no more! No, because I shan't be here," he added more mildly. "You mustn't come here anymore."

"No, no," they answered.

Daniel pointed: "Look here, when you go back you must follow the scrub all the way and not go on the bare slope where you'll be seen. Now, don't be silly, follow the scrub the whole way."

"All right!"

"And thanks again!" said Daniel, turning away from them.

The boys left him. They had done their part and hauled down the flag of truce. There's no doubt they were full of their mission and proud of having shaken hands with the robber chieftain. . . .

Daniel still held the mountain, for the third day now. He wasn't even afraid to move farther down towards the sæter and the houses, and here again he held the position with his long rifle. The people were helpless, at last they went down to Helmer in the village and said: "You must try and get him by fair words, Helmer!" No, Helmer backed out, it was beyond him, he couldn't bear to see Daniel again in such a state. And Daniel continued to hold the mountain, the crazy lad raised his rifle and called out that he would shoot anyone who came within range; it was almost like a man defending his hearth and home.

The two women at the sæter put their heads together and pondered, hoping to God Daniel would seize a chance of coming down and getting something to eat; they themselves dared not stir a step on account of the police and the villagers. Now and then they heard shots on the mountain, when he was shooting at somebody no doubt.

The Sheriff's officer had ordered them to put some food out for him on the door-step. Oh yes, they did that. "And now one of you go and tell him where he'll find food!" he then said. No, they durstn't do that, said Marta, said the lady, not for dear life, said they. All the same the Sheriff's officer sat in the barn door a whole night keeping an eye on the door-step in case Daniel should come, and he wasted a whole night over it, but Daniel didn't come. And so this innocent experiment was abandoned and the food was taken in again.

But one rainy evening he came.

It so happened that Marta and Julie were chatting quietly in the kitchen, when the door opened and he slipped in. Julie gave a little cry and started back when she saw him. He was wet and perishing with cold, a pitiable sight, his face streaked with the rain, hollow-eyed and worn out for want of sleep. He did not look up, but put a blue hand before his mouth and gave a bashful laugh; then he flung himself upon the table, seized a loaf of bread, and began to bite at it. He stood the rifle by his side.

Marta was equal to the occasion: "It was a good thing you came, here's the coffee!"

He bit away at the loaf without cutting it and left the meat till later. The coffee stood there steaming.

"I can take this with me, can't I?" he said, putting the rest of the loaf under his arm as he rose from the table.

"Won't you drink your coffee?"

"No, it don't matter. It's so hot."

"Well, now we've been questioned," Marta went on to say. "We told him it was reindeer you went out to shoot that morning. That was why you took your rifle, we said."

"Ah," he replied.

"It wasn't to shoot anything else. So now you know."

"I don't care!"

"For if it was it'd be a hanging matter," said Marta.

"Oh, all right."

Julie, from the other side of the room: "You'll try and get away, won't you, Daniel?"

"I don't know," he replied. And he gave a sidelong look at her feet and asked: "Is Julius asleep?"

"Yes, he's asleep."

CHAPTER THE LAST

"I'd like just to have a look at him."

God knows what his idea was, whether he felt drawn to the child or only wanted to show that he was not a man that was in a hurry and afraid. He snatched a jacket that was hanging on the wall, picked up his rifle, and strode to the door, Julie after him and into the new cottage. It was all done in a rush. He just looked at the child, nodded, and stepped to the door again.

Julie: "Here—stop a moment!"

The fact that he was pursued and hunted affected her deeply, that he did not accuse her or say an angry word made her ready to throw herself at his feet. She opened her trunk, took out some banknotes at random, and thrust them into his hand, begging him to get away, over the mountain perhaps, "we'll meet later—"

He looked at her for the first time and said: "All right—thanks!"

Marta came, she had filled a bottle with coffee and handed it to him, but as he was reaching for it, it fell on the floor. From old habit he groaned over the breakage: "Ah, there goes the bottle, but my hands were so numb!"

Then he flung the door open and dashed out. . . .

He held the mountain for a couple of days yet; the Sheriff's officer was in despair, he clung to the hope of dealing with this affair without having to call in outside help. Together with his wife he now came up towards Torahus Sæter, and they had no guns or anything to show they were police, but just walked up. When they came within range, where Daniel usually shouted his warnings, the Sheriff's officer halted and let his wife go on. A strange emissary for such a mission, the one who had jilted Daniel and all! But Helena must have said that now *she* would try what fair words could do.

The two women at the sæter had seen the couple and now kept their eyes on Helena, to see how far she dared go. It looked as if Helena would go right up, although Daniel shouted a warning to her.

"He won't shoot Helena," said Marta.

"But it's no joke going near him!" said Julie enviously. "I ought to have been the one to do it. But, then, you and I were not allowed."

Helena continued the ascent.

"What does that Sheriff's wife want there?" sniffed Julie. "He doesn't care a scrap about her!"

Suddenly Daniel did an unexpected thing: he started to come down, he walked towards her, they met and stood talking, Helena and he.

Poor Fröken d'Espard, she was liable to such childish and fatuous aberrations; at this moment she was furious with him for being still on the mountain; why had he not made his escape as she asked him? They might have met later on, she would have found him sure enough! "Will you just look, Marta, how busy they are chatting away? Ah, now he's got rid of her, sent her about her business, none too soon either—"

Helena descended the mountain again, walked on and on, and Daniel stood watching her. She rejoined her husband far below and the couple went on their way to the village. What in the world was the meaning of it all?

Fröken d'Espard boldly marched up the mountain in her turn, in defiance of his orders. Daniel saw her and came to meet her as he had done with the other.

"Are you still here?" she said. "Why didn't you try to escape?"

No, Daniel must have seen how impossible this plan was, he just shook his head and made no reply. How far would he have got before being caught? Not at all far, perhaps to some little town, and what was he to do there? Perhaps to Christiania; what was he to do there? He had realized that sooner or later he would have to bow the knee, perhaps he had at last seen the foolishness of his whole proceeding—trying to defend himself against the law with a rifle. It was intelligible that in his distraction immediately after the crime

CHAPTER THE LAST

he had hit upon nothing better, but in the long run, many days and nights together—no. This must be the end of it, he was worn out and beaten. And, besides, it would save Julie's money, this could now be added to the rest for redeeming his father's farm. A big help when the time came; if not for himself, then for little Julius.

He walked homewards with Julie.

"Dare you come with me?" she asked.

"Yes," he replied despondently.

"What was it that woman wanted—Helena?"

"She brought a message."

"Oh, indeed! I was waiting all the time to see you hug her."

"Helena?" he cried. "I was thinking of giving her a couple of bullets! She brought a letter from the parson. Here it is, read it!"

It was just a few words, a cordial little note: Daniel must come down from the mountain and be good, then perhaps it would not be so bad for him, everything was in God's hand. He was making his case worse by persisting in threats and violence. The clergyman himself would offer evidence as to his good character, and several others would do the same; God and men would show him mercy, he would see!

"What will you do?" asked Julie.

"I'll just go home and get a bit of food and a sleep, then they'll come for me."

"Are they coming for you?" she whispered.

"Three o'clock," he nodded. . . .

He came home, took the bullet out of his rifle at once, ate, and slept. When he got up he washed himself and changed into his best clothes. He also gave Marta some instructions about the cattle and how the sæter was to be worked when he was away. Then the Sheriff's officer came and another man with him.

Fröken d'Espard was now of no account, she drifted between the kitchen and the new cottage, wringing her hands and whispering, whispering, grey in the face. O God in heaven, and it was all her fault! Daniel was in for a moment to look at the child, then he shook hands with both women, putting a tolerably good face on it, the same to each of them.

Then the three men went away.

However, Daniel's last words did something to cheer the lady up. He turned to Marta and said: "Those people at the sanatorium want to have the big bull, but you're not to sell him till well on in the autumn. Remember that!"

All might have gone well and went amiss—

You see, Fröken d'Espard was now free to visit the sanatorium as much as she pleased, but there was nothing to take her there. Why should she go? To meet the same summer boarders and holidaymakers and patients as before, the lawyer, the Rector, perhaps Fröken Ellingsen, perhaps the newly-married Bertelsen and his wife, formerly Fru Ruben—what had she to talk to them about? To flirt with the youngsters, the curly-pates, the new Norway with the toreador's calves and records in high jump? She was no giddy young thing. For that matter Fröken d'Espard had by no means done with the case, with the court, the jury; she had enough to think about.

She received an application about the corpse, Herr Fleming's corpse. There had been a post-mortem, all was in order; but what was to be done about the burial? Was the corpse to be sent to Finland?

She had thought of this, oh, the lady could be very clear-headed when she chose. Of course she would have paid for the unfortunate Herr Fleming's funeral, no question about that; but could she venture to interfere in the matter? Prudence urged her to refrain; supposing she paid, might it not raise the question of where the money came from? The dead man would remain dead whatever she did.

"What have I to do with it?" she asked the emissary, to get rid of

CHAPTER THE LAST

him.

Ah, but the fact was, Herr Fleming hadn't left a penny. That was the queer part of it.

"Well, what business is it of mine?" she exclaimed nervously. "I'm not his mother. I didn't even know him well."

No, no. But then he'd have to be buried at the public expense.

"Why?" she asked. He surely left enough to pay for the wretched funeral. "I seem to remember that he had several trunks, he showed me some expensive clothes, he carried a diamond ring in his waistcoat-pocket which may have been worth a fortune."

No, the emissary informed her; the ring had been tested, it was not genuine, it was worth nothing.

The lady: "You don't say so!" Then she had the presence of mind to add: "Well, but his clothes—ask at the sanatorium—"

So there her suspicion was confirmed: it was not the first valuable ring, he must have been forced to sell that; and he came back with another, which was valueless; as a matter of fact she had seen it at once, at their first meeting in the summer; the ring had no sparkle. Oh, that poor Herr Fleming, he too was down, a man on his knees—holding his head high, but on his knees. This gave her even more to think about, soon her little head would split....

The days went by. Fröken d'Espard helped with the work more than before and relieved Marta as far as she could, she treated it as a cure. It was hay-making time, Helmer came up early one morning and mowed the meadows with his machine, the two women spread the hay, turned it, and carried it, little Julius lay in the field. It was not so bad, thought Julie; and how would her head have been without this outdoor work? Really, she had known things more boring than this, her garret in Christiania was often worse, the empty loafing about the streets was often worse. After the examination and the trial she positively began to regain heart and spirits; Daniel's sentence was extremely humane and just, he got seven years; by the mercy of God and men, and Fröken d'Espard, who before had wept with vexation over her misfortunes, now wept with joy at the good turn things had taken. Of course, seven years' penal servitude was no boon, but at any rate it was not sheer destruction and death, thanks be to God!

The days came and went and it was a blessing how they passed, Julius was growing, he took notice, followed her with his eyes, smiled, howled, sucked, and slept. The whole year had been full of harrowing events, nothing in her surroundings was stable, all had been subject to violent changes, she had been hurled from one side to the other, and the lines of her fate had been relaid many times in the course of the year. When she reflected upon them, many of these stages had almost faded out, the things seemed to have happened long, long ago. In the last few days she had reached firmer ground, she could now take an interest in getting the hay in before the rain came.

They had not forgotten her at the sanatorium, no, at that great holiday home and health resort they took compassion on her and sent her a note. No doubt they wished to cheer her in her desolation, and the idea was certainly Lawyer Rupprecht's, though the note was signed by Andresen, her former employer.

What should she have to talk to him about? Had he seen her with the missing tooth and the glaring scar on her chin? And were not her hands those of a working-woman, was not her whole appearance coarsened? But above all she had become flat-chested.

She did not go.

But then one day she received a bill, the bill for Herr Fleming's last weeks at the sanatorium. Yes, it came to her, and now what was she to do? Could she venture on another blunt refusal? It so happened that she had some small share in this last bill of Herr Fleming's: she had dined with him one day and they had drunk an expensive wine. She looked at the bill, began to examine it carefully;

scandalous prices, she thought, rank profiteering—her thriftiness was outraged, she appealed to Marta, pale with anger: "Just see what those people at the sanatorium charge for a meal and a bottle of wine, twenty crowns! It was French wine, and oughtn't I to know the price of French red wine, when I come from there?" said Fröken d'Espard in her indignation. Marta backed her up, she had never heard anything like it either, did they think they could do as they chose at that place? "No," said the lady; "if you'll look after Julius meanwhile, I'll go across and have it out with them!"

She smartened herself a little and went.

She was lucky enough to meet the director in the big veranda; he was delighted, greeted her effusively, and said: "Herr Andresen would be very glad to see you again, he was your chief once, wasn't he? This way, Fröken!"

She stopped him: "No, thanks, I only came to say something to you. I've had this bill sent me."

Lawyer Rupprecht put on his glasses and read it. "Ah, I see," he said doubtfully.

The lady: "Is it your intention to send me Herr Fleming's bill?"

"Mistake!" said the lawyer.

"I'll pay for my dinner if you like."

At this the lawyer cried: "Oh, it's beyond bearing, all the blunders they make here! A mistake, Fröken!"

"That's what I thought. For I suppose you can pay yourselves out of his effects."

"No, his effects—but we won't talk about that—his effects have been claimed by the authorities. Well, it was really a good thing I got hold of this bill and was able to stop it, now it's mine!" he said, putting it in his pocket. "That you could suppose for a moment that Torahus Sanatorium was capable of sending you—! To go from one thing to another: when are you coming back to stay with us, Fröken d'Espard? We miss you, and we won't send you other people's bills anymore, I'll have a word with the person concerned. Your room shall be ready for you."

In the face of this cordiality Fröken d'Espard was somewhat mollified. She was not easily duped, there was no doubt the lawyer had known all about the bill and where it was sent, but after all she could not be surprised at that; the main thing was that she would save her money. "Thank you," she said; "I must stay where I am."

The lawyer: "Some of your friends are still here; Fröken Ellingsen hasn't come and Rector Oliver has left, but Herr Bertelsen and his wife are here—I don't think you have met them since their marriage? Fröken Ellingsen writes that she'll come later, she can't very well come as long as certain other people are here—you understand! However, we shall have Eyde, the composer, you knew him, Selmer Eyde, the pianist? He has finished his studies in Paris and we look forward to getting him back for our winter visitors. Ah, and then we have a new engineer, a sportsman to his finger-tips, a new doctor, you've met him, lots of new faces, capital young people. And of course you've seen how we're building and adding to the place? Oh, we shall make Torahus the leading sanatorium in the country! Can you guess what our fire-insurance stands at already? You'll never guess, hundreds of thousands! Now we're devoting our whole energy to laying on water and electric light—"

The lawyer chatted on, enumerating one thing after another, he was full of his own affairs, but did not forget to send a maid for Andresen: "You must really allow Herr Andresen to say how d'ye do, Fröken! He wanted to go and see you at the sæter, but I didn't know if you were receiving."

Andresen came. What made him so pressing? Did he want to get her back to the typewriter?

A big man with thin hair, very pale and very fat, he had come to drink the Torahus waters and go through a cure and already his face hung in pouches, drained and empty. He was very friendly, but the lady did not fail to notice how disappointed he was on seeing her again. Alas, yes, she was no longer the same! And all at once a thrill shot through her: she would go home again to the child, to little Julius, home this minute!

He: "I thought I'd say how d'ye do to you as I was in these parts."

She: "That was very kind of you!"

"Are you getting on all right, Fröken d'Espard? We've got a lot of new people at the office, you must look in some time when you're in town."

Words, words, it was not as in old days at the office when this same gentleman leaned over her on the pretext of seeing what she'd written, and then kissed her like a madman. No, today he no longer wanted anything of her, he started back on seeing her. He even stood on his dignity, let it be seen that he was her former employer and was condescending: "It seems to me such an infinite time since you were with us. Let me see, were typewriters and steel pens invented then?"

Fröken d'Espard did her duty and laughed loudly at this. But when he wanted to go on entertaining her with recollections of her bygone life at the typewriter, which she had almost forgotten, she was bored and was not sorry when Herr Andresen rose and took a friendly leave of her: "Now, don't forget your French, Fröken d'Espard! Your successor is far from being such a dab at the language as you were, but she has other good qualities. Well, good-bye! It was pleasant to meet you again and hear you're all right."

She could not avoid another encounter with the lawyer: "Ah, has Herr Andresen's desire been gratified? I saw how delighted he was! I say, Fröken, didn't you tell us that Herr Magnus went to Christiania? Well, but he hasn't come back. Isn't it a month ago? You were the last to speak to him; but now it appears that somebody has been here inquiring for him, a lady; who can she be? I didn't see her, but she's been here twice, it looks like something important, she's telephoned too. I really don't know what we ought to do. What do you think?"

"I don't know. He'll come, no doubt."

"Ah, you think so? But now if you were here, you found him for us once before, you're so clever! Can't you be induced to come back to us? We miss you."

What did the man mean by being so persistent? He meant nothing. He made himself amiable to Fröken d'Espard and to everyone else and meant nothing by that either, he was only interested in getting as many boarders as possible, full house, and just now he had a poor house. No, Lawyer Rupprecht had no private ends with her, he never thought of setting up house, never fell in love, he was just as much taken up with getting young Selmer Eyde back as with housing a young lady—perhaps rather more.

"So the rest of your friends are not to be allowed a word with you today?" he said. "Herr Bertelsen and his wife won't like me for that, indeed they won't. They're in Number 107, in case you'll look them up. You won't, then?"

Number 107! Oh, that Director Rupprecht, he had added a hundred to all the numbers in the sanatorium to make them look big on the doors.

Save that Andresen might have shown less disappointment in her appearance, the visit had been a fortunate one for Fröken d'Espard, but it did rankle a little to find she was already such a thing of the past. What would she be in seven years' time? Oh, but she'd manage to be healthy and pretty again, charming, there was nothing she wouldn't do to recover her looks; when the time came, she'd have a tooth put in.

Yes, in everything else the visit had been a success. Everyone had spared her, no one had hinted that she was living in the house of a murderer, Herr Fleming was never mentioned. And in any case the visit had paid, she had saved money.

So she turned back to the sæter, hurried back; she was more afraid than ever that little Julius might be awake and waiting for her. Poor little creature, he had such pretty hands—

Marta met her outside and whispered: "There's a visitor here."

"A visitor?"

"A man. He's sitting in the wood-shed waiting for you."

"I don't know of anybody. Is Julius awake?"

"He woke up and had some milk, then he went to sleep again. There's the man!" whispered Marta.

It was the Suicide.

"Is it you, Herr Magnus! We were just talking about you at the sanatorium, wondering when you'd come back—"

The Suicide did not answer.

XVII

The Suicide looked distracted and as if he had not been under a roof lately; his clothes were new, but untidy, creased, and covered with pine-needles. But at any rate the sore on his hand was healed at last.

"Where have you come from?" asked Fröken d'Espard.

"Where have I come from? Ah, what shall I say?" replied the Suicide, looking about him. "Can anybody hear us?"

"No, nobody."

"I've come from home. You know, I went there to put something right, settle a score. Excuse me if I'm worrying you!" he said suddenly.

"You're not worrying me. What's the matter with you, are you afraid of something?"

"Yes."

"Will you come in?"

"Yes, thanks."

They borrowed Marta's little room and sat down; this seemed to make him calmer, but he kept a look-out through the window. To begin with, there was no method in what he said: "I slept somewhere in the forest last night," he told her with an embarrassed laugh. Shortly after, he impressed on her earnestly that medical men—"we doctors"—were invariably humbugs, he had just had fresh evidence of this. "Oh, I forgot, Fröken, you've had some painful experiences since I saw you, I read about it in the papers. How much of the blame is our own and how much other people's? Each of us has his own troubles and we all make mistakes, we're all human."

CHAPTER THE LAST

Perhaps she was afraid of his starting one of his usual long discourses, so she asked: "You must have been away about a month, haven't you?"

"One month, two months, I don't know. You see, I was to try that new remedy, but do you think I was man enough to go through with it? Kept putting it off day after day, couldn't make up my mind, and didn't bring it off. So it was not the fault of the remedy, you will say? And in a way you're right. But what do I want with a remedy I can't use?"

"What sort of a remedy was it?"

"The cane, you know. Didn't I tell you?"

"The cane—?"

"Didn't I tell you one day about the cane? I can't remember anything now, my memory's gone. Yes, the doctor praised this new medicine, it was so efficacious and all that, a safe cure. But what if one isn't man enough to use it? Is it two months, did you say? To take two months over it and not bring it off, and then at last to go away again with one's errand unaccomplished. It was another story with the blacksmith. Did I tell you about the blacksmith?"

"No."

"It wasn't anything either, only doctors' nonsense. What was that moving over there? Did you see it?"

She threw a glance out of the window. "It can't have been anything. But, by the way, Herr Magnus, have you had anything to eat, have you breakfasted?"

"Breakfasted? No."

She knew how hard he was to please about food, but all the same she went out to Marta and asked her to get ready a little country fare, whatever she could find. When she came in again, the Suicide was growling like a dog and staring out of the window. "There's a bush stirring over there at the edge of the wood," said he.

"It must be the wind. What are you afraid of?"

He did not answer.

Of course this man could not be quite right in the head, but his suffering was not a matter of indifference to Fröken d'Espard; she could not forget that, together with another sick man, he had once rescued her and a certain wad of money in the neatest way; and many a time since then the unhappy Suicide had been her support in hours of despondency.

"If you would tell me what you are afraid of—I don't know, but perhaps Marta and I might be able to help."

"It isn't anything to talk about, perhaps I ought to hide and not show myself by daylight. No, you wouldn't think it was anything either; but suppose it was you she was after?"

"Who?"

"I was told it at the station. I arrived at the station yesterday and the station-master asked me my name and said that somebody had come by train and had made inquiries about me; she also borrowed the telephone and rang up the sanatorium. She had come two days before me and she's still going about here watching for me."

"Don't you wish to meet her?" asked Julie in a low voice.

"Wish? Yes!" cried the Suicide. "But do you know what it is you're asking? Whether I will resume the old life, whether I have really come down to that, whether I have lost all shame. Yes, that is the real question. But do I wish to see her? Yes, Fröken d'Espard, that is the moment I have been waiting for day and night for the last fifteen months. Yes. But now, you see, I'm unnerved, I'm destroyed with waiting and have lost all courage, she has delayed too long."

Silence.

Julie: "Perhaps it would be best after all for you to meet her."

"Isn't it lovely?" the Suicide went on; "is it possible to hatch out anything dirtier and more impudent?—after fifteen months of silence, without a word, without a Christmas card! And then to come in person, in broad daylight, in sunshine, to come openly by train!"

"I expect she found it easier to come than to write."

"She besieges the sanatorium, I can't go up to my own room and take refuge."

"I don't know, Herr Magnus, but I believe you'll have to speak to her."

"Never!" he cried. "So you believe that? Never! Now I've said it!"

That unhappy Suicide, at last he had attained what he wished and now he shrank back. Could anything more malicious be imagined?—he was pursued by the very thing he desired, was hunted by it and ran away from it! Why didn't he make an end of it all and go to Australia? Once more, he can't have been man enough, he was a moth about a candle. He had this one thing to occupy him, the only thing he knew of from which to squeeze all the suffering, he saw life through this crack; more he did not see, but perhaps this was not a little. Seen through a crack, the thing would look sharp and clear, urgent.

Marta came in with the tray of food. The Suicide gave a look of dismay, as though he could not spare the time to eat. "I'm giving you far too much trouble," he said unhappily.

Julie: "What bush was it? Let me keep an eye on it while you're eating."

He pointed out the bush that had stirred. "But for that matter it isn't only that bush, you must watch the whole edge of the forest, where the cattle-track runs." Whereupon he turned to the food. He ate rapidly and heartily several boiled eggs, bread, waffles and butter, and drank a great deal of milk. It was evidently his first meal for a long time.

Fröken d'Espard kept a look-out at the window. Ah yes, now she could see what was moving, no mistake about that; the lady yonder was coming slowly towards the houses, timidly, swaying slightly, with a feather in her hat and a loose dust-coat which was buttoned all the way down. The lady was now very near and Julie let her come on. Not without excitement.

"Thank you!" said the Suicide, rising from the table. "That was the best meal I've eaten in the mountains. Waffles, too!"

Julie: "Now sit down where you were before and light your pipe."

"I haven't a pipe, I haven't anything to smoke. And how are things going with you, Fröken d'Espard? Keeping a good heart?"

"Yes," she replied, "keeping a good heart. Yes, I can say that."

"I'm sure you chose the better part when you left the sanatorium."

"I don't know!" And in order to say something and fill up the time, she added: "They're building tremendously at the sanatorium."

"Yes, but we're all dying there!"

She nodded: "There have been many deaths, that's true."

"One after another, I've lost count. Ah yes, Death makes a clean sweep of us, we're not fit to live, we're too small for the boots we wear and so we stumble over them."

Suddenly Marta opened the door and called Julie out; while she was away the Suicide took her place at the window. He was calmer now, the food had done him good, his memory returned, and he remembered to leave a tip on the tray for Marta. Then he turned again to the forest and scanned it keenly.

Fröken d'Espard came in and said: "Well, now she's here!"

The Suicide knew at once who it was and screamed: "What—!"

"Outside here. Marta has spoken to her. She must have come by the sanatorium road."

The Suicide said with a gulp: "Good, let her come! Just let her come in here, then by God I'll—!"

A lady in a loose coat with a big ostrich-feather in her hat. She was young, fair rather than dark, quite pretty after her walk, with a candid face; the only defect was two of her front teeth which were

CHAPTER THE LAST

crooked. She stopped in the doorway and said nothing, but her lips moved.

There was a little clock on the wall with weights and a brass chain, the Suicide suddenly took it into his head to pull the weights up with a long rasping sound—he did that, in the middle of the day and in a strange house. Then he turned half round and saw her. "Is that you?" he said, but turned back to the clock as though he hadn't quite finished with it. "This clock's wrong, I see!" he said, whereupon he left it and went to the window, fumbling at his chin as though he had a beard. "All well at home?" he asked, and went on, terribly nervous and not knowing what to say: "Why don't you take off your coat and sit down? There's a stool."

"I'm cold," she answered, and sat down as she was.

He: "Is she alive, the little one, I mean—is she alive, I ask?"

"Yes, she's alive and well, talks quite a lot already. Oh yes, she's very much alive."

"Talks—that doesn't sound likely!"

"Yes, talks, prattles."

"What's her name?"

"Leonora. She's called after you."

"What nonsense! You might have hit on something else," he said, turning scarlet.

She said nothing.

"You might have hit on something else, I say."

"Yes," she answered simply. Oh, she was so humble, but all the same she twisted him round her little finger.

He chattered on in his embarrassment: "Leonora, eh, a fool name! And you want me to believe she can talk? She'd have to be properly born first."

"She's so clever—"

"Yes, yes, yes, I don't care, I have other things to think about. But Leonora—! Where are you staying here?" he asked all of a sudden.

"At the store. I slept there last night."

"You must have slept there two nights."

"Well, perhaps it was two nights. I—yes, I remember now, it was two nights."

"Why don't you stay at the sanatorium?"

She, almost inaudibly: "I will—thank you!"

"That was an extraordinary idea, to put up at the store, a hole like that. Then I suppose you had to sleep with the maid?"

"No, on a sofa. They made up a bed for me on a sofa."

"I never heard of such a thing! And you were always so scared about your health!" he said, meaning, no doubt, to be really spiteful. "Perhaps you haven't had anything to eat either?"

"Not today. But it doesn't matter."

"No," he mimicked, "it doesn't matter! Of course not! Did you have anything to eat last night, if I may ask?"

"Yes."

"Oh! But anyhow that's eighteen hours ago. Yes, that clock's fast, but to go without food for nearly twenty-four hours—that's a sensible thing to do! Get up at once and we'll go to the sanatorium and get something for you. It's dinner-time now."

They both left the room, and the Suicide put on a very fierce and manly air, but in reality he was feeling very foolish. To Marta he said: "My wife's afraid of the bull, is he out?"

"Yes," replied Marta, "but he's up on the mountain now, a long way off."

"Fröken d'Espard isn't in?"

"She's in the new cottage."

"Say good-bye for me!"

They walked across to the sanatorium and spoke but little on the way, but one or two things were said, questions and answers. She asked timidly: "Were you in Christiania a week or so ago?"

"How do you know that?"

"Somebody thought she'd seen you, the maid."

"I was there buying these clothes, if you want to know."

"Yes."

"Well, what then?" he asked snappishly.

"Nothing."

"Of course you were out searching for me when you heard I was in town?"

"Yes, I was."

"Ha ha ha!" laughed the Suicide.

"Oh yes, Leonhard, I was. For two days. And inquired at the hotels too."

"Oh, stop that nonsense! What was I going to say—?" He made a pretence of trying to remember, but he had certainly forgotten nothing, he only wanted to cover his ill temper.

When they reached the sanatorium, there was no one to be seen; the Suicide, who knew his way about, guessed that the few boarders were at dinner.

He rang the hall bell and asked the maid for a room for his wife.

At that moment the lawyer came out of the dining-room, clapped his hands, and bowed. "I heard the bell ring and had to see who it was. Welcome back, Herr Magnus! You've been away a long time. This is Fru Magnus, no doubt? Glad to see you, ma'am! Get ready Number 106 for Fru Magnus," he said to the maid. And he turned to the Suicide and explained: "It's the floor below you, but you shall be moved down, to 105, the adjoining room. I don't know whether you have had dinner?"

The Suicide: "No. And my wife is very hungry."

"Pray come in at once then, we've just sat down. Oh, you're quite nice enough as you are, Fru Magnus; we haven't many boarders at the moment, but a lot more are coming soon. Perhaps you would like to take off your hat and coat? No?"

"No, my wife's cold," said the Suicide.

"Yes, the autumn air is getting keen now in the mountains, a splendid tonic; but we have to dress accordingly. This way!"

The lawyer showed the couple in. He had a happy air, as he brought more visitors; they were but two, but they helped to swell the little party at the table.

After dinner the Suicide sent a messenger for his wife's handbag from the store. The lawyer was there again and said: "I told the maid to serve your coffee in your wife's room. I was right, I hope?"

The Suicide did not answer him. No, he would rather have avoided this officious patching-up, perhaps he thought he had gone quite far enough himself. When the lawyer asked if they might move his things down to Number 105 at once, he curtly answered no.

The lawyer looked at him.

"I shall stay upstairs," said the Suicide. "My wife has to go home again, she's leaving at once."

The lawyer: "That's a disappointment, I must admit. Oh, but, Fru Magnus, we shall be all the more anxious to make you comfortable the short time you are here. Unfortunately I myself have to go back to my office in town, but I shall leave orders."

The blinds were drawn in Fru Magnus's room. The Suicide dashed to the window and sent them flying up. "They seem to think you can't stand the sun here," he growled. "How was it, by the way, didn't you say you were cold? Are you ill?"

"No, I'm only a little cold, it's nothing."

"Well, but one oughtn't to come up to the mountains in silk stockings and open shoes."

He hurried over his coffee and said: "If you've been sleeping on a sofa for two nights, you must want to take a siesta. Now I come to think of it, it must have been three nights, not two?"

"I don't remember, perhaps it was three."

He shook his head in despair and said as he was going: "Well, undress and lie down now!"

She coughed as he was leaving so that he had to turn round. "No, it was nothing," she said; "but don't be angry with me, forgive me for the last time!"

"The same old yarn!" he replied with a sniff. "Forgive and forgive!"

"He's gone away now," she said.

"Gone away?" He knew well enough whom she meant and replied scornfully: "That's very sad! Fancy, he's gone away!"

"No, it's not sad, I drove him away."

"Ha ha ha!" laughed the Suicide.

"Yes, I drove him away, it's several months ago now. I would have told you long ago but—"

"But you grudged me this piece of news?"

"I was afraid."

"Ah, was there really so much shame and honour in you that you were afraid?"

"Yes, yes, afraid. I have written hundreds of letters to you and not sent them—"

"O God, what an untruth!" he exclaimed. "When I sent you a card at Christmas and you didn't even answer that!"

"No, it's true, it's true! But at that time I was still off my head and hadn't come to my senses; it's eight months since Christmas, remember. But now it's several months since I sent him away."

"Where did you send him to?"

"Where? I don't know, he's gone, I haven't seen him since, it was in the summer, he may be in America perhaps. I'd rather he was dead."

"Ha ha ha!" laughed the Suicide again.

"Stone-dead, oh, deep down underground!"

"Why, I wonder? The darling boy, the first love and all that!"

"We were to have been married," she said. "Yes, that was the agreement. I was to ask you to divorce me and then we were to marry. That is what we had agreed—"

"Well, I won't hear any more!" the Suicide interrupted suddenly.

"He laid a trap for me—"

"I won't hear any more, I tell you!"

"No!" she replied and stopped obediently.

"And now perhaps you'll excuse me if I go," he said. Curiously enough, he was no longer excited, no longer embittered, the news that a certain person was out of the way had had no disagreeable effect on him. He even turned in the doorway and said: "I advise you to lie down for a while. You shouldn't be so obstinate."

She was not obstinate, she began at once to turn down the bed-clothes as he went out.

The Suicide had been given something to think about and went up to his own room. Here all was unchanged, only rather dustier, as the room had not been cleaned in his absence; he was looked upon as a queer fellow who hated washing and so the maids respected his love of dirt. He looked out; one of the annexes was being extended to double its length, and another storey was being added, the carpenters were sawing and hammering with a terrific noise. From the tarns came the distant reports of blasting as the charges were fired. But all this left him unconcerned.

This room had been his home for fifteen months, he might show it to her, she might come up and see what a comfortable time he had had. As yet he had not heard that she felt sorry for him, that she thought him badly treated, not a word. What did she want here after all? Beg forgiveness for another last time! The Suicide sniffed as though he were utterly sick and tired of this sentimentality, here in the privacy of his room he pretended to find it distasteful, but he would certainly have been more dissatisfied if she had not asked his forgiveness. Can it have distressed his ears to listen to her entreaties?

Yes, it seemed so, without a doubt! And now the whole discussion bored him, he was sleepy into the bargain, he hadn't slept too well either, he had passed the night in the forest—

Strangely enough he was not awaked either by the blasting or by the noise of the builders, but by a much fainter sound; he heard a vehicle drive into the yard and somebody say whoa to a horse.

He went to the window and opened it; it was Fröken Ellingsen who stepped out of the trap. What had she come back for? It was nothing to him, but this woman too must have had some motive for coming. They all came and went, they all crawled, hurrying hither and thither, busy with their own concerns. And what was it all for? He felt cold and gave himself a shake, it was late already; in a very depressed state of mind he went downstairs and stopped outside his wife's room. Was she still asleep, he wondered. He heard sounds of weeping and went boldly in.

He feigned surprise: "What in the world—?"

"Excuse me," she said; "just a moment—"

"What are you doing? Lie still if you like, you can have breakfast sent up. Haven't you slept?"

"Yes—oh no, I don't know!" She seemed to be trying to find the answer that would please him best. "Oh yes," she decided; "I'm sure I slept, at first, quite a long time. It was so good to get a sleep. And you?"

"I?" he sniffed.

"Yes, Leonhard, you need it, you have had so much trouble, I know well enough—"

"We won't talk about me!"

"No, no. But your hair's turning grey, I thought about it in the night—"

The Suicide thundered: "We won't talk about me, do you hear?"

"No."

If he objected so strongly to being pitied, why was he moved by her words and why did his resolution give way? A kind of silly sweetness actually came over him. How was he to explain her not having shown her sympathy before? Perhaps she did not dare, God knows. He excused her to himself; if it was forgetfulness on her part, it was pardonable. On the other hand, he couldn't stand there like a stuffed owl and smile and say hum and ha. Not to be thought of!

She was to give him a great surprise with her next words: "I understand why you wouldn't move down to the room next this."

"You understand—how—?"

"Yes, I see why you don't want to, and I'm not surprised. I'm not what I was."

He was quite at sea: "Not what you were? You mean that you've disgraced yourself?"

"You've seen the change in me," she said.

At this a ray of light must have penetrated his brain and he did what she did not: he blushed and dropped his eyes.

Neither said any more.

He stumbled across to the window and looked out. "Ah, so the lawyer's going away again," he muttered, and his voice was unsteady. "Hm. I see he's taking Fröken Ellingsen's trap—Fröken Ellingsen, who came just now. Well, he's made a long stay this time. The doctor's down there too. Hm. I wanted to speak to the doctor, by the way; there's another letter from Moss, Anton Moss, and I get the doctor to read them. What was I going to say—?"

Long silence.

Then he turned and came away from the window. "What is it you want with me after this?" he asked, calmly enough. "What have you come here for?"

"No—!" was all she answered, shaking her head.

"I haven't—that is, you must have some idea?"

"Oh no. Well, of course you want to divorce me now, that goes

CHAPTER THE LAST

without saying."

"Yes, we can do that. There, the lawyer's gone off, I see. Oh yes, we can do that. You must think it over. What day is it today?"

They both frowned and tried to remember; at last he said: "Oh well, what does it matter?"

And indeed it did not matter, it was of no importance to him, it just slipped out of his mouth. It was not a good thing to be in his shoes.

Perhaps it was not good to be in hers either. . . .

He strolled along the familiar path to "the Peak." Here was the juniper-bush, here was the white stone slab, and here the little gully, all as before. After all, he was not broken down, nothing had really come upon him unexpectedly, it was only that now it had come. And now after the catastrophe she found it was time for a divorce. Very well; but how about the child, little Leonora? She talks already, she's so clever, of course she's learnt to walk long ago, she can run even, she has little shoes on her feet, a frock—eh, what a queer thing it was. Mamma and Papa, she would be saying. Hm, enough of that! So that's why we've come, that's why we wear a dust-coat, we've altered so. The whole thing is not very savoury, and, oh, what shall we do with ourselves, where shall we hide our face? And little Leonora doesn't say Papa, what bosh, how should she have learnt that? Don't let us make fools of ourselves. The whole thing, therefore, is not too savoury. Admitted! However—however—

There she comes, that is she, walking nicely, with a slight sway, in a big hat, small shoes, gloves—mind the gully, it's not meant for ladies—bravo, she clears the gully easily, hops over it, lovely creature! How should he receive her? Sit up here on the Peak and look down on her and be on one's dignity? Nonsense, we get up and wait till she's here, and then let chance decide. On closer consideration the affair looks not quite so crude: she had not lured him back to her in time; on the contrary, with the greatest nonchalance she had waited too long before coming—now that at once made it less disgraceful, less dishonest, there was no denying that. And as regards the root of the matter, the lovemaking part, it was not so strange that she should yield when she was promised marriage. Let us just look all the circumstances full in the face—

He asked as she came up: "What are you doing out here in your thin shoes?"

"I have a message for you," she replied, in order to disarm him at once. "I met the doctor, he told me to tell you that there's a letter for you."

So she had made that a pretext; for he knew about the letter. "It's from Moss," he said; "there's no hurry."

"Is this where you come when you take a walk?" she asked.

"Yes, this is where I come."

"Nice to see how you spend your time," she said, looking about her with interest. "Do you sit on that stone?"

"Yes, here I sit."

"Here you sit and look at the view. Oh yes."

He: "So you didn't sleep?"

"Yes, I did. But it was so lonely. And then there was so much noise and chatter in the next room."

"In 107? That's Bertelsen's. He generally has that room. A man named Bertelsen."

"I was thinking," said she, "whether I should go home and bring back Leonora for you—?"

"Here?"

"No, perhaps not, no, no. But I suppose you won't come into town and see her, you won't do that. But you have been so long alone, I didn't know whether she might be a little company for you."

"We can always think about that. Won't you sit down and rest?"

"Yes—thanks!"

All humility. Which had its effect on him; his resolution softened, became flexible, he asked: "What was your idea, did you mean to come here with the child and stay here?"

"No, not I! Dear me, no, I had no such big thoughts!"

"But I couldn't have her here alone, could I?"

"Well, I wasn't thinking of myself. No, nothing of the sort."

"This is no place to stay at either," he said with his old dissatisfaction. "There's a chronic meat famine, we live on trout and canned stuff, the child would die of malnutrition."

"I don't know what we are to do. You must say that."

"I have said that we must think it over," he replied, getting up. "This wind will be cold for you, let's go back."

"I'm not cold, I have this thick coat."

"Get up! There's a mountain breeze here, you don't know what it's like."

She was on her feet long before he had finished speaking, obedient as ever. Then they came down. On reaching the gully he gave her a hand to help her over, but to do the thing properly he had to give her both hands and receive her in his arms. This was more than she expected; her knees gave way and she sank to the ground. "Rest a moment," he said.

"No, it's not that. I'm in despair. Here you are, so good and kind—if only I had been like my old self, come here like my old self, but I'm so changed and ugly. And then I've behaved so badly—"

He: "Rubbish! It's getting dark, let's go down!"

They had supper served in her room. There was again a party in 107, with laughter and talk.

She asked: "Am I to leave tomorrow morning?"

"Do you ask me that?"

"Yes, you must say."

"No," he replied shortly.

"When does the morning train go?"

"Fearfully early, you'd have to get up at four. There's no sense in that, I think."

"No, no—thanks!"

They talked for some time longer; both were now calm and he hinted that a lady could not very well travel all alone by train, it was not quite the thing. Not that he offered to take her home, though that did not appear to be totally impossible. When he said goodnight he added, with a kind of worry in his voice, looking away: "Well, well, we'll see each other tomorrow."

She seized his hand and thanked him, thanked him impetuously for his kindness. She was trembling, and when he asked if she was cold she answered yes.

"That's your walk up to the Peak. Go to bed at once, you want sleep."

She began immediately to unbutton her coat and before he had reached the door she had it off. He showed some surprise and stopped for a moment.

"I'll do as you say," she declared hurriedly; her teeth were chattering with cold and she unbuttoned more and more—

He stood still. It surprised him that she was so slim, as she had always been; then why had she worn that long coat?

"That's right, undress yourself quickly and go to bed, then you'll get warm," he said for the sake of saying something.

And she was obedient and complied, struggling with her clothes, tearing them off, and piling them on a chair.

Then it was that he asked in the greatest astonishment: "But—why have you kept that coat on all day long?"

"My coat? I'm cold," she replied. "It must be the mountain air, as you said. Would you rather I had taken it off?"

"No, why should you? But—"

"No," she said, shaking her head; "I'm so changed in every way, I can quite well wear a matron's coat like this. It makes no difference."

"How changed?"

"Oh dear me, can't you see it? Ugly complexion and flat-breasted, they're hanging down. Suddenly she looked at him with eyes wide open and asked: "What was it you thought?"

"I? Nothing."

"You look so surprised. Tell me what you thought."

"I can't see that you're changed," he said.

"Oh, now I understand!" she exclaimed; "you thought I was obliged to—that I wanted the coat to hide something."

"Well, but it's not so."

"No, no, no, what a thing to believe! But it's bad enough anyhow —making you blush like that."

"There now, lie down!" he ordered, pulling the blankets over her and tucking her in.

No sooner had he finished this than she started up again: "No, Leonhard, I was in love, I suppose, and frivolous and silly, I know that, and I was drinking wine then, but I never did it again. No. And I haven't been so bad as you think."

"All I say is that you're to lie down," he said, feeling miserably foolish, and tucked her in again. A great joy fluttered within him, he had got her back, got possession of his own wife again, he wanted to do something for her in return and said: "I'll sit here till you go to sleep."

"Yes, will you?" she replied and thanked him again; it seemed to be a real boon. "But then you must wake me up when I'm to lock the door."

He thought this over: yes, he would have to do so. But what a pity to wake her again after she had fallen asleep; she wanted sleep so badly. What if he locked the door on the outside and took the key with him?

"Yes!" she agreed gratefully, giving his hand a good-night

grasp.

"I'll unlock you again in good time in the morning," he promised. . . .

When she had gone to sleep he slipped out with infinite caution, locked her door, and took the key. He was in a mood of sheer rapture as he went downstairs, out into the big veranda and on across the yard. He smiled and said foolish things to himself; it was queer, when you thought of it, that such happiness should be permitted in this world!

He noticed now that it was a damp evening, with driving mist, there was a taste of autumn in the air, the stars were few and had a kind of bitter look; what did that mean? Stars are quite capable of being bitter, their expression is not always a sweet one.

There was a light in the doctor's consulting-room, he might look in there for a moment and hear what Moss had to say. Not that it interested him any longer; a letter from Moss was now a thing of minor importance, but in his present mood of exaltation he could afford once more to bestow a little scorn and spitefulness on his old crony. Here goes!

Moss had written with his own hand, neatly, in straight lines, with well-formed letters, stops and all; he seemed to have quite got back his sight. He announced that he had entirely recovered from the barber's itch and was now going home for a spell. It would give him pleasure to meet Suicide Magnus in Christiania as completely restored to health as he was himself!

"He shall have that pleasure," said the Suicide. "I'll really look him up now when I go home."

The doctor: "Are you going home?"

"Yes. Tomorrow."

The doctor made no reference to their former conversation, he spared the Suicide, did not mention his wife, or let him see that he remembered anything. He said: "A good deal has happened since

CHAPTER THE LAST

you left us, a serious business, murder."

The Suicide did not answer.

"Did you know the parties concerned?"

"With regard to Moss," said the Suicide, "that's cheerful news."

The doctor thoughtfully: "I don't know."

"You don't know?"

"I think you'd better not look him up in Christiania."

"Why not?"

"Because he won't be there," replied the doctor.

The Suicide, put out: "Ugh—just when everything seemed all right! You're making me doubt again. Why should there always be something bad?"

This time it was the doctor who was silent.

"Why don't you answer?" asked the Suicide.

The doctor with a smile: "Because of course I don't know. Don't you think, Herr Magnus, that good and bad are relative concepts?"

"No," cried the Suicide, "they are absolutely concepts, things you can lay hold of."

"Good, let us leave it at that. Your friend Moss has recovered his sight and that in itself is no small thing."

"So it wasn't barber's itch after all?"

"No, it certainly was not."

The Suicide got up. "You've given me an uncomfortable feeling, Doctor, and now I'll go. That is to say, I don't want to think anymore about it on this particular evening."

No more was said, there was no exchange of wit, no offer of a whisky and soda. "Good-night!" said the Suicide.

He strolled back to the big veranda. It struck him there was a lurid gloom in the air, a chill came down from the Peak, the mist still hung over the ground, but soon it would be driven away, as a breeze was springing up. Over by the servants' quarters he saw a light, a man was moving about with a lantern. It made a little round gleam in the fog, the lantern was scarcely powerful enough to light up anything, only itself. It had quite an uncanny look.

He went across and saw it was the postman.

"Are you looking for something?"

The postman: "Don't talk of it!"

"What have you lost?"

"I've lost a five-crown note. I was out here just now for a minute and must have dropped it. But now the wind's getting up and it'll blow away. It was five crowns!"

"Don't stay out bare-headed in this bitter weather looking for a trumpery thing like that. Here's five crowns for you."

"It's not possible—?"

"Yes, it is possible. You've brought me a great many letters and cards, and now I'm going home tomorrow."

He had made the poor fellow happy and that raised his spirits. Strange how cold and dismal it was, ugh, but that should not get the better of him this evening. The wind was beginning to whistle round the Peak, it was cold, but clean; the fog rolled off in blankets through the forest. It should not make him dismal, he would not have it; he buttoned his jacket defiantly and stood with his hands in his trouser-pockets watching the drifting fog, a diverting sight; the plateau was swept clean, the sanatorium buildings were visible once more. What could it all mean? Storm? Perhaps storm.

Lights were out in the castle, except in Number 107, and of all silly things to happen, Bertelsen opened his window and shouted to him to come up: "Come on and have a glass with us!"

The Suicide did not answer. It was a nice thing of that half-intoxicated person to stand there waking the other boarders with his yelling! What if she had been waked by it and could not get to sleep again?

As he went in he stopped outside his wife's door and listened a long time. No, thank God, all was quiet; oh, she must have been dead tired. "Good-night!" he whispered and went upstairs to his room. He was tired too.

It was the end of a momentous day. And all might have gone well, but Death came between.

XVIII

It was a mistake of the lawyer to go away, he might have kept order.

Bertelsen was in a festive mood, he began with wine directly after dinner, he got hold of Fröken Ellingsen and wanted to make a great splash with her, wanted it to be as before, only more so, wanted to drink with her, "Cheer-o, Fröken Ellingsen!" and make love to her.

And of course she on her side could not hang back, she had to show an easy jauntiness at this painful meeting. Fru Bertelsen, who was once Fru Ruben, took it none too well, but by no means tragically, she was too clever for that, had plenty of brains when she chose to use them. Bertelsen had been going a pretty hot pace, perhaps he was not the best investment she had made, but she didn't feel daunted, she was the woman she was, and her separate estate was secure.

Ah, that separate estate, maybe it had already been subjected to assaults!

Besides Fröken Ellingsen and Bertelsen and his wife, there was a fourth person present at the revel, the widow of a district judge or whatever it was, secretary of a certain undertaking that was concerned with a table-cloth. She had been invited in order that she might sit in the fourth chair and fill up the number, and she understood this very well herself. At first she tried to make her voice heard and praised Fru Bertelsen's appearance, but as this was nothing to boast of, that lady merely answered: "Indeed!" Fru Bertelsen herself knew how it was with her appearance; it was betwixt and between: she was eating again, carefully and a little at a time so as not to get too fat, but enough to keep herself in health more or less. Such treatment did not lead to bloom and loveliness; but at any rate Fru Bertelsen had her eyes, and they could look deeper and more charming than anyone else's.

"Yes," said the widow, "it's amazing how well you're looking, Fru Bertelsen. For I can remember how you looked before, last year, I mean, when you first came—"

But again Fru Bertelsen said: "Indeed."

After that the widow was very modest and reserved in this wealthy company and simply hung on Fru Bertelsen's lips.

Fröken Ellingsen on the other hand did not show the older lady any particular attention, nor indeed had she any reason to do so. She had her own affairs to occupy her; when she had had some wine she began, unprompted, to speak about her book, that collection of short stories which was to come out in time for Christmas. She had at last been given this holiday to get it finished.

Bertelsen had heard of the collection often enough, but the ladies asked out of politeness what it was to be called. "*The Shriek in the Night*," replied Fröken Ellingsen.

"Fancy!"

She had not yet chosen a publisher, but she knew how big the book was to be and she had the whole of it in her head.

"How you can do it, how you can manage it!" said the ladies.

"That's what everyone says," she replied. "But the fact is, one must have the gift. It comes to me, I don't have the slightest difficulty in finding material. For instance, would you like to hear what happened to me in the train on my way here?"

"Yes," said the ladies, and "Cheer-o, Fröken Ellingsen!" said Bertelsen.

"Well, there was a man sitting on the seat right opposite me, I should know him again among thousands, he made such an impression on me. He did everything with his left hand."

"Yes?" said the ladies excitedly.

"With his left hand!" Fröken Ellingsen insisted.

"Well, was that so extraordinary?"

"That man," she said, "had certainly done something that could only be done with the right hand."

The ladies were quite at sea.

Fröken Ellingsen, impressively: "His left-handedness was simulated."

"Simulated?" queried Fru Bertelsen. "Indeed. Well, but how do you know that? What in the world—I don't understand—"

Fröken Ellingsen began to flounder again, questions were more than she could bear, it was no use pressing her. And when Fru Bertelsen asked: "But what was the rest of the story?" she shook her head and replied: "There isn't any more—as yet."

Bertelsen came to her rescue. God knows if the worthy Bertelsen wasn't playing a private game of his own, trying to beat down his wife over some other matter; he said: "I can't see why we need be so pedantic and expect to have everything explained. Fröken Ellingsen's scent is of the keenest, as I know; you may be sure she knows what she's talking about. Your health, fair lady!"

"It seemed to me a lot of rubbish," said Fru Bertelsen. "Excuse my saying so."

Fröken Ellingsen's eyes dropped, but the lady, usually so calm, was trembling slightly and she shot a sidelong glance of her narrow eyes from the floor to Fru Bertelsen's knees. "I have something to go upon," she said, "from my work in the Telegraphs. It may be that I know something about the man in the train. But I must not say more, I am under oath."

"There, you hear that!" said Bertelsen to his wife. He got up, yawned, and said: "There's so much smoke here that we can't see each other. Do the ladies object to my opening the window a moment?"

CHAPTER THE LAST

It was true, the room was thick with smoke, the widow's eyes were smarting with it, and neither the big hanging lamp over the table nor the candle in the corner by the door made much impression on it.

It was at this moment that Bertelsen opened the window, caught sight of the Suicide down in the courtyard, and called him up.

A chorus of screams from the room—and Fru Bertelsen cried: "Shut the window! Can't you see the lamp's blown out!"

With great difficulty he pulled the window to again, cursing the high wind. Now the only light in the room came from the candle. The widow tried to light the lamp again, but burnt her fingers on the hot chimney and gave it up. They agreed that they had light enough and went on talking in the semi-darkness. Bertelsen fell to abusing the Suicide, who hadn't even answered his invitation, swore at the wind, which had nearly torn the window out of his hands, and growled at the wretched candle, which gave such a poor light that he couldn't see the way to his glass—a lot of annoyances, a string of misfortunes; and after a while Bertelsen fell asleep.

Yes, this hale, strong man always required a nap when he was getting on in his cups. The ladies took no notice of it, they went on chatting and seemed to find more to say to each other now they were alone. Fru Bertelsen was the one who was best posted about theatres and music; she sat playing with one of her expensive rings and told an interesting story of a singer, a great star who at her last concert in Christiania turned out not to have a note in her voice and caused a sensation.

The widow briefly expressed her wonder that singers did not retire in time.

Fru Bertelsen: "It's a melancholy fact that they're forced to take one farewell after another. They make a fortune in their good years, but they always spend it, and when they're old they're left with empty hands."

"Yes, so it is," Fröken Ellingsen agreed, from courtesy.

And the ladies chatted on and on, while Bertelsen slept. Thus passed a couple of hours or more, the widow watching for a sign from Fru Bertelsen, on seeing which she would show her breeding and get up at once, so she would; she owed that to herself and the distinguished lady whose guest she was.

At last Bertelsen's snoring grew rather too loud and his wife said: "I don't know, perhaps it's getting late? Not that I would drive you away—"

They all rose.

But now Fru Bertelsen dropped her ring. She looked about the floor, and the other ladies helped her to search. Fröken Ellingsen fetched the candle and held it, circling round Fru Bertelsen; it was extraordinary that the ring should have totally disappeared. She came round behind Fru Bertelsen with the candle. "Here it is!" she said. At that instant Fru Bertelsen burst into flames—

The next thing was a confusion of screams and fire, Fru Bertelsen dashed into the alcove in search of water, blankets, setting fire to the portière on the way, everything around her caught—screams and fire, screams and fire.

Bertelsen woke up at last and in his half-drunken state screamed louder than the rest: they were not to shriek so, they were to take it calmly! As he went into the alcove to help his wife he too caught fire from the portière, he ran back and was going to jump out of the window, but set fire to the curtains, then he turned to the table and emptied the rest of the wine on his burning clothes, but it was pure futility and had no effect at all. Fröken Ellingsen had the sense to snatch the cloth from the table, sending glasses and bottles crashing to the floor, and wrapped it about the burning man. But this was insufficient, the cloth did not cover him, he did not stand still either, but tore about, and the next thing Fröken Ellingsen knew was that she herself was alight. She threw herself on the floor and rolled, shrieking, howling, and upset the table. The only one left who might have done something stood stock-still and hiccuped, the widow did not attempt to do anything, but stood paralysed and hiccuped. Suddenly Bertelsen freed himself of the burning table-cloth and heaved it from him as far as he could, over towards the widow; it fell in a long flame at her feet and set fire to her too—

Now the whole room and everyone in it was blazing.

Over in the servants' annex they noticed the bright light in the castle; when they ran out and saw smoke they understood that a disaster had happened. A gale was blowing, they could not walk upright, but had to butt their way along with heads bent, they called "Fire!" to wake everybody and then stopped at the veranda door waiting for it to be opened from within and for someone to come out. No. It was such a long time that the porter fetched an ax from the wood-shed and broke in the door. But nobody came out. The porter, the manager, and the, postman ran in through the passages and staircases of the castle shouting "Fire!" till at last they were turned back by smoke and had to take refuge in the veranda.

Flames now shot high into the air from the roof, the gale spread the fire up and down, the great timber-built house burnt like paper. What were the servants to do? Put up two ladders to windows chosen at random and then look on. They were helpless, they could only shriek, pails of water were of no use. Visitors in their nightclothes threw open the windows on every floor, they called down, but nothing could be heard in the storm; one or two of them jumped frantically, their fluttering shirts took fire on the way, and they came down like meteors. The servants crept up the ladders and tried to lift out a victim, but could get hold of none; a lady with her hands full of clothes handed these out first, but dared not follow; all was hurricane and destruction, now the walls were on fire, the ladders were cut off, the men had to descend step by step.

"This way with the ladders!" It was the engineer with his men from the electric-light works who took command. All right, the ladders were taken from window to window, from place to place, a young man, a dare-devil, ran up each ladder, thank God they got right up, they looked into a room full of fire and smoke, but no people, the people were one with the fire and smoke and were no longer themselves. The dare-devils hurried down again, their own clothes were on fire, even the ladders had caught.

The doctor turned up, in underclothes and bare-headed; he could do no more than the rest, but he did not shriek, he held his tongue. Then at last a couple of boarders came flying out of the veranda door, two or three more followed, they were all undressed, but some had clothes in their hands. They were screaming and on fire, all ablaze, but they got out. Only just in time, then the flames swept out of the veranda door.

At the corner up at the top under the roof a fully dressed man appears at a window. He looks down and doesn't take a second to think, but clutches the rain-pipe and swings himself out. He could have been saved by a ladder, but there are no ladders left. He lowers himself hand over hand down the pipe and comes nearer and nearer the ground. When the flames from the first floor stop him he seems lost, he hangs by his hands, evidently hesitating to let go. Suddenly he is lost to view, hidden by smoke and fire, and he reappears in the courtyard. Smashed? Not smashed, but on fire; he rolls over on the ground, tears off his jacket and puts it out, beats out the fire with his hat and his bare hands, beats it out—

There he is. It is the Suicide.

He had saved himself by getting a purchase on the rain-pipe as he sprang off; this spring carried him obliquely against a first-floor balcony, which broke his fall, so that the last part of it was only the remnant of a fall. A marvellous piece of luck, the terrified Suicide had had the courage to save himself from a dizzy height and through a sea of fire!

CHAPTER THE LAST

He tried to enter by the veranda, but had to turn back. "I've locked her in!" he screamed. "I have the key, she can't get out! It's 106!"

But 106, where is it? Room 106 is burnt.

He could get no help, there were no more ladders, there was no wall to rest ladders against, no window, nothing, only a sea of flame. He kept roaring his number, holding a key on high with both his scorched hands, and tried again to get in by the veranda—which was no longer a veranda, but a blazing bonfire—

Even now a face would appear high up, a pair of waving hands, a woman's hair on fire, then the vision was gone.

Then the whole place was gone and everyone in it.

The storm made it a conflagration on a grand scale, the fire spread from the castle to the annexes, to the storehouse, to the cowhouse; these five buildings, great and small, were all in flames except the wood-shed. There was no saving anything; the engineer and his men rushed about on the roof of one of the annexes for a while, trying to put out the flames as they burst out, but when the gale began to hurl great brands across from the castle, they had to give it up. Another party of men came up from the village without being able to do anything, their goodwill was of no avail. What could be done was done: the porter let out the cows in time and drove them down towards the forest. And the doctor sent the village folk home again for vehicles to take away the few survivors.

Four o'clock in the morning.

The storm had subsided, having done its work, the scene of the fire lay still, the injured had been driven away, only two of the engineer's party were left as watchmen. From the forest below, the plaintive lowing of the sanatorium's cows was heard now and again.

The place was abandoned to darkness and smoke.

The Suicide was wandering about the site. He had refused

to leave with the others, he walked up and down in front of the façade foundations, stopping now and then and muttering, looking up at an imaginary wall and going on again, still with a key in his hand—a hand that had grown stiff round a piece of iron. The watchmen would rather have been without him and tried several times to get him away, but he would not go.

"What are you looking for?" asked the men. "What are you waiting for?"

"I'm not waiting," he replied. "That is to say, I'm still here, but I'm not waiting. My wife was asleep in 106."

"Ah, so your wife was in there?"

"Yes. Locked in. Here's the key."

The men were mollified and shook their heads. They let the man stray about in peace, he was not stealing, there was nothing to steal; they sat down and chatted quietly, wondering who was the genius that had started this blaze; they spoke of the insurance and prophesied that the sanatorium would be rebuilt sure enough. And wasn't it a sad thing—in a month's time the engineer would have had the works finished and all the water they wanted to put it out with! But it was not to be.

The Suicide wandered past.

"Wouldn't it be better for you," they said, taking pity on his distracted look, "wouldn't it be better for you to go over to the sæter and have a roof over your head?"

"Yes," he answered.

"Then you'd get some coffee and something hot."

"Yes."

But he did not go, he continued to stray about. At about five o'clock he went of his own accord; it was now getting light, the men kept an eye on him, he went to the wood-shed, the only house left standing on the plateau.

He did not look about, but went straight to a little sleigh that was standing in there against the wall, the same that had been used as a bob-sleigh the winter before, yes, that was it; and now he began to unfasten the cord from the sleigh.

The men came up and said: "What are you doing here?"

He went on with his work without answering.

"You mustn't touch anything. What do you want with that cord?" they asked.

"What do I want with it?"

"Do you want to tie up something?"

"Yes," he muttered; "I'm going to tie up something!"

"Where have you got it?"

He made no answer, but did not drop what he was doing; it seemed he had picked out this cord and did not intend to let it go.

The men probably did not give it much thought, perhaps they were willing to let him have this bit of cord in order to be rid of him. "All right, take the cord!" they said. And the Suicide went off with his prize.

He went across the plateau, past the posts with the white placards, showing the way and giving the latest weather forecasts, these few naked remains of Torahus Sanatorium; he took the well-known path to the sæter and walked fast, as though he had important business. When he came to the little barn, he turned down into the wood.

Strange, it was only now that he felt a severe smarting in his burns and as he walked he blew on his hands to cool them. When he was deep enough in the wood he began to look out for a tree. He muttered as he went; 106, he said, 106. In the course of the night he had got so much in the habit of muttering this number that he kept on at it without thinking. The key was still in his hand.

It was not so easy to find a suitable tree and he searched for a long time. But it had to be found. What he had in his mind was the only thing to do and it must be done now. What purpose would be served by postponing it? Did not Death lie in wait for him in any case, behind every tussock, behind every tree, ready to fling himself upon him?

Something chafed him in his boot, pricking him at every step, and at last he sat down and pulled the boot off. It was a fir-needle sticking in his sock. When he had taken it out he put the boot on again and laced it as usual.

Evidently it was easier to find a tree with a serviceable branch higher up, he had passed some that were not too bad, by no means impossible. He turned round and went uphill again; no, he mustn't be so particular, here was a dead pine which had a branch. He threw the cord over the branch and put his whole weight on it to try. Of course the branch broke. He searched higher up and found another pine, tried it as before, and seemed to have what he wanted, the branch held. He even took some trouble to break it, but it held. Then what was wrong? He should not have taken all that trouble, he should have thought of his burnt hands, they could not stand it, they were bleeding, they ached and smarted and throbbed with fresh pain. But what of it? He arranged the cord, tied it to the branch, made the noose, 106, 106.

In a day or two there would be a great cawing of crows above this fir, people would follow the cries and find him hanging. His feet would now have sagged nearly to the ground, he would have stretched, his neck would be unnaturally long and thin—

Even if he did not do it now, Death would come for him today or some other day, Death was not to be avoided, so why fly from him, why not put one's neck in the halter and have done with it? He startled a bird, a thrush—there it rose, a little thrush so droll and innocent; but good-bye all, and good-bye little Leonora in town—

The next thing is that he doesn't do it. No, he does not. He sits in the heather and blows on his hands and weeps. God help us, we are wretched creatures, we are human! When death is nothing to stick at he sticks to life. The Suicide has nothing to live for, he does not see the sun, nothing on earth makes him happy, 106, 106, smarting hands, dead tired, he is utterly done and falls into a doze, shivering with cold.

The pain wakes him almost immediately and he rises to his feet. He looks anxiously about as if something is after him, leaves the cord hanging on the branch, and walks off in the direction of the sæter. "Hound," he says to himself; "hound, hound. . . ."

They were up at the sæter, Fröken d'Espard had already settled her child and was standing over the wash-tub in the yard. She straightened herself as the Suicide came up, and stood looking at him in amazement; he gave no greeting, his clothes were in tatters, his hands were bleeding. What in the world—!

At the little out-of-the-way sæter they knew nothing of what had happened during the night, they had gone to bed the evening before and slept till day-break, undisturbed by the hurricane, then they got up and went to their work. Fröken d'Espard was taking lessons from Life, she was capable in her way, she too was human.

The Suicide uttered a few words, so queer and strange: "Fire, there's nothing left, 106 is burnt, she was locked in and couldn't get out, here's the key—"

"The sanatorium burnt? Marta, the sanatorium's been burnt down!"

Marta came out of the kitchen and received the news with distraction in her face. "And the people?" she asked.

"The people—" echoed the Suicide; "they are burnt. She was asleep in 106."

"I thought I noticed a smell of smoke this morning," said Marta. "Didn't I say so?" she appealed to Fröken d'Espard.

"Yes, you did."

"The moment I came out, I noticed the smell of smoke so plainly."

"You came in and said so."

"Yes, didn't I?"

The two women discuss the point over and over again as if it were important, and although the Suicide is not really listening; but far too much occupied with his own trouble, the words insinuate themselves into his ears and little by little change the direction of his thoughts. It is human chatter, the two women cling to earth and the day's doings, now and again Fröken d'Espard plunges a garment into the water so as not to interrupt the work. She is careful about worldly things.

The Suicide had his hands smeared with tallow and bound up in rags, he was given food, he grew drowsy and dozed off for a few minutes as he sat. As he was going he asked: "Is the bull out?"

"He's on the mountain," replied Fröken d'Espard; "a long way off. Now you're going to the station, aren't you?"

"I don't know," he answered. "To the station?"

"Yes, and then home?"

"Oh? Well, perhaps," he said, shaking his head. "It's beyond me."

"That will be best, you'll see."

"Why? What am I to do at home?" he asked abruptly. "The fire has ruined it, she is dead, utterly wiped out. Don't you remember? She came after me on the Peak yesterday, came walking up to me, it's hardly any time since that, only a few hours. We talked together and went home again. Last evening we talked still more, I hadn't understood her till then, she said something, I don't remember the words, but everything was cleared up and I was so happy. God bless you, can't you hear?" he wailed.

"Yes, poor thing!" she said.

"I sat with her till she fell asleep, I was so happy. And then I went out. And now she isn't anywhere, it's past conceiving; no, I can't grasp it, do you hear?"

Fröken d'Espard said cautiously: "I wonder if you haven't a little girl?"

"Yes, Leonora, you mean. Oh yes."

"You mustn't forget her, must you? And of course you won't forget her either, perhaps she'll be lifted up to the window, looking out when you come. That will be fun. Oh dear, yes, I understand so well how sad it is for you, but we must not despair!" she encouraged him. "We all have our troubles, as you used to say. For my part I have many years to wait for something."

"Oh?"

"Yes, many years, seven years."

It was now quite light and gave promise of a fine day after the stormy night. Around the sæter all was still, not a bush stirred, only the hens pecked about on the ground, and the brook murmured softly a few paces away.

"I'm a hound!" exclaimed the Suicide, and said no more.

She gave him a frightened glance. He had such a look of conviction, as though he had said something profoundly true, and he turned pale at his own words, as though they had gone straight home.

To calm him she adopted a practical, everyday tone: "I think you'll go down to the station and take the train home, Herr Magnus. No, you needn't look so alarmed, the bull's on the mountain today as he was yesterday, he's out at fell pasture—so we call it here."

"Good-bye!" said the Suicide and went out.

"If you go through the forest you can still catch the morning train," she called after him.

He went through the forest, he came to the cord, dangling empty from its branch, he walked past, walked on and on and disappeared.

Fröken d'Espard had followed him with her eyes as long as she could, then she set about her washing again—so quick to learn in good as in evil, so careful about worldly things. So we call it here—

THE END

www.ingramcontent.com/pod-product-compliance
Lightning Source LLC
La Vergne TN
LVHW032046070526
838201LV00084B/4726